Koenig's Wonder

Linda Kuhlmann

Mickey —
Enjoy the journey !

L Kuhlmann

Llumina Press

ISBN: HC 1-59526-259-8   PB   1-59526-258-X
Printed in the United States of America by Llumina Press

Acknowledgments

During the years I took to write this novel, I received assistance from so many people that it is impossible to name them all. To all of them, I express my deepest thanks.

In addition, I would like to express my gratitude to the following people for their expertise, help, and encouragement. Although the final responsibility for the accuracy of the text is mine, I could not have completed this novel without these special people: Steve Barham, past Executive Director of the Oregon Racing Commission; Eric Witherspoon, DVM; J. L. (Buck) Wheat, of Churchill Downs; Rich Gresham; Lynda Schar; Gloria Carson; Wallace P. Carson, Jr.; Gardner Mein; Cynthia Whitcomb; Twyla Poppleton; Judith Braaten; Chad Wade, of CWS Freeze Branding Service; Julie Bouché-Forbes; Galen McBee; Anne Koenig; Gary Olson; Carl Odiam; and Janet Williams. Also, I would like to thank the Women Writers of Newberg (WWN) for being relentless and encouraging.

Finally, a special thank you goes to my husband for his infinite patience and support.

For Mom and Dad

PROLOGUE

1937

Georg Maseman sat on the deck chair of the ship as it approached his new world, the lights of the harbor in the distance shining like bright jewels across the dark water. He pulled his heavy, wool coat closer to keep out the icy wind, but it didn't help against the chill that burned inside of him. He knew he had to tell his brother the truth, all of it.

It was a frightening and confusing time in their country. A new power was rapidly growing in Germany like a wildfire that threatened to change their lives forever. Some people embraced it; others ran in fear.

George thought back, as he had numerous times on this voyage west, to see if he could have done it any other way. Hermann's engagement to Hannah would not have been broken, if it hadn't been for George. But, then, Hermann would not be with him now on the ship to New York.

When George had told his father that Hermann refused to come with him to America because of Hannah, his father became very angry. Martin Maseman wanted his two elder sons to leave Essen before it was too late and find a home for his family in America. He did not tolerate disobedience, and he did not approve of Hannah Siemens. George now shook as he remembered the fury in his father's face as he gave him his instructions. George always feared his father, a strong man steeped in traditions; but, this was the first time he had ever questioned his father's command. When George told his father to do it himself, his answer was the back of his father's hand across his face and a demand to be obeyed.

That was the night he had decided to take the painting, just as he left his parents' home for the last time. He remembered now when his father had bought the Friedrich, one of the last oil paintings the German artist had finished before a stroke ended his career. George had seen the changes in his father after a few months of owning it. Later, he'd learned what it had cost his family. When he'd taken it from the wall, George had enjoyed the thought of how much it would hurt his father to find it missing.

Once it had been in his possession, George had seen that he held the means to his dreams in his hands. Now, he was afraid of what Hermann would do when he learned it was on the ship.

Before they had left Germany, Franz, George's younger brother, had begged to come with them. George had refused, explaining to Franz that he was too young and their parents needed him to stay to help with the farm. Franz had been furious with George and said he would never forgive him. George shivered deep in his soul as he now thought of the hatred in his younger brother's eyes and how they'd reminded him of their mother's brother, a very evil and dangerous man.

Now, as the ship was nearing Ellis Island, George knew the time had come to confess all to Hermann. The only question was how. He knew Hermann's temper and cringed at the thought of provoking it, but he had no choice.

George stood and walked to the railing of the ship. Tears sprung into his eyes as the cold wind bit his face, and he angrily brushed them away. His first thoughts of coming to America had been exciting and adventurous. Now, he found his heart heavy and sad at the sight of the lights on the tall spires of the city breaking the dark horizon, framing the harbor as the ship slowly came near the famous Statue of Liberty.

He turned and saw his brother approaching. Though Hermann was older, he was smaller than George, blond and blue-eyed like Franz, resembling their mother's father more than their own. George saw the dark circles under Hermann's eyes and knew that he had spent most of the voyage in their cabin or down in the cargo hold, where Conversano was sequestered.

"Hello," George said in German. "Are you ready?"

"Yes. I was checking Conversano before we disembark. He has traveled well, but I am most anxious to remove him from the ship and settle him into a stable soon."

Hermann had purchased the white Lipizzaner stallion when the horse was retired from the riding school in Verden, where he'd taught dressage. After his training at the Spanish Riding School in Vienna, Hermann had returned to Germany and worked in Verden for three years, against their father's wishes. Hermann had told George he'd decided to use the stallion's fine blood lines for breeding in America, since Germany no longer held a future for him.

Nervously, George looked away and placed his hand in his pocket, fingering the coins there – a habit he'd had since he was a child. He saw that the ship's crew were preparing to dock, and people began coming out onto the deck to watch.

"We should get our luggage," Hermann said.

"Yes, but first, there is something I must tell you." George motioned toward the chairs on the deck behind them, but Hermann shook his head, leaning both elbows on the railing to watch the men on the shore. George looked down for a moment at the dark water along the side of the ship, then looked at his brother and said, "It is about Hannah."

George watched as Hermann turned to face him, his eyes darkening and the muscles in his jaw tightening.

"I should have known what type of woman she was. It is too painful to think that I was betrothed to a woman that would throw herself at my own brother."

George flinched at the hatred in his brother's voice.

"No, Hermann, I must explain..." George began, then stopped, searching for the right words. He took a deep breath and slowly continued, "I lied to you about Hannah."

Hermann stared at his brother's face, a face so embedded in his mind over the years that he could always tell what was behind the brown eyes — or so he had thought.

"I don't understand," Hermann said.

"She....we, that is...." George had to look away from his brother, shoving both hands into his pockets. He couldn't bear Hermann's eyes any longer. All at once, he blurted out, "She never approached me in the manner I told you. I only said that, because...because, I needed you to come to America with me." George couldn't tell his brother that he had followed their father's orders.

Hermann stood before his brother, his arms hanging at his sides, his face white, an anger welling up inside of him. He thought of the terrible things he had said to Hannah when he broke off their engagement, the hurt in her face as she denied his angry accusations. Hermann pulled his right hand into a tight fist before he swung it with all his strength into George's face.

"I believed you. My own brother!" he spat at George, who was lying on the deck with blood pouring from his mouth. Then, fear grabbed him as he thought of how he'd believed George over the woman he loved, the woman he had decided to spend the rest of his life with. The fury inside of him had come not from this new truth, but from deep within himself - his own inextricable sense of guilt which engulfed him because he had falsely accused Hannah.

George pulled himself up and stood next to the railing, a few paces from Hermann. He could see how much he had hurt his brother, but he was not finished. He had not told him everything.

"There is more I must tell you," George began, wiping the blood from his face with the back of his hand.

Hermann's eyes flared at George, but he was silent.

"I took the Friedrich from our parents' home," George said quickly and softly. He didn't want to be overheard.

"You did what?" Hermann yelled.

"Took the—"

"I heard you," Hermann said, holding up his hand to stop George from speaking further. "But, why?"

George thought for a moment about the anger he'd felt at their father, the sting of his hand. His brother would understand, since he had also experienced it. However, he decided not to reveal his reason of revenge – not yet. Finally, he said, "On the chance that we would need money to survive in the new country."

George watched Hermann closely. At first, the expression on his face looked as if he was confused; then, Hermann looked squarely into George's eyes with a hatred that now frightened him.

Hermann stood before his brother as a fire began to burn deep inside, furiously raging and fueled with fear. What his brother had done to break up his engagement to Hannah was unforgivable. But, Hermann had been unable to make peace with his father before they left, and now he was afraid his father would think that he had been the one to take the painting. He knew that the Friedrich was the one thing his father valued most in life, even more than his own family.

"Not only are you a liar," Hermann hissed softly, "but a thief, as well." He stared at his brother's face, then added, "I never want to see you again as long as I live."

Hermann ran across the ship's deck and disappeared through a door leading to their cabin. He quickly gathered his bag and started to leave, but paused for a moment, looking around the room, turning over in his mind what he felt he must do. When he saw George's case lying open on his bed, he knew. He went to the case and found the painting, no longer in its frame, wrapped in a muslin cloth at the bottom. Hermann gently took it out and placed it inside of his own bag. Then he closed both bags and ran from the room.

Hermann turned and went down the stairs that led to where Conversano waited. Later, as he led his stallion from the ship, he thought to himself, "*Maybe now Papa will forgive me.*"

◆ ◆ ◆ ◆

George, still standing on the deck, wiped the blood with his handkerchief. A crowd of people had gathered around him, checking to see if he needed assistance. He tried to leave the deck, but there was no room now to move. People from numerous countries filled every open space on the deck like water flowing through a channel, seeping down toward the gangplanks that led to the soil of their new home.

He leaned against the railing and saw Hermann, standing out in the crowd as he led the white stallion down the ramp, away from the ship.

George stood and watched his brother disappear into the crowd with Hermann's last words ringing in his ears. He turned and began shoving his way through the sea of people and ran back to his cabin. He retrieved his case and ran to the long queue of people going down the ship's ramp. When he was finally on the dock, he could not see his brother amongst the vast bodies crowded around him.

At the U.S. Customs counter, a tired, old man, with graying hair and small, wire-rimmed glasses, quickly scanned George's papers and asked his name.

"George Maseman," George answered in broken English.

The man at the counter made some notes and handed George his entrance papers.

At last, George ran through the gate, toward the new city that had represented freedom and prosperity to their family. His brother was nowhere in sight. He searched, but was unable to find anyone who knew where Hermann might have gone.

Later, George took a taxi to the hotel where he and Hermann had booked a room, but Hermann had not checked in. Inside the room, George placed his bag on the bed and emptied his pockets next to it. Then he opened the case. He saw his clothes had been shuffled. Frantically, he dug through it, the pit of his stomach burning. The painting was gone! His anger flared and he slammed the case shut, swearing in German. He knew it had to have been Hermann who had taken it. George paced the room, not knowing where to turn, images running through his mind of what he was going to do when he saw his brother again.

Finally, sitting on the bed next to the case, he put his head in his hands. Out of the corner of his eye, he saw his entrance papers lying on the bed near him. He picked them up and noticed that the old man had mistakenly written MASON down for his last name. With the paper still in his hand, he stood up and went toward the door, thinking he would return to the dock to correct the mistake. Then he stopped.

George smiled as he stepped back away from the door, and thought to himself, *What a twist of fate. Now, I can locate my brother, but he won't be able to find me.*

PART ONE

CHAPTER ONE

1957

A t the end of the Arlington Park shedrow, where George Mason's eight
Thoroughbreds were temporarily stabled for the late summer races, Fred
Jamison was talking on the telephone. The cool September day was a relief
after the hot humid summer that had just passed.

"Thanks, Chris," Fred said into the receiver. "We knew we could count on
you. I'll pass this on to George."

In the backside of the North Chicago race track, George Mason stood nervously next to the stall holding Koenig, his prize two-year-old colt. As Fred
walked quietly up to where George stood, he watched the large, dark-haired man
place his forehead against the white blaze below the star on the tall horse's head,
softly talking to the animal as he stroked the long neck. George did this before
each of Koenig's races. Today, his voice had a hint of melancholy.

Fred waited patiently, as he always did. He was George's trainer at Essen
Farms in Kentucky. He'd first met George Mason in New York at Belmont Park,
when Count Fleet won the Triple Crown. They had been friends ever since.
When George purchased McKenzie Farms, he'd called Fred and asked if he'd be
his trainer. Fred knew about George's past and would do anything he asked of
him.

The voice over the loud speaker filled the air as it paged a steward to the superintendent's office. George looked up at Fred; his eyes were dark and tired.

"Chris just called," Fred said softly. "He said that Hermann is bringing his
family to Chicago and are on their way here to the track, just like you wanted."

Fred knew how important this meeting was, and how long it had taken
George to get to this point in his life. Today, George would see his brother for
the first time in twenty years.

"Good," George said after a moment. "Chris is a good man."

A few years back, Fred had seen a man at a horse auction near Chicago that
reminded him of George. He'd learned that the man's name was Hermann
Maseman, who owned a riding school near Rockport, Indiana. Fred was the
only other person who knew that Maseman was George's true name. When
Fred told George about Hermann, George had sent Chris Schmidt to work on
Hermann's farm to be his eyes and ears.

"My niece, Emma, turns eighteen today," George said. Fred noticed the envy
in his friend's voice, and he hated how George always reminded himself of what
Hermann had that he did not. Although the farm took all of George's time, Fred
knew that this was not the reason George had never married.

As the knots in his stomach tightened, George sat down in the chair next to
Koenig's gate. Emma was their mother's name. He'd never written his family
back in Germany. He had been too ashamed. A few years after the war, he'd

flown back to find his family. He would never forget the devastation he'd seen in
Essen. Most of the city had been destroyed by the bombs. His childhood home
was ruined.

After some time, George had located Johann Meier, a man who'd lived on
the farm near their home. Johann had told George that his parents had died after
a bomb hit their home. The horses had been scattered and he'd tried to locate
them, but later, he found that the army had seized them. When George asked
about his brother, Franz, Johann's face had turned gray.

'He joined the Nazi's,' Johann had said with disgust. 'I heard that he was
killed at one of their concentration camps, when some prisoners attempted to
escape.'

George had immediately returned to America. His attempts to locate
Hermann at that time had been futile. After their arrival in New York, Hermann
had simply disappeared. The old anger had welled up inside of George as he'd
remembered that night he'd found the Friedrich missing from his luggage in the
hotel room, after going through immigration. George had then vowed to himself
that someday he'd locate Hermann and get it back. However, life had gotten in
the way and he'd never had a chance – until now.

♦ ♦ ♦

George looked up at Fred, still standing next to him in the backside of the
track. His friend was tall, like himself, but more slender. He saw the slight graying in Fred's curly, sandy hair, which he hadn't noticed before. He thought to
himself how little we see the changes in the people around us every day, until
one day, we see them in a different light due to some change in our own perspective.

"I fear my brother will learn that I am here, before I am ready," George said.

"No, the *Racing Form* will list George Mason, not Maseman. As long as he
doesn't see you, he won't have any idea you're here. That is, until you want him
to know."

George sighed and smiled a little. He could always count on Fred to help him
see things more clearly. He had been careful not to have his photo in the press
over the years. Nodding his head, he said, "That is true. I had forgotten."

He laughed softly and added, "Then, my friend, I must send you to the Winner's Circle, since Hermann will be in the crowd watching when Koenig wins."

"Aren't you being a little optimistic?" Fred asked, smiling.

George sat upright and said with a strong voice, "When have you ever seen
me not optimistic?"

"That's true," Fred said, shaking his head and laughing. "What are you going
to do when you see him again?"

George was silent for a moment, looking down at the ground, his elbows
resting on his knees. "I'm not sure," he finally said. The smile was now gone
from his face.

♦ ♦ ♦

"Oh, Dad, thank you!" Emma said, kissing her father on the cheek as they sat
down in their seats in the grandstand.

Hermann smiled, reminded of his own excitement at seeing a large race track for the first time. He knew his daughter couldn't wait to see the horses.

"This is so exciting," Emma said, bubbling with joy as she looked at the throng of people around them.

Hermann watched Emma with pride. Her black hair, hanging down the back of her light, blue dress, glistened in the sunlight that streamed in from the side of the grandstand. His heart swelled as he saw her profile, the same as her beautiful mother, who sat on the other side of his daughter.

"Your mother and I thought you might like this, Emma," he said, winking at his wife.

Sophia was still a stunning woman, tall and slender in her cream blouse and long, dark green skirt, her long, dark hair pulled up underneath the wide-brimmed hat. She always wore hats when she went out. That was the first thing that had caught Hermann's eye at the concert hall in New York many years ago, but then her large, brown eyes had captured him completely. Sophia smiled at Hermann as she caught his eyes watching her.

Another face flashed in his mind, a face of a woman he'd known years ago. He could never forget her, even though he'd tried. She had been his first love.

He smiled back at Sophia, then quickly looked away. He wanted to stay in the memory for a moment longer, remembering Hannah's beautiful long, red hair waving down her back and over her shoulder as she'd turned to him when the photograph had been taken. Hermann could still see the love in her blue eyes smiling at him over the photographer's shoulder, just before the flash had blinded him.

Suddenly, a chill came over him as he remembered his brother's words, tearing his very soul. His brother had lied to him.

Hermann had rushed to ask Sophia to marry him, shortly after they had met in New York. When he'd taken her to Indiana, he'd thought it would put the bitter past behind him. Yet, he still found himself heaped in the middle of his memories when he least expected it.

An announcement came over the loud speaker, bringing Hermann back from his own thoughts.

"This is the happiest day in my life," Emma said as she hugged both her mother and father.

Emma loved her parents more than anything and felt very proud sitting there between them at that moment. Most of her friends at school felt their parents disapproved of them, so they never confided their true feelings to them. She was fortunate that she could tell her mother anything. Her father was more restrained, but he would open his arms to her, if she needed him. He was a wise and gentle man, always loving and caring. She had seen this same gentleness when he taught the students in his riding school. The only time he seemed stern with her was when she had begun to date boys at her school. In her mind, he'd seemed overly strict.

The smell of hot dogs and roasted peanuts was in the air as vendors walked by with their trays hung around their necks. Her father bought peanuts and lemonades, while Emma watched the crowd around them. She listened to the loud hum in the air, which reminded her of a giant bee hive as the excitement grew with the anticipation of the race.

"Here's Karen and Oliver," Sophia said in her soft voice, waiving her gloved hand to the couple advancing toward them. The man was tall and high wasted, with long legs and black hair combed straight back from his high forehead. The woman, a tall and slender redhead in a yellow, flowered dress, her hair softly curling under at her shoulders, waived back to Sophia with a smile on her face. Emma knew that Karen Stenson and her mother had been friends at the conservatory in New York, where her mother had studied the cello. Emma longed to someday find a friend like Karen of her own.

The two women hugged and kissed each other on their cheeks. Hermann and Oliver shook hands.

"Hello, old friend," Oliver said in a crisp voice. "I'm glad we found you in this crowd."

Oliver looked at Emma and winked. "Hello, young lady."

"Hello, Uncle Oliver," Emma said smiling. She had called the Stensons aunt and uncle ever since she could remember, because she had no real aunts or uncles. Her mother's parents had come alone to America, and Sophia was an only child. Her father had told her once that his family had been killed in the war. He rarely talked about his past.

"Are you having a good time?" Oliver asked.

"Yes, it's wonderful."

After they sat down, Emma's father looked at her and asked, "Would you like to bet on the horses?"

"Oh, could I?" she begged, her eyes wide with joy.

Sophia placed her hand on her daughter's arm. "I have an idea, dear. You and I will decide which horse we like best." She looked over at her husband. "Maybe your father will not mind placing our bets for us. I'm sure he will want to go down and listen to the touters before making his decision."

Emma looked at her father. "What are touters?" she asked.

"Henry Miller told me about them one day, when he and I came here for the races," he answered. "Touters are men that go to the backside of the track and talk to the trainers and jockeys, getting information on each horse that would be racing that day. Then the touters go to the betting areas and sell this information to the bettors."

Emma knew Henry. He owned the farm next to theirs. He and her dad played cards every Friday night.

"How much can we bet?" she asked.

"I think ten dollars, Em," her father said.

Emma and Sophia bent their heads together over the *Daily Racing Form*. It looked confusing at first, but Karen explained the columns and rows of names and numbers. Emma noticed that one of the races was listed as a "Claiming Race."

"What's a claiming race?" she asked Karen.

"It's a race where the horses are listed for sale. After the race, any horse can then be purchased for the claimed price for that race. It is also a way to classify a horse."

"But, why would anyone want to sell their horse at a race?" Emma asked.

"It's a chance the trainer takes with his horse, but it opens the eyes of the other trainers and owners. Usually, the price is placed well above where they think anyone would want to buy."

Emma thought for a moment. Then she said, "I don't think I'd like it if I took that kind of risk and actually lost my horse. How do you know so much about races, Aunt Karen?"

"My father owned a large breeding farm in Kentucky and had been involved with racing for a number of years."

"Does he still have race horses?" Emma asked.

"No, dear, Mother sold McKenzie Farms years ago, after Father's heart attack."

Emma watched as Karen's eyes darkened. She didn't know that Karen was still angry at her father for leaving the farm to that German while she was in Paris with Oliver. It meant nothing to her that Mason had worked for her father for almost twenty years and that she had not stepped foot on the farm since she was twelve. She still believed McKenzie Farms should have been hers.

Emma saw Karen look at her and reach out her hand to stroke Emma's long, black hair. A few years ago, Emma's mother had told her that Karen and Oliver could not have children. Emma liked being spoiled by them.

"Emma," Karen said. "You look wonderful today. Are you ready to enter your new school?"

"Yes, Aunt Karen. Mom and Dad brought me here as a surprise for my birthday, before taking me to register tomorrow." Emma loved the emerald green of Karen's eyes and had wished hers was that color, instead of dark brown.

"I am so glad you have decided to major in the arts. You have such a natural talent, and it is much more appropriate for a young lady than playing with horses."

Emma didn't agree. She loved being with the horses more than anything. She wanted to stay on the farm and help her father in his work, but her mother was adamant about her going to school. Sophia felt it was important for a young lady to have an education before she decided on her life's career. Emma had chosen art because of her mother. She'd watch Emma sketch the horses in their arena at home while her father was training. Her father had told her once that he especially liked Emma's watercolors of the woods behind their home.

He frequently mentioned that Caspar Friedrich was his favorite artist. Emma loved the story he'd tell her of a painting that he thought was priceless, containing a solitary man walking through a grove of naked oak trees in the winter at dusk, his long, heavy cloak trailing behind him in the fallen leaves on the ground, nature dying all around him. But, to her father, the painting's waxing moon and Venus, its star, symbolized the promise of rebirth and hope. Emma had never seen the painting, but she saw the change come over her father's face whenever he talked about it. She'd noticed a wild look would come into his eyes that she had never seen before. Sometimes, it frightened her.

♦ ♦ ♦ ♦

A bugler's call came over the loud speaker. The crowd began to cheer as the two-year old Thoroughbreds came onto the track to begin their parade before the grandstand, the sunlight shining on the sleek animals' coats and the colors of the silks on the jockeys riding them. A gentle breeze played through the long manes on the horses' necks as they slowly turned. Some of the riders stood up in the stirrups and brought their horse to a canter or trot as they passed the grandstand on their way to the gate.

Emma looked at a tall, dark colt passing by with a number seven on the blanket. The jockey on his back was wearing a red silk shirt with a large, gold 'V' in the center. The horse held his head high and pranced in line with the other animals, but somehow he stood out from the rest. Emma couldn't describe it, but he seemed to have some magical brilliance about him.

"I like Koenig," Emma said, after finding the number of the horse on the *Racing Form*. "That means 'king' in German, doesn't it, Mother?"

"Yes, love. I like him, too." Sophia took a ten-dollar bill from her handbag and handed it to Hermann with a smile. "Would you mind placing our bet on Koenig to win?"

"Yes," Hermann said, standing up. "Care to join me, Oliver?" The two men walked down the stairs of the grandstand.

"Oh, I love this," Emma squealed and clapped her hands as she watched the horses. She didn't want to miss a thing. Something was in the air, and she knew this would be a day that she would never forget.

♦ ♦ ♦ ♦

As Hermann and Oliver approached the betting area, the noise became deafening. People stood yelling in queues before small windows, money in their hands, trying to hurry the person in front of the small attendant behind the bars at each window so that they would not miss their chance to place their bets before the race began. To Hermann, the attendants looked frazzled, trying to smile and stay pleasant throughout the pandemonium, knowing that it would all be repeated once again before the next race. Hermann thought what it would be like to be one of those attendants and sent up a prayer of thanks that there were people in the world who didn't mind doing that type of job. He knew he would hate it himself.

As they inched closer to the window, Hermann was looking at the *Racing Form*, trying to make his decision when a tall, thin man came up to him.

"Are you interested in a bit of news about the horses today, sir?" the man asked with a slight Western accent. "I've just been in the backside and have some valuable inside information. It'll only cost you a sawbuck, but it's a sure thing."

"What do you know?" Hermann asked, handing the man a ten-dollar bill.

"Prince Hannover's the favorite. I secretly clocked him myself during his exercise, and I guarantee he'll be our winner today." The shrewd man winked an eye, which made Oliver nervous, but Hermann was taken in.

"Thank you, sir," Hermann said.

Then Hermann walked up to the window and said, "I'd like to bet ten dollars on Prince Hannover to win, please."

He placed his hand back into his pocket and felt the bill that Sophia had given him. He pulled it out and said, smiling, "Oh, and also bet this other ten on Koenig to win, for my wife and daughter."

◆ ◆ ◆ ◆

The horses were being loaded into the gate when Hermann and Oliver returned to their seats.

"Which horse did you decide on? " Emma asked her father as he sat down next to her.

"A nice man told me to bet on Prince Hannover, and I liked the horse's name. We shall see now, won't we?" He motioned toward the starting gate as a large bay horse began to back out of his stall, dancing around behind the gate until the jockey regained control. Finally, the animal was led back into place.

Sophia, reading a pamphlet she had picked up earlier about the track, said, "Did you know that in 1940, Arlington Park was the first race track in Illinois to install the electric starting gate?"

Before anyone could answer, a bell rang as the gate opened, and the horses bolted down the track, their hooves thundering above the loud crowd. A chestnut horse, carrying a jockey wearing yellow and green silks, broke out in front, while the others ran closely behind in a tight band.

"That's Prince Hannover," Hermann yelled with pride, pointing to the leader.

Emma was on her feet, looking for Koenig. She watched as he attempted to free himself from the other horses that had him boxed in. Her father's horse continued out ahead of the rest. Another chestnut tried to catch Prince Hannover, but the leader widened the distance between them. As the horses passed before the grandstand, Emma could feel the thunder in her heart. Then the field of horses made the first turn and seemed to disappear in the backstretch.

As the horses made the last turn toward the final stretch, Emma stood and saw Koenig swing out around the pack, his long legs stretching ahead of him, trying to close the gap to the leader. He came up alongside the red colt, and the two rode side by side. Prince Hannover's jockey was heavily striking him with his whip. Emma noticed Koenig's rider carried no whip and had both of his hands on the reins, letting the animal have his head as the pair approached the finish line. Emma was sure that Koenig had pulled slightly ahead of Prince Hannover just seconds before they crossed the line, but PHOTO FINISH came up on the board in the infield.

"Now, what?" Emma asked, breathlessly. "Which horse won?"

"They're not sure, yet. That is why they are holding a photo finish," Karen explained. "Since the race was so close, the judges are looking at the photo that was taken on the finish line, just as the horses crossed under it."

"Oh," Emma sighed.

"The winner will be announced momentarily," Karen added.

Emma held her breath until she saw Koenig's name appear as the winner. She threw her hands in the air and screamed with joy, then wrapped her arms around her mother.

"We won! We won!" Emma exclaimed. She watched as the crowd in the infield parted to allow the young, black horse into the Winner's Circle, lights from the photographers' cameras flashing around him like fireflies at night.

Emma turned and kissed her father's cheek and hugged him. "What do we do now?" she asked, her eyes dancing with excitement.

"We go down and collect your winnings," Hermann said, tearing up his ticket and letting the confetti fall to the floor. He took Emma's arm in his hand and led her down from the grandstand, while Sophia and the Stensons followed.

"Oh, thank you," she whispered into her father's ear, her arm now tucked in his. She had never known such joy, except when she had received her first pony on her eighth birthday.

◆ ◆ ◆ ◆

In the betting area, after retrieving their winnings, Emma saw a tall, young man walking toward them, his dark hair combed back at the sides, one curl falling down on his forehead. His eyes were as blue as a summer sky, and she couldn't take her eyes off him. When his eyes locked onto hers, his smile seemed to light up his handsome face. Feeling awkward, she looked down at her feet, then back up to see that he was now standing near her.

"Oliver," the man said in a soft voice. "I didn't expect to meet you here."

"Sam!" Oliver said in surprise, then heartily shook the young man's hand.

"Hello, Mrs. Stinson."

"Hello, Sam," Karen said, laying her hand on the newcomer's broad shoulder. "It's been quite some time since we've seen you. Are your parents here at Arlington?"

"No, I'm here alone."

"How is your mother?" Karen asked.

"She's well, thanks," Sam said, then turned again to Emma and smiled, hoping Oliver would catch the hint.

"Sophia and Hermann Maseman," Oliver said, remembering the others in their party, "I'd like you to meet Sam Parker. He's the son of Harold and Joanna Parker, friends of ours from Oregon."

Sam made a slight bow toward Sophia, smiled, and reached out his hand to Hermann.

"Hello," Hermann said coolly, shaking the young man's hand.

Emma liked the way Sam looked in his dark jeans and white shirt. Then she saw her father glance at her, and she looked down again.

"Harold and I met through racing years ago; he has some fine horses," Oliver added.

Sophia nodded and smiled at Sam. She reached out a soft, gloved hand to him. "It's nice to meet a friend of Oliver and Karen's." Her voice rang out like music over the clamor of the crowd.

"What are you doing at Arlington? I heard you were going for basic training in the Air Force," Oliver asked Sam.

"I am, sir. I'm leaving soon for my pilot's training in Arizona. However, I wanted to visit the backside and bet on a race one more time before I leave." Sam looked at Emma again and smiled. "Are you going to introduce me to this beautiful young lady?" he asked Oliver.

Emma felt her heart jump in her breast and she shyly looked away for a moment, feeling as if her face was on fire. Then, remembering herself, she turned back to him and smiled.

"This is Emma, Hermann and Sophia's daughter," Oliver said.

Sam took Emma's hand in his and gently held it as if it was a small, fragile flower. He looked into her deep brown eyes and fell into their darkness. He smiled as he saw that Emma had her mother's beautiful eyes. The sweet smell of lavender flowed around him. It was the same perfume his mother wore.

"I'm Sam Parker," he finally said.

"I know," Emma said, her voice shaking. Then she asked, "Are you one of the touters my father told me about?"

Sam laughed. It was rich and hearty. "No, my dad owns race horses in Oregon. I've spent most of my life in the backside of a race track."

"You said you bet on a race," Emma began, watching Sam's eyes. "Which horse did you bet on?"

"Koenig."

"We did too, my mother and I. Do you always bet on the horses?" Emma was curious about this man.

"You've got to," Sam said. "I mean, you can't just watch a horse race and not bet."

"Well," Hermann said, clapping his hands together. "We must be leaving."

The sharp sound seemed to awaken Emma from some deep spell.

Oliver interjected, "We will be meeting the Maseman's at the Drake Hotel for dinner around seven this evening. Would you mind, Hermann, if Sam joined us, since he's alone in the city?"

Emma saw her father stiffen. She knew he hated to see her around boys. When she had begun to date in high school, he'd been protective and demanded to know where she was going and who she would be with. But, her shyness prevented her from dating very much. She looked at her father for the first time with a pleading face, hoping that he could not resist.

"I guess that would be all right," Hermann said, reluctantly.

"That would be great," Sam said, looking at Emma, "if you don't mind, that is?"

"No, I don't mind," she said shyly, amazed that he would even ask her.

"Do you need a ride, Sam?" Karen asked.

"No, I'll take a taxi later. I have a few things I need to do first."

Sam turned and looked at Emma. "I'm looking forward to it," he said with a smile.

Emma's knees weakened. "Come along, Emma," she heard her father say, as he pulled on her hand. She was glad her father had accepted, and she couldn't wait to see Sam again.

Just as she turned to follow her family, she noticed a man watching them from the shadows by the betting booths. When the man saw her looking at him, he stepped back into the dark.

♦ ♦ ♦ ♦

In the betting area, George cautiously watched Hermann from the shadows. Just as he was about to approach Hermann, he saw Karen McKenzie and stopped. He knew she hated him because he now owned McKenzie Farms and didn't want to bring that into his first meeting with Hermann. He wondered who the young man was that Hermann was talking to.

He saw his young niece, Emma, for the first time, and he could tell that the woman standing next to her was her mother. They were a carbon copy of each other. When he saw that Emma was as beautiful as her mother, his heart ached. He wanted a family, but had used his success as the owner of a large Thoroughbred farm as his excuse. He blamed his constant attention to the farm, but he knew that wasn't the whole truth. There had been only one woman that he wanted to share his life with, but now she was gone.

When he saw Hermann, George noticed his blond hair was a little thinner, his shoulders still strong from working with his horses, the steel-blue of his eyes sharp. The years had been good to his brother. Tears came to George's eyes, which he abruptly wiped away in an attempt to once again harden his heart. He wasn't going to allow himself to be sentimental now.

As Hermann led his family and friends out of the building, anger gripped at George as he watched. He had waited for this opportunity to get his brother alone, but now it was too late.

"Someday, my brother," George said under his breath, "we will meet again."

♦ ♦ ♦ ♦

Later that evening, Sam arrived at the same time as the Stensons at the Drake Hotel. Sam had never been there before and was impressed with the plush, red carpet and crystal chandeliers in the lobby. A large, circular marble table, containing an enormous Oriental vase filled with tall, colorful flowers, stood in the center of the wide area. Sam saw people standing at the registration desk to the right of the entrance. He looked into a mirrored lounge, with a large fountain in the center on his left as he followed Karen and Oliver toward the dining area. He could hear violins playing somewhere.

"Look in there," Oliver said as he paused before the open doors to what was labeled the Camellia Room. Sam looked inside and saw a vast ballroom with tables set on either side of the oak dance floor. A row of huge, crystal chandeliers hung high over the tables, casting a warm glow against the golden wallpaper. To the left of the door, a small orchestra played on a dais as couples in their finest dress swayed to the music below the soft light.

"I've been told that the roof was created so that it could be pulled back at night to allow their guests to dance under the stars," Oliver said. He continued down the hallway to a smaller dining room where the Maseman family waited.

At the dinner table, Sam sat across from Emma. The dimples in his cheeks deepened when he smiled in the candlelight, and Emma found it difficult not to stare at him while the others talked. She much preferred listening, hanging on every word Sam said.

"How many horses does your father have now, Sam?" Oliver asked later as the waiter was clearing the salad plates from the table.

"Ten. Six of them are owned by a doctor."

"Does he still have O'Leary?"

"Oh, yes, sir." Sam's tanned face beamed. "He's a bay stallion that my father prizes," he explained to Emma and her parents. "He's going to keep Dad busy at the track next year."

"Where is your father's farm?" Emma asked, glad that her voice seemed strong, even though her hand shook as she took a sip of water.

"In Eugene, Oregon. We call them 'ranches' out West."

"I've never been to Oregon," Emma said shyly, looking into Sam's blue eyes. He had changed into a dark suit, with a white shirt, and a tie the color of his eyes. He looked very distinguished, like the college boys she'd seen in the movies.

As the entree was set before them, Sam looked intently at Emma and said, "You would like Oregon. It's very beautiful there."

"Doesn't it rain a lot in Oregon?" Hermann said from the end of the table.

Sam looked at Hermann and smiled. "Yes, sir, that's why it's so beautiful. Everything is green and alive. We have high, snow-capped mountains and deep, rich farmland in the valleys." He turned and looked at Emma again. "And, the ocean's just over the coastal range, an hour away from my parents' ranch."

"I've never seen the ocean," Emma said, her heart soaring.

"Do you have any brothers or sisters, Sam?" Sophia asked.

"No, Mrs. Maseman. My parents had a baby girl when I was five, but sadly she died shortly after she was born."

Emma looked quickly at her mother and saw the sadness in her eyes. Her brother, Martin, had died before she was born, and she knew the pain that was always in her mother's heart. Emma watched her mother look down at the other end of the table at her father. Then she saw the look in Sam's eyes, and knew that he understood.

"So," Sam said to Sophia, feeling awkward in the silence and wishing he could take the pain from her eyes, "how long are you planning on staying in Chicago?"

"We will only be here for a few days," Hermann said, his voice sharp and loud. "Emma is entering art school here in Chicago. We will be taking her to the Art Institute for registration tomorrow."

Emma looked across at her mother and smiled softly. Sophia smiled back, and Emma felt her love in her glance.

Sam cleared his voice, then asked Emma, "What made you decide on art?"

"I guess it was my mother's influence," Emma said as she smiled at her mother. "Ever since I was five years old, she took me to galleries whenever we traveled around our state for competitions. This is my first time in Chicago."

"What type of competitions?" Sam asked.

"Dressage," Emma said proudly.

"Where will the Air Force be sending you, Sam, after your pilot's training?" Hermann asked. He wanted to make sure he knew where this young man was.

"I'm not sure yet, sir. I won't get my assignment until after graduation."

Emma knew her father was becoming uncomfortable. She saw that he was beginning to fidget with his silverware, and she knew it was because of Sam.

"What type of plane will you be flying?" Emma asked.

"Jets," Sam said, smiling.

Emma's birthday cake arrived at their table, with eighteen lit candles. Everyone sang to her as she blushed and made a wish. When she attempted to blow out the candles, Sam leaned across the table and helped her. When he sat down and winked at her, she didn't see her father watching them.

While the waitress cut and served the cake, Karen handed Emma a small package, wrapped in a white-brocade paper with a shiny, gold ribbon and bow. Emma slowly removed the ribbon and opened the paper, being careful not to tear the beautiful wrapping. Inside was a book, covered in a deep purple cloth, with "For Your Dreams" scrolled across in large, gold letters. When she opened it, she saw the white, empty pages and imagined the images she could draw there, a private place for her thoughts. Tears came to her eyes as she read the inscription, which was written inside the cover in Karen's lovely handwriting:

> 'Emma, dear.
> These empty pages await your lovely art
> and adventures in your new journey. Remem-
> ber to write down your dreams for the future.
> Love always,
> Aunt Karen and Uncle Oliver.'

"Oh, thank you!" Emma exclaimed, wiping her tears away. She got up and walked around the table, hugging Karen and Oliver.

As she stood near Sam, he took her hand and stood up so that he could whisper in her ear. "I didn't know this was your birthday. Happy Birthday, Emma."

She smiled back at him and thanked him. His hand felt warm in hers, and she noticed her heart was beating in her throat. She gently pulled her hand away and walked back to her seat, her face on fire.

"I read that there is a jazz concert tonight on the waterfront," Karen said, as the table was being cleared. "Let's all go there."

◆ ◆ ◆ ◆

It was a cool night when they left the hotel. The city lights were so bright, it seemed to Emma as if the sun was still shining. When they walked past a small coffee shop in the next block, Sam stepped in next to Emma, and they fell a little behind the other couples.

"I have been waiting to talk to you alone all night."

"Why?" Emma asked, a little nervously. Sam was older than the boys she had dated before. She never really liked the boys in her high school, they were so immature. Sam, on the other hand, was very intriguing. It annoyed her that she felt so shy around him.

"I wanted to ask you if you'd like to go to a movie with me tomorrow night? They're playing the new film, "*Funny Face*" with Audrey Hepburn. My mom used to take me to musicals when I was a kid, and I haven't outgrown them yet."

"Oh, I'd love to, but I'm not sure my father will permit me."

"How old are you now?" Sam said, smiling.

She thought for a moment. Realizing that she was no longer a child, she began to see new doors opening before her. It was like stepping out of a fog and seeing the world more clearly for the first time, seeing much further than she had ever seen before. Then she saw her father's face ahead of her as he turned to look her way.

"I...I don't know..." she began. "My parents are taking me to my school to register tomorrow, and I don't know what they have planned." She thought about what her father's reaction would be when she asked him and shivered. She took a deep breath, squared her shoulders, and said softly, "Is there somewhere I could telephone you, to let you know?"

"Yes." Sam quickly wrote a number on a folded copy of the *Racing Form* from the track that day and gave it to Emma. She smiled, carefully refolded it, and placed it in her jacket pocket.

"What time is the movie?" Emma asked, excited now at the idea of going.

"It's at seven."

"I'll let you know, thanks." Then she added, "I'd really like to go."

◆ ◆ ◆ ◆

Later, as Emma and her parents walked into their hotel lobby, she thought about her evening with Sam. At the waterfront, the jazz musicians had played late into the night, but her father insisted that they leave early. She knew he had watched her and Sam sitting nearby, their heads together and laughing as they talked. She had overheard Oliver tell her father more about Sam and his family as they sat on the grass before the waterfront, but she knew it didn't matter. All he could see was Sam was pulling his little girl away from him.

In the sitting room of their suite, Emma sat down in one of the wing-backed chairs. Her bedroom was off to the left of the sitting room, while her parents' room was on the right. Her father stood at the small bar, pouring himself a glass of port, one of his evening rituals.

"Here, darling," her mother said, handing her a long, slender package wrapped in silver paper with a purple bow on top. "Happy Birthday."

"Oh, Mom..." was all Emma could say.

"Your father picked it out," Sophia said softly, gently touching her hand to Emma's cheek.

Emma looked at her parents standing together, her father's arm wrapped around her mother's slender waist. "You have given me so much already today."

She bent her head and slowly unwrapped the package. When she lifted the

lid to the gray, felt box, a silver bracelet lay on the dark blue velvet, a small figure of a horse leaping into the air hung from the center of the chain. Tears began
to swell in her eyes as she leaped out of the chair and hugged her parents.

"Oh, thank you both so much. It's lovely," she said, wiping the tears from
her face. Her mother helped her to place the bracelet around her wrist. Emma
went to a tall mirror that stood above the fireplace and looked at her reflection,
holding her hand up to the light. Her father walked up next to her and looked
with her at her reflection.

"Well, now," Hermann began, overwhelmed by his daughter's tears. "We
will need to leave around ten tomorrow morning to take you to your school. Afterwards, we could see other things of interest in Chicago; maybe spend time in
the art museum."

"Oh, I can't wait!" Emma exclaimed.

"So, you'd better get yourself off to bed."

"All right," Emma said. She was just about to tell them about Sam's invitation, but hesitated. She wanted time to rehearse what she would say.

"Good night, Mom and Dad, and thank you for a wonderful birthday." She
kissed both her parents on their cheeks.

"Good night, *mein liebchen*," her father said. "Tomorrow is another day in
paradise."

Dreamily, Emma went into her room, softly shutting the door. Her father
said that same thing to her every night before she went to bed since she was
small.

Emma was still wearing her jacket. She put her hand into the pocket and
pulled out the *Form* that Sam had given her, noticing the way he signed his
name, carrying the line after the last initial up in a high arch over the entire
name. She was surprised to see that his handwriting was so precise and beautiful.
The writing she'd seen from the boys she knew back home was more like a rustic
scrawl compared to Sam's. Emma smiled and placed the *Form* on the table next
to her bed, then took off her jacket and hung it up.

As she began to change into her nightdress, still wearing her bracelet, she
stopped in front of the long mirror and looked at herself. She saw something
different in her reflection, a sort of glow about her that had never been there
before. She also saw that she was smiling to herself and her eyes sparkled. A
veil had been lifted and she no longer saw the tom-boyish, young girl that used
to stare back at her in the mirror. In her place was a young woman, a younger
version of her mother. She turned and looked at her profile and smiled secretly.
Yes, she was no longer a child.

Emma climbed into her bed, sitting up against the pillows. She wrote in her
new journal, entering everything that had happened on this magical day. Then
she added the events that, she hoped, were yet to come.

*"Was it my birthday, or was it Sam Parker that had created this change in
me?"* she wrote at the end.

As she slipped under the covers and turned out the light, Emma's thoughts circled around Sam, and his was the last face she saw in her mind before falling asleep.

◆ ◆ ◆ ◆

Hermann sat quietly gazing out of the window of their hotel room. Sophia had already retired for the night. He was restless, and couldn't sleep. Puzzling over what was bothering him, he first thought it was because he would have to say goodbye to Emma the next day. Yes, he admitted to himself, this was going to be very difficult, since they were so close. But, he knew that wasn't the only reason.

He saw in his mind the newspaper headlines on the night Emma was born. 'Hitler invades Poland,' the newspapers had said. On a single day when his heart was filled with pride and joy, a dark shadow had quickly turned it to sorrow and regret.

Hermann had then written a letter to his family in Germany, telling them to begin preparing to come to their new home in America. That was over eighteen years ago. He had not posted it right away.

He sighed heavily. His family never sailed. When he received the letter from his mother's brother, telling him that they were all dead, he never would forgive himself. Even now, he knew that there was nothing he could have done then. Yet, in his heart, he knew he could have brought them over sooner, before the war had started. He'd waited because he'd wanted everything to be perfect, especially for his father.

Years before, shortly after he'd arrived in New York, Hermann wrote his parents, reassuring them of their safe arrival. It was hard for him to explain to his father that he had the painting, but knew it was important that his father knew of its whereabouts. He did not explain to them what had happened between him and George on the ship. All he'd ever wanted was for his father to be proud of him.

When Hermann had learned that he'd lost his family was the first time he'd felt the desire to search for his brother, George. He'd returned to the immigration office in New York. It seemed smaller than he remembered, with fewer crowds than when he'd arrived. He'd been told that there was no record of George ever entering America. He'd inquired if George had possibly left on the next ship sailing for Germany, but still nothing was found. The clerk had suggested that possibly his brother had signed on as a crew member on a shipping vessel going back to Europe, using an assumed name. Disappointed and blaming himself, Hermann had returned to his farm in Indiana. Now, all he had left was his own small family.

Hermann sat with his face in his hands. His shoulders began to shake as he sobbed. His daughter's birthday was a constant reminder of his own failures.

CHAPTER TWO

T he next day was busy and long, the longest day Emma had ever spent in her life. The bustle of the large city was overwhelming to her, and yet, somehow exciting as crowds of people and busy traffic swirled around her. They rode on the El, an elevated railroad, that made her head spin as she tried to see everything as the train moved through the city. All the while, she kept trying to decide when the best time would be to tell her parents about Sam's invitation to the movies that night.

Emma found the Art Institute was perfect for her. Housed in an old building in the heart of Chicago, it reminded her of one of the large museums she had visited with her father in Indianapolis. The tall steps were guarded by two large lion statues, leading up to giant pillars at the entrance. Wide, colorful banners hung across the front of the building, advertising the Monet exhibition that was on display in the Institute's museum. The building was on Michigan Avenue, near the waterfront of Lake Michigan, which Emma liked very much. She could see the tall buildings of the city behind her and the park where they had been to the jazz concert the night before. This made her think of Sam, and a warm feeling ran through her body.

As she stepped inside, they were greeted by an elderly woman who was handing out pamphlets containing a map of the building, along with information about the exhibits in the museum. Emma looked up and saw the high ceilings filled with more colored banners, then she heard her father ask the woman which way was the school. He led the way through the museum.

"Oh, this is wonderful," her mother said, grasping Emma's hand in hers. "I know you will like it here."

"We will return to the museum later today to see the Monet paintings," her father said, looking around at the art exhibits as they wandered slowly down the hallway.

The smell of linseed oil and clay filled the air as they entered the school. A young girl, with short, straight brown hair, stood behind a semi-circled reception desk. Her white Peter Pan blouse, tails hanging out over her jeans, had different colors of paint smeared across the front, as if she had carelessly wiped her hands while painting. Emma looked around the room and saw booklets and newspapers stacked everywhere with information about the school and the city, her fingers beginning to itch to reach out and gather them all, hungry to know everything. The girl looked up and smiled at Emma and her parents from behind large, round glasses.

"Good morning," Hermann said as he handed the acceptance letter to the young girl, his hat in his other hand. "I am Hermann Maseman. And, this is my wife, Sophia, and our daughter, Emma. We are here to register Emma for her classes in the school."

The girl read the letter, then looked at Emma and nodded. She picked up a folder containing a large booklet and forms and handed them to Emma. Then she pressed a button that rang a bell somewhere down the long hall to the right.

"You will need to fill out these forms and return them to the Admissions Office by tomorrow," she said, pointing to a windowed door behind her. Just then, a tall young man came out of a door in the hallway and walked toward them.

"Jeremy," the young woman said to the man, "this is Mr. and Mrs. Maseman and their daughter, Emma. Emma is one of our new students."

Jeremy reached out and shook hands with all three of the newcomers, his dark hair falling down over his eyes.

"I'm the aide to the Admissions Superintendent," he said to Emma as he pushed his hair back and smiled. "Unfortunately, Mr. James is out of town this week, but he had advised me that you would be coming. I'll take you on a tour of the facility and show you your new quarters, if you would like."

"Oh, yes," Emma said, filled with excitement. "That would be wonderful!" She and her parents had been to the school on their initial visit last spring to get the admissions papers, but it had been exam week. Yet, the short tour they received had been enough to convince Emma that this was the right school for her. She had wanted to see more, but they were restricted from certain areas.

They followed Jeremy back down the same hall. Special classes were in session in some of the rooms that they looked into. Emma strained to hear what the instructor was saying before they moved on. Other rooms were empty and Jeremy led them in to look around. One was set up for sculpture, with small, wooden models standing on a sideboard waiting for the next class. One of the painting classrooms had tall lockers where students could leave their supplies. Paints were splattered on the long tables where the students had worked, and some of their paintings were leaning against a green wall or still standing on easels. Emma could see from the canvasses that some of the students were very good and she felt apprehensive about her own abilities.

The dormitory Emma would be living in was separated into numerous rooms with two students in each. They were sparsely furnished with two beds and desks pushed against the walls. Her room was painted a light blue with bright, yellow chintz curtains on the solitary window that overlooked the lake and the city.

She saw the other students were near her age. But, when she asked about her roommate, Jeremy had said that she would be rooming with a second-year student. Emma was a little frightened by the enormity of it all and the volume of students, but her mother reassured her she would adapt, once she found herself a new friend.

Emma stood in the empty dormitory room and began to fear that she would miss her home. Then, from her window, she saw a large park with people horseback riding.

"Look, Dad. There must be riding stables in that park over there. Can we go see it?"

◆ ◆ ◆ ◆

At the stable office, Hermann talked with Henry Jones, the manager, about arranging for Emma to ride whenever she wanted while she was at school. Emma looked through the office window and saw the long line of bright, white stalls with the tall, horses' heads leaning out over the gates. This was the first time Emma would be living away from her home; yet, now she felt that her home was not so far away and that she was ready for her new adventure.

"We have over thirty horses here at our stables," Henry said proudly as he led Emma and her parents from the office, through the archway of ivy, toward the sounds and smells of the horses. He was a short, balding man with dark, curly hair on his bare arms.

"Some of the city's residents board their horses with us, but we have about fifteen horses that are available to the public. We'll find one that your daughter will like," Henry said as he winked at Hermann, noticing his stern and concerned look.

Emma walked up to a stall where a tall, gray horse stood, his head turning toward her. The gelding nickered softly to her as she approached him and reached out her hand to his forehead. She stroked his long neck and smiled into his big blue eyes. As she looked at the gold plate above his stall, she saw that his name was Grenada, which reminded her of the small island off the northern coast of Venezuela that she had studied in school. She had wished that someday she could go there.

"Hello, Grenada," she said softly.

"I don't think he'd be a good one for you, miss," Henry said. "He's got too much spirit for most young ladies."

"My daughter is an accomplished rider, Mr. Jones," Hermann said, looking into the stall at the animal. "Would you please lead him out of the stall so we can get a better look at him?"

Henry snapped the lead line onto Grenada's halter and opened the gate. The horse followed his lead easily as Henry walked him around the open exercise arena. He then gave the lead to Emma to walk with the horse.

Hermann nodded his head in approval, then looked at Emma.

"What do you think, Em?" he asked.

She ran her hand over his smooth back, feeling the horse's muscles ripple at her touch. She smiled and said, "I think Grenada will do very nicely."

While her parents returned with Henry to the office to finish the arrangements, Emma walked the horse around the stables, watching his gait as he followed her. She led him back to his stall and released him inside. As she closed the lower gate, the big animal walked up to her and touched her hand with his soft muzzle.

"We're going to be good friends," she said. "You'll see." Silently, she reminded herself to bring an apple each time she came to ride him.

Emma turned and walked toward the office. She stopped to watch as people returned on horseback from their ride around the park. She saw a young girl around her own age with long, curly blonde hair and a warm smile sitting on a brown filly, staring at her. The girl rode over to where Emma stood.

"Hi, I'm Jennifer Spencer," the girl said, leaning down in the saddle and holding out her gloved hand to Emma.

"I'm Emma Maseman," Emma said, a little shyly. "Do you ride here often?"

"Oh, yes," Jennifer said as she stepped down from her horse and handed the reins to a groom that had come out of one of the stables. The filly followed the lead of the groom back to her stall.

"I'm a second-year student at the Art Institute," Jennifer said

"I'm a student there, too. This is my first year. I'm a little frightened by it all." Emma wished she wasn't so nervous and talkative. She wanted to be so grown up.

Jennifer looked at Emma for a moment with her green eyes. "This is your first time living away from home, isn't it?" she asked as she pulled off her riding gloves.

"How did you know?" Emma asked, staring at her.

"Call it a hunch. I remember when I first went to New York with my aunt to live for a few months in the summer. It was kind of scary and exciting at the same time."

"You went to New York? How old were you?"

"Oh, about ten. My aunt took me there to watch a Broadway show. Where are you from, Emma?"

"A farm near Grandview, Indiana. My father has a dressage riding school there."

"I once saw a traveling tour of white Lipizzaner stallions perform in Portland. Could you show me how to ride like that sometime?"

"Yes, if you'd like. Where is your home, Jennifer?"

"Portland, Oregon. Been there since my parents were killed. I lived with my aunt and uncle – after the accident."

"Oh, I'm so sorry," Emma said. "What happened to your parents?"

"An auto accident."

"How terrible for you."

"It was a long time ago," Jennifer said, shrugging her shoulders. "I was only one. I don't remember much about them, except for what my aunt told me and the pictures I have of them. Aunt Charlotte is wonderful, always happy and smiling."

Emma wondered what she would do if something happened to either of her parents, but couldn't even think of the possibility. She admired Jennifer's ability to go on, as if nothing bothered her, even though she knew she had to have some feelings tucked away inside. Maybe she was the type of person who kept her feelings private.

"I love Oregon," Jennifer said, looking sideways at Emma. "Maybe I'll take you there, someday."

"I'd like that." Emma smiled as she thought of Sam telling her she'd like Oregon, the mountains, the farmland in the valleys, and, of course, the Pacific Ocean.

Jennifer and Emma began to walk down the row of stalls, petting each tall head that looked out over the open tops of their gates.

"What do you think of Chicago, Emma?"

Emma smiled. "Oh, I like it very much," she said. "I met a nice young man yesterday who is from Eugene, Oregon." It was the first time Emma had talked to anyone about Sam. Suddenly, she found she was bursting to share how she felt about him.

"Oh? What's his name?"

"Sam Parker. He's going into the Air Force to fly jets."

"Parker? I've heard of a Harold Parker from Eugene. I think he races Thoroughbreds. Where did you meet Sam?"

"At Arlington Park Race Track."

"Now, there's a coincidence. So, tell me more about Sam Parker," Jennifer said as she sat down on a bale of straw at the end of the stalls, picking out a piece of straw to chew on.

Emma looked around her, making sure her parents weren't looking for her. She took a breath and began. "He's tall, dark, and handsome, and has a great smile. He's going into the Air Force to be a pilot - oh, I said that..." She stopped and laughed. "I like him very much, and he has the most wonderful blue eyes I've ever seen, except for my father's..." Emma caught herself for a moment. She'd never met this girl before in her life, and here she was telling Jennifer things she would only have shared with her friends at home. Yet, somehow she knew it was all right.

Jennifer noticed how Emma's face changed and her voice became softer, when she talked about Sam.

"He asked me to go with him to the movies this evening," Emma confided.

"Wow, he moves fast," Jennifer laughed. "Are you going to go with him?"

"Oh, I don't think so," Emma said nervously.

"Why not?"

"Because, I don't think my parents will let me."

Jennifer's eyes were sparkling. "Did he give you a telephone number where you could reach him?" she asked.

"Well, yes."

"Then call the man!"

"But, what will my parents say?"

"Probably 'no,' if you tell them." Jennifer smiled at Emma with a sly look on her face, as if she was remembering her first moment of rebellion.

"Not tell them?" Emma was shocked. This had never occurred to her.

"Sure, I used to sneak out of my bedroom at night and meet Jason, when I was in high school."

"Who's Jason?"

"He's the man I'm going to marry someday. I've known him since grade school." Jennifer's face beamed as she talked.

Emma wondered what it would be like to actually know who she would marry. "Did you ever get caught?" she asked.

"Oh, yeah, but my aunt and uncle were okay. They remembered what it was like to be a kid, so they gave me 'the speech' and grounded me for a week."

"What was "the speech?" Emma asked.

"Oh, you know, stuff about boys and sex and decisions. I'm not sure I would miss an opportunity like this one, if I was you."

Emma sat and thought for a moment, her heart beating in a panic at the thought of disobeying her parents. Then she smiled as a small light began to shine in her mind. Her new friend had made her point, and Emma had caught it.

"Maybe you could give me his number," Jennifer said, laughing, nudging Emma gently with her elbow. "Just kidding!"

Emma laughed, but her mind was racing. Her father was very strict. Before, she would never have even considered doing something like her new friend had done. She had always been too afraid - of her parents and the consequences. If she could only wait to see Sam until her parents returned to Indiana, then they would never know. Just then, Emma heard her mother calling her.

"I need to go," She said, then stopped and looked at Jennifer and smiled. "It was nice meeting you. I hope we will be friends."

"You can count on it," Jennifer said with a smile and hugged Emma before she ran off. Emma didn't know that she had just met her new roommate.

♦ ♦ ♦ ♦

Emma saw her mother looking at her at different times during the rest of the day with a curious look on her face. Emma's mind was elsewhere, even while they toured the museum and the city. They went inside the Chicago Theater, a beautiful Beaux-Arts style building that had been built in 1921. The gilded decoration and elaborate, winding staircase took her breath away. She told her parents about meeting Jennifer at the stables when they stepped outside again into the sunlight. She looked up and noticed the marquee listed *"Funny Face"* in bold letters. In her hand, inside of her jacket pocket, her fingers wrapped about the *Form* with Sam's telephone number.

On the taxi ride back to the Drake hotel, Emma was silent.

"Are you all right, darling?" Emma's mother asked her, as they walked into their hotel, leaving her father behind to pay the driver.

"Yes, I'm fine. It has all been very exciting."

"Yes, I know. You just look different today, Emma. It wouldn't be because of Sam Parker, now would it?"

"Oh, no," she blurted out, after being stunned for a moment. Then she hurried to go through the revolving doors ahead of her mother. She didn't know what else to say.

It wasn't until dinner that she found the courage to ask.

"Mom. Dad...," Emma began, after the dessert was placed before them. She knew if she didn't ask now, she would never be able to. "Yesterday, Sam asked me to go with him to the movies tonight. It's an Audrey Hepburn musical that sounds like a lot of fun. I told him I thought it would be okay." She knew she had not told Sam this, but felt it was the only way she would be able to convince her parents to allow her to go, if they thought she had already accepted. This is what she had rehearsed in front of her mirror before dressing for dinner. Besides, this wasn't the first date in her life, but it was the first time she had ever lied to her parents.

Hermann exploded, slamming his hand on the table, making the silver and glasses clatter and people around them stare. "I will not hear of it and forbid you to go. This is Chicago, young lady. Besides, we know nothing about Sam Parker." His German was beginning to come out, as well as the veins in his neck.

"But, Oliver knows him and his family, dear..." Sophia began, but Hermann cut her off.

"No, Emma. You may not go." His face was now beginning to turn red.

Emma could not stand the look in his eyes. She looked away and put her hand in her blazer pocket. She felt Sam's note and wrapped her fingers around it tightly. She looked back at her father and said, "I'm eighteen, Dad, and I want to go with Sam tonight." She hated the ache in her heart, but knew this was something she wanted.

"You will do nothing of the sort, young lady," her father said. "Go to your room immediately."

Emma stormed from the dining room, embarrassed at the numerous pairs of eyes turned toward her, and ran the four flights to her room. Slamming the door behind her, she locked it without thinking and began to pace the floor. Finally, she slumped down onto her bed and cried, feeling like she was eight years old again.

After a few moments, she went into the bathroom and washed her face. Taking a deep breath, she looked at herself in the mirror. Staring into her eyes, she asked herself what she should do.

"Am I still a child or an adult?" she asked her reflection. She saw a glint of hope, and a small, silent voice inside of her answered. She thought of what she would say while she combed her hair and replaced the blush on her cheeks. She went to the telephone and asked the hotel operator to dial Sam's number.

"Sam, this is Emma," she said, a little nervously into the receiver as she heard his voice. Her stomach was in knots, but she knew she had to do this.

"I would like to go with you tonight, if it's not too late. I could meet you at the coffee shop that we walked past last night, the one near my hotel." She paused, looked at her watch and listened to Sam's instructions.

"Ok," she said breathlessly. "I'll see you there in about fifteen minutes."

She hung up the telephone and took a deep breath. She noticed her hands were shaking. Quickly and quietly, she got up and began to change her clothes, putting on a pretty, red dress and a pair of short heels that her mother had bought her that day for her birthday.

She grabbed a tan raincoat and scarf, then remembered the hallway door and decided to leave through it. She wrote a quick note to her parents, in case they came in while she was gone. She unlocked the inner door, then stopped to look at her reflection in the mirror and smiled.

"*Yes*," she said to herself, "*I'm no longer a child*."

◆ ◆ ◆ ◆

"Hermann, I think you handled that very badly," Sophia said softly, yet bravely. It wasn't the first time she had needed to intervene for Emma. Hermann was pacing the floor of the sitting room of their suite, his hands clasped behind his back. He stopped and turned to his wife.

"What would you have done?" he demanded in a sharp tone. "Our daughter wants to go out with a strange, older man in a strange city. Would you have let her?"

Sophia knew that Hermann was desperately trying to convince himself that he was right and she loved him for it.

"Yes, I would," Sophia said, as she sat calmly in the red velvet, wing-backed chair, watching the fire dancing around the logs in the fireplace. "She is old enough to decide for herself what is right for her, and I think it is time we learned to trust her. Besides, tomorrow we will be leaving, and she will be making her own decisions from now on."

Hermann stopped pacing and stared at his wife. All of a sudden, he saw himself as he stood before Sophia's father when he was asking permission to take Sophia to a concert at the conservatory. He had received the very same reaction that he had just displayed to his daughter. He remembered how terrible he had felt when Sophia's father yelled at him to leave their house. Tears came to his eyes.

"Oh, Sophia, you are right," he said. "Do you think she will ever forgive me?"

Sophia walked over to him and hugged him. She looked into his eyes and said, "You could ask her."

Herman went across the room to Emma's door and knocked. There was no answer. He knocked again, calling out her name. After receiving no answer a second time, he walked back to his wife.

"Maybe you should go talk to her, Sophia," he said, with a pleading look in his eyes. "She does not answer for me."

"Very well," Sophia said and went to her daughter's bedroom door, as Hermann watched.

"Emma, it's me," she said, her soft voice almost singing. "May I come in?"

After she also received no answer, Sophia opened the door with Hermann following her. Emma was not there. Hermann saw the note on her bed and picked it up. After reading it, he slowly handed it to Sophia.

> *Dear Mom and Dad,*
>> *I have decided to go with Sam to the movies after all. Please do not be angry with me. I promise I will be careful.*
>> *Love, Emma*

Hermann became furious and stormed back to the sitting room. After a few moments, Sophia closed the door to their daughter's room. She had quickly called Karen and Oliver, and was assured that Emma would be safe with Sam Parker.

She found Hermann standing at the window, staring out into the night. She walked up to him and put her arm gently around him.

"She will be all right," Sophia said with a true sense in her heart that Emma would be okay. She was not surprised by her daughter's note. She thought of her first date with Hermann and smiled.

"Remember, dear?" Sophia said softly, smiling. "We did the same thing."

◆ ◆ ◆ ◆

In the dark theater, Emma was mesmerized by the images on the large screen. The music was alluring and she liked Audrey Hepburn, with her large, dark eyes and wide, beautiful smile. Later, when Sam put his arm around her shoulders, she stiffened at first, then relaxed, realizing she liked it. She gently relaxed against him, hardly noticing the arm of the seat pushing into her side. As Audrey ran down the stairs of the Louvre in her beautiful, flowing, red dress in front of the statue of Venus, Sam pulled Emma to him. When she looked up at him in the light from the big screen, he brushed his lips against her cheek.

"Happy Birthday, Em," he whispered in her ear.

Her father was the only one who had ever called her 'Em' before. Sam handed her a flat, shiny black box with no wrapping, only a gold ribbon around it. She looked up at him in the light from the screen and smiled. Then she took off the ribbon and opened it. Lying on a white satin cloth was a long, gold necklace with a locket covered in a leaf pattern of different shades of silver and gold.

"It's Black Hills gold," Sam whispered as he took the necklace from the box and leaned closer to her to place it around her neck. She looked up at him, and his lips were soft and gentle as he kissed her. She gasped a little, when his tongue touched her lips, then she relaxed and let him pull her closer. The world disappeared and a loud noise, like the El passing overhead, roared in her ears. When he released her, her head was swimming and she gasped to catch her breath.

"Are you okay?" Sam whispered, seeing her face in the faint light.

"Mhm," she sighed, waiting for her heart to stop hammering in her breast. Sam smiled and took her hand in his.

"Thank you," Emma whispered and they finished watching the movie with their fingers intertwined, her head resting on his shoulder. She liked the ending of the movie, hoping that someday she would find someone like that for herself. When Sam's arm pulled her closer to him before the lights came on in the theater, she smiled to herself, wondering if she had.

◆ ◆ ◆ ◆

After leaving the theater, they walked along the waterfront. Sam helped Emma into her raincoat, as the cool night air blew across the water. He placed his arm over her shoulders, which she liked very much. Then he talked about his father's ranch and horse racing.

"We have forty acres on our ranch in Eugene. Grandfather had built our house and stable when my dad was small. I remember when my dad used to talk about his dream to race horses. His face would light up and the lines around his eyes seemed to disappear when he watched his horses train. I could tell it was his heart's dream. Dad took me to the races in Portland a lot."

"After seeing the race yesterday, I think I like horse racing, too," Emma said, smiling.

"My grandfather worked at the Oregon Racing Commission. That was a great job for him."

"What is the racing commission?" Emma asked.

"It's a state agency that protects the horses from being harmed for the sake of winning the game. Each state in America has one. There's also a Thoroughbred Racing Protective Bureau I heard of once - it's more on the national level."

"You like racing, don't you?" She could see the spark in his eyes as he talked; the excitement in his voice told her this was his dream.

"Yes. Someday, I'd like to own a large Thoroughbred farm, bigger than my dad's ranch."

"Then, why are you going into the Air Force to learn to fly jets?"

He thought for a moment, searching for the words.

"I've been flying most of my life, either on a horse or in a plane. My grandfather was a pilot, and he took me up with him whenever my parents would allow it. I grew up learning to love flight. Being airborne to me was more comfortable than being tied to the earth. Being up there," he said, looking skyward "is like walking on the clouds."

Emma felt she understood what Sam was saying. When she rode Gandolf in the open fields around her home, the world disappeared around them and they seemed to float through the air in perfect harmony.

"My friend," Sam continued, "Jim Barolio, and I hung around the local airport when we were kids, and we vowed that someday we'd fly jets together. We've known each other since grade school. Jim joined the Air Force when I did and is coming with me to Arizona."

Emma was silent for a moment, thinking of her own dreams. She knew Sam was watching her, as she leaned on her elbows on the railing, watching the lights on the shore dance on the black mirror of water.

"I hope I'm doing the right thing," she said with a heavy sigh, as she thought of her choice to go to art school.

"Care to share?" Sam asked.

Emma told the first person in the world her dream of what she really wanted to do. "My father brought Conversano Regina, a white Lipizzan stallion, with him from Germany to use as breeding stock. All Lipizzaners are descendants of the white stallions bred for the Austrian Empire hundreds of years ago. They were first bred for the cavalry, but later were used to perform dressage for the emperors.

"Dad learned dressage at the Spanish Riding School in Vienna. Later, he taught at one of the riding schools in Verden. I hope that someday I will be able to teach dressage, like my father."

"Dressage - that's a very intense and formal style of riding, isn't it?" Sam asked.

"Yes."

"I've never seen it before, just heard about it around the tracks from some trainer."

"It's usually performed in an arena, where the horse and rider move in perfect unison, following a specifically designed pattern. It's very beautiful to watch. Oh, I wish I didn't have to go to school. I'm afraid I'm going to miss the farm." She was beginning to have doubts about the next day.

"First time away from home?" Sam asked gently.

"Yes."

"Why are you studying art?"

"I told you," she began, then looked out over the water again. "My mother wants me to. She was studying the cello at the conservatory when she met my father. I think that sometimes she's trying to finish what she started through me." She stopped, feeling guilty that she had thrown the blame onto her mother so quickly.

"I see."

Feeling that she needed to explain, she continued. "I've always liked to draw - horses, mostly. My mother's talent is in music. She plays the cello so beautifully. Some evenings, she will play for us, but I know that mostly she plays for herself. I can see it in her face. Sometimes, when she is finished, I can see the tears in her eyes. I guess you could say I'm doing this for her." She stopped for a moment, then added, "I'm looking forward to studying different mediums in art, even though I prefer working with the horses more."

"I understand," Sam said. "I've always been torn between horse racing and flying."

Emma thought of Jennifer. "I met a new friend today, who is also going to the Institute. We met at a riding stable in the park near the school. She's from Oregon, too. Her name is Jennifer Spencer. Do you know her?"

Sam laughed. "The name doesn't ring any bells. But then, Oregon is a big state with lots of wide, open spaces."

"I've always believed," Emma said a little wistfully, "that every person you meet adds another piece to the puzzle of your life. At the end, it all comes together - as if by design."

"Yes," Sam agreed.

Emma smiled as she looked at Sam under the light. His hair was the color of dark sable, the light catching the highlights created by the sun. She thought he was handsome in his blue uniform, as he flashed his incredible smile at her. She wondered why he was wearing it tonight, but had been too afraid to ask.

"What are you going to do after the service, Sam?"

"I don't know yet. Probably continue racing, like my dad. It's in my blood."

They were silent as they watched a small boat coming into the lights of the harbor below them. Emma wondered where the boat had been and felt that it would be wonderful to just step onto one and take it anywhere she desired, never thinking of where she'd been. For the first time in her life, she was feeling a sense of adventure awakening deep within her. She was beginning to see the possibilities opening in front of her.

"Hungry?" Sam asked softly.

"Starving!"

"There's a little all-night diner in the next block. Let's go."

Inside, the air was warm and the flourescent lights bright. Sam and Emma sat down on the red, plastic stools in front of the long, oval counter. A short wait-ress, with brown hair and red lipstick, walked over to them with a coffee pot in one hand and menus in the other. The white apron, barely covering the front of her black dress, was stained with ketchup and mustard. Sam turned over his cof-fee cup for the waitress to fill, but Emma motioned that she did not want any.

"We're famous for our burgers and fries," the waitress said in a high-pitched voice, as she quickly chewed gum.

"That sounds great," Sam said. "How about you, Em?"

"Yes, I'll have the same." Just before the waitress walked away, Emma added, "Do you have milkshakes?"

"Sure do, honey. What flavor would you like?"

"Strawberry, please."

After the waitress left, Sam asked Emma, "What did you wish for?"

"What?"

"Before you blew out the candles on your cake last night."

"I can't tell you or it won't come true." She couldn't tell him she had wished that she would find someone to love, who would love her in return - like the love her parents had.

Their food arrived and they ate slowly, talking of when they were young.

Emma shared what she had learned from her father on the process of training a young foal in the ways of dressage, how their muscles needed development at different stages to achieve the balance to perform the exercises from the Training Level to the Grand Prix.

Sam talked more about flying and his home in Oregon. As he spoke, Emma could see how much he loved both. He told her about his friendship with Jim Barolio and their adventures at the small, local airstrip. He described the snow-capped mountains surrounding his parent's ranch, and the rushing river running next to it. She marveled at being anywhere that had mountains with snow all year long. She placed her hand on her locket and promised to herself that one day she would go there.

After they finished eating, they exchanged their future addresses, writing them on clean napkins, promising they'd write. They left the diner, and slowly walked back along the waterfront toward Emma's hotel.

"The last two days have seemed like a lifetime," Emma said. "It's as if time stopped, so we could treasure each moment, like in slow motion. So much has happened."

"Yeah, I know what you mean."

They came to the street where the Drake Hotel stood high above the other buildings, the shoreline white in the moonlight. They stopped, waiting for the traffic light to change.

"When do you have to leave for Arizona?" Emma finally asked, hopeful that it would not be for some time. She now had an urgency to know.

"Tonight."

They stood under the light in silence. Emma's heart sank into the depths of her body. *That's why he's wearing his uniform*, she thought. She hated the other thoughts running through her mind, the panic of Sam leaving, of how much she had started to care for him, how much she wanted to give to him, and her unwillingness to look past this night.

He reached over and gently placed his arm on her shoulders again as she shivered. Sensing her fear, he engulfed her in his arms in an attempt to hold onto this moment forever. He put his hand under her chin and tipped her head up, slowly lowering his lips to hers, tasting her young sweetness. His body ached for her. He wanted to lose himself in her black hair, her dark eyes, holding back each moment that encroached to pull them apart.

He wanted to say, *I love you Emma*, softly into her hair. It was the first time he'd ever felt his heart swell so large that he thought it would burst, but his head began to get in the way and he remained silent. He'd never let a girl get this close to him before, he'd always managed to pull up his guard before it was too late.

Just then, some people bumped against them as they clung together.

"I should get back to the hotel," Emma said finally, placing her hand to her hair.

Sam nodded and they began to walk. Just before they reached the building, Emma tucked the necklace under the neckline of her dress, so it hung close to her heart. They stood near the front doors looking into each other's eyes, searching for an answer to the hope in their hearts.

What Sam saw made his mind spin. He was beginning to feel confused, afraid. Emma was getting too deep inside of him, too fast. In college, he'd always been loose, no ties. Whenever a young woman had tried to tie him down, he'd run the other way. Now, for the first time in his life, he didn't know what he wanted to do.

Just as Emma was about to speak, a taxi drove up to the curb next to them. The car door opened, and a beautiful, blonde woman in a dark blue suit called out, "Come on, Sam, honey. We'll miss our plane."

Sam looked at the woman, then back at Emma. He tried to smile, but it appeared more as a smirk. "I've gotta go," was all he could say. He'd seen an escape. He quickly kissed Emma. Then, just before he turned away, he saw her father's face through the window in the lobby, red with fury. Sam ran to the cab and sat next to the woman. As he closed the door, he waved back to Emma. His heart broke when he saw her face.

Emma stood stunned, her face frozen with shock as the car disappeared into the city's traffic. She wasn't sure what had just happened, how one person could change so quickly. She thought she knew Sam, knew how she felt about him, but realized she must have been wrong. What she had seen in his eyes had shocked her, but she had seen when he'd begun to pull away. She held herself, feeling the ache in her heart.

Quickly, she turned and ran into the hotel and up the stairs, tears streaming down her face. She was glad her parents were not in the sitting room when she arrived at their suite. Once she was inside of her room, she locked her door and threw herself down onto her bed and sobbed. Sam had left just as she was about to tell him she loved him. She suddenly became afraid of her own feelings, the stirring deep inside, a feeling she had never known. She had wanted to stay in Sam's arms and forget everything – school, the farm, her dreams – until the woman had appeared. Then, everything had changed. Emma knew she would never be the same.

◆ ◆ ◆

Her father stood in the hotel lobby, hidden by a large pillar. He'd watched as his daughter was being kissed. He'd been upset that she had disobeyed him, but now he was furious after seeing Sam leave with the other woman. He vowed then to himself to protect his daughter from this man, at all costs.

CHAPTER THREE

Spring, 1958

The light flickering from the red-brick fireplace danced on the walls, creating shadows that reminded George of the race yesterday at Churchill Downs. Koenig, his favorite three-year-old colt, had pulled away from the other horses from the start of the race, taking the lead and keeping it until the finish line. Having his own horse win the Kentucky Derby was a dream George had kept alive ever since he first owned Essen Farms.

He picked up the prior day's newspaper and re-read the article. "Mason's 'Koenig,' Juan Martinez up, won the eighty-fourth Kentucky Derby today." His heart swelled with pride. He removed his reading glasses and leaned back in his chair, remembering where it all began.

George had been around horses all his life, helping his father with the warm-bloods on their breeding farm on the Ruhr River outside of Essen. Even though Essen was a mining and industrial city, their farm was a small haven away from the invasion of the technical world. Their horses were originally bred as work horses, which they sold to the German military.

Always hating having to follow in his older brother's footsteps, George never felt that he measured up to their father's ideals. Hermann had been the favored one, immersed in dressage since he was sixteen and given the opportunity to learn to ride at the Spanish Riding School in Austria, even though it cost their family dearly. Hermann was to return to their farm when his training was completed to begin a new sports riding program that their father thought would meet the upcoming future of the horse farms in Germany. Instead, Hermann went to the equestrian city of Verden to train others in dressage. Their father became angry with Hermann, vowing to never speak to him again. Franz, the youngest, had then become the favorite. George was forced to grow up that year, taking on more responsibilities on the farm. He had to give up his dreams, and he'd never forgiven Hermann.

George dreamt of notoriety and vowed that someday he'd make his mark in the world in a different way than Hermann. George had a competitive spirit, and he always liked winning.

In America, George learned that he was a betting man. Shortly after his arrival in New York, he'd heard about Belmont Park race track and took the train to Elmont. He began eating and sleeping at the track, exercising the horses, working as a stable hand, whatever jobs he could find to be near the horses. That was when racing became his life's desire. He'd kept his eyes and ears open, eager to learn how to win at the game of gambling, and he was good at it. He knew what to watch for, what horses and odds would be the best bet. Sometimes he lost, but he'd gain it back again another day. Because he had few expenses, he stockpiled his winnings.

After a few months, he'd heard of a job as a stable hand at a large breeding farm in Kentucky. He wasn't afraid to begin at the bottom to achieve his dream. On the train ride to Louisville, he found that this part of his new country was not very different from Germany. Upon taking the job, he learned to love McKenzie Farms and believed that one day it would be his. It was more than a Thoroughbred farm to him – it was his home.

Through the years, George became caught up in the thrill of the race and paid attention to the horses on the circuit, learning all he could from the owner, Bob McKenzie. George became obsessed, keeping to himself and his goal, never letting anyone get close to him, except for Bob. Betting with the inside knowledge he'd gained at Belmont, George began creating a hidden hoard of his winnings for his future plans. His dream became a reality when Bob had a heart attack, but George's own heart ached that day. Bob McKenzie had been more a father to him than his own.

George's eyes grew dark in the firelight as he now thought of seeing Bob's daughter, Karen, at Arlington Park on the day he'd arranged to see Hermann. If she hadn't been there, he may have approached his brother that day. But, because of what he knew about her father, he'd hesitated. Bob had left a reputation around the Louisville racing circuit for years known only to those inside. He'd allowed his horses to be drugged for the sake of winning. George knew about it and had tried to convince Bob that it would ruin him some day, but Bob shrugged him off, explaining that he ran his farm his way. It didn't reach the public until the Racing Commission charged Bob with a violation. That was the day Bob fell over dead. When Karen learned about it, she'd blamed George and not her father, but an investigation had cleared George.

Mollie McKenzie knew what kind of man her husband was, and she wanted nothing more to do with the farm. She was glad when Bob's will had left the farm to George, providing he made a settlement to Mollie and Karen. When George took over the farm and renamed it Essen Farms, he vowed that the abuse would never happen again. He'd instructed his riders to never carry a whip and let the horses run with their hearts during a race. When Koenig was born, George had begun to work toward his next dream that one of his horses would win the Kentucky Derby.

Now, after the elation and celebration of winning was over, while he sat with his long legs stretched out in front of him in the office of his large home at Essen Farms, a deep sadness filled his heart. There had been only one person to share the most exciting day of his life - Fred, his trainer and friend. Fred and the other employees were now George's family. His farm was over five hundred acres of prime Kentucky land, with fifty stallions standing at stud that would have made any man content, but it wasn't enough.

George stood and walked to Bob's old liquor cabinet and poured himself a shot of Kentucky bourbon. He had learned to drink it straight, no ice. He went to his massive oak desk, took off his tweed jacket, loosened his tie, and sat down. Looking around the office, he saw the trophies and ribbons that all of his horses had won over the years, their photos hanging above each one. That was before he'd turned Essen Farms into a breeding farm. Koenig was his last colt he would use for racing, but he was sure that this horse was going to be the next Triple Crown winner.

The tall Derby trophy stood amongst the other trophies, Koenig's name engraved on the cup. The golden horse on the large cup gleamed in the firelight. George looked up at the photo of Koenig, already mounted on the wall above the trophy. He could see Juan Martinez, his jockey, sitting on the horse's back in the red silks with the gold 'V', the colors of Essen Farms.

Then, in the firelight, George thought of his brother again. Karen McKenzie hadn't been the only reason he'd hesitated in going up to Hermann at Arlington. His own fear of his brother, if he really knew, had stopped him. George shook his head, and was lost in his memories.

◆ ◆ ◆ ◆

"I can't believe this," Fred said, shaking his head as he and Simon Day walked up to the large, white-columned entrance to George's home. "It's never happened since this was Essen Farms. You'd damned well better be right," he warned Simon with a side glance at the short man with dark, brown hair, who was having a hard time keeping up with his own long, hurried stride.

"I am," the smaller man with spectacles said, pushing his shoulders back in an attempt to muster up some courage. He knew what George Mason was like when he was angry. "I wish there was something I could do, but facts don't lie."

Simon hadn't been to this house since the last time, after another race when he'd had to charge Bob McKenzie with using Phenylbutazone on one of his stallions. 'Bute,' as the drug had been nicknamed, contained an anti-inflammatory agent that was used in the racing industry to help injured horses complete a race. Simon knew the racing commission was considering changing its rules about the use of this drug on horses, but the changes never came soon enough according to him. He had no tolerance for animal abuse. This case was much more serious and an altogether different matter.

As Fred opened the large, red doors, Simon looked around and saw that it hadn't changed very much, which didn't surprise him. George had worked for Bob for many years and had become the son Bob never had. Bob's daughter, Karen, was always jet-setting around the world and had no time for the farm. Molly McKenzie never liked the horses or Kentucky and had no qualms in the settlement, quickly selling it all to George when her husband died, leaving almost everything of the farm behind and returning to Boston, where she had grown up. Simon remembered the fierce anger Karen McKenzie had thrown at George during her law suit to try to get McKenzie Farms from him, but the judge had let Bob's wishes in his will stand.

The wide entrance, with the tall ceiling and marble floor was still rather intimidating to Simon. He remembered that Mollie always had a tall vase of bright flowers standing on a long narrow table in the entrance. He noticed the same narrow table stood there now, but it was bare.

Fred led the way down the hall, through the foyer and knocked on the closed door of the den.

"Come in," a voice behind the door said. The two men entered the room.

Simon saw the light in the room was dim. Most of the floor-to-ceiling mahogany paneling was covered by the large bookshelves filled with old leather-bound books, trophies, and brass statues of horses bred on the farm. A liquor cabinet stood in a corner, containing a silver tray of glasses and an open bottle of bourbon gleaming in the soft light from the fireplace across the room. When he looked over and saw George look up at him from behind the large desk, his mouth went dry.

"Hello, Simon," George said, stretching his hand out to the Kentucky Racing Commissioner. George knew Simon didn't make house calls unannounced, unless there was trouble. When he saw the look on Fred's face, he felt as if a fist had clenched around his heart.

Simon walked over to George and shook his hand. The soft light of the floor lamp behind George cast the large man's face in shadows.

George could see that Simon was forcing a smile on his face and felt the sweat from the palm of the hand he'd just shaken.

"George," Simon said, avoiding the dark eyes.

"Can I get you some bourbon?" George offered, as he got up and walked over to the cabinet carrying his glass.

"No, thanks," Simon refused, swallowing hard, wishing he could have a shot.

Fred simply shook his head when George lifted the bottle towards him in an invitation.

George poured another shot of bourbon and slugged down the golden liquid, feeling it burn as it went down his throat and into his stomach. He placed the glass on the tray and took a deep breath, preparing himself for the question that he knew he had to ask. He turned and stared at the small man.

"What brings you here, Simon?"

"It's about Koenig," Simon said. He was glad his voice didn't waver.

"Wasn't that a grand race he ran yesterday?" George said, knowing that he was stalling, but he wanted to postpone the inevitable as long as he could. He walked back to his desk, in an attempt to separate himself.

"Yes, it was," Simon said, looking over at Fred.

George saw the look on Simon's face as he'd turned toward Fred. He knew his farm had been clean of illegal drugs since he'd taken over – he'd insisted on it. But, he was still worried.

Simon turned his eyes back to George and cleared his throat.

"I'm afraid I've got bad news, George," Simon said. "Koenig's post-race urinalysis showed 'Bute' in his urine."

"What?" George roared.

"There's more..." Simon started, then looked away from George. He wasn't sure how to break this to the man he'd come to respect in front of him. "There was another substance we're not able to pinpoint yet, but it doesn't look good,"

Simon added. "We're still checking the sample. I've called Brad Jones in to take a look at Koenig."

George stared at Simon. Then he looked at Fred, not believing his ears. Fred nodded his head in agreement to Simon's verdict. George slowly sat down and looked into the fire. The crackling logs and a clock ticking on the mantel were the only sounds in the dark room. His world was breaking apart and falling in small pieces around him.

"Are you sure you have the right horse, Commissioner?" George's voice boomed in the stillness of the room, an anger rising from deep inside of him.

"Yes, George," Simon said, aware George had used his title. "You know the results of the saliva and urine tests are tagged immediately after they're taken and assigned a number before they are sent to both the steward's office and the technical lab for testing. The guys in the lab don't know which horse they're testing; they just know it was a horse that ran in one of the races that day."

"How did this happen?" George questioned Fred, pounding his fist on his desk.

"I don't know for sure, George" Fred began, looking George straight in the eye. "Simon said they've tested Koenig's stall at Churchill Downs, thinking that maybe something had been put into his feed somehow, but no trace of anything was found there. I've already started checking everyone that was near him yesterday."

Karl Strauss' face came to George's mind, a tall, slender man who was the newest member of his team. Karl had come to work for George as his vet recently, just after McKenzie's old vet, Henry Phillips, retired. Strauss, like George, was a German immigrant. He'd arrived with good credentials, listing his work at tracks in both Venezuela and New York. Yet, George still didn't know much about the man. He always kept to himself, unwilling to talk about his past. Karl had reminded George of himself.

George thought of Fred's words at the track yesterday, just after they'd left the Winner's Circle. He'd had asked Fred where Karl was.

'He's gone into town. Said he needed to get some supplies,' had been Fred's reply before he'd walked to the testing barn with Koenig.

George hadn't thought anything of it at the time, but now he turned this over in his mind. It had seemed strange to him that a vet would leave his horse and not send someone else for the supplies, especially when the colt had just won the Kentucky Derby. Yet, at the time, George's mind had been on other things.

Simon cleared his throat, beginning to feel uncomfortable in the silence.

"I'm going to get to the bottom of this," George yelled and stormed out of the house toward the barn where Koenig was stalled, Fred and Simon following.

Simon noticed the crisp night air. The full moon lit the way to the barn, and faint, yellow lights streamed from the windows as they approached. He could smell the sweet hay and knew that this serene setting was about to explode as George slammed open the barn door.

"Everyone, get out here, now!" George roared.

George went to Koenig's stall and saw that he was standing with his right, front leg cocked. He went into the stall and knelt down beside the horse, feeling the swollen limb.

Johnny Blair, one of George's grooms who cared for Koenig, came out of his quarters at the other end of the barn, rubbing his sleepy eyes in his dark face with one hand and pulling a suspender up onto his shoulder with the other. Hank and Tony, two young stable boys, joined Johnny as he walked over to where George stood.

"What's up, Mr. Mason?" Johnny said in a slow, southern drawl.

"Where's Conrad?" George yelled, his face red with rage. Conrad Schultz had been the farm foreman since Bob McKenzie's time.

"I don't know, probably at his house. It's late, Mr. Mason." Johnny was wide awake now, his eyes wide and frightened. He'd seen his employer's anger before, but never like this.

George took the man by the shirt and began to shake him. "Koenig was drugged yesterday, before the race, and now he's injured. I want answers and I want them now..." George began to rant in German at the groom, shaking him until his eyes were filled with fear.

"I don't know nothing about any drug, Mr. Mason," Johnny stammered back, unable to look at George's face. He remembered Bob McKenzie taking the whip to him, accusing him of the same thing, but he'd known that time it had only been a performance for the benefit of the Commissioner. He knew what McKenzie did to his horses.

Johnny looked nervously at Simon. He was a different Commissioner than before. He'd seen him around the track, but never had any cause to talk to him. This time, Johnny was really scared. He knew George Mason would never let his animals be hurt, for any reason. And, a groom was the first to be suspected.

"You're lying, Johnny, I know you are." George threw him down onto bales of straw sitting in the aisle that would be used for the stalls in the morning. He reached over and grabbed an old riding whip hanging on the wall behind Johnny and raised it in the air.

"Tell me the truth, or I'll beat it out of you."

Fred grabbed George's arm. He knew George's temper and what he could do when blinded by it. It wasn't the first time he'd had to stop him.

"George, stop this. You won't get any information this way," Fred said.

Fred threw the whip down on the ground and reached to help Johnny to his feet. The other young grooms stepped back, hands in their pockets.

"Johnny, tell me what you know about this," Fred said in a soft voice. "Did you see anyone near Koenig before the race yesterday?"

Johnny stepped from one foot to the other in a nervous manner, looking down at the ground. He knew something had happened when he'd groomed Koenig after Fred brought him back from the test barn. The horse was different somehow, but he'd kept quiet. Now, he was afraid to say anything.

"Johnny, I'm Commissioner Day," Simon said, placing his hand on Johnny's shoulder. "You remember me. I don't think that you are in any kind of trouble, but did you see anything out of the ordinary before the race?"

"The only thing I know is that I saw Doc putting something back into his coat pocket after he checked Koenig for the last time – just before I walked him out to the paddock. I didn't think nothing of it, since he's the vet an' all. Didn't tell nobody, cause I didn't want nobody to get into any trouble." He let out a sigh. It was mostly the truth.

"Did you see anything else, maybe later, after the race?"

Johnny was quiet for a moment, looking from Simon to Fred to George. He felt cornered, but he knew he couldn't keep it inside now.

"I knew there was something different with Koenig after you brought him back from the tests, Mr. Jamison."

"Why didn't you say something then, Johnny?" Fred asked.

"I was gonna keep an eye on him and see how he was later. Sometimes, a race takes everything out of a horse. Usually, though, Koenig's pumped and ready to run again. This time, he just seemed sad or something."

"Did you see anything out of the ordinary before that?" George asked, calmer now.

"Just when I was getting Koenig's stall ready for his return, I seen Doc leaving the track in a hurry. That horse run a fine race, he did. I'd thought it was mighty strange. Doc said something 'bout running for some supplies, but I knew he'd gone and got them all the day before."

Simon turned to George. "Where's Strauss' office?" he asked.

"This way," George said, as he led the way out of the stable to the small building to the right.

"He sleeps in the back room behind the office," George said as he entered the building. He knocked on the door that had a gold plate with VET written on it, but there was no answer.

"Karl, open up," George yelled. "We need to talk to you."

Fred put his hand on George's arm, then knocked again.

"Doc, it's me, Fred. Open up, will ya?" After there was still no response, Fred opened the door. The room was dark, with the strong smell of alcohol and liniment in the air. A small light could be seen from under the door at the end of the room. Fred turned on the overhead light and walked past the cabinets of medical supplies to the inner door and knocked.

"Doc, are you awake?" Fred asked.

George was getting impatient and pushed Fred aside. He turned the handle and opened the door, stepping into a room that was like a small hotel room, containing a brown plaid couch, one chair, and a single bed. The room was empty. The drawers on the dresser near the bed were hanging open, also empty.

Simon noticed a door off to the left. "What is that room?" he asked.

"A bathroom," Fred answered.

Simon went to the bathroom, turned on the light, then disappeared into the room.

"Looks like he left in a hurry," Simon said, walking back where the other men stood. "He left a few things behind that could easily be replaced. I found this in the pocket of a jacket hanging on the back of the door."

Simon held out his hand, which was now covered with a glove. A short, blue jacket hung over his arm. George saw the syringe in Simon's hand and his heart stopped.

"Why?" George asked, looking between Simon and Fred. "Why would he do this?"

"I don't know, George," Fred said, placing his hand on the large man's shoulders. "But I'm going to get to the bottom of this."

"What gets me was why he was so careless," Simon said, dropping the syringe into a plastic bag that he'd pulled from his coat pocket. He had learned in his business to always be ready for anything. "It's almost as if he wanted us to find it."

◆ ◆ ◆ ◆

Karl Strauss sat on the plane taking him back to Venezuela, smiling at the pretty blonde stewardess in First Class.

"Here's your coffee Mr. Maseman," she said as she handed him a cup.

He just nodded to her as he took the cup. He wasn't in any mood to talk. After she left, he sat back in his seat, closed his eyes, and took a deep breath. He knew he could relax now, but it always took his body a long time to release the adrenalin he needed to do a job. He'd learned that back in Germany, when he and Franz Maseman had stood together during the war. When young, they had become part of the Hitlerjugen, a semi-military group of young people who were taught how to be soldiers.

Franz was like Karl's adopted brother and his friend. The war had thrown their lives together when they were young. Karl was only sixteen when his parents brought Franz Maseman to live with them, after Franz's parents had been killed. He was older than Karl by three years, and they looked as if they were blood brothers.

Karl opened the passport and looked at the photograph of the young man inside. He closed his eyes and laid his head back against the seat, remembering the day he'd learned that Franz had disappeared. That had been the saddest day of his life.

Franz had told Karl how his brothers had left for America, abandoning him and his parents. Franz blamed his brothers for his parents' deaths, and he'd vowed his revenge. He'd told Karl about the stolen Friedrich painting, and about the letter his brother, Hermann, had written to explain that he had it with him in America. Franz believed it was his true inheritance and he'd sworn he'd get it back, no matter what the cost. That passion had driven Franz when they were in the Nazi army. Karl wasn't proud of what he'd had to do for the Third Reich, but he'd seen the sick pleasure in Franz's face as he tortured each victim. There were times when Franz scared Karl.

Then, one day, when there was an attempted escape at the last camp they were assigned to, some of the Germans were killed. Karl hadn't been able to find

Franz anywhere. When they'd given him Franz's passport with what was left of his belongings, Karl had begun his plot to carry out Franz's revenge on Hermann and George Maseman.

The prior year, he'd decided to leave his job in New York and explore more of North America. It was when he was walking near the end of a shedrow in the backside at Arlington Park race track that he'd overheard two men talking and made the connection between Franz Maseman and George Mason.

'Hermann won't know you, because of your name change,' he'd heard one of the voices say. 'The *Racing Form* will list George Mason, not Maseman.'

Karl had continued to listen, being careful not to be seen. Later, he'd learned that George Mason was the owner of Essen Farms in Louisville, Kentucky. The name of the farm intrigued Karl, since Essen was where he and Franz had lived in Germany as brothers. It was then he'd begun to form his strategy. He'd been around horses most of his life and knew he could forge the vet documents he'd need.

Later that same week, after George had returned to Kentucky, Karl warmed up to Fred Jamison, George's trainer. After Fred had prepared the horses for the return to Kentucky, Karl invited Fred to a small bar near the track and began to buy him whiskey. The more the man drank, the looser his tongue became.

"George," Fred had said, his words a little slurred, "he's a great guy. I've known him for years. We're like brothers. George owns Essen Farms in Louisville."

Fred was beginning to slide lower in his chair, and Karl had continued to fill his glass. As Fred talked about the horses they had raced, Karl began to realize that the man was a fool as a trainer. Fred didn't seem to know what drugs to use to make a horse run to win, like he did.

"I'd like to meet George," Karl said. "I'm a veterinarian, and I'm looking for work."

"Well, isn't that a coincidence," Fred said. "Henry's just announced his retirement, and we're looking for a new vet."

"That is convenient," Karl had said with a smile

Karl now smiled to himself in the cabin of the plane, thinking just how convenient it had been. When he'd first seen George Mason, he wasn't sure if he had the right man. Franz was blond and blue-eyed, like himself. George was a much larger man, with dark hair and eyes. But, life had taught Karl to be a very patient man.

Karl looked at his watch. The drugs would have been found by now in the post-race test. He knew how much George Mason wanted Koenig to win the Triple Crown and what this loss would do to George. Karl had learned of the drug combination in Venezuela and used it once before, when it was necessary. When he'd seen the slight swelling after Koenig's prior race, involving hypertension of the front, right pastern joint, he knew exactly what he had to do when the horse raced again. He knew the leg should have been X-rayed, but he'd minimized the problem to Fred and simply medicated the horse. The pounding from the race would most likely fracture the horse's short pastern bone. It could be surgically repaired, but it would bring the animal's racing career to an end.

Karl got up and went into the toilet on the plane. He knew he'd never be able to work again in America, but he didn't care. He'd done this for Franz. He'd do anything for Franz.

"Now, little brother," he said to his reflection in the mirror, thinking of Franz. "I have done something for you."

◆ ◆ ◆ ◆

George sat behind his desk again. Simon and Fred had just left, with Brad Jones, a vet that worked for the Commission. After Brad had looked at Koenig, he'd determined that Koenig had a fracture of P2 or the short pastern bone. He figured the horse was so drugged up that he didn't feel the pain in his right, front leg during the race. There was no question about the surgery for Koenig. The horse would receive the best of care.

He knew exactly what this meant. There would be no Preakness. No Belmont. No Triple Crown. George didn't mind that he would lose the Derby winnings, nor that this would leak to the press. It wasn't the suspension that would follow that bothered him. George knew now that Koenig would never race again.

George's mind began to swirl with a collage of images of his parents' faces, of when he'd seen McKenzie Farms for the first time, Emma's face at Arlington, Koenig in the Winner's Circle, Chris Schmidt, Karl Strauss, Hermann. He brought himself up short and stared out in front of him.

Could Hermann have sent Strauss to him, just as he had sent Chris to spy on Hermann? he thought to himself. *Is this Hermann's revenge?*

George opened the drawer of his desk and took out a print. The image of the Friedrich painting was bent and a corner was torn from the years that he'd continually looked at the copy. When he had seen the print in a small gallery in New York, he couldn't believe his eyes. It was the thorn in his side that he now believed his brother had put there.

He slipped the print back into the drawer and slowly closed it. It was time to finally visit his brother.

CHAPTER FOUR

Summer, 1960

"**C**an I give you a lift?" David Storey asked Hermann as he was leaving Henry Miller's house, his blue eyes shining a little more than usual from the beer he'd consumed during the poker games. "I'll be ready in a few minutes, after I talk to Henry for a moment about his new tractor."

"No thank you, David," Hermann replied, looking at the summer night around him as the half-moon rose overhead. "It's such a beautiful night, and I prefer walking."

Hermann liked to walk home after their Friday-night poker games at Henry's farm. He smiled to himself as he walked, fingering the fifty dollars in his pocket that he'd just won. He'd been playing poker with this same circle of friends for five years, a harmless game where the money that was won would eventually return to each player.

It was a dark, warm night, and the white-painted fence surrounding his farm glistened in the pale moonlight. When he saw the lights of his house in the distance, he smiled. Emma was home from college for the summer. Next year was her last year at school. He had missed her. Secretly, he hoped that someday Emma would continue his riding school after him.

There was still a small, but distant ache in his heart as he thought of his son, Martin. The sadness was the fact of never knowing him, what type of person he would have been. He'd hoped for a son and had decided to name his child after his father, when he was born. Then, after his death, Hermann had learned the seemingly cruel fact that life went on. As a blessing, Emma was born the following year, whom he treasured.

"What a good life I have," Hermann said to the night as he walked down the gravel road, taking a deep breath of the warm air. He was proud of his farm. It had taken many years to make it productive, but he didn't mind the work. He'd always kept the vision of his dream in mind, driving him forward until the day he'd opened the riding school.

When he'd sent for Sabrina, a mare from a southern Austrian breeding farm, his dream was complete. Conversano, his stallion, was from one of the six foundation sires of the Lipizzaners. With his new mare, Hermann planned to the sell her foals to Simpleton Farms in Indiana, the largest Lipizzan dressage training farm outside of Austria. He didn't like admitting to himself that he'd had to use the Friedrich, his father's painting, as collateral to finance Sabrina, but he'd felt he had no choice. It had almost killed him until he had been able to get the painting back in his possession.

He thought of the day he'd found oil on his property. It had been an exciting day. He and Chris had toiled for weeks down by the old bridge, helping to build the test pump. When it blew, Sophia and Emma were there. They had all been covered in oil as they danced under the shower of black liquid. Even though they'd drilled more wells, he never struck oil again. But, he didn't mind.

The only thing he felt still missing in his life was his family he'd left behind in Germany. He thought of his relationship with his father, a stern man who was grounded in tradition. His father had inherited the large horse-breeding farm from his father, carrying on the tradition of providing warm-bloods to the military. But, Hermann had always wanted to learn to ride the Lipizzaners in Austria, after he'd seen a performance. He had been forced to work while going to the school to help with the costs, but he didn't mind. He would always be grateful to his instructor Rudolf Hinteregger, who was more like a father to him than his own. Rudolf had given him the job that would help him stay in the school.

When Hermann returned to his home in Germany after finishing his training in Austria, the Friedrich painting hung on his parents' wall. Hermann knew that Caspar Friedrich was a Romantic painter, whose paintings had at one time been commissioned by a Russian Czar. When his mother told him how much it had cost and that his father had sold a large portion of their land to purchase it, Hermann had realized then how his father valued this painting more than his own family. That was when he had left for Verden.

Now, when his life was at its fullest, Hermann hated the fact that he and his father had not spoken to each other since his decision to work in Verden, instead of staying on the farm as his father wished. It was a scar that he would carry to his grave. But, he knew, at the time, that he had made the right decision. When he'd left for Verden, he remembered wishing that he had been as strong as his brother George and had taken the Friedrich with him. Now it was his!

In Verden, he'd begun to see his future when he learned that the school sold retired performance Lipizzaner stallions, and he knew that someday he would own one. His work as a trainer and performer helped him to gain the money to later buy his stallion. He'd also been able to send his mother some money over the years. Her letters had told him about his father's drinking, but that he still refused to allow Hermann's name to be mentioned in the house. She had hidden Hermann's pictures, since his father demanded that they all be destroyed. As far as his father was concerned, Hermann was dead.

Hannah's face flashed in his mind and his heart leaped. Whenever he allowed himself to think of his homeland, she would always be there. He'd met her after one of his performances in Verden. She was so beautiful, and being young, he'd been swept off his feet. He knew that her memory would never be erased and that she would never age for him. Yet, the love he had with Sophia he knew he could never have had with Hannah. They were very different women.

He and Sophia had only disagreed once during their marriage – when she'd told him she did not want the Friedrich in her house. She knew it had been stolen from his parents. The argument came after she realized he had used it to finance his mare. She did not approve of their gain from something that had been stolen. She had said that he was obsessed with it and that it belonged in a museum.

When the loan had been paid and the painting was back in his possession, Hermann knew that he could never part with it again. He had lied to Sophia and told her that he had sent it back to a museum in Germany. But, late at night, when he knew he would not be disturbed, Hermann went to the stable and took the painting out of its new hiding place. Hannah's photograph was kept there, as well. He'd sit for hours, staring at the painting with such pride, reveling in the reality that it was his alone to enjoy.

He wondered at himself as he walked down the gravel road at this desire for rumination tonight.

Suddenly, headlights illuminated the road from behind him and he heard the roar of a car's engine approaching very fast.

"Kids," Hermann said out loud and stepped closer to the edge of the gravel. Just as he turned to look at the vehicle, he realized it was coming directly at him. He felt the impact, but didn't feel his spine snap. Through the slow motion of time, he felt himself fly through the air and land jarringly on the gravel. He lay there and watched as the dust from the gravel swirled around him like clouds through the lights of the vehicle, the engine hammering in his aching head. He heard the car door open and saw someone slowly walk to him and kneel over him. He wanted to cry out, but he couldn't speak, lying there as the warm wetness of his own blood trickled out of the side of his mouth.

"Ah, good, you are still alive," the man's voice said in a German that Hermann hadn't heard in years. In the light from the car, Hermann saw the face of a man that he had seen when he was younger.

"Where is the Friedrich?" a voice hissed in the dark. "It is mine."

The voice had a chill that froze Hermann. Fear gripped him as he watched the man pick up a large rock in his black-gloved hands. Hermann tried to move, but he was immobile.

Hermann thought about the painting, about Sophia and Emma. Then he saw the anger in the face staring at him now.

"I destroyed it," Hermann lied, almost in a whisper. He knew he would never let it be taken from him.

"You are lying," the man yelled. "No matter, I will find it. You, my brother, are responsible for our parents' deaths." Just before the rock came down, Hermann heard, "Now, join them."

◆ ◆ ◆ ◆

Emma sat on the porch swing, looking at the small lights from the distant farms shining in the darkness, the half-moon barely lighting the fenced yard around the brick house of her childhood home. Fireflies twinkled everywhere, like tiny stars near the earth. Her hand was deep in Patsy's fur, the old black and tan shepherd lying next to her whom Emma had loved since she was twelve years old. Patsy had become more her mother's dog since Emma went to college, but when she was home for the summer, Patsy stayed near her side.

The locusts, in the heat of the night, harmonized with her mother's favorite Bach cello suite floating through the open window, the soft, yellow light from inside the room resting on the porch at Emma's feet. It was her mother's habit to play in the evenings. Whenever Emma heard it, it reminded her of when she used to ride in a show or was painting, she would always hear *"Lightness,"* *Bach's Suite No. One* in her head. There was silence as her mother came to the end of the piece.

The sweet aroma of hay came to her from the barn, and she smiled. *"Home,"* she sighed to herself. She loved the way time seemed to slow on the farm, driven only by the cycles of the seasons, unlike the city where the clock was the dictator.

Sophia came through the screened door and stood on the porch, staring at her daughter, an apron now tied around her waist over her green flower-printed dress, her dark hair piled on top of her head in the warm summer night. Emma could see a few strands of silver shimmering in the pale light.

"Emma, dear," Sophia said, a hint of the old German accent still in her voice. "I was going to slice some of the peaches I picked today to put on our home-made ice cream. Would you like that?"

"Oh, yes." That was her favorite summer treat, one that she remembered through numerous other summers in her life. "Can I help?"

"No, love, just sit there with Patsy and relax." Sophia looked out into the darkness toward the road. "Your father should be home soon," she said. Then she opened the door and paused with her hand on the frame, smiling at Emma. "It's good that you are home." She disappeared into the house, letting the door softly shut behind her.

Emma heard a horse whinny from the stable. She hadn't realized how much she missed the horses, until this summer. She knew it would become more difficult to return to her college in Chicago. She really preferred to be here, but her father and mother insisted on the importance of her finishing school before deciding what she would do with her life. When she returned home each summer, she would immediately go to the stable and walk by each horse, talking to them, patting their heads or necks. Chris Schmidt, her father's hired man, would always follow closely behind her and update her on each one. It was becoming harder to leave them each fall, but this next term was her last year at the Institute.

Emma remembered that she was thirteen years old when Chris first came to their farm, looking for a job. He was a large, gentle man with a big smile and a generous laugh that shook his entire body. He had told her father that he'd worked as a groom on one of the bluegrass farms in Kentucky, but had decided to leave and travel west. Chris said that he needed work and believed he might be of use, helping with the chores around the farm to give Hermann more time to teach his students. Her father had agreed and given Chris a room in the stable. Once, Chris had told Emma about his sister that lived alone in Kentucky, but he rarely spoke of her.

When she was very young, Emma's father had taught her to ride dressage. She became very good and moved to Grand Prix level within a few years with his tutoring. She thought of the young foals born each year, their dark coloring masking their true beauty until they were eight to ten years old. Gandolf, the colt her father had given her when she was fourteen, was now six years old. At sixteen hands, his dark markings were almost faded now and the white coat of the Lipizzan was beginning to come through. He was an offspring of Conversano and Sabrina, her father's horses. His full name was Conversano Sabrina, but she liked to call him Gandolf. She really wished she could stay here and work with the horses again. That was what she truly wanted to do.

From the porch, she looked up as she heard a car in the distance, traveling rapidly down the road toward their house. She was too far away to see anything else. The car stopped for a moment, then, eventually continued, racing past their house and disappearing through the grove of trees by the creek. She heard the tires go over the wooden bridge, a sound she had heard since she was a child. Later, she realized she would never forget that sound.

The screen door opened again, and Sophia came out onto the porch. Shooing the dog down, she sat on the swing next to Emma and reached over and held her daughter's hand. Sophia looked down and saw the small, brown spots on the skin and the veins on the back of her own hand. She remembered when her hands were as young looking as Emma's. She had met Hermann when he came to the concert hall in New York during her third year at the conservatory. She had instantly fallen in love with him. She was much younger than Hermann, but that didn't seem to matter. He was charming and witty, and she left her studies to marry him.

"Where are you?" Emma asked softly, seeing that her mother was in her own little world.

Sophia looked at Emma and smiled. "I was thinking of when I first met your father."

"At the Bach concert in New York," Emma added. She'd heard the story numerous times in her life.

"Yes. He was so handsome, and gentle. He made me laugh."

Emma could see the love in her mother's eyes and knew what her mother meant. She had seen that same love in her own eyes in the mirror on her eighteenth birthday in Chicago, after meeting Sam Parker.

Sophia was watching her daughter's face. "Have you heard from him yet?" she asked.

Emma looked up quickly.

"Who?"

She knew who her mother meant, and it scared her how their thoughts could be so connected at times.

"Sam Parker," Sophia said.

Emma was silent and stared down at the porch floor. She had written Sam from school, once she'd found the courage. When her letters to Sam returned unopened, she never wrote to him again. She could not forget the blonde woman she had seen in the taxi that Sam had disappeared with into the city on the last day she had seen him in Chicago.

"No," she sighed. "He knows where I am. He'll write to me."

But, he never did.

Suddenly, a car raced up their gravel driveway. Emma recognized David Storey's pickup and figured he was returning their father home from the game, but she couldn't understand why he was driving so fast. The pickup stopped and David jumped out, running up to the house, his face white and frightened.

"Sophia! Emma!" David yelled as he came through the gate in the fence. "Call an ambulance, quick. There's been a terrible accident. Hermann's been hurt."

David knew that Hermann was dead, but he didn't want to be the one to tell his family.

◆ ◆ ◆ ◆

Chris drove Sophia and Emma home from the hospital in Evansville, then left the two women alone. Emma made tea for her mother, and they both sat at the kitchen table, staring into space, numb and exhausted, their clothes stained with Hermann's blood.

"I have to go to the church early tomorrow," Sophia said after awhile, "to arrange the flowers on the altar for the Sunday service. Janet was going to help me."

Emma placed her hand on her mother's arm. She could see that her mother was still in shock and her mind was now working as if nothing had happened. Emma had seen this with her friend Jennifer at school, when Jennifer's uncle had died last spring in a terrible accident.

"Mom, I'll call Janet and ask her if she could take care of them for you. I don't think we will be going to the church tomorrow."

Her mother's eyes were becoming heavy-lidded; the medication the doctor had given her at the hospital was beginning to take effect.

"Come on, Mom, it's time for sleep."

Emma helped her mother to her room and into her bed. Just as she was about to turn out the light, she saw her parents' wedding photograph on the dresser and tears came to her eyes. She looked over and saw that her mother was already asleep. Emma felt so alone and afraid, when she closed the door to her parents' room.

As she walked into her own room, Emma felt that it was not the same. The wood panels on the walls had not changed, the pair of horses she had painted as a child were still in the old frames, hanging on each side of her closet, the stuffed animals lay waiting on her familiar chenille bedspread with the small crocheted flowers of pink and green, but she saw everything differently now. They were childlike and unimportant. She lay down on her bed without changing and cried herself to sleep.

◆ ◆ ◆ ◆

In the stable that night, Chris placed a collect call to Essen Farms in Kentucky. Fred Jamison answered the phone.

"Fred, Chris here. I know this is late, but I need to talk to George."

"He's not here," Fred said in a sleepy voice.

"Where is he?"

"Yesterday, he said he had some personal business to take care of and left."

"Did he say where he was going?"

"No. It's the craziest thing. He's never done this in all of the years I've known him."

"Well, when you hear from him, tell him his brother was killed tonight."

◆ ◆ ◆ ◆

The day was overcast and humid as Emma and Chris walked out with her mother to the grave site on the hilltop, the canopy erected next to Martin's grave. Their friends stood around her father's casket, suspended over the gaping, dark hole in the earth. The colors of the flowers on the casket were a contrast to Emma's grief in her heart. A single dove cooed in a nearby tree, his song mournful in the early morning light. Sophia stopped next to her friends, Karen and Oliver Stenson. Jennifer Spencer, Emma's friend from college, was also there. Jennifer reached over and took Emma's hand as she came to stand next to her.

While the voice of the minister droned across the air, Emma's knees went weak and her body began to shake as the grief ran through her. Her mother stood strong, her face hidden behind the dark veil of her hat. Emma noticed the lilies on the casket and remembered they were her father's favorite flower. Tears ran silently down her cheek. As she brushed them away with her black, gloved hand, she saw her father's face in her mind: the pride in his smile when he had brought her first pony to her, and as he watched her in her first show, his patience in her training; the days when they would disappear into the woods with small, silver buckets to pick the blackberries for a pie that her mother would make; the joy in his face when he surprised her by taking her to the Arlington race track, watching her excitement as she watched the horses race; the tears in his eyes when they said goodbye at her school in Chicago. In her mind, Emma heard her father's voice saying to her as he had every night when she was small: "Good night, *mein liebchen*." Then, he would kiss her forehead and turn out the light. Now, she would never hear his voice again.

Emma looked away from the casket onto the hilltop in an attempt to separate herself from her grief. She noticed a tall, large man in a dark suit standing alone by a tree in the distance with his hands behind his back in a gesture like her father's when he was deep in thought. She felt as if the man looked at her for a moment, then dropped his eyes to the ground.

She heard her mother cry out as the casket was being lowered into the ground. Emma reached over and put her arm around her mother, comforting her. Then she turned her mother away and walked toward their car.

When Emma looked back at the top of the hill, the man had disappeared.

◆ ◆ ◆ ◆

The Stensons and Jennifer stayed with Emma and Sophia until the next morning after the funeral. Oliver had taken the telephone call from Stephen O'Hara, the Rockport sheriff.

"The vehicle that hit Hermann has been found," Oliver said to the women who sat around the kitchen table. "The police said it was a stolen car owned by a man in Evansville. They found it abandoned at the oil well, just beyond the small bridge."

Emma shivered when she remembered the sound of the wheels crossing the bridge that night.

"No evidence of the thief could be determined from the vehicle," Oliver continued. "Many car thefts have been reported lately in the Evansville area, so they think Hermann's death was an accidental hit and run by some thief.

"O'Hara also said the coroner's report revealed that Hermann had received multiple internal injuries on the impact and died from hitting his head as he fell on a rock that was found near the scene."

When Emma saw her mother's face, she knew what she must do. Suddenly, she felt grown up and knew it was time to put her own needs aside. She went up to her room for a little while, then returned to the kitchen, where Jennifer was just finishing the dishes. She asked Jennifer to walk to the stable with her, as she grabbed an apple from the bowl on the counter.

"Are you okay?" Jennifer asked, once they were inside the stable.

"I think so. God, it hurts," Emma sighed, tears coming into her eyes again as she looked around the familiar surroundings, expecting her father to walk out of the tack room at any moment. She went over to the open top of the gate where Gandolf stood.

The tall horse lowered his head and nickered softly. Emma wrapped her arms around his large neck and hugged him. Then she took the shiny, red apple out of her pocket and held it out for Gandolf to take with his soft muzzle

Jennifer came over to Emma and gently hugged her, then stepped back, tears in her eyes. It hurt her to see the pain in her friend's heart.

"Is there anything I can do?" Jennifer finally asked.

Emma was quiet for a moment. She thought of the first day she and Jennifer had met at the stables in the park. Later, Jennifer had helped her to get over her home-sickness, taking her around Chicago to see the city – to get her mind off of Indiana. Emma could tell Jennifer anything. She wiped her face with a handkerchief, squared her shoulders, and turned to look her friend in the eye.

"Yes, Jenn," she said, using the pet name that she had begun to use after they'd become friends. She took a deep breath and continued, "I'm not going back to school."

"What? But, Em—"

"I've made up my mind. I'm staying here with Mom. I can't leave her now." She took an envelope out of her pocket and handed it to Jennifer. "Will you take this letter for me to the dean? It will explain everything."

"But, what about your mother—"

"I'm sure that once I've explained it to her, it will not be a problem. There is no way she and Chris can run this farm alone. They need someone to teach."

"Are you sure that's what you want?" Jennifer looked down at the letter in her hand. She admired her friend's decision and was unsure if she could have done it herself if she'd had to.

"Yes, I'm sure. Would you mind packing up my things at school and sending them to me? I've got some money I could give you."

"Don't worry about that. If I need some, I'll let you know." Jennifer looked away and patted the neck of the big stallion. "I'm going to miss you, Em," she said, trying to smile.

"I'll miss you too, Jenn," Emma said, tears welling in her eyes. "You can stay here anytime."

The two girls looked at each other in the stable aisle, then hugged with tears running down their cheeks. Emma had never had a friend like Jennifer before. They knew everything about each other, no secrets and no pretenses.

◆ ◆ ◆ ◆

Later, after everyone had left, Emma and Sophia sat in the swing on their porch, the same place they had been when they first learned of Hermann's death.

Emma looked at her mother and saw the weariness and pain in her face, making her look much older now than ever before. It saddened Emma to see her mother this way, and frightened her to see her strength gone. She had relied on her mother's ability to shrug off life's disappointments and get on with her work, and had incorporated this attitude in her own life. Her father had also clung to that strength throughout the years of their marriage. Emma reached over to her mother's hand that lay on the porch swing and was glad to see her smile for the first time that day.

"We have had a wonderful life together," Sophia said, staring ahead. "It's a shame it had to end this way. Your father was a good man." Her voice quivered and she stopped, raising her hands to her hair and quickly wiping the tears away. Emma sat silently listening, knowing that her mother needed to talk.

"I wish I had known his family," Sophia continued as she looked at Emma. "Did you know he came to America with his brother, George?"

"No!" Emma exclaimed "He talked very little about his family and only told me about his parents and brother, Franz, who had died in Germany."

"He made me promise to never tell you, but I don't think he'd mind now."

"Why did he do that?" Emma asked. Then, for some reason, she thought of the man she had seen on the hill at the funeral and a chill went down her spine.

"Your father was older than George. He always felt that his brother was bitter about the fact that your father was able to go to school in Vienna and he'd had to stay behind to work on the farm in Germany. He told me once how he and George had argued on the ship as they entered New York Harbor. He never told me why. He only said he had learned something terrible about his brother and vowed to never see him again. Later, quite a few years ago, your father tried to locate George, but was unable to find him. According to the immigration records, he never arrived in America."

The two women sat in silence for awhile.

Emma thought about the day before the funeral, when she had gone to the tack room in the stable to where her father's old trunk sat in a corner, the brass hinges dark with rust spots. When she had opened it, she could smell the old leather of the bridle straps that he had used while performing in Verden. His uniform was also there, the white, buck-skin breeches and red coat, the black, bicorne-style hat. When she picked up the coat, tears had come to her eyes. She sat there sobbing, seeing her father's face before her. The equipment was outdated now, but she knew she never would part with it. It was a reminder of her past, her father's past.

At times, she knew that there was something her father had wanted to tell her, but never could find the words. When she was fourteen, while they were in the stable watching the birth of Gandolf, her father had confided in her about his family. He'd told her he grew up on a large horse-breeding farm near Essen. His mother's brother was forbidden to come to their home because of a dispute between his father and his uncle. He never explained why. Her father had come to America, to make a new home for their family. But, when he had sent for them, telling them about the farm in Indiana, it had been too late. They had been killed in the war. He'd never told her about his brother, George. She had so many questions she wished she could ask her father. But, as she closed the lid of the trunk that day, she felt that his life was then closed to her.

"Mom," Emma said, placing her hand gently on her mother's shoulder. "I've made a decision." She waited for her mother to look at her. "I'm going to stay here with you. I want to continue the riding school."

Sophia was silent for a moment. Emma saw her face, the glint of hope at first, then the shadow. "But, what about your art, Emma, your school? You only have one more year."

"I will continue my art, but my main work will be here – with the horses, as my father's was. It is what I've always loved."

"I think we should not decide for now." Sophia patted her daughter's hand nervously. She had never regretted her own decision to leave the conservatory to marry Hermann, but she wasn't sure if her daughter would regret hers. "Let's wait and see."

"No, Mom," Emma said strongly, looking squarely into her mother's eyes. "I know what I want, and it is to stay here and work. I've already written a letter to the dean, and Jennifer said she will send my things home. I am needed here, now."

Sophia looked away toward the horizon and was silent for a moment. Then she turned to her daughter and smiled. "Yes, I can see that you have made up your mind. I guess I'm not surprised. You always were like your father." Sophia knew her daughter would excel in carrying on Hermann's work, like her husband.

◆ ◆ ◆ ◆

A few months later, Sophia sat on the train nearing the Evansville station. She opened a window and felt the cool air on her face. This was her favorite time of year, and she was glad to be home. The farmers were now busy in their fields, finishing the harvest. The big leaves of the sycamore trees were now turning red and gold. She smiled as she remembered Hermann once saying that the sycamore leaves were as large as dinner plates. Oh, she missed him.

She had gone to visit Karen and Oliver in Chicago the prior week. Emma had told her she thought the trip would be good for her. Sophia knew it was because this was the first time she'd left the farm since Hermann's death, but she had not been able to tell her daughter the real reason for her visit.

As the train stopped, Sophia saw Emma standing on the platform and noticed how beautiful she was. She became sad as she thought of how busy Emma stayed with her work and seemed to have no time for fun – or love. *If only Sam Parker had written to her*, Sophia thought. She knew that Emma had fallen in love that summer and that her daughter had never really gotten over it. She didn't like the thought of Emma being alone.

She sighed and hoped Emma wouldn't notice the weariness in her face as she rose to leave the train.

"Hello, dear," Sophia said, hugging her daughter closely to her.

"Oh, Mom, I've missed you."

"I know, Emma. I've missed you, too." Sophia stood back and smiled, taking Emma's chin in her gloved hand. "We're together, now," she said. "Come, let's get my bags and go home."

On the ride, Sophia watched the familiar landscape pass by the window with new eyes. *Oh, I wish I hadn't gone to Chicago*, she thought to herself. But, she knew she'd had no choice. The doctor had confirmed what she already knew.

◆ ◆ ◆

A few days later, Sophia went to the training arena and watched Emma with pride as she helped Tom Shafer, a young boy of thirteen, riding his brown gelding. Emma slowly and gently trained the rider and animal to work together as a team. Sophia could see Hermann in Emma's training style, the same soft tone in her voice, encouraging and correcting the signals the rider was giving the horse to make a specific movement. Emma had been working with Tom for a year now, and Sophia could see the fruits of his training. He was preparing for his second-level riding test the following month.

Sophia thought of the day when Emma decided to use music in conjunction with her training. She had found a consistent pattern in a horse's gait based on the beats to music. Therefore, some days, Emma would ask Sophia to play her cello in the riding area when she was training a student.

Sophia missed Hermann. She had been very careful to keep her illness from him in the year before he'd died; pretending nothing was wrong when he'd asked if she was all right. She was glad for the years she'd had with him. She spent most of her nights thinking back over cherished events of their lives together, which for her, kept Hermann alive in her heart. *If only I could find the Friedrich before I go*, she thought to herself.

Shortly after they had moved to Indiana, Sophia learned about the painting Hermann had taken from his brother, George, but she would never tell Emma about it. Sophia wanted to destroy it or place it in a museum before it destroyed her daughter, as it had her husband. She had watched Hermann's obsession with the painting grow over the years, pulling him further away from her and Emma.

He'd used it as collateral to finance the new mare. The private lender had insisted that the painting be held in a secure gallery in Chicago until the loan had been fulfilled. Hermann's obsession did not really surface until it was returned to him from the lender. He'd begun to change; a haunting wariness had taken over him. He would disappear for hours, long after his family went to bed. One night, she had found him sitting up in the attic, staring at the painting and totally unaware of her. When she had confronted him, telling him to get rid of the painting, Hermann had hidden it somewhere. She had not been able to find it, but she knew he would not destroy it. That had been shortly before Hermann was killed.

Now, when she went to bed each night exhausted, she would cry herself to sleep. She was beginning to feel afraid that her time was running out.

Chris walked through the large doors on the other side of the arena, making sure Patsy did not come in. Emma felt the dog sometimes distracted the horses during their training, so she had asked Chris to keep the dog out of the arena. Chris understood and went to stand near Emma, watching Tom and his horse go through their paces.

"He's come a long way," Chris said to Emma, nodding toward young Tom.

"Yes, I think the pair of them will do nicely in their tests."

Sophia smiled when Emma looked over at her. She knew that her daughter was worried about her, seeing how much weight she had lost, but she always shrugged it off and continued her work during the day - and her search at night.

She thought of their argument the previous night at the dinner table. Emma had asked her to see a doctor. Sophia had become very angry and refused, leaving the table without clearing the dishes. She had gone to her room, afraid that Emma would see that her answer had come too quickly and sharply, learning what she was hiding. Later, Emma had softly come to her door and knocked, but Sophia didn't answer. Now, she needed to apologize to her daughter and tell her the truth.

Tom's horse snorted, bringing Sophia's thoughts back into the arena. Standing at the railing, watching her daughter, a sharp pain shot up the side of her head. This wasn't the first time she had experienced this. She put her hand to her head and rubbed the temple. This had helped in the past, along with the morphine, but this one was much stronger. She hadn't told Emma what the doctor had said. She was too afraid – for her daughter and for herself.

She stepped back and sat down on the chair behind her. She was beginning to have trouble getting her breath, the pain was so severe. She held her head in her hands, closing her eyes to the lights that flashed in front of her, then she fell forward and onto the ground.

"Emma!" Chris yelled out, as he rushed to Sophia lying on the dirt of the arena floor.

Emma looked over and saw her mother. Fear grabbed her heart and she ran to her side. She kneeled, taking her face in her hands and calling her name.

"Chris, call an ambulance," Emma yelled after receiving no response. She didn't know what to do. Should she move her, leave her to get the car and take her to the hospital, find some way to revive her, let her be? All she could do was call her name, holding her hand tightly in her own and watch her mother's face grow ashen.

Tom ran over and stood next to her.

"What's wrong with her?" he asked.

Emma looked up at him, tears running down her cheeks. "I don't know, Tom. We have to wait for the ambulance."

Just then, Chris returned with a blanket, which he gently laid over Sophia to keep her warm. Sophia had confided in him about her spells when she'd asked him to drive her to the doctor's office. He had watched her hide her pain from her daughter, but he kept his promise to Sophia to not tell Emma. Now, he felt he had to break that promise.

"Tom," Chris said to the young man, steering him and his horse toward the arena door. "You probably ought to stable Gunner and go home now. We'll call you later, OK?"

As Tom opened the door, Patsy ran inside and went to Sophia's side.

Chris walked back into the arena; his heart ached when he saw the two people he loved very much. Sophia had seemed like a queen to him, regal and slightly out of reach. He'd watched Emma grow from a small child to this beautiful, young woman and felt as close to her as if she were his own daughter. He had never had any children of his own.

His thoughts shifted to George Mason, his employer. He knew he would have to call George as soon as he had a chance, but right now, he was needed here.

"Chris, what should I do?" Emma said, with tears streaming down her face.

Patsy began to whine softly, as she lay close to Sophia's side.

"What's wrong with Mom?" Emma pleaded.

"Right now, honey, you're doing the best you can for her. We shouldn't move her until the ambulance arrives." He had to say it; he had to tell her what he knew. He placed his hand gently on Emma's shoulder.

"Emma, your mom's got cancer."

Emma's eyes widened and looked at her mother before returning to Chris. "What?" she asked, with a puzzled look on her face. "How do you know?"

"I've been taking her to the doctor in Rockport for her appointments, whenever we went for supplies."

"What appointments? How long has this been going on?"

"She made me promise not to tell you, Emma. I'm sorry. She's been seeing Dr. Benson for six months now, but she refused to do any of the treatments he recommended. All she wanted to do was to take the drugs for the pain."

Emma looked at her mother in fear. Now, she understood why her mother had been so distracted lately. Emma had noticed how tired her mother looked all the time, but when she'd asked, her mother would only laugh and say she wasn't as young as she used to be. Emma hadn't realized that her mother was dying. Now, she would never forgive herself. She had let her work get in the way of seeing how her mother had pulled inside of herself, losing her will to live and allowing the cancer to take over.

◆ ◆ ◆

Emma spent most of her time now at the hospital, unable to concentrate on her work. She had asked one of her advanced students, Jerry Jones, if he would take over her beginning classes for her. Jerry had been delighted to help.

Emma hated the hospital, but knew she needed to be there for her mother. Dr. Benson told her there was nothing anyone could do, except keep her mother as comfortable as possible. Each day, Emma would walk into her mother's room, with crossword puzzles and coffee, trying to smile and choke back the tears. She pretended that nothing was out of the ordinary, that this was the way they had always spent their days together. When her mother became tired, she would leave, waiting until she was alone in the car to allow her tears to finally spill down her cheeks.

After six weeks, Sophia finally closed her eyes for the last time. Emma was there at that moment, holding her hand, as her mother silently slipped away, her pain-ridden face now peaceful.

Later, her mother's last words rang inside of her as she left the hospital.

"*My darling, I hope you find the happiness I had with you and your father. Family is everything.*"

CHAPTER FIVE

Fall, 1962

Patsy died on Emma's twenty-third birthday.

On that day, Chris was in Louisville, visiting his sister. Emma had finished the chores and changed to go to the riding show that she was judging in Evansville. As she drove past the house in her father's truck, she yelled to the old shepherd who ran next to the vehicle.

"Patsy, take care of things for me. I'll be back shortly after dark." Patsy barked in response.

As she drove away, Emma thought it was funny how humans talk to their pets as if they understand every word, finding some sense of comfort in knowing that their animals would follow their instructions.

"Silly," she said to herself, as she drove down the gravel lane.

♦ ♦ ♦

At the arena, Emma was the only judge who sat inside at one end of the fenced area. Today was a small show of beginning riders. Jana Page was her scribe today, a young girl of seventeen, who had been taking notes for the dressage shows at the fairgrounds for three years, allowing the judges to fully focus on the horse and rider. Emma had only started working with her recently, but they seemed to work well together. Jana would note the score for each movement of the test, as well as any comments that Emma quietly gave to her.

Since the beginning of dressage, the various white cards, with large black letters, had been placed around the inside of the fence according to the rules, representing the points where each movement of the test either began or ended. The county fairgrounds were used for these smaller shows to prepare the young riders for the bigger events they were working towards. They were called shows, not competitions, because each student and horse was being individually judged on their performance for each movement during the tests. Their scores at the end of the day would then be tallied and the best score basically was the winner of the day for that level of test. The tests were indicators of the capabilities of the horse, and were changed only to show the refinement of the judging.

Emma quickly reviewed the new test that she had studied the night before, knowing that each rider and horse had practiced the movements as laid out in the test for weeks in preparation for today.

The arena was humming with voices. After Emma rang the bell, a signal to the next rider, the arena became still. A new horse and rider entered at the area where the card with the letter 'C' hung and slowly circled around the arena, then trotted in a straight line toward Emma. Prince, the large, gray gelding, stopped abruptly at 'X,' standing tall and quiet in halt directly in front of Emma. The rider, Kathy Shore, wore her long blonde hair neatly braided beneath the black, velvet cap, the braid hanging down the back of her dark jacket. She sat tall in the saddle in her white breeches and Spanish-top dress boots. Emma smiled slightly at the girl, but then checked herself. Kathy and Prince had studied with Emma at her farm. The young girl's face remained without expression as she stared straight ahead, just as Emma had taught her. Then Kathy dropped her right, gloved hand to her side and bowed her head to Emma in the traditional salute.

The young girl began to take the horse through the sequence of movements, using the letters in the arena to clearly show where each transition took place. The rider and horse appeared as one as they moved around the arena, the soft sound of the animal's hooves in the dirt echoing through the large building.

Emma remembered thinking how nervous she had been in her first test, her father standing on the sidelines watching her. She'd had to keep reminding herself to focus on the back of Saber's head, the horse she had learned to ride on, each new section of the test embedded in her memory. She shook her head now, returning her focus to the rider in the arena before her.

Kathy moved through the series of transitions, according to the current test. At one point, during the rein change, Prince seemed to resist, but Kathy anticipated it and moved the animal through to the next series on the other rein. It had been almost imperceptible except to the experienced eye.

The test completed, Kathy and Prince once again stood in halt before Emma. With a final salute, Kathy walked her horse from the arena, a smile on her face. She knew that the scores were seldom a perfect ten, but generally she had received sevens and eights in her prior tests with Prince. This time, they had completed the ten-meter circle, which was more difficult than in her last show.

This continued the rest of the afternoon, one horse and rider after another, until all had completed the required tests. Dressage tests enabled the riders to know how they were progressing in the development of their horse's training. After the final rider had left, Emma took a few moments to go through Jana's notes. Emma could see the riders nervously waiting around the arena. Then, finally, she stood and stretched, and walked over to the billboard to post her results for the riders to see.

◆ ◆ ◆ ◆

In the dark, Emma drove home. She shivered slightly as she passed the place in the road where they had found her father that horrible night, a sense of foreboding sweeping over her. She turned on the radio in an attempt to break the memories flooding back into her mind, until Carmen McRae began to sing *"Ghost of Yesterday."* Quickly, Emma turned off the radio and drove in silence.

That's strange, Emma thought to herself, as she drove up the lane to her house. Patsy didn't come to the fence around the yard like she usually did. The dog was always the official greeter to anyone coming to the farm. Emma drove her father's truck into the open garage and turned off the engine, the quiet was deafening. Crickets made the only sound in the still night.

Emma stepped from the truck and walked slowly to the house.

"Patsy," she called, as she stepped through the small gate in the fence around the yard. There was no answer. Emma started to whistle, but stopped when she saw the large dog lying in the light near the back door of the house. She knew immediately that something was wrong. She ran to the animal and, as she leaned over her in the light, she saw the blood around Patsy's dark head.

"No!" Emma cried as she shook the animal, trying to awake her, but there was no response. She felt for a pulse, but there was none. Patsy was dead.

Emma looked around her. "Who did this?" she said softly into the night.

Then, fear grabbed her, as she thought that they may still be around. In a panic, she ran into the house and switched on the light in the kitchen. She saw the drawers and cabinet doors standing open, their contents scattered all over the floor. She picked up a large knife and slowly walked into the living room, stumbling over something in the dark. She felt for the wall light switch. When the bright light came on, she saw that the room was in a shambles; papers were lying all over the desk in the corner that had been neatly stacked before, books had been tossed from the shelves, pictures were ripped from their frames and thrown onto the floor.

Frantically, she ran to the telephone on the desk and called the police.

"Jane," she said, knowing the night telephone operator's voice from high school. "This is Emma Maseman. Someone has killed my dog and ransacked my house. Please call Stephen O'Hara."

She hung up the phone, and stared around her, holding herself with her arms, her knees shaking. She stood there for a moment, unsure of what to do. She took deep breaths, trying to calm herself, but it didn't help.

Just as she was about to go upstairs to look through the house, a car drove up the lane and stopped in front of the house. Emma knew the police couldn't have arrived that soon, there wasn't enough time. Quickly, she turned off the light in the living room and crouched down in the shadows next to the desk. She was shaking, her hand clutched tightly around the handle of the knife. She heard footsteps on the sidewalk approaching the front porch. Emma held her breath as the screen door opened and the doorknob turned, the door slowly opening in the dark. She was about to scream, when she heard Chris call out, "Emma, are you home? I saw the light on..."

When Chris turned on the light switch, he stopped. He saw the same disarray that Emma had walked into only moments ago. Tables were turned over, lamps thrown onto the floor; paintings were strung around the room. Then he saw Emma crouched down by the desk, tears running down her face and a knife in her hand.

"My god, Emma. What has happened here?" Chris asked, going to her. "Are you all right?"

She dropped the knife and ran into his arms. "Oh, Chris. Patsy's dead," she cried.

"What?"

"She's out by the back door. I called the police. I thought you were them, coming back."

"Them? Who?"

"Whoever did this," she said, sweeping her arm around the room.

They heard the sirens and watched as the police drove up.

Stephen O'Hara stood before them with his hat in his hands. His short, stocky frame was overstuffed in his tight uniform, the hair at his temples starting to gray, like his father's. He and Emma had gone through high school together. He looked around the room now and shook his head. He'd seen vandalism before, but this looked like it was done with a vengeance.

His men entered, and began going through the other rooms. "Call for the crime lab fellows to come here and get prints and photos," O'Hara told one of them. "And check the other buildings."

"Hi, Emma," O'Hara said. The last time he'd been here was when Emma's father had been killed in that hit-and-run accident.

"Any idea who would do this?" O'Hara asked.

"No," she cried. "They killed my dog, Patsy! She's out back by the kitchen door."

O'Hara nodded to one of his officers to go out back, then began asking her questions, which she answered mechanically about where she had been, what time she had arrived home, who was here when she arrived. Chris told what he knew to the sheriff. Then he went out to the back to see Patsy.

"Who could have done this terrible thing?" Chris helplessly asked the officer. The officer shrugged, then left to inspect the other buildings. Chris had also grown to love the dog over the years. Tears welled in his eyes, but he brushed them away and went back into the house to help Emma.

Chris found her in the living room, slowly picking things up in an attempt to put some order back into her life. She seemed dazed and confused.

"Emma," O'Hara cautioned, "Don't touch anything."

Chris led her to the chair next to the window, avoiding the sofa that was covered with broken glass from a large, broken picture frame. He then stood next to her, holding her hand in his.

"The upstairs looks just like this, sir," one of the officers said to O'Hara, as he entered the living room.

Emma watched as the blue-uniformed men walked around her house, going from room to room, the feeling of invasion grabbing at her, even though she'd known the officers through most of her life. Finally, she wanted to do something. She couldn't just sit there, so she got up and walked out to where Patsy was. She knelt down and looked at the gray around the muzzle, the lifeless body lying as if she were only sleeping. Emma reached out and slowly brushed the soft fur, noticing that her body was already cold. She placed her face in her hands and sobbed. Patsy was all that was left of her family. She had probably been trying to protect the house when she was killed. Tears streamed down her face, dropping off her chin.

She stared ahead of her into the darkness, thinking of when Patsy had come to live with them. It was her birthday party, and Patsy was just a puppy, cute and full of energy, chewing on everything in sight. She and Emma had grown up together, but Patsy had begun to shadow Emma's mother, once Emma had gone away to school.

"Come on, Emma, don't do this," she heard Chris say. His gentle hands were pulling her to her feet and helping her back into the house. One of the officers was taking photos of the kitchen.

"Who could have done this?" she asked again. "Why? Why would they need to kill Patsy?"

"I don't know," Chris said. She saw his sad, gray eyes, and thought how his eyes had always looked sad, even when he had first come to their farm looking for a job. It was as if he knew something that she didn't; something in his life that he felt he needed to keep from her and her family. She never really knew much about Chris, even after all these years.

"Emma," O'Hara said as they entered the living room, his voice soft and gentle now. "We've searched the house and found that all of the rooms have been torn apart like this one. After the lab boys are finished, we'll need you to go through and take an inventory. Let us know if anything is missing."

"Yes," she said. "I understand."

"It's really weird," O'Hara added. "All of the paintings have been taken out of their frames, as if they were looking for something specific. I've never seen this before. Whoever did this also went through the tack room in the stable. We found an old trunk out there that had been gone through."

"That's my father's tack trunk," Emma said. "He brought it here with him from Germany."

"Well, there doesn't seem to be anyone about now. Would you like us to have someone stay around here tonight?"

Emma looked at Chris, her eyes pleading for his help. She didn't know what to answer.

"No," Chris said, taking charge. "I'll be here with her and help her clean this up."

"Okay. Well, we've done as much as we can for now," O'Hara said. "So, we'll be going back to the station now." As he started to go out the front door, he stopped and turned. "Sorry, Emma, about your dog," he added awkwardly. "It seems she was hit over the head with a rock we found near the back door. They must have done that to keep her quiet."

"Thank you, Stephen," Emma said. "She was a great watchdog, and a good friend."

◆ ◆ ◆ ◆

After the police left, Emma asked Chris to help her bury Patsy. Even though it was dark out, she knew where she wanted the dog's grave. Patsy had always loved to lay in the pansy bed at the north side of the house, a cool place on hot summer days. Under the front porch light, Chris began digging. Emma placed Patsy on an old blanket and lovingly wrapped it around her, then Chris helped her carry the dog and place her into the hole. Emma walked onto the front porch and found a rubber teddy bear, one of Patsy's favorite toys, which she placed in the grave. As Chris began to toss the dirt over the animal, Emma began to softly cry again. Unable to move, she stayed until Chris was finished.

"Goodbye, old girl," she said. "I'm really going to miss you."

Emma and Chris walked back into the house and began the slow process of cleaning up. She found that her parents' sterling silver set that they had purchased for their twenty-fifth wedding anniversary was missing. Upstairs, a few pieces of her jewelry were gone. They weren't worth much, but they had sentimental value - like the silver bracelet her parents had given her on her eighteenth birthday. Emma was glad that she was wearing her mother's opal ring that day. Her father had given it to her mother when they became engaged. She'd told Emma that she hadn't wanted a diamond. Emma was also wearing the necklace that Sam had given her. It was her favorite treasure.

In the stable, Emma saw that her father's old trunk had been emptied onto the dirt floor. As she slowly put everything back, she noticed that nothing seemed to be missing. The police couldn't figure out why the stable's tack room had also been disturbed, but they thought the thief had simply been looking everywhere for anything of value.

◆ ◆ ◆ ◆

Stephen O'Hara called a few days after the incident to advise Emma that they had determined the incident to be a theft. Other farms in the area had been subjected to similar thefts about that time, but as yet, they had been unable to locate anyone in connection to them. Emma reported to Stephen the few things she had found missing. As she hung up, she remembered the Friedrich painting her father had once told her about and was glad that she did not have it.

◆ ◆ ◆ ◆

Since her mother's death, Emma had begun to think differently about the farm. Now, the loss of Patsy was the last straw. She was seriously considering leaving her home and living somewhere else. She needed a change.

One sunny day, as she wandered around the farm, a restlessness came over her. She walked out behind the house, which sat on a hilltop, a large valley opening up below her. She stood at the edge, pulling her sweater closer around her as the autumn wind whirled by. She looked out over the field of hay stubble that she leased to Henry Miller's son. They had an agreement that he would give her enough hay for her horses as partial payment for the use of her land. The soil lay dormant now.

The old chicken coop that her mother had kept stood to her right, but Emma had sold all of the chickens. Next to it lay the garden plot her mother had planted her vegetables in every spring - until she'd become too ill. Emma didn't have time to manage everything now and was feeling overwhelmed by it all.

If I could just get a new start, Emma thought to herself, *a place of my own.*

Turning, she walked toward the old large, red barn, where the hay was stored. At one time, her parents had kept a milk cow inside the barn and a hutch of rabbits just outside. Emma stepped inside the barn and found the dark air cool compared to the sunshine outside. There were still telltale odors of the animals, but the strongest was the sweet hay. The long, rope swing hung from the center beam, the red paint on the seat peeling.

As she walked back to the house, she thought of the memories that still lived there for her and wondered what life would be like away from it. A melancholy swept over her.

When she opened the kitchen door, the phone was ringing.

"Em, is that you?" a familiar voice said on the other end of the line.

"Jenn. How are you?"

"Great. I'm going to be in Chicago for an exhibit this week, but wondered if you'd mind if I came down to see you first. I can only stay for a couple of days."

"Mind? I can't wait. Do you need me to pick you up somewhere?"

"No, I'll fly into Evansville and get a car. I know where you live," Jennifer laughed. Emma realized it had been some time since she'd heard laughter.

"When will you be here?"

"Is tomorrow too soon?" Jennifer'd had a feeling that she needed to see Emma for some reason. Their friendship had grown so close that they seemed to know when to call each other. It was like having ESP, only more personal, like twins when they sense something is wrong with their other half.

Tears came to Emma's eyes. She really needed to see her friend.

"Not at all," she said. "What time do you think you'll arrive?"

"I'll probably be there around noon."

"I'll have lunch ready." Emma paused, then said, "Jenn, it's good to hear your voice." Emma hoped her friend wouldn't hear her voice quivering as her throat tightened.

"Are you Okay, Em?"

"Yes," Emma said, trying to sound cheerful. "I'll see you tomorrow."

She didn't want to tell her friend over the phone what she had been thinking about on her walk. Just before she hung up, Emma said, "Jenn, I'm really glad you called."

◆ ◆ ◆ ◆

When Emma saw the rental car Jennifer was driving come up the lane, she flew out of the house to meet her friend. They hugged each other, then took Jennifer's bags inside.

"Mother was always the strong one," Emma said, as they sat in the kitchen. She hardly touched her sandwich as she told Jennifer about Patsy and the theft. "I could always talk to her. I'm just glad she wasn't here to see Patsy."

Jennifer put her hand on her friend's arm and nodded in agreement.

"I haven't had anyone to talk to in so long," Emma continued, "except for Chris and my students. But, I don't like to bother them with my troubles."

"That's why I'm here," Jennifer said softly. "I just had a feeling, you know."

They looked into each other's eyes and smiled. Sometimes, after they'd gotten to know each other, there were times when they seemed to have the same thought at the same time. Jennifer had always admired Emma's strength; but, it frightened her now to see her friend so fragile.

Emma felt the tightness in her throat and the tears beginning to well in her eyes. She bit her lip, fighting to keep the tears from spilling over. Finally, they fell, and she began to sob.

Jennifer went to her and put her arms around her shoulders.

"Tell me, Em," she said softly. It was a phrase she'd used numerous times when they were in college together - whenever Emma had tried to keep something to herself.

"All I can think of is that my family is gone now. I can't keep up this farm by myself, and my heart's just not in my work right now."

Jennifer pulled Kleenex out of her pocket and handed them to Emma. "I should have been here sooner."

"You were busy—"

"Not too busy for you."

"Oh, I'm not sure what's wrong with me, but I keep thinking..." She paused. She was frightened that if she said it out loud, it would become a reality.

"What?"

"Oh, I don't know." Emma sighed and squeezed Jennifer's hand, then let go to pick at a piece of meat hanging out from the bread on her sandwich.

"I'm just glad you're here," Emma finally said.

"Me, too." Jennifer knew not to push Emma. When she was ready to talk, she would.

"Tell me about your work," Emma said, to change the subject.

Jennifer began telling Emma about her favorite pastime now, which now had become her life's work. She would drive to remote areas of Oregon and photograph the beautiful valleys and rugged coastline that appeared from the hilltops she liked to hike. She talked about the changes in her art since she began developing her skills with the camera to portray the world she loved. Art school had given her the design and colors, but the camera was the medium she found that truly enabled her to show her perspective of the world.

They placed their dishes in the sink and walked into the living room. Jennifer walked up to a photograph of Mt. Hood.

"Hey, I know this one," Jennifer said.

Emma smiled. "Yes, that's yours. I found it in a studio on a business trip in Chicago."

Mt. Hood stood facing the sunset, a pink glow vibrant in the evening sun. The still, blue sky around it was cloudless. It was Emma's favorite. Indiana didn't have mountains, only small hills that broke the monotonous horizon. When she first had seen Jennifer's work, Emma had wondered if she'd made a mistake in her decision to leave art school. Then, she would think of her mother and knew that she hadn't.

"Hey, this has been scratched," Jennifer said, looking more closely at the photograph.

"Yes, it was done during the theft. All of the pictures had been ripped from their frames."

"That's odd," Jennifer said, looking more closely at the other pictures, some oil landscapes, hung around the room. One was of the farm, which she remembered Emma had painted when they were in school.

"I still have the negative of that photograph, so I can print a new one for you. I'll even autograph it. Promise."

The two days went quickly for Emma. During the day, she and Jennifer explored the farmland and outer buildings. Jennifer always took her camera bag on their walks.

"I'm experimenting with Polaroid now," Jennifer said as she pulled out a folded rectangle from her camera bag. She pulled the rectangle open and checked to make sure it had film inside. Emma was amazed to see how small the camera was.

"I got this new camera that lets me take instant photos without the processing. They're still only in black and white film, but I bet they'll have color out in a year or two."

Jennifer asked Emma to sit in the rope swing that still hung in the center of the old, red barn.

"I'm not sure this rope is going to hold me now," Emma laughed as she gingerly sat down. When she found it held, she slowly began to swing, which brought back memories of younger days. Jennifer waited for the right moment. She watched as the look on Emma's face made her seem like she was a young teenager again, her eyes closed and hair following in her wake. The pain had disappeared, and Emma was softly smiling. Jennifer took the photo.

Emma stopped and watched in amazement as the film came out of the camera. Jennifer grabbed it by an edge and peeled off the backing. Then, as they waited, Emma's image began to form.

"Where's the negative?" Emma asked.

Jennifer held up the backing. "Isn't this great?" she asked, smiling. She laid the photo and camera on a bale of straw.

"Now, it's my turn."

Jennifer sat on the old swing and pushed back, swaying until she had enough height she could pump with her legs. The rope groaned with each pendulum motion.

"You're going too high," Emma warned.

"Now you sound like my aunt," Jennifer laughed. Just then, the rope snapped and Jennifer fell to the ground.

"Are you all right?" Emma said, running over to her. She helped Jennifer get up and untangle the rope from around her.

Jennifer laughed and brushed off the dirt on her jeans. "Sure," she said, rubbing her backside. "I just bruised my ego. Guess I'm not a teenager anymore, huh?"

Both women laughed.

"Let's go pick some berries for dinner," Emma suggested, grabbing some silver buckets and running out of the barn. She suddenly felt young again.

Jennifer quickly grabbed her camera and ran after Emma out into the sunlight.

In the woods behind the barn, with the small buckets in hand, Emma and Jennifer walked under the large oak canapé. Emma led as they walked up a trail toward the blackberry patch, talking of the days when she and her father did this.

There weren't many berries left, but they had filled their small buckets and their bellies, their fingers stained with purple. Then Emma showed Jennifer where a small stream was located. They could see small crawfish slowly walking on the bottom below the water. Emma told Jennifer some of her tales of when she used to go fishing in this stream, when it had been much larger.

"Of course, there were no fish," she laughed. "I only caught crawdads. I used to have nightmares about them when I was little."

Emma and Jennifer went down to the site where the only oil well stood, still slowly pumping. Jennifer remembered seeing photos of the well when it had gushed. She had been impressed with the photography.

"Do you get much from this?" Jennifer asked.

"No, not anymore. But, even if I sold the farm, I'd still get the royalties from it..." Emma stopped, realizing that was the first time she had mentioned her plans – selling the farm.

The colors of the leaves were brilliant in the afternoon sun, which was still warm. As the sun began to set, the air grew cooler. Jennifer took a sequence of photos with her Nikon, catching the changes in the light as the last rays slid sideways across the tops of the hills, the colors bursting around them.

◆ ◆ ◆ ◆

On their last evening together, Emma and Jennifer sat sipping coffee in front of the fireplace, the golden light dancing on the walls around them.

"Tell me about your show in Chicago," Emma said.

"Oh, it's just a collection of some seascapes I did of the Oregon coast. It's not what you normally think of – like the warm beaches of California. Oregon has sandy beaches, but the air is cool and the water is icy cold. Areas of it are very rugged, with beautiful tide pools containing starfish and anemones. It takes your breath away."

Jennifer decided that now was a good time. She handed Emma a package wrapped in shiny white paper, tied with a purple bow.

"What is this?" Emma asked.

"A late birthday present."

Emma took off the bow and wrapping and held a large journal in her hand, covered in dark, red leather. She slowly opened it and saw that every few pages, Jennifer had inserted photos of places Emma had only seen in magazines. One was labeled 'Cape Foulweather,' that looked like it was taken from a great height. She looked at the deep blue ocean against the white clouds, the coastline weaving south with a large inlet that was dotted with rocks in a large, perfectly symmetrical arc, as if they had been placed there by giants. A huge rock, which Jennifer had noted was Otter Rock, stood out against the sea's horizon. There was another photo taken that Emma recognized as looking further down the same coast, since Otter Rock was in the foreground. A long stretch of white beach and blue ocean led to a point where a lighthouse stood. Jennifer had captured the moment when the brilliant beam emanating from the lighthouse winked at her.

"Oh, this is beautiful," Emma said, looking up at Jennifer. "Are these some of the photos from your show?"

"Yes," Jennifer said with pride in her voice. "These are the originals. I blew them up for the show. I wish you'd come with me to Chicago."

"I can't. I have three students coming tomorrow."

"Maybe next time," Jennifer said, smiling.

"Yes," Emma said, hugging her friend. "Thank you so much."

Jennifer just smiled.

"I'm so proud of you," Emma said, after she had spent some time looking through the journal.

"Do you miss your art?" Jennifer asked.

"No. I did at first, but the school keeps me busy. Lately, though, I've been thinking about bringing out the paints again."

They were quiet for a moment, listening to the crackling of the logs in the fire.

"Are you thinking of selling the farm?" Jennifer finally asked.

Emma looked quickly at her friend. "Yes," she finally said with a sigh. She felt as if a huge weight had been lifted from her. "It's not the same now, and there are so many memories here – some memories that I wish had never happened. I feel so restless, like a caged tiger that can't seem to break free."

"You'll know when the time is right," Jennifer said. Then she stood up and yawned, stretching her long, thin body. Her golden hair hung in soft curls down her back.

"I'm going to hit the sack," Jennifer said. "See you in the morning, Em." She went upstairs to the guest room.

Emma sat by the fire, saying a prayer of thanks for the day she'd first met her best friend.

The next day, just before Jennifer got into her car, she said, "If you ask me, Em, I think it's time you sell this place and move on with your own life."

Emma hugged her friend. "I'm so glad you came."

"Me, too. See ya," Jennifer added, after she'd climbed into the car. Then, as she started the engine, she said, "You'd love Oregon." She waived her hand and drove off. Jennifer never said goodbye.

Emma stood and stared after her friend. She had heard those words before, when she was eighteen.

◆ ◆ ◆ ◆

The snow fell gently outside the window. Emma watched the soft flakes float slowly to the ground in the yard light outside by the old sycamore tree. On its branches hung dark seed clusters, which her mother had used for winter floral arrangements. Emma's eyes followed a solitary flake that entered the light from the dark sky, seeing it almost suspended in air for a second as everything else became a blur until the flake landed softly on the Japanese yew outside the window, blending into the white cloak that was painting the world with a halo reflected in the pale winter moonlight. She sipped the dark, sweet, Kahlua liqueur she'd poured for herself, in an attempt to chase the chill and sadness away. It had been her mother's favorite winter's evening tonic.

Emma had been thankful each day for the choice she had made to stay with her mother and work with the horses. She'd continued the riding school that her father had begun in her drive to keep him alive in her heart. Whenever she began working with a new student, she felt her father with her, guiding her decisions on the training that the particular pair needed. Being around the stable and near the horses had kept her close to her father, until now. Emma had also thought the house would keep her mother near, but she was now finding that it all felt very empty and cold.

A sultry woman's voice sang "*How Long Has This Been Going On?*" from the collection of jazz tunes on the record player. Emma sighed. All was peaceful with the world – except within herself. This song always reminded her of Sam, ever since she'd heard it sung in the movie he'd taken her to.

I wonder where he is now. She could see his face again clearly in her mind, his blue eyes and dark hair in the sunlight of her youth. Her heart still swelled as she thought of his intoxicating smile. She shook herself, annoyed at how little things; a voice, a sound, a song, brought back images of a time in her life that she had tried hard to forget.

The Chicago she had first seen five years ago was just a memory now, but a nagging one that would not go away. She had been young and confused, her heart had been broken. Once, after she'd left her school, she had thought about writing Sam again, but her stubborn German side would not let her. Like her father, she had immersed herself in her work to forget.

Now, as Emma sat alone in her parents' living room, watching the snow falling outside, she began to look inside herself. With both of her parents gone, there was little keeping her here. Every room she walked through was another painful reminder that she missed her parents terribly.

Maybe Jennifer was right. Maybe, it was time for a change.

The hardest part now would be telling Chris. If she sold the farm, she figured he'd go back to his sister's in Kentucky. The thought had occurred to her to ask him to come with her, but Emma had decided against it. She knew she needed to make this change for herself.

◆ ◆ ◆

The next morning, Emma walked to the stable. The sky was a brilliant blue and the new snow glistened in the sunlight. She looked around her and felt at peace for the first time in a very long time. She had made her decision.

Before beginning her chores, she went into the tack room, looking for Chris. He was not there, but she saw her father's trunk and walked over to it. Looking inside, she gently picked up her father's riding coat. A photograph fell onto the floor from one of the coat pockets. Emma picked up the photograph and stared at it. It was of her father and Conversano performing in Verden. At that moment, it occurred to her that it was time to return to her art.

Once I'm in my new home, she thought to herself, *I will paint again.* She smiled and placed the photograph in her sweater pocket.

The papers for the purchase of Conversano and Sabrina were lying to one side in the trunk. Both of those horses were now gone. She remembered the stories her father had told her of riding Conversano in Verden, Germany.

She slowly closed the lid of the trunk and walked out of the tack room. Gandolf brought his head over the top of his stall gate. She went to him and placed her arms around his neck, hugging him, burying her face in his silver mane.

"Don't worry, Gandolf," she said softly to the horse. "You're coming, too."

"Are you okay, honey?" Chris asked from behind her. He had watched her walk over to Gandolf and hug the big stallion, just as he had seen Hermann do over the years with Conversano when something was on his mind.

Emma hadn't remembered Chris getting old, but she now saw how bent his shoulders were from the years of work. His gray hair was thinning, and his eyes looked tired.

"Yes, Chris. I was just thinking about my folks."

The old man nodded and smiled.

"Chris," she began, a pained look on her face. "I have something I need to talk to you about..."

"So do I," Chris said. Fred Jamison had called him that morning. George Mason wanted him to return to Essen Farms. Fred hadn't said why. Chris really didn't want to leave Emma. But, he'd always obeyed George. "You know about Annie, my sister in Louisville," Chris added hurriedly. "I received a call this morning, and...well, I've got to move back there." He turned and looked away from Emma. He didn't like to lie, but he couldn't tell her the full truth, either. He couldn't tell her that he'd been working for her father's brother all these years.

"Oh, Chris," Emma said, placing her hand on his shoulder. "I'm so sorry. Is your sister okay?"

"Yeah, she's okay, but I'm needed there now. I've talked to Doug Miller and he's agreed to help you around the farm."

Emma was surprised how sometimes life worked out in mysterious ways.

"What did you want to tell me?" Chris asked.

"Well, I've been thinking about selling the farm and moving somewhere out west."

"Sell the farm? But, you love it."

"Yes, I know, but it has a different meaning to me now," Emma looked around the stable she'd grown up in.

"Where will you go?"

"I've been thinking about moving to Oregon."

Chris handed her a small piece of paper. "Here's a phone number I can be reached at in Louisville. Let me know if you ever need anything." He'd written the number of Essen Farms down before he'd walked into the stable.

She hugged the older man. "I'm really going to miss you, Chris." She really meant this, but was happy at the thought of moving on with her own life.

PART TWO

CHAPTER SIX

Spring, 1964

Portland was a beautiful, but small city, compared to Chicago. From Emma's apartment window, she had a view of Mt. Hood in the east. The gray, winter skies hadn't shaken her, like it did so many others she'd met since her move. At times, during the winter, she had missed the snow, but she knew she only had to drive to the mountain if she wanted to enjoy it. She liked the way spring came early to the Northwest. The azaleas and rhododendrons were in full bloom all over the city.

Emma had just bought her new ranch on Chehalem Mountain, a few miles southwest of Portland and was boxing the few things she'd brought with her to the furnished apartment. The majority of her things were still in storage, and her horses were boarded at a stable near Jantzen Beach. She was looking forward to having them in her own stable – in her new home.

Jennifer had found the empty ranch on the mountain during one of her photographic adventures. The owners had moved to Arizona and had just placed the ranch on the market that morning. She took Emma there that same day, excited about her find. Emma fell in love with the house, the red-brick style with white-fenced borders. It reminded her of her parents' home. The fifty acres and a large horse stable helped Emma to see the potential for the riding school she wanted. She'd already created in her mind the riding arena she planned to build as she and Jennifer had walked around the property.

In the house, she'd liked the oak-paneled den off the main, wide entrance to the house. It had ceiling-high shelves and a river-rock fireplace. There was a guest bedroom down the hall, with a small bath next to the stairs leading to the next floor. The large kitchen had a dining area that looked out toward the white stable. Upstairs, she'd found three bedrooms. When she walked into the room with two skylights facing north, she could see Mt. Hood from the window. She had decided then that this room would be her art studio.

That very same day, Emma had jumped into her new car, a silver Buick Skylark, which she'd bought after arriving in Oregon, and drove to the realtor's office to make an offer. The owners had eagerly accepted.

At last, she'd finally found a home of her own.

Now, Emma sat on a red, velvet chair in her apartment and thought of the day she'd gone to the bank in Newberg. She'd chosen a smaller bank in Newberg near the new property, instead of going to one of the larger banks in Portland.

When she'd walked into the old granite building of the Chehalem Bank, she liked the wood wainscoting and trim, stained to a dark hue and shining from years of polish. Large, brass chandeliers with Alabaster glass hung from the high ceiling, casting a soft, warm glow around the open lobby.

"May I help you," the dark-haired secretary had said as Emma approached her desk.

"I have an appointment with Mr. Johnston. I'm Emma Maseman." Emma was nervous, but she forced herself to relax her grip on the envelope of papers she had brought with her and took a determined deep breath. She was glad she'd worn the black suit and crisp, white shirt. She'd learned in her negotiations with the people at the bank back in Indiana that she had to look professional to get anywhere with them.

The secretary ushered Emma into a large office painted in a pale blue color.

"Would you like some coffee, Miss Maseman?" the secretary asked.

"No, thank you."

The secretary smiled and softly closed the door.

On the desk before her, Emma saw a picture of a lovely, young, red-haired woman. She was reminded of Karen Stenson and smiled, then sat patiently waiting until a tall man appeared in a dark, pin-striped suit.

"Hello, Miss Maseman," Mr. Johnston said. His face was stern and Emma's stomach jumped from nerves.

"Hello, Mr. Johnston. I am here about a loan for the Grandhaven property on Chehalem Mountain."

"Yes, I see you've brought the papers I asked for."

She handed him the envelope she was clutching and was glad her hand didn't shake.

Johnston took some time leafing through the report of her financial background from her bank in Indiana. Emma took slow, deep breaths and tried to relax. She knew she was doing the right thing and she had done her homework. Slowly, her confidence began to return.

The loan officer at the bank sitting across from her looked at her with a scowl on his face.

"You understand, Miss Maseman, that I must protect my institution's investments." He was about her father's age when he had died, his hair and mustache graying. She liked his eyes, even though he seemed stern.

"Yes, Mr. Johnston, I do." Emma cleared her throat and leaned forward, looking directly into the man's eyes across from her. "As you can see, my records from the Indiana farm prove that I have run a lucrative riding school on my own for over three years."

"But, you are single, and a—"

"That should not have any bearing on my acceptance for this loan. I am basing my application solely on my own ability to produce income from the farm...ranch." She remembered that people out west called their properties ranches, not farms.

"And, you do not have a job to support the loan payments until the school is established. How much time do you feel it will take you to begin seeing a profit from the school?"

"As I'm sure you know, I have opened an account with your bank with the cash from the sale of the farm in Indiana, from which I will pay the down payment for your loan. There will be enough left for the riding arena that I plan to build and pay for my living expenses for the next year. I anticipate, after seeing the need for dressage training in this area, I will have seven or more students by the end of the year, which will bring more than enough income to pay my loan, Mr. Johnston."

Emma had been doing her homework. Jennifer had warned her about the stiffness of the banks in the area, so Emma had looked around, asking questions at the rare dressage shows she'd been able to find. She knew she would be able to make this work.

"In addition, I have one of the oldest blood lines in the Lipizzaner stallions," she continued, "which I plan to use for breeding. I'm sure the director of Simpleton Farms in Indiana would have no difficulty in continuing to purchase young stock from my sire. After all, they are the leading Lipizzan training farm in America. I currently have one yearling that has already been sold to Simpleton and will be delivered later this spring." Emma planned to continue her father's work, to the letter.

The large, gray-haired man sitting across from her looked again at the array of reports she had produced. He liked her marketing style. Emma reminded him of his daughter, who had gone to New York after college and was now a top journalist for a big magazine. He was proud of his daughter and now found himself smiling at Emma, seeing the same drive and persistence in her that his daughter possessed. He had made his decision.

"Well, Miss Maseman, I feel that this institution would be willing to work with you to develop your business."

"Thank you." Emma smiled. She finally saw that one of her dreams was becoming a reality.

"We will draw up the papers for you and give you a call when they are ready. I will contact your realtor to advise that you have been approved for the loan."

Johnston stood up and reached his hand out to Emma.

"We will need to have full inspections for any necessary repairs or modifications prior to closing," he added.

"I understand," she said as she shook his hand. "This means so much to me, Mr. Johnston."

It was one of those moments in her life that she knew she would never forget. She noticed everything around her as she walked out of his office. It was like watching a movie in slow-motion: a small, elderly couple held hands as they walked up to a teller; small dust particles danced in the sunlight that beamed through a tall window as she passed; Mr. Johnston's secretary was talking to one of the tellers about her weekend.

"Goodbye, Miss Maseman," the secretary said as she waved to Emma.

Emma smiled and said goodbye, then pushed open the heavy, gold doors of the building and walked into the sunlight. It felt warm on her skin as she went to the parking lot. The air smelled sweet from the daphne blooming in large bushes around the base of the tall lamp posts near where she had parked her Buick. A little white dog barked ferociously at her from the car next to hers, protecting his master's property. Emma smiled at the dog, then slid into her car and sat there for a moment, letting the reality sink in. She pulled the rear-view mirror toward her, looked at herself and sighed.

"You did it, girl!" she said, smiling at her reflection. She let out a yelp like she had done at her first riding competition when she found she had passed. She looked up at the sky and said, "Thank you."

She had started the engine and drove to Jennifer's house to share the news.

That was the third luckiest day of my life, she thought now to herself as she looked out of her apartment window towards Mt. Hood. The second was when she'd met Jennifer at the riding stables; the first had been when she'd met Sam.

◆ ◆ ◆ ◆

It was a gray, spring day, with heavy clouds overhead. The sun was shining through an opening in the west over the hills just behind the stable as Emma and Jennifer drove up the lane to Emma's new home.

Emma knew she would always remember the first time she used her key to open the door. The house was still empty and her footsteps echoed on the oak floor. She noticed a built-in gun rack at the left of the entrance. As she and Jennifer walked through each room of the house, they decided where Emma's furniture would best fit. Emma was caught up in the excitement of a dream come true.

When they'd entered the wide, square kitchen, Emma sighed.

"Look how those cabinets go up to the ten-foot high ceiling," she said. She heard a pop and turned as Jennifer was pouring champagne into the glasses they'd brought to celebrate.

"To new beginnings," Jennifer toasted and clanked her glass against Emma's.

"New beginnings," Emma repeated and sipped the golden liquid. With the bottle in her hand, she walked toward the door that led outside and looked out the window. A large white building stood with small windows on the side, facing the house, which she knew was the stable. She saw the larger, red barn across the lane that reminded her of the old barn at their farm in Indiana.

"Where are you going?" Jennifer yelled after Emma as she ran out of the kitchen door.

"To the stable!" Emma exclaimed.

Jennifer followed out the door and down the lane, finally catching up to Emma standing next to the open field next to the large, white building.

"It will need to be covered," Emma said. She lifted her face to the soft rain that had just started, feeling it fall gently on her cheeks. She poured more champagne into her glass and handed the bottle to Jennifer.

"What will?" Jennifer asked, then sipped the bubbly liquid.

"The new arena," Emma said as she mentally measured how large it would be. Dressage arenas were twenty meters by sixty meters.

A large pond shimmered in the sunlight down toward the stable. Tall cattails stood like sentinels along one edge, while a large weeping willow dipped its branches in the water on the south side.

Emma turned and walked into the stable. The large tack room stood open on the left, and a small room on the right that could be used by a stable hand. There were twelve stalls in all, six on each side of a wide aisle down the center.

"This will be Gandolf's," Emma said to Jennifer, walking into the largest stall next to the tack room. "He'll like this one, because the sun will shine through the window first thing in the morning."

"Don't plan on sun every day here, Em," Jennifer warned. "Remember, this is Oregon."

Emma laughed and continued walking down, looking into each of the stalls. She stopped once in awhile and took a sip from her glass. Looking up, she smiled when she saw the hay loft and the drop chute that would help her to manage the straw and hay herself.

"You've got your work cut out for you now," Jennifer said, placing her hands on her hips.

"No problem. I like work."

At the end of the building was another set of large, double doors. She opened both of them and walked out into the fresh air, smelling the rain. She saw Elvin Coffee and waved. He was the farmer who was currently leasing the farmland. She had already talked to Mr. Coffee and arranged that he would continue leasing her land, as long as he provided her with hay for the horses.

She closed the doors and walked back into the tack room, looking around at the shelves and hooks on the walls. She began picturing where her tack would hang when the moving van brought her things from storage the next day.

Emma went back out into the empty center aisle and hugged her friend.

"Thanks, Jenn, for getting me here."

"What're you talking about?" Jennifer asked, looking around her. She opened her arms out to her sides, indicating everything around them. "You did this all on your own, lady." Jennifer hugged Emma back.

"Yeah," Emma said, looking into her friend's eyes, "but you were the one to convince me I should come here."

Emma turned to the door. "Come on, I'm getting hungry. I'll buy dinner. It'll probably be the last one I'll be able to afford for a while." She and her friend laughed as they walked back up the lane toward the house.

"I know a great builder out of Newberg," Jennifer said, as they passed the arena area. "He could help you with the arena. He's really cute, but very married. I'll get you his number."

◆ ◆ ◆ ◆

Emma carried the last box into her new home. It'd felt good to hand in the key to the landlord of her apartment. At the same time, it was also a little scary. Emma knew now that if anything went wrong, like plumbing or wiring, she would have to fix it herself or pay someone else to do it for her. She wished now that Chris could have come with her, but then laughed at herself.

She took the box to the spare bedroom behind the den. She knew it contained the last odds and ends of the things she'd found at the farm in Indiana. As she began to unpack it, she came across her father's small Mauser pistol and a box of shells that he'd kept in his truck for years. He had always told her that it was good to have, in case it was needed someday. But, he'd always cautioned her to keep the clip out of the pistol, for safety. She'd learned to hunt with her father, but wasn't fond of killing. She preferred skeet shooting and had become very good at it. She reloaded the clip and placed it next to the pistol in the box -- *just in case it was needed someday*, she'd thought.

Earlier that day, Emma had driven to the stable at Jantzen Beach and loaded her horses into the large trailer. She thought of when she and Jennifer had driven her father's truck from Indiana, hauling the horses to Oregon. It had taken them four days, since they had to stop often to let the horses rest.

"We're going to your new home," she'd said to Gandolf as she'd loaded him in last. "I think you're going to like it very much."

The first project she undertook was to reinforce the old fence on the corral. She was able to use this as a temporary arena while the construction of the larger one was underway. The new one would be the same size as a show arena. She was surprised to see how quickly the contractor and his crew worked. The ground for the new arena had been prepared, and now the roof was almost finished.

Her new students started filtering in from her advertisements at the local feed store and county fairgrounds, where she had visited a few dressage shows when she'd first arrived in Oregon. She now had five full-time students. She'd worked out a deal with some of her students to receive a discount for their training if they would board their horses at her stable, providing they would help with the maintenance of the horses. This would allow her to board a number of horses without having to hire someone else to help.

Emma had even begun to paint again. Her inspiration had come one rainy day, while she was unpacking a box of photographs. She'd found the old photograph of her father's performance in Verden. In full uniform, Hermann stood proudly holding the lunge line of Conversano, as the white stallion leaped into the air. The capriole leap was the most difficult to master. She knew immediately that she had to paint this. She took it into her studio, found a new canvas, and placed it on the easel. With the photograph nearby, she quickly sketched the outline of the images, studying the photo. When she looked into the face of her father, she stopped. It was the same expression she had seen in a photo of herself, when she had won her first competition. Emma smiled as she began to paint the back colors onto the canvas.

She was happy for the first time since her parents had died. She no longer felt the restless itching under her feet, and the memories of Indiana no longer lingered. Everything was bright and different. Each day, when she awoke in her own home, she felt the surge of pride.

◆ ◆ ◆

Emma had never done anything on impulse in her life, except when she was eighteen in Chicago and she had defied her parents and met Sam Parker. Now, seven years later, she was repeating herself. Life was good. She loved her new ranch and was consumed with work that she fully enjoyed. Yet, late at night, she still felt as if something was missing.

Six months after she had settled into her new home, she was cleaning the spare room closet. She found the box that Jennifer had sent from college when she'd left the art school. The purple journal that Karen Stenson had given Emma for her eighteenth birthday was inside. Emma opened it and saw Sam's address in Eugene, Oregon he'd written on the napkin in the diner after the movie in Chicago. That was the spark that made her decide to look him up.

While she drove south on I-5, Emma rehearsed what she would say to this man after all these years. Every so often, she would feel foolish and she'd consider turning around, but something made her continue.

She could see the Coast Range Mountains toward the west and the foothills of the Cascades to the east. The green fields of young, winter wheat glimmered in the sunlight, reminding her of the photos of Ireland she'd once seen. Tall, sleek Thoroughbreds stood in a pasture in front of a breeding barn, their heads held high and the wind whipping through their dark tails and manes. Through the side window, she saw a red-tailed hawk soaring in the azure sky, looking for prey.

Oh, Sam and Jennifer were both right, Emma thought. *I love Oregon.*

When she reached Eugene, she stopped at a coffee shop near the highway to find a phone. It was an old-style diner with private phone booths inside. Her hand shook as she wrote down the phone number of Sam's father, the address matching the one she had received from Sam in Chicago. Then, she sat at a table and fortified herself with a strong cup of coffee. She needed some additional strength before she made the phone call.

Once again, she rehearsed, taking notes, scratching them out, frowning, and laughing to herself. She looked up and saw the waitress watching her. Emma smiled, then put her notebook away. She placed the money for the coffee on the table and went back to the phone booth. When she sat down and closed the door, a small light came on. She took a deep breath, carefully dialed the number. Then waited.

"Hello," a woman's voice said on the other end. It was a soft voice, like Emma's mother's.

Emma dropped a nickel into the phone's coin slot, and said nervously, "Is this the Harold Parker residence?"

"Yes. May I help you?"

"Is Sam there, please?" It was all she could think of.

There was a pause at the other end. "No, I'm sorry, dear. Sam is in Texas, in the service. This is his mother. May I help you?"

"Do you have an address for him?"

"How do you know Sam?" the woman asked.

Emma's heart went to her throat when she thought how silly it would sound. How did she explain to Sam's mother that she had met him in Chicago and that she had fallen instantly in love with her son?

"We met many years ago in Chicago. I was hoping to find out how he was doing now."

"Well, at the moment, he's about to get married."

The word stopped Emma dead. *Married*? This had never entered her mind. She believed that he hadn't written to her in all these years because she had been such a young child when they first met. She was hoping that by seeing him now, it would be different. Emma was a grown woman. Her hand went to the locket he had given her that hung between her breasts. *Married*?

"Hello," the voice said in the phone. "Are you still there? Can I tell Sam that you called?"

"Nooo, thank you," Emma quickly said, then hung up. She sat in the booth, her heart pounding. *Married*? If only she'd had the chance in Chicago to tell him that she knew she loved him. *If only...*

Tears rolled down her cheeks, which she quickly wiped away with the back of her hand. She now felt angry with herself for even believing that he might still be interested in her, after all this time.

"What was I thinking?" she said aloud in the space that now seemed to close in on her. She pulled out her keys from her handbag and left the phone booth and the diner. Once inside her car, she sat there for a moment, numb and suddenly very tired.

Married? Emma thought again in disbelief.

"You idiot," she angrily yelled at herself. She turned on the car's ignition and pulled onto the highway. Now, she let the tears flow, sobbing, gasping for air, as she drove furiously toward home, racing by the other vehicles. Visions flew through her mind of how she'd imagined it would be. Eventually, the tears stopped and she slowed down to the pace of the other cars, not seeing anything but the long, straight road ahead.

Dreams shattered, one by one, like a broken colored glass window. Her heart ached. Her stomach hurt. She had decided that he was the one thing missing in her life. She had everything else that she could ever need, but not the one person she wanted to share it with. Sam was gone forever. He was getting married - to someone else.

When she arrived home, she dragged herself inside. It seemed colder now, emptier than before. She went to the small bedroom behind the den and looked at herself in the mirror. Her eyes were red, her face swollen. Sunlight streamed through the window, shining in the mirror, catching the gold of Sam's necklace. She had never taken it off since Sam had placed it around her neck so many years ago, except when she showered. Slowly, she raised her hands and undid the clasp. A sob wrenched from her as the last bit of hope that she'd hung onto over the years died. She gently placed the necklace in the top drawer of the dresser. As she slowly shut the drawer, a small light inside of her went out.

CHAPTER SEVEN

January, 1965

Sam walked off the commercial jet onto the tarmac and looked toward the Louisville terminal. A tall, blonde woman stood behind the fence waving to him, holding a small baby. He smiled, waved back, and walked towards them.

"How's my girl?" Sam said, after dropping his bag and hugging the woman.

"Which one?" the woman asked, as she laughed when he picked her and the baby up together and twirled them around.

"Both of you," he said. He first kissed the baby wrapped in a pink blanket, then the woman.

"We're doing just fine, Sam. We missed you."

Sam smiled, then bent down and picked up his bag. He placed his arm around the woman's waist as they walked out of the airport toward the parking area.

"Nan, you're as beautiful as ever."

"Glad you noticed. You don't look so bad yourself, handsome." She knew he'd know she was lying. He'd never looked so terrible – his eyes had dark shadows under them and he looked thinner. This man was nothing like the Sam Parker she'd met eight years ago in Chicago.

"Where's Jim?" Sam asked as they climbed into a Jeep with a canvas top. He watched the light snow beginning to swirl around them in the wind, and the air inside the car was cold enough to see his breath.

"He's at home working on the Chevy. That's why Amy and I brought the Jeep to pick you up. This is the car Jim usually drives, but I need the bigger car by tomorrow."

Nancy knew she was babbling, but when she'd looked sideways at Sam, she could tell he wasn't in the mood to talk. She chatted about her new infant, Amy, who was now sitting in the car seat between them, her little, mittened hand touching Sam's arm. As she drove, Nancy talked about their move to Louisville to help take care of her mother.

When they finally pulled up in front of the large, green house Nancy had grown up in, she took Amy from her seat and walked around the Jeep. As Sam stepped out, a tall man with black, curly hair, wearing a beat up, brown leather, flight jacket approached, wiping his hands on a greasy towel. Sam shook Jim Barolio's hand. Nancy smiled, then carried Amy to the house, leaving the two men alone.

"Damn, it's good to see you, Jim," Sam said, placing his arm around Jim's shoulders and giving him a hug. They'd known each other since they were kids and had no secrets.

"You keep getting uglier every time I see you," Jim said.

"And, you're getting shorter," Sam retorted.

This had been a long-standing joke between them ever since they were teens, but this time Jim could see the strain in Sam's face. He was still trying to figure out what Sam was doing here. Sam didn't say much on the phone when he'd called from his parents' house in Oregon. Jim knew that Sam had spent the last two weeks in Oregon.

"How's the life of a racing commissioner going?" Sam asked.

Jim had asked for an early out of the military, after his commission was up, when Nancy's father had died and her mother needed special medical care for her heart. Nancy had been pregnant with Amy. Jim had taken the job as Racing Commissioner for Kentucky when Simon Day moved over to the Racing Bureau in Baltimore.

"Never better," Jim replied.

"Do you miss flying, Jim?" Sam asked, looking overhead at the contrails streaked across the crisp, blue sky.

"I miss the jets." Jim looked skyward and was silent.

Sam could see the longing in Jim's eyes. He didn't know himself what it would be like to have to give up something you loved. When he and Jim had flown their jets, wing to wing, the world had been theirs and nothing was going to stop them. *Life has a strange way of proving you wrong sometimes*, Sam thought.

"I keep a Cessna at a small airstrip near here for when I get the itch to go up," Jim said after awhile. "Maybe you should get out of that uniform someday and join forces with the Racing Commission yourself."

"Nah, I like to fly too much," Sam said. He looked toward the horizon and thought of where he was going to be the following week.

Jim noticed the shadow that had come over Sam's face – he suddenly looked very tired. Now, he knew why Sam was here in Louisville, and he swallowed hard, a knot forming in his stomach.

"Hey, why don't I show you to your room and you can rest up a bit. Then, after dinner, we'll have a beer and talk about old times." Jim was trying to keep the conversation light.

"How's the car?" Sam asked, nodding over at the green sedan with the hood still up, evading Jim's suggestion. He walked over to it and leaned in over the V8 engine.

"She's purring like a kitten," Jim said, leaning in next to Sam. The engine gleamed and hummed. He was proud of his work and always kept his equipment in good running order. "Just had to change the fuel pump. Why don't you close her up?" he asked Sam.

Jim got in and turned off the ignition, as Sam slammed the hood down.

"You always were good with engines. And women," Sam said, nodding toward the house where Nancy and Amy had disappeared. "I remember that old '34 truck you bought after we got out of high school. I lost money on that truck when I bet you it would never run."

Jim smiled as he thought of the old, red truck. Then he looked at Sam again and frowned. He picked up Sam's bag and headed toward the house.

"Come on, Sam. You look like a Mack truck ran over you, backed up, and did it again."

"That bad, huh?" Sam asked, as he followed.

"Yep."

The house was a Bungalow style with a large porch that wrapped around one side. The ceilings inside were high, with dark beams and the walls in each room were painted different soft and warm colors. Sam could hear Nancy in the kitchen and smelled fresh coffee.

"Great house," Sam said.

"Thanks," Jim replied. "This was Nancy's mother's house, until we bought it from her. I built a small apartment for Mom in the back."

"Hey, boys, would you like some coffee?" Nancy called from the kitchen.

"Um..." Sam began, then looked at Jim.

"I think Sam would like to go upstairs and stretch out for a while, first" Jim said, giving his wife a hug and kiss as she walked out into the hallway. "He looks pretty beat." Jim cringed as soon as he said it, seeing the pain in Sam's eyes.

"Sounds good, Jim," Sam said, relieved. "I could use some time alone. I hope you two don't mind."

"Not at all. What're friends for?" Jim smiled and led the way upstairs.

◆ ◆ ◆

Sam lay on the small, twin bed of the paneled room that looked like a teenager's bedroom. Looking around, he noticed the blue and white yearbook, and the band letter stacked among old textbooks. He realized he must be in Nancy's old room.

He thought of Susan and decided that breaking his engagement with her had been the best thing he'd ever done in his life. He hadn't liked the way it had hurt so many people. He'd wanted to simply make a phone call to the church, but knew that was a coward's way out.

He'd first met Susan Delaney when he went to Texas after flight training. She was the first woman Sam had become involved with after leaving Chicago. He'd been hurt when some of his letters to Emma had returned unopened, and he'd closed himself off from every woman – until he met Susan. He never told Susan about Emma, until now. He wasn't really sure why.

Susan was a nurse on duty at the infirmary on the base, when he'd been sent there after a crash in the Gulf when the fuel control meter failed in the new F-4 he was testing. He was glad it had only caused a flame-out without exploding. Those planes were called "Thuds" for a good reason - they were fast, but not very reliable at first.

She was a gorgeous, tall, and slender brunette.Later, Sam learned she was looking to marry a pilot. The Delaney family had money in Texas oil, and Susan was used to getting what she wanted. He'd thought he was in love with her, and before he knew it, he had agreed to get married. The wedding had been planned for the previous summer, but they'd had to postpone the wedding because Susan's grandmother had fallen and broken her hip. The wedding was rescheduled for December. During that time, Sam had begun to question what he was doing with his life, and he was scared to death.

The morning of the ceremony, Sam's mother had told him about the woman who had called their home in Oregon asking about him. His mom had said the woman had known him in Chicago, but she wouldn't leave her name. Emma's face had flashed in his mind as he stood in the church before his wedding, and then he knew. He knew he couldn't marry Susan, because he would always be comparing every woman to Emma. He knew then that he was still in love with Emma.

Seeing Nancy again today had reminded him of the last time he'd seen Emma. He replayed that night he'd spent with Emma over and over in his mind, trying to see if he could have done something differently. *Why would she return his letters? What had he done that night to cause it?*

He'd wished he'd told her then that he loved her. He was about to say the words, when Nancy's taxi had driven up in front of Emma's hotel. But, there hadn't been enough time. *If only I could get another chance*, he thought to himself.

Suddenly very tired, Sam closed his eyes and slept.

◆ ◆ ◆ ◆

"You did the right thing," Jim said later, as the two men sat in front of the warm fire in the living room. Nancy and Amy were asleep upstairs.

"Oh, I know that. I just wish Susan would get over it." Sam took a swig of his beer. "She's been dogging me since that day, begging me to change my mind."

Jim nodded. In December, Jim and his family had all been in Texas for the wedding – Jim was to have been Sam's best man. He remembered the large cathedral where Susan had attended when young, the flowers everywhere and the large number of guests waiting on the bride's side for the ceremony to begin. Sam's parents and a handful of friends from the base sat on the groom's side. Jim shivered when he thought of the anger he'd seen in Susan's face after Sam had told her. *Yes*, he thought. *Sam had made the right decision.*

"I figured it had to be big to get you away from your jets – for now," Jim said. When Sam had called to say he was coming to Louisville, Jim knew it wasn't Sam's broken engagement or the love of horses that had brought him here. He knew there was more, and a chill ran down his spine. Sam was leaving the country again.

"Well, you know I've wanted to see Churchill Downs ever since we were kids," Sam began, then he saw Jim's face. "It was a lame excuse, huh?"

"Yep."

There was a long pause as the two men looked at the fire. Then Sam spoke again.

"I'm going on a special mission, Jim. Top secret."

Jim looked over at Sam. Jim knew that the uncertainty of deployment made each moment precious.

"Thought so," Jim said. He knew his friend like the back of his hand. This was what he was waiting to hear, the real reason Sam was so tense.

"You know I can't talk about it - except to say that I may not be back."

The two men looked into each other's eyes. When they had joined the Air Force ROTC program in Portland, they'd thought of nothing but the opportunity to learn to fly jets. Once they'd graduated from pilots' training, they both knew their lives were on the line. This was the real reason that Jim had bailed out before Sam. He and Nancy had married while they were at Marana in Arizona. He had to think of Nancy, too, since she became pregnant shortly after their wedding.

"Well, you know where we'll be," Jim said, fighting back the tears that threatened to begin. He'd let them come later. "I hope you'll be able to keep in touch."

Sam nodded and winked at Jim.

"How much time do you have before you leave?" Jim asked.

"Just a few days," Sam replied. "I need to be back at base by o-nine hundred next Sunday."

"OK, so what're your plans while you're here?" Jim asked, already knowing the answer.

"I'm thinking about driving to Churchill Downs tomorrow and see the track and horses."

Jim nodded, and waited. He knew that wasn't all. Sam had talked about Emma Maseman all through their flight training, and he remembered that she lived on a farm in southern Indiana, just a few hours' drive from Louisville.

"Then I think I'll go up to Indiana and check out the countryside." Sam smiled as he saw the twinkle in his friend's eye. "I hear it's a sight to see."

"You could take the Jeep. The rag top's a little breezy this time of year, but the heater works and I've got some gear that'll fit you, if you need any. Maybe you'll just find what you're looking for."

The men smiled at each other and tapped the necks of their beer bottles together.

◆ ◆ ◆ ◆

Sam had wanted to see a live Kentucky Derby ever since he was a kid. As he approached the large track in the early morning light, his blood began to warm and he felt an urgency in his heart. The white, twin towers came into view, their gray roofs dull in contrast to when he'd seen them shining in the afternoon sun on television during the Derby each May. Now, he drove the small Jeep through the lane of tall, bare sycamores, leading to the parking area. Sam thought of the three-year old horses that had traditionally raced their hearts out on the oval, mile and a quarter track each year, the new winners proving that they were the best, with the hope to go on to win the Triple Crown. He wasn't surprised that the guard at the entrance simply waved him on, since it was months before the main event in May. Sam made a silent wish that he could be here for it, but he knew the odds were against that happening.

He'd seen a couple of horses exercising on the track as he drove in, so he walked up to a gate in the white railing and leaned against it. The cold air chilled his face as he watched a light mist dance around the strong, wrapped legs of the animals and steam roll off their heated bodies. A large, roan colt thundered by as his jockey gripped the reins to hold the animal back on his training run, the horse's breath blowing from his nostrils as his long legs stretched out over the earth. Sam's heart raced along with the animal, feeding one of his childhood dreams.

Sam had to move when a rider on a lead horse came through the gate with a tall, dark mare and her jockey, guiding them toward the backside to cool down the horse. Sam walked to the paddock area behind the clubhouse and stood, remembering the noise of a crowd of over a hundred-thousand people on the day of the Derby, as the horses were led into this area.

Just then, a tall slender woman passed Sam. She had long, flowing black hair. He stood for a second, his pulse thundering as he stared after her. For a moment, he thought she was Emma. He called out Emma's name, and his heart leaped into his throat. The woman ignored him and kept walking. He watched her until she was out of sight. Then he wondered if Emma would ever disappear from his mind, let alone his heart. He let out a long, slow sigh, then turned and continued to walk to the backside.

In comparison to the frantic activity during the Kentucky Derby, the backside today was deserted. Only a few horses and grooms were in the area. Sam saw the dark horse he'd seen earlier walking counter-clockwise around the walking ring, covered in a blanket. Bandages that had been washed were flapping stiffly in the cold air to dry. Sam pulled the collar of his coat up around his neck and pulled his baseball cap down tighter.

"I'd bet my life on my next colt winning the Derby," Sam heard a loud voice roar from around the shedrow he was approaching.

"How much you willing to put up, George?" another voice said.

"Fifty grand too much for your blood, Harry?"

"You're on."

Sam heard the man called Harry walk away, laughing to himself. When Sam came around the building, a broad, tall man stood with his hands on his hips, his dark hair dancing in the cold breeze. The man turned and looked at Sam. Their eyes met. Sam froze where he stood, struck by the intensity in the large, brown eyes. He felt he'd seen this face somewhere before.

"Who're you?" the man growled.

Sam didn't answer at first. He saw that the man's hair was only slightly graying at the temples, but his weathered face made him look much older. His body was strong and muscular. Sam wondered what secrets were hidden behind those dark eyes.

"Are you lost, son?" George Mason asked. He thought he'd recognized the young man, but wasn't sure. His mind worked to find the link.

"No, sir," Sam finally said. "I was just wandering around. I've never been to Churchill Downs before."

"Well, you picked a hell of a time of the year to do it." George looked at Sam over the top of his glasses. "Most people come when the Derby is running."

"Well, sir, I won't be around then," Sam said, holding out his hand. "My name is Sam Parker. I've always dreamt of owning a horse farm like the ones here in Louisville. My dad has a small training ranch back in Oregon."

"George Mason," George said as he shook Sam's hand. "Glad to make your acquaintance." George chuckled to himself, softening a little. He remembered that same dream himself. "Have you ever been to Louisville?"

"No, sir."

"Well, son," George said with a big smile, patting Sam on the back. "Why don't you come back to Essen Farms with me? We could have a drink and talk about that dream of yours."

"Yeah!" Sam exclaimed, then caught himself. "Yes, sir. I'd like that very much."

"What're you driving?"

"I have a friend's Jeep over in the parking area."

"Well, we'll be pulling out shortly with a four-horse trailer. You won't be able to miss it. It has the color of my silks, red with a gold 'V'."

"Thanks, Mr. Mason. I'll be ready."

◆ ◆ ◆ ◆

Sam was impressed with Essen Farms. The long, tree-lined drive, flanked by acres of white fence, had led up to the enormous Colonial-style home with tall columns in front. The numerous, long stables were covered in a thin layer of new snow, but Sam could still see the dark green roof underneath. A few horses stood in the meadow, grazing on the small amounts of grass peeking through the sheer, white blanket.

George waited until Sam had closed the door of the small Jeep, then he asked, "Would you like a tour of my farm?"

"Sure," Sam said, looking at the number of stables. "How many horses do you have at Essen Farms, Mr. Mason?"

"Almost a hundred. And, please, call me George."

As they walked to one barn, George said, "We can hold twenty stallions here."

George opened the door and they walked down the wide aisle. Sam saw the rows of white stalls with the Essen colors painted on each gate. Everything was neat and orderly. George stopped before one stall that was larger than the others. A tall, dark colt, with a white star and blaze on his forehead, poked his head over the top of the gate.

"This is Koenig," George said.

Sam could hear the pride in the older man's voice. There was also a sadness.

"I read about the mishap with the drug after Koenig had won the Derby," Sam said, remembering the breaking news. He reached up his hand to let the horse smell; then, he gently stroked the muzzle.

When George didn't respond, Sam continued. "I can only imagine how angry you must have been, when you learned that your vet had drugged your horse." Sam saw that George still held that anger inside with a short tether. "Someday," Sam continued, "I want to find a way to help protect the horses from people who think they can mistreat animals like that."

George only nodded as he placed his big, gentle hand on Koenig's neck, then walked out of the barn. His thoughts now were focused on his private vow of what he'd do to Dr. Karl Strauss, if he ever met him again.

He led Sam to the breeding barn, and then the mare and foal barn. As they walked between the two barns, Sam saw a pair of yearling foals racing each other in a fenced meadow, their bodies beginning to catch up with their long legs.

"That one on the right is Koenig's Pride," George said. "A colt, sired by Koenig. He's fast."

Sam looked at the young horse, his head held high and his mane and tail blew as he sniffed the cool air. His coat was dark, like his sire's, with a long, white blaze down his nose. Then, in a flash, the animal took off in a dead run, racing with the other young colt. Sam could see the long stride as Koenig's Pride took the lead. Sam turned to follow George.

In the foaling barn, George pointed out a chestnut mare from Caracas, Venezuela, owned by a Frank Reichmann.

"Never met the man," George said in a rough voice. "The mare was sent to us by air with two grooms and a request to breed her with Koenig. I don't approve of this practice. I like to meet the owners personally first, but the man paid handsomely. That new colt at her side was just born this morning."

Sam saw the dark, almost black colt. Oddly, there were no markings on the small animal.

"Aren't there usually some unique markings on a foal, something that's used to identify it with The Jockey Club?"

"This little fellow is very rare. He and the mare will be flown back to Venezuela when the time is right. The owner has indicated that the colt will not be raced in America, so our Jockey Club doesn't get involved."

An older, middle-sized man, spewing something that Sam recognized as Gaelic to a young, blond man, came out of the birthing stall nearby. Sam's father's trainer was Irish, so he recognized some of the conversation.

"Eric," George said, stopping the older man. "This is Sam Parker, a young man from Oregon."

"Hello, Sam. I'm glad to meet you. Eric Muldoon is my name, and this fine young man is David, my assistant."

"Eric used to work as a vet at the McHenry Farm near Dublin, Ireland. Now, he's here working for me. He was highly recommended to me and I trust him with my horses - and my life." George and Eric exchanged glances.

"I hear Ireland is so beautiful, it's hard to leave," Sam said.

"Ah, well, you're right there, lad. I do miss her sometimes, but I get back once a year to see the Emerald Isle again. I have some family still there."

"I'll have to go someday," Sam said, smiling.

"You do that," Eric said. "George, you'd best look in on Classy. She's missing you."

"A true winner will come from her," George said to Sam as he walked down to a stall across the aisle. A beautiful, chestnut mare stood with her sides bulging.

"She's my best broodmare, also bred by Koenig. The foal is due anytime. She's produced many a winner in her lifetime." George walked in and touched the tall animal's cheek, talking softly to her. Sam recognized that tone of voice. It was the same one he himself used with his dad's horses.

"This is the one I've been waiting for," George said with a big grin on his face. "Koenig's Pride is fast, but I know that Classy's foal will be a winner."

George patted the mare's neck as the horse turned her head into him, almost as if giving him a hug. Sam was struck by the closeness of the man and horse.

"Come on, Sam," George finally said, leading the way to the outside. "I'll take you to the yearling barn."

Once inside the building, Sam heard George's voice roar, "What is the meaning of this?" Sam looked and saw George pointing down at a bale of feed sitting in the aisle.

"This feed is moldy!" George yelled.

Sam was startled by the change in the large man. It was as if a switch had been flipped and a different person had emerged. But, he could see himself that the hay was ruined and should not be given to the horses.

A short, round boy came running out of an open stall with a pitchfork in his hand. He was fairly young to be a groom, Sam thought, but he'd been about that age when he'd begun working with his dad in their stable. The boy looked at the bale that George was pointing to.

"I'm sorry, Mr. Mason," the boy said, leaning the fork against the stall. Sam could see his hand shake. "I don't know where that came from. Usually, all of the hay is checked with a hydrometer before it is brought into the barns."

"I don't want any of this hay given to my horses," George boomed. "Do you hear me?"

"Yyyes, Mr. Mason. I'll see to it personally."

"Have Conrad look into this and check the rest of that shipment. I want to know where we bought it right away."

"Yes, Mr. Mason. I'll tell Mr. Schultz." The young boy's hand was still shaking when he pulled down a bale hook that hung in the empty stall next to where they stood, then walked to the bale. Snagging it with the hook, he drug it out through the door.

George stormed out of the other end of the building and walked toward the house, with Sam hurrying to keep up.

"I'm sure the young groom didn't know the hay was wet, sir. It was probably an accident."

George whirled on Sam, about to yell at him. Then he remembered himself and fought to calm down. Sam was amazed at the abrupt control in the older man.

"You're right, Sam," he said between his teeth. "It probably was an accident." George didn't allow accidents in his stables, and knew that when he got to the bottom of this, he'd never buy from that supplier again. He looked at Sam, rolled his shoulders and smiled slightly.

"Let's have that drink now," George suggested and continued walking.

Sam took off his cap and followed George into the enormous house, through the large, double doors with tall, beveled glass on each side. Shiny marble floors gleamed from the overhead light in the entry hallway.

As they continued through the hallway, Sam glanced through the open door to the right, but the room looked cold and unused. Red-velvet wing-backed chairs stood before a dark fireplace and the long, curtains of the same red velvet were drawn. The door to the left of the hallway was closed.

"When was this house built, George?" Sam asked.

"Sometime in the 1830's."

They entered a large foyer with a wide staircase leading up to the next floor. Sam looked up at the enormous crystal chandelier that sparkled overhead in the sunlight streaming through the tall windows at the head of the staircase - a great contrast to the darkness in the room he'd just seen.

Sam followed George into the den, a room that looked as if it was truly lived in.

"How much time do you have before you have to report back, Sam?" George asked as he poured bourbon into two glasses, his anger only simmering now.

"I have to be back tomorrow to catch my flight out of the country." Sam wished he hadn't said that.

"Where are you flying to?" George asked, handing him a glass.

"I can't say, sir," he said, hoping he'd been able to keep the grim look from his face that he'd seen that morning in the mirror. He didn't want to think about it right now.

Sam looked around the room. It suited the man that handed him his glass. He walked over to the wall that held numerous trophies and photos of horses who had won in prior races. He was impressed. Then he saw the photo of Koenig and his jockey.

"Do you have any family, George?" Sam asked as he sat down in the large, overstuffed leather chair next to George. He saw George's face grow dark, as if a cold shadow had passed over it. George sat quietly for a moment, gazing into the fire.

"No," the large man finally said. "I have no family."

George remembered now where he'd first seen Sam Parker - at the betting area in Arlington Park when he'd watched Hermann's family.

"Tell me about your career with the Air Force, Sam," George said to quickly change the subject. "Where did you go for flight school?"

"Marana Air Base, near Tucson, Arizona."

"I noticed you have an insignia on your cap. What does that mean?"

"Each instructor at Marana gives a new group of four students a name. My squadron was the Scorpions. Whenever I'm on leave, I wear this cap. After our first solo flights in a T-34, we were given a white, silk scarf with red polka dots on it. Then, we were all thrown into the club swimming pool with our green flight suits on."

"Where are you stationed now?" George asked.

"Lackland Air Force Base, near San Antonio, Texas." Sam had almost forgotten that Susan was back there. He flinched as he thought again about her last words to him. 'I'll hate you, Sam Parker, as long as I live,' she'd yelled.

Just then, a loud commotion came from the hallway.

"George," a man yelled with a lilt in his voice. "George, come quick."

Sam saw the tall man who appeared in the doorway, his sandy hair beginning to gray, curling at his collar.

"Fred, come in and meet Sam Parker..." George began, until he saw Fred's face. "What is it?"

"It's Classy, she's about to foal."

The sun had come out, warming the air and slightly melting the snow on the rooftops. When they entered the foaling barn, the moans of the mare could be heard. David was standing outside of the large stall where the chestnut mare stood, the top of the door open. His eyes were wide and curious as he watched Eric in the stall with the mare. Eric looked up with a towel in his hand, as George, Fred, and Sam approached. The vet walked over and leaned against the gate.

"How's she doing?" George asked, his eyes watching the mare nervously.

"She's going to be fine, George. I'm surprised she's started now, but Mother Nature decides when." Eric grinned, his blue Irish eyes flashing.

Classy began pacing back and forth, her breath coming in quick gasps and her coat sweaty. Just then, she sighed heavily and began to paw at the extra-thick bed of straw under her, water dripping down her hind legs. Eric walked behind her and wrapped her tail, then went to stand near the others and watch her, leaving the mare to her work. She slowly laid down, heaving another sigh.

David, as if on cue, walked over to a small table outside of the stall. He checked the pile of towels, disinfectant, and scissors, making sure that all would be ready when needed. Then, he returned to the gate and watched quietly with the others.

Eric stood just inside the stall, talking softly to the mare in a soothing voice.

"You're going to be just fine, lass," he cooed in his Irish brogue. "Take your time and let the little fellow do his work."

The mare's eyes opened wide and she looked around her wildly, attempting to get up, then stopped. She lay back onto her side, waiting; her breathing coming in heavy, fast pants. Sam saw two tiny hooves push through the placenta. Then a small amount of the muzzle appeared. Eric walked over to Classy and continued to talk her through each contraction until finally a slippery, wet foal lay in the deep straw next to her. The sweet smell of newborn and blood filled the stall.

The foal laid shivering and gulping air, the severed cord separating him now from his dam. David handed Eric some clean towels. Then the vet slowly walked up to the small foal, softly talking to him as he wiped him down, clearing his nose and mouth. Even though the foal's hair was wet, Sam could see that his color would be as dark as his sire's. His only marking was a small, white star on his forehead.

David entered the stall now and handed Eric the disinfectant for the foal's navel, then backed away and watched with Eric as the mare began to lick the foal, bonding with her offspring.

He laid there, his long legs sprawled around him, his breath coming easier now. A short while later, the mare stood. Then, she encouraged her foal to also stand. He began to struggle to his feet, his skinny legs hardly able to support him, slipping, falling, trying again, and falling again. The mare nickered encouragingly as the foal finally stood on his own, shaky legs. He thrust his dark muzzle into the air. Classy walked near her foal, and he instinctively began to nurse.

Classy Elegance, Sam thought to himself. That would be the name of his mare that he wished some day he would own. He stood in awe, watching the young colt and his dam. This was the first time Sam had watched the birth of a foal. At home, they usually came in the middle of the night, when no one was around the stable. He'd find the newborn standing next to their dam the following morning.

Sam looked over at George, his face was unreadable. Sam thought he would have shown concern or joy, but George simply stood, watched, and waited. Sam wondered how he could be this distant, after seeing him with the mare before.

"He's a fine colt you have here, George. What will you name him?" Eric asked.

George was quiet for a moment. He looked up, as if he were searching the sky, which was visible through the skylight overhead, for his answer. Then, he turned his face back to the stall with a large smile.

"Koenig's Wonder will be his name," George said with pride. "And he will win the Triple Crown," he predicted.

◆ ◆ ◆ ◆

Later, as George and Sam walked out of the foaling barn, George asked Sam to stay for lunch.

"Thank you, George," Sam said, looking at his watch. "But, I really need to be going." He had one more mission before he returned to his base.

"It's been a pleasure, George. I don't know when I've enjoyed myself more. If you're ever in Oregon, please look me up." Sam handed George a card that his father had made for him to give to the people he met in his travels during his duty in the service that he wanted to keep in touch with. It was something his father had done when he was in the Army.

"Thank you, Sam. Keep your dream alive."

"I will, sir."

Sam got into the Jeep and drove away.

◆ ◆ ◆ ◆

Once George was back in his den, he sat in the large chair before the fire-place and looked at the wall with the trophies. Pride swelled within him, but something was still missing. The last time he'd seen Sam Parker was when he'd planned to meet his brother, Hermann. His parents and brothers were all dead now, and he was alone in the world – except for his niece. Maybe it was time he went to meet her. He knew where Emma was. He always knew where she was, and where the Friedrich was.

◆ ◆ ◆ ◆

After Sam left Essen Farms, he headed northwest, away from Louisville. He already knew how long it would take him to get to Grandview, Indiana.

The sun was well overhead now, warming Sam's shoulder through the Jeep's window in spite of the fact that it was January. It was one of those rare days with the promise of spring. He passed numerous horse farms until he crossed the Ohio River. Eventually, the landscape gave way to the farming community. He turned straight west and drove toward Emma's hometown.

Grandview was small, located north of Rockport. As he entered it, he passed a large, white church with a tall steeple and small, clapboard siding. Over the large, double doors, Sam saw that the church had been built in 1824. The sun, now lower in the sky, burst through the colored, stained-glass win-dows. He noticed a small drive-in diner stood across the street.

As he continued through the town, Sam stopped at a gas station and asked di-rections to Emma's farm from the address Emma had given him in Chicago, telling the young man it was the Maseman farm. The man didn't know of the name Maseman. He said he'd just arrived from Rockport and was new in Grand-view. But, when Sam told the young man about the riding school, he told Sam where one used to be.

Driving up the hill away from Grandview, the farmland opened around Sam, and he could see for miles. The sky was a bright blue, with white, cumulus clouds hanging over the land. His heart skipped a beat when he saw the red-brick house sitting on the hill in the distance to his right, just as Emma had described it.

On the drive, he had practiced what he was going to say when he saw Emma again and he thought of those now:

Hi, Emma. Do you remember me?

Hello, Miss Maseman. It's me, Sam Parker.

Emma, it's good to see you again after all these years.

Emma, I've loved you from the first moment I met you.

He stopped and sighed, beginning to feel foolish. He wondered if she was still living with her parents. Or, worse yet, maybe she was married! Sam hoped he wasn't too late. He could turn back now and she'd never know. But, he knew he couldn't.

He drove up the lane to the house and his heart sank. The paint on the trim of the house was peeling, and the gate on the fence around the yard hung on one hinge. He stopped his car and got out, looking around him at the other buildings nearby. They were also in bad repair. The air was still. He listened for sounds of horses coming from the stables, but there were none.

Sam slowly walked up to the house and knocked. The screen door had a large hole in the mesh, as if someone had thrust their foot through it. He waited, but no one answered. He knocked again. Still, there was no answer.

He turned and began walking to the outer buildings, calling out, in case someone was around. He heard no reply. The air was warm, even though there were deep patches of dirty snow on the ground in shady areas where someone had plowed from the driveway.

The door to a large building that looked like a stable was closed. When Sam walked over and tested it, the door was unlocked. He slowly walked inside. It was a large riding arena with stalls attached, but the stalls were empty and looked like they hadn't been used for some time. Dust and cobwebs had begun to take over, and it felt cold and damp. He went into the tack room and saw empty hooks on the walls where bridles and saddles used to hang.

"Hello," Sam called out. "Is anyone here?"

Still, there was no reply.

He walked back out into the sunlight, feeling the warmth again. He continued to the large, red barn. He noticed the paint was fading, and there were boards missing in some areas. Inside, the stale smell of old hay hung in the air. He walked up and down the center aisle, saddened by the empty stalls. Then, at the other end of the aisle, he found a rope swing lying on the floor, the ends of the rope frayed.

He was about to leave when a small flash of something white caught his eye. He walked over to it and looked closer. It looked like a piece of paper, stuck between two wallboards, possibly the kind used for a photograph. He looked around, as if to see if anyone was watching, then took out his pocket knife and dug the paper out of the wallboard. When he pulled the paper out, he turned it over. His hand trembled and his heart thudded in his chest. Emma's face stared back at him.

She was beautiful, just the way he remembered her. Her skin was creamy white against her long, black hair. She was swinging in the rope swing; the smile on her face was the same smile she had given him on their date in Chicago.

Sam's hand shook as he tucked the photo into his shirt pocket. He wondered at the thudding in his chest and stuffed his hands deep in his pant's pockets as he walked out toward the open valley behind the house. He could see that crops had once grown there, but now the soil lay in a mass of weeds covered in a light blanket of snow. He stood next to a small, gray, chicken coup, which was almost devoured by the blackberries. He saw a pile of old, rusty farm machinery nearby that was also being reclaimed by the land.

Sam heard a vehicle coming up the lane, so he walked back to where his car stood. A large man in bib-overalls, a white T-shirt, and a red baseball cap stepped out of the dirty green truck. The man placed his hands in the front of his overalls and walked over to Sam, his face stern, almost angry.

"What're you doin' here?" he asked gruffly. Black hair curled out from under the cap and his face was tanned like leather from the years of farming.

"I'm Sam Parker," Sam said, extending his hand. The man kept his hands where they were. "I'm looking for Emma Maseman."

"Don't know any Maseman," the man grunted.

"I think this used to be her father's farm, Hermann Maseman."

"Look, mister. I've only been here a few months. I bought the place from a man named Jenkins last fall. Don't know any Maseman."

"Well, I'm sorry if I bothered you," Sam said, as he turned to get into the Jeep. "Thanks for your help, Mr., huh..."

The man didn't answer. He just watched Sam as he got into the Jeep and drove away.

◆ ◆ ◆ ◆

Back in Grandview, Sam stopped at the small diner he'd seen earlier, the smell of frying grease and ice cream came to him as he walked up to the small window. A short, round woman with a hairnet on her dark hair walked up to take his order. He asked for a hamburger, onion rings, and a chocolate milkshake. He looked around inside the small building and saw colorful plates leaning on a shelf along one wall; all of them had "Indiana" written in gold letters across the front.

While Sam was paying for his order, he asked, "Do you know a Hermann Maseman?"

"No," the woman said. Then, she pointed to a small room in the back where Sam could see a few men, sitting around a table, sipping coffee. "They might know of him," she added and turned to make his milkshake. After handing it to Sam, she went to prepare his food.

Sam walked around the diner and entered the back room from the side door. Three older men looked up as he entered. There were four men around the gray table with marbled, Formica tops and chrome legs. The walls were a faded gold color with streaks of grease that looked like they hadn't been painted in years.

"Hello," Sam said, nodding his head and smiling to the men. He sat down in an empty chair near the men. "I'm looking for Hermann Maseman."

Two men shook their heads, indicating they didn't know him.

"I knew Hermann," a tall man said, sitting with his back to the wall. His eyes were like steel and just as cold. "A damned good poker player. He had a riding school, but it's been closed for years now."

"I remember young Emma," another piped in. "She and her mother were sure pretty things. I liked sittin' behind them in the old church on Sundays."

"Do you know what happened to them?" Sam asked the two men, sipping his milkshake. He felt a small hint of hope as he watched the men.

"Sophia died shortly after Hermann was killed in that hit-and-run accident..." The man paused and shook his head. "I never believed it was an accident, but nobody would listen to me."

"Where's Emma now?" Sam couldn't sit still, he felt so close.

The man scratched his gray beard and looked at the others, his blue eyes seeming to question them whether he should tell this stranger or not. He leaned back in his chair and placed his hands in the suspenders at his chest.

"Why're you lookin' for her?" the old man asked, squinting one eye at Sam.

"We knew each other when we were young. I'd met her in Chicago before she enrolled in school." Sam figured this was the man who knew the most about Emma and her family and was just about to ask another question when the waitress came in.

"Here's your order, mister," the waitress said as she handed Sam the sack with grease already staining the outside. Sam nodded to her and thanked her, giving her an extra dollar as a tip.

The woman put the money in her apron and walked back to the front of the building.

"She sold the farm some two years ago to Gary Jenkins," the tall man continued. "He wasn't much of a farmer, so he sold it about six months ago. Don't know the new guy. He keeps to himself."

Sam was getting impatient. He didn't care about the farm.

"Yeah, I've met him," Sam said, rolling his eyes. A couple of the men snickered. "What happened to Emma?" Sam asked, trying to steer the man back to what was important to him.

"She moved out west somewhere."

"Do you know where?"

"Nope, I don't."

Sam's heart ached. He'd felt so close, but now he had to search the entire western part of the country for her.

"Well, thanks for your help," Sam said as he stood up and held out his hand to the man. "What's your name, sir?"

"Storey's the name. David Storey."

"You're not the first to ask about her," one of the other men said. He was a small man who had been quiet during the conversation. "There was another guy here just about a month ago, a foreigner with a heavy German accent. Said he was a relation."

◆ ◆ ◆ ◆

As Sam left the small town, his heart was as heavy as the clouds that had rolled in. He stopped at a small park near the river. He couldn't eat now, his stomach was in knots. He ached inside, as if a part of him was lost.

He watched the water flow calmly in the center where the river was deepest, creating a dark, smooth ribbon, that went on for miles, reflecting the tall, dark trees surrounding the river. A small, white, empty boat dock stood a few yards away, the dark pilings standing strong against the water's current. Near the bank, the current was rapidly moving, with light dancing on the water. Visions of Emma's face flashed before Sam and he swore he could hear her laughter in the sounds of the river. He remembered watching her face in the light of the movie theater, the strong line of her jaw, the soft curve of her lips.

A large, flat barge drifted by and Sam wondered what his next move would be. The smaller man wouldn't say any more about the German who'd been asking about Emma.

Just then, the sun broke through and flashed brilliantly on the water, causing Sam to look down at the ground to shelter his eyes. The light shone on a dime lying next to his shoe and he reached down to pick it up. Turning it over in his hands, he thought about when he was a kid and the many wishes he'd made every time he found a coin. He made a wish now and put the coin into his pocket. His heart felt a little lighter. Hanging onto a childish belief, he felt that all hope wasn't lost yet. Smiling to himself, he got into the Jeep and started the drive back to Louisville. A gentle snow began to fall. He knew in his heart that someday he'd find Emma.

CHAPTER EIGHT

Fall, 1965

Joanna Parker smiled as Sam kissed her on the cheek on his way to the back door of their home. She watched as he grabbed two apples and slip them in the pocket of his uniform, then leave for the stable. She shook her head. He hadn't taken the time to change, just like he'd always done after he'd come home from school. He couldn't wait to see the horses.

She didn't like the changes she'd seen in her son after he'd returned home from his mission in Vietnam. He looked exhausted and somehow very sad. She knew the missions he'd flown were classified, but it hurt her to see what those years had done to her son. She sighed and put her hand to her dark, brown hair, tucking in a stray gray strand that had fallen next to her cheek. Then, she continued rolling the crust for an apple pie. She was just thankful he was finally home.

Outside, Sam could smell the smoke from the wood fire burning in the fireplace. The crisp, autumn evening air was refreshing after the warm kitchen. Looking around in the light of the setting sun, he saw the leaves on the large oak turning gold and brown. In his mother's large garden, pumpkins lay ready for harvest and the drying corn stalks rustled in the breeze. In the distance, the golden, cut hayfields, the dark green evergreens, the blue sky above the hills to the east, and the soft pink clouds all reminded him of the colors of Africa he'd seen. Overhead, a flock of Northern geese began their southern migration, flying in a similar formation Sam had used with his squadron. He could hear the rushing rapids of the McKenzie River near their farm as he approached the large red stable. He looked over at the oval track his father had built when Sam was ten. Many a horse had been trained for racing on that track. It all seemed so very long ago.

His father's ranch was much smaller than the Kentucky farms Sam had seen. Harold Parker had said he wanted to keep it that way. He'd seen what the racing circuit did to some families and didn't want that to happen to his. 'Racing is my second love,' he'd said. 'My family is my first.' Sam's grandfather had worked for the Oregon Racing Commission, and because of it, his father had spent most of his life on a race track.

In the darkness of the stable, Sam waited for a moment for his eyes to adjust. He'd missed being with the horses, the smells of the stable. Then he saw his father and Doc White, his father's vet. They were both bent over, looking at the right foreleg of O'Leary's Bluff, an old, retired bay stallion. A bucket of ice stood nearby. Sam could see the swelling beginning in the leg and knew that this horse would run his heart out for his father, if he was having a good day. This horse would sometimes shy at the slightest sound, but put him on the track and he was unstoppable. He'd won numerous races at the tracks in Oregon and California.

"What do you think, Doc?" Sam's father said with concern in his eyes. Harold was a tall, slender man in his early sixties, the sides of his sandy hair showing silver. Sam's heart swelled at the sound of his father's voice and seeing his tanned face, furrowed with concern for the large animal.

The vet smiled, his brown eyes twinkled in the light from the bare light bulb overhead. When he'd first come to America from England, he'd been shocked by the Americans' careless way of addressing him. At Epsom Downs, no one would have ever called him 'Doc.' But, after the first year, he'd decided he liked the sound of it.

"I think he's going to be fine," Doc said in his British accent. Sam knew that Emerson White had come to Oregon with his wife in the fifties, after he'd heard about the Northwest from a young fellow racing at Epsom Downs, where he had been the track veterinarian. Doc knew a good race horse when he saw one, and had worked with Sam's father for years.

"Keep the ice on his leg for a while longer, just to be safe." The small man placed the horse's leg into an empty bucket, then gently packed ice around the swelling.

Sam remembered when his dad had first let him ride O'Leary when the colt was training as a young racer. He'd loved the wind in his hair as he and horse raced around the track at full speed, his father watching from the side. That was when Sam had begun his dream of owning a racehorse of his own.

"Thanks, Doc," Harold said. "I appreciate you coming out so quickly."

"Good Morning, Sam," Doc said as he turned around. "When did you arrive home?"

"Hello, Doc. I just got in." Sam smiled first at his dad, then at the old vet.

"Well, in that case, I best be returning to my practice. Glad to see you are back safe and sound, lad. Goodbye, Harold."

"Bye, Doc. Thanks, again."

When they were finally alone, Harold and Sam stood looking at each other. Harold was reminded of how much his son looked like Joanna, the same dark hair and high cheekbones.

"Hello, son," Harold said with a smile that warmed his face.

"Hi, Dad."

The two men in the stable first started to shake hands, then father hugged son. Quickly, Harold turned and wiped his eyes - so that Sam wouldn't see.

"How was your flight home?" Harold asked.

"Long, but I'm glad it's all over." Sam took an apple out of his pocket and gave it to O'Leary, stroking the horse's long, dark neck.

"So are we."

Harold stepped back and looked at his son in his uniform. It brought back memories of his gunner days with the 637th TD in the Philippines. His tank division had been one of those that helped in the recapture of Corregidor, which stopped the Japanese from advancing into Australia in WWII. He still owned the Japanese carbine rifle that was taken from a soldier killed in one of the caves on the island. It was his reminder of the tragedy of war. His tank commander had been called home on an emergency furlough, and Harold had given him the money to get home. Harold was appointed to the commander position, but never received the commission. The war ended before it was ever put on paper.

A high whinny came from the back of the stable. Harold smiled, then began to walk toward the sound, motioning for Sam to follow him.

"Come here, I have something to show you," he said, stopping in front of the last stall. As Sam came up next to him, Harold opened the top gate and stepped back.

Sam walked up to the gate and looked in at the shy, young filly inside, her chestnut coat aflame in the last sunlight coming in through the window behind her. He looked at her sleek, strong legs and proud head.

"Hey, girl," Sam said in a soft voice as he placed his hand in his pocket, and raised it out to her. The horse nickered and began walking up to Sam's hand, taking the apple he offered with her soft muzzle.

Joanna walked into the stable just then and came up to stand next to her husband, placing her hand in his.

"She's beautiful, Dad. Who does she belong to?" Sam asked, thinking his dad may have taken her on as a boarder.

"She's yours, son. Came from the Whiteson Ranch."

Sam looked at his father and mother and saw their smiles. He could tell by their faces that it was true, but he had to ask. "You're kidding, right?" The horses at Whiteson had produced great racers for generations and cost a pretty price.

"Nope," Harold said. He turned to the yearling in the stall. "Lady, meet your new owner, Sam Parker."

The filly whinnied again and nodded her head, as if she understood.

Sam laughed, then walked into the stall and placed his hands softly on her. She turned her head to watch him with her big, brown eyes as he circled her, checking every inch of her, talking softly in a low voice all the while. He'd learned when he was young that he had a special way with animals. She was tall for a yearling. When he came up on the other side of her and placed his forehead on her neck, she softly nickered again. He wrapped his arms around her neck and hugged her, wiping his tears into her mane, smelling the sweet odor of horse flesh that he loved so much. He looked at his parents.

"What a great homecoming. Thanks, Mom and Dad."

"Glad you're home safe, son. Your mother and I missed you."

Harold clapped his hands together and said, "Now, the work begins. We've got to get this filly ready to race by next spring. What're you going to name her, Sam?"

"Classy Elegance," Sam said without hesitation. It had been a name that had come to him at Essen Farms in Kentucky.

◆ ◆ ◆ ◆

Late that night, Sam and his father sat in front of the large fireplace in the den, each sipping a shot of Jack Daniels. Sam's mother had already gone to bed, leaving the two men to talk.

Sam looked around the oak-paneled room of the house his dad had grown up in. It was a long, ranch-style house, and the den was his dad's favorite room. The rock in the fireplace had been pulled from the river near their property.

"Your mother and I are very proud of you, son," Harold said with a smile. "You've certainly come a long way from pilot training."

Sam laughed, remembering his primary days at Marana, learning to fly the single-engine props. He'd managed to still have the ball cap he'd worn with the Scorpion insignia, which now hung on the wall of his bedroom upstairs, along with numerous photos that he'd taken during his training. His favorite was the one taken of him and his friend, Jim Barolio, just after their solo flights.

"Thanks," Sam said. "Remember when you and Mom flew out for my graduation when I received my wings?"

"Sure do. We were so happy for you that day. I never understood how you became so good at formation flying."

"I just kept the lead's tip tanks as close as possible to the front wind screen. That way, I could detect the slightest changes the other pilot was making."

Then, Sam thought of the Quemoy-Matsu crisis, which occurred off mainland China - across the Formosan Strait from Taiwan. That was the first mission Sam was sent on that he couldn't tell his parents about.

"It's been a real adventure," Sam sighed, then was quiet for a moment. He stared into the fire as visions of what he'd seen on those missions flashed through his mind. He wished he could forget them, but knew he never would.

"Dad, you know I can't divulge classified information about my missions, but there are some things that I can share with you, now that they're over."

Harold sat forward in his chair, elbows on his knees, holding his glass of whiskey between both hands as he watched his son. He knew it was time he remained silent and let Sam talk. He saw a shadow come over Sam's face, but he remained quiet.

"It was a time to forget, a war that didn't make any sense," Sam continued. "I was flying with one of the first squadrons in Vietnam. We weren't allowed to tell anyone what we were doing. They were classified missions..."

Father and son talked late into the night. Harold had only heard small pieces of what happened in Vietnam through the media. During that time, he'd understood more how his family had suffered while he was in the Pacific, not knowing whether he was dead or alive most of the time, as they sifted through the meager news reports that only highlighted a handful of battles the military would feed them. What Sam told him was inconceivable. It was nothing like the war he'd fought in.

Sam told him of one night when they were camped at a small, hidden airstrip. A young Vietnamese girl, about the age of ten, had walked into their camp one night with a live grenade strapped to her. Sam had had to make the split-second decision to shoot her before she came any closer and destroyed his men. He'd always carry the scar from the shrapnel that had caught him as the grenade exploded, but he'd never forget the fear in the young girl's eyes when he'd fired.

Hours later, Sam and his dad sat quietly, staring into the fire, trying to let the whiskey erase the sour taste in their mouths from Sam's words.

"I hope we never see a war like that one again," Sam finally said. He raised his glass to touch his father's. "Here's to world peace," he toasted, then finished the golden liquid, feeling it burn as it went down to his stomach.

"Did you ever hear from Susan again?" Sam's dad asked in an attempt to change the subject.

Sam laughed. "No, but I talked to a Captain she'd married shortly after I broke our engagement. He told me it didn't last very long. When they were divorced, she took him to the cleaners."

"Good thing it wasn't you," Harold said, smiling.

"You got that right."

"Well, better get some sleep, son." Harold rose and put his hand on Sam's shoulder, needing to touch his son. It reassured him that Sam was really home.

"Goodnight," Harold said, smiling.

"Night, Dad. It's good to be home."

◆ ◆ ◆ ◆

Sam was unable to sleep. He walked out into the cool, autumn air and headed toward the stable where a soft light shown. His dad always kept a small light on in the tack room at night. Once inside, Sam turned on a switch that only lit the aisle way between the stalls. Then, he walked back to where his mare stood.

She nickered in the still night when Sam opened the top door to her stall.

"Hey, Ele," he said, looking into the shadows of the stall, lit only by the light over his head. He was surprised at the nickname he'd used, but he felt it fit so naturally on his tongue.

The mare nickered again softly and walked to the gate, her head coming out to meet Sam's outstretched hand.

"Sorry, girl," he said. "No apple this time. Just me."

When he placed his hand on her forehead and scratched, her eyes closed. She seemed to lean into his hand, enjoying the sensation. They stood like this for some time, then the mare nodded her head and nickered. Sam looked into her large eyes.

"You and I are going to lots of places, Ele. I can see in your eyes you want to run. So do I."

Sam buried his face in her mane and let his tears finally fall quietly. He wasn't a man who cried, but there was much more inside of him that he couldn't tell his dad. Now, it was only between him and his horse. Ele stood still, almost as if she knew what he needed.

Once Sam was back in his room, his mind raced around in numerous directions as he relived the day. He kept circling back to one event. At the dinner table, his mother had asked him if he had ever heard from Emma Maseman. In his letters that he'd sent to his parents while he was in Arizona, he'd mentioned meeting Emma in Chicago. His mother had said she'd wondered if that could have been the girl who'd called for him before.

Now, in the dark, he thought of Emma. He could never forget the way the light had shone on her dark hair and how soft her hand felt in his. His stomach had tied in knots as he'd tasted her lips before they parted. Then, he remembered the look on her face as his taxi had driven away from her hotel. Sam was sorry he had been so stupid not to introduce her to Nancy. He had been scared then. Scared of how hard he had fallen for Emma.

Once he had arrived at the air base in Arizona, he'd written Emma, pouring out his heart. She hadn't responded. When he wrote his second letter, he'd asked her to marry him. Sam still had the letter he'd received from Oliver Stenson, which said that Emma had asked him to tell Sam she didn't want to hear from him again. Sam had been crushed, his heart broken. He thought how angry he'd been, feeling rejected. He had almost written Oliver, telling him what was in his heart, but he never got the courage. Now, after all he'd seen in his life, he knew that had been a mistake. Oliver would have understood and helped him reach Emma, but now it was too late.

He picked up his wallet and pulled out the photo of Emma he'd found at her old farm in Indiana. He stared into her face and knew now that he needed to find her. He had to. He'd already checked with her art school and found that she had not finished, that she had left before her last year. He didn't have a clue where to begin, but he had no choice. He still loved her.

◆ ◆ ◆

The following March, Sam, his dad, and Mike McKeegan, his dad's trainer, stood near the railing around the track at Portland Meadows. Shane McKeegan, Mike's son, was exercising Sam's two-year-old mare. On January first of each year, every Thoroughbred across America turned one year older, no matter when they were born the previous year.

Shane, a thin, young boy with fiery, red hair, had worked for his father for the last three years. Sam remembered that was how he'd started in the Thoroughbred world with his father.

Sam had learned that Mike and Shane had begun Classy Elegance's training the prior year, before Sam arrived home. Mike had been careful not to put too much weight on the filly before her legs were ready. Mike had been his dad's trainer since Sam was twelve years old. Before that, Mike had worked at various horse farms near Lexington most of his young life. He'd joined Harold Parker after leaving Kentucky to move to Oregon with his wife. Sam had always liked the stories Mike told him about Kentucky.

Sam watched Ele race by. He liked the gait of his horse, her long legs stretching out in front of her as she ate up the track. She kept her head low, even though Shane was trying to hold her back. Finally, when Shane pulled Ele up in front of Sam, his mare still seemed ready to go on.

Mike took hold of Ele's rein and Shane jumped down.

"She's going to make you proud, Sam," Mike said, a slight southern drawl still in his voice.

"I think you're right," Sam replied.

"It's time we find her a rider," Harold said.

Sam nodded, then, looked over his shoulder as something caught his eye. He turned, facing the backside as a man with black, curly hair walked up to Sam and slapped his shoulder.

"Sam Parker, so this is what you've been up to," the man said.

"Jim!" Sam hugged Jim Barolio, his best friend, noticing he'd changed a bit since he last saw him in Kentucky. He was a little rounder now, with a touch of gray beginning at the temples, but he looked much happier.

Sam turned to his dad. "Dad, you remember Jim."

Harold reached out a large hand to Jim. "You bet. I'm glad to see you again, son." He and Joanna had enjoyed watching the friendship grow between their son and Jim when they were young.

"It's nice to see you too, sir."

"You remember Mike McKeegan, my trainer?"

"Sure. How's the training going, Mike?" Jim winked at Mike. He'd known about Harold Parker's decision to buy Sam a horse before anyone. Sam's dad had called him and asked his opinion about the Whiteson Ranch horses.

"Very well," Mike said with a big grin.

"Looks like you've really got something there," Jim said to Sam, nodding towards the horse.

Sam looked between Jim and Mike. He wondered how Jim knew about Ele. "She's got a heart of gold," Sam replied.

Just then, Ele started to dance around. Mike pulled on her rein and softly talked to her until she settled down. "I need to go cool her down," he said. "See you later, Jim."

"What'd you name her, Sam?" Jim asked, as the chestnut filly was being led toward the shedrow.

"Classy Elegance. But, how did you know..." Sam stopped when he saw the smile between Jim and his dad. He began to understand the conspiracy and laughed with them.

"What're you doing here, Jim?" Sam asked.

"I work here. Well, actually, I work all over Oregon now. After Nancy's mother died a couple of months ago, I took the Racing Commissioner job here." Jim had always known where Sam was, but the mail in the military could sometimes be slow.

A large, burly man walked up to Jim.

"Commissioner," the man said. "There's a phone call for you from Salem."

"Thanks, Jerry." Jim turned to Sam. "I'll check back with you after I take care of this."

Just as Jim walked away, Sam saw a small man in a tan jacket coming toward him from behind the grandstand, his short, sandy hair cut close to his head and his hands in his pockets. Sam then recognized him.

"Remsky, what the hell are you doing in Portland?"

"Looking for you," the short man said as he stopped in front of Sam.

"Dad," Sam said. "This is Joe Remsky. We met at Marana Air Base in Arizona. Joe was a jockey in California before he enlisted."

Sam's dad nodded to Joe. He was searching his mind why this man looked familiar. He looked over and saw Jim looking their way before turning into the office.

"Nice to meet you, Mr. Parker," Joe said, then turned to watch Sam's horse. "She's a beauty."

"What brings you to Portland?" Sam asked.

"I heard in the backside you were looking for a jockey."

"Yes, Ele's ready."

"I've been riding the Western circuit again, since I got out. So," Joe said, looking at Sam with his dark eyes, "can I ride for you?"

Joe wasn't about to tell Sam about the time he'd drugged Sloan's stallion in a Pomona race to make some extra cash. He hadn't gotten caught, so why open it up now. That was the second time he'd been lucky. The first time was in San Francisco, when he'd been arrested for beating a Mexican woman, but the charges were dismissed because she wouldn't testify. He'd worked hard to keep that one quiet. Joe never got his wings, he'd washed out and was transferred to supply school, which he'd hated.

Sam thought for a moment, then said, "Why don't you come back tomorrow and we'll see."

"Ok. I'll see you early tomorrow," Joe said as he saluted Sam and his dad, then turned and walked back behind the grandstand.

"You've been awfully quiet," Sam said to his dad.

"Well, she's your horse, son. And, what you decide to do is your business. There's just something about him that I can't put my finger on."

"He's all right. Had a few problems with the authorities in the service. That's why he never made it as a pilot." Sam didn't add that Joe had a wandering passion that always got him into trouble, usually involving some very young girl.

"Just keep your eye on him," Sam's father said, then walked toward the backside.

◆ ◆ ◆ ◆

The next day at dawn, Joe arrived at the race track, just when the sun was beginning to rise over the rim near Mt. Hood. The clouds were aflame with the early light. Sam and his dad stood near the track, the breath of the horses visible in the cool air. They were going to run Ele with two other horses in a set together to prepare her for the races coming up in April.

"Hey, Sam," Joe said as he walked up to him. He had on an old pair of whites that he'd used during training and a black, silk shirt. He carried his helmet and a whip.

Sam saw the whip and frowned. "You won't need that, Joe. I don't want you using it on Ele."

Shane and Jimmy, another exercise boy, held the reins of their horses while Mike checked the tack on Ele once more. The boys watched Joe hesitate before he tossed the whip onto the ground near the railing.

"She's trained at the gate, so you won't have any trouble loading her. Are you ready?" Sam asked.

"You bet."

"Mount up."

Mike gave Joe a leg up and the mare pranced around in a circle, excited to begin her exercises. The other horses impatiently pawed the ground.

"She's going to want to race ahead, but hold her back a little," Sam cautioned. "I don't want her injuring herself."

Joe nodded, then led Ele slowly around the track, warming her muscles, the other riders following close behind. When it was time to test her for speed, they finished the first turn, then came up to the gate. The horses lined up together and waited.

As soon as the bell rang, and the gate sprung open, Ele shot out ahead of the others. Shane and the other rider followed closely behind in a close pack, but were unable to close the gap. Sam could hear Joe yelling at Ele, hugging close to her neck on her reins as she reached for the ground before her, stretching her long legs, staying strong as they came around the first turn. Her red mane was afire in the morning sunlight that burst across the sky.

Sam watched Ele with a stopwatch running in his hand, but he didn't take his eyes off of her. Joe seemed to be holding back on the reins, but Ele lengthened the distance between her and the other horses. Harold had never seen anything like her. She was showing no signs of stress, flying on the wind as if she was born to run. He looked over at his son's face and saw the pride in his eyes.

The horses came to the third furlong with Ele far in the lead. Sam pressed the button on the watch as Ele passed him. He stood there staring at the clock's face, unable to believe what he saw. Joe and the other riders pulled up the horses, standing in the stirrups as they continued around the track. Sam handed the watch to his father and walked out onto the track. When Ele came back around toward him, Sam grabbed her rein and held her still for a moment, patting her neck.

"Good job, girl," he said in his soft, soothing voice as he looked into her big eyes that still held the excitement of the run. Her nostrils were flaring and she pranced in place. "I knew you had it in you."

"She's fast," Joe said as he dismounted and handed the reins to Mike. "What'd she do?"

Sam was quiet for a moment, stroking the animal's tall neck with pride. "Thirty-six," he said with a large grin.

Joe whistled. "I could have sworn she was more like forty seconds. She was flying, even with me pulling on her. I had a hell of a time holding her."

"Mike," Sam said. "You'd better take her to the backside to cool down and get her washed."

Sam and his dad watched as Mike and Joe slowly walked away with Ele, Joe talking wildly with his hands waiving in the air.

"She's going to surprise the world, Sam," Harold finally said, patting his son on the back.

"Damn right," Sam said, smiling after his chestnut mare.

◆ ◆ ◆ ◆

Jim Barolio hung up the receiver. He now understood why his gut had both-
ered him since he'd seen Joe Remsky walk up to Sam yesterday at the track.
He'd remembered Remsky from Marana and knew he'd jockeyed in California.
Jim had then called Mark Williams, the commissioner down there, to check on
Joe.

Mark had just called and told him about Joe's reputation on the tracks down
south. 'There wasn't any hard core evidence,' Mark had said. 'Only speculation.'

Jim didn't trust the small man. He was afraid that some day, Joe was going
to do something that would hurt his friend.

Later, he thought to himself. *I'll talk to Sam about it.* He didn't know that
he'd never get the chance, before it was too late.

◆ ◆ ◆ ◆

Spring, 1966

Del Mar had a slick, seven-furlong turf track, but Sam wasn't worried. He'd
seen Ele run on anything and still win. He was totally convinced that his mare
couldn't lose, even though his dad had tried to caution him about getting too con-
fident. Sam thought otherwise; he knew Lady Luck was with him. Classy
Elegance had won three races consecutively at California tracks, and Sam knew
she wasn't finished yet.

The night before the Del Mar Futurity race, George Mason walked into the
small tavern near the track and sat at the bar. He looked around the room and saw
Sam Parker. George remembered Sam and overheard him talking to the two men
sitting at his table about his mare's winning streak. George had been watching
Sam's mare. She was a fine animal and had the potential of a Derby winner.
When the two men left, George walked over to Sam and offered to buy him a
drink.

"Hello, Sam," George said with a smile.

"George Mason," Sam said in amazement. "What're you doing at Del Mar?"

"I'm running Koenig's Pride tomorrow in a claiming race."

Sam thought of the young colt he'd seen racing in the meadow at Essen
Farms in Kentucky.

"I'll bet you, George, that my Classy Elegance can beat your boy tomorrow.
She's running in the same race." Sam's words slurred slightly, but he looked
George in the eye with pride.

George had seen pride like that once - in the mirror, after Koenig won the
Derby.

"Classy Elegance," George said. "Where did you get that name?"

"From the day I watched your Classy give birth to Koenig's Wonder." Sam
thought about that night at Essen Farms and smiled.

"You're in no condition to bet anything, Sam."

"Afraid I'm right?" Sam asked, sitting straighter in his seat.

"I didn't say that." George knew the gambling edge, he'd been in the game
longer than Sam Parker. "What stakes are you willing to put up?" he asked.

"The claim on the race is for forty thousand. Nobody'll touch her," Sam took a deep gulp of his beer. He thought of his dad's warning, but he knew Ele wouldn't let him down. "But, on the side, I'll bet you a thousand she wins."

George thought of another claiming race. It was a race that trainers and owners used to classify a horse and determine its value. The unfortunate outcome of the race is that someone could claim your horse and you would lose it. Once a claim was filed, there was no way to withdraw it. He'd taken a chance with one of his favorite two-year-old fillies then, but he'd been very lucky that time.

"A man would be foolish to risk a valuable horse in a claiming race," George said. He was willing to let Koenig's Pride go, but he wasn't so sure Sam wanted to lose his filly. Koenig's Pride had not been able to match Koenig's times in past races. George was in the market for a winner.

"Are you calling me a fool?" Sam asked, anger rising inside of him.

"Yes."

Sam shrugged his shoulders to shake off the sting. "Then, why do you have your horse entered in the same race tomorrow, if I'm such a fool?" Sam asked.

"I have my reasons. And, I can afford to take the risk. Can you?"

Sam thought for a moment, then thought of Ele racing her heart out in the last race. He knew she couldn't lose and luck was with him.

"Nobody'll touch her," Sam said. "So, do we have a bet?"

George agreed. He could afford to lose the smaller cash, but he wasn't so sure that he wouldn't buy Sam's filly, if he liked the way she ran in tomorrow's race. After all, he was a businessman first. He shook Sam's hand in agreement and left the bar.

While the two men had talked, Carlos Madera, a jockey who rode any horse for the right price, sat at a table nearby. He was scheduled to ride Mason's colt the next day. His rugged, dark face was shadowed by his dark hair hanging down. He pushed it back with one hand, the muscles in his forearms and shoulders strong and tight. With his back to their table, he'd overheard Mason and Parker talking. When Mason left, Carlos walked out after him, keeping a few paces behind him.

Mason went into the secretary's office. Carlos waited outside. Watching through the window, Carlos saw Mason place a claim certificate into the box. Carlos hid in the shadows as Mason came out of the office. Before closing the door, Mason said to the pay master, "Classy Elegance will be mine tomorrow."

Carlos waited until Mason was out of sight. Then, Carlos shook his head. The job he'd been hired to do, just got complicated.

Carlos walked to his car and drove out of the track gate. Then he pulled into a small, single-story motel that looked like it had been there for a hundred years. He wondered why this motel had been chosen. It looked like some he'd seen back home. There was a much nicer one closer to the Del Mar track, but he knew he'd never ask the question. Walking up to a green door that needed paint, he knocked. A tall, thin man in a dark suit could be seen from the light in the room as the door opened. Carlos shivered, then went inside. The overhead light was bright, making the shabby furniture marked with numerous cigarette burns look even worse. The worn spread on the bed was a mass of gaudy fall colors, threads hanging loosely where they had broken in the quilting. A voice on the news station on the television talked about the upcoming weather.

"We have a problem," Carlos said to the man standing in the middle of the small room.

"Tell me," Karl Strauss said in a heavy accent, as he turned off the television.

"Mason just put a claim on Classy Elegance."

Strauss stared at Carlos, disbelieving his words. "Mr. Reichmann wants that filly for his breeding stock."

Carlos remained silent.

Strauss paced up and down the small room, the faded, red curtains matching his mood. He knew why he was here and what motive was driving his actions, but he kept those to himself. There were too many factors in this type of race to leave everything to chance. He had dealt with George Mason once before. Then he stopped pacing, a grin starting across his face.

"Wait here," Strauss hissed, and walked into the bathroom, closing the door.

Carlos put his hands in his pockets and took a deep breath. He had met Karl Strauss and Mr. Reichmann at a track in Venezuela. Both of these men made him nervous, but they paid him well to do what they asked, and he never questioned their requests. When the bathroom door opened, Carlos took his hands out of his pockets.

Strauss walked up to him and held out his hand, which was draped with a wash cloth. On the cloth lay a small object that fit in the palm of his hand.

"I want you to give this to Parker's jockey. Instruct him to give it to the filly just before the race. This will guarantee that she will win, but she will be disqualified after the results of the post-race test are found. Tell her rider that Mason gave this to you, which will cause an investigation."

Strauss stopped and looked at the ceiling. "You and Parker's jockey will receive twenty thousand, if you both do this," he added. "Tomorrow, I will place a claim on Koenig's Pride."

Carlos looked down at the syringe as Strauss wrapped it in the cloth. When it was placed in his hand, Carlos slipped it into his jacket pocket. It wasn't the first time he'd been asked to do this kind of job.

"What is in this?" Carlos asked, before he could stop himself.

"It is none of your concern," Straus snapped, his voice shaking. He was not used to being questioned for his actions. "Just do as you are told. We will get the filly later."

Carlos nodded and walked out.

In the backside of the race track, Carlos stopped at the stall holding Sam Parker's filly. He looked at the chestnut and could see in her eyes that she was ready to run.

"Have you seen your jockey?" he asked the young man who had just walked up to the horse's gate.

"Joe Remsky? He's down in the jockey room." Shane McKeegan didn't know this man, but because of his size, he assumed he was another jockey.

When Carlos entered the jockey room, the humid heat and smell of liniment hung in the air. Three men stood by the lockers, talking softly amongst themselves. Carlos walked over to them and asked for Joe. One of them told him Joe was still in the shower.

Carlos walked to the shower area, steam rolling from the only stall where a small, muscular man stood lathered in soap.

"Remsky?" Carlos called out above the sound of the rushing water.

"Yeah?" Joe wiped the water from his eyes to see the man in front of him. He recognized Carlos from other races. All jockeys knew each other and their style of riding. They were a close group of men, but this one was a loner. Joe had met Carlos six months ago, when Carlos had just arrived in the states from Venezuela.

"I need to talk to you," Carlos said, lowering his voice so only Joe would hear. "Meet me outside when you're done."

"Okay," Joe said.

Joe finished showering, then quickly dressed in a pair of tight jeans and a black shirt. He liked black. Walking out of the jockey room, he stepped into the cool night air.

"Over here," a voice whispered from a shadow at the side of the building.

"Why all the hush, hush?" Joe asked, after his eyes adjusted to the dark and he saw Carlos.

"I just heard something I think you and I can use to our advantage."

"What?"

"How would you like to make a lot of money on tomorrow's race?" Carlos' voice was now only a soft whisper.

"What the hell are you talking about?" Joe asked. He was starting to itch for a drink in a bar.

"Keep it down, pal," Carlos cautioned. "Your owner was back at the tavern, boasting about his filly. I heard him make a bet that his filly can beat Essen Farms' young black. I'm scheduled to ride for Essen tomorrow. Maybe the two of us can make our own bets on the side, actually knowing which horse is going to win."

Joe had dreamt of making his fortune with this filly. She was fast, and he knew it. He started to see the green money in his hands, lots of it. He had a stash that he'd been keeping for just this opportunity.

"What've you got planned?" Joe asked, curious now, daring to see his dream come true. He wanted to see what Carlos was up to.

"We both get someone to place our bets on your horse to win. Then, we take our money and run."

Joe thought for a moment, running over the details in his mind. "Who's going to place our bets?" he finally asked.

"My girlfriend will do it."

"Oh, yeah, sure. And, I'm really going to see my winnings from her?"

"Yes." Carlos looked squarely at Joe, his jaw tight. He was growing impatient with Joe, but he needed him.

"All right," Joe finally answered. "What's going to guarantee that my horse will win?" He'd seen the Essen colt run before.

Carlos sighed. It was very tedious working with amateurs. *Rookie*, Carlos thought, as he pulled the small syringe out of his pocket.

"Give her this, just at the last minute before you have to go to the jockey room," Carlos said, handing Joe the package. "It is what my man wants," he added. Carlos didn't want to use Mason's name, he might need to continue riding for him in the future. But he figured Remsky would make the connection.

Looking down as he unwrapped the package, Joe asked, "This ain't going to show up in her drug test after the race, is it?" In the past, he'd seen other trainers give drugs to horses he'd ridden, some got caught and some didn't.

"No," Carlos lied. "It's only a mild anti-inflammatory drug they don't test for. It won't harm her." Strauss hadn't said what drug this was or what it would do to the horse, but it was not his concern. Carlos knew that the tracks were watching for this type of manipulation during races by trainers and owners, but he had a job to do.

"You do this," Carlos added, "so that the filly wins the race, and you will also get an additional twenty thousand dollars for this."

Greed took hold of Joe now. He carefully tucked the syringe into his shirt pocket, looking around to make sure no one saw him.

He began to reach into his back pants pocket for his money, which he always carried with him. Then he stopped.

"On second thought," Joe said. "I'd like to go with you to give my money to your girlfriend and watch her make the bet. I'm not sure I trust you."

"We won't have time tomorrow, and we'll be watched all of the time."

"You're right," Joe said, as he handed over the wad of large bills. He knew that if he ever needed to find Carlos Madera, he'd have no trouble.

"When do I get my twenty thousand?" Joe asked, licking his lips.

"Tomorrow, after all the races are run. Hang around the jockey room and wait until everyone has left. I'll meet you there."

"Okay. Now, where do I meet your girlfriend to pick up my winnings?"

"She will be at the Paradise Club in town tomorrow night at ten o'clock. Her name is Maria Sanchez, and she has long, black hair. I have some other business to take care of and will meet her later."

Joe was now looking forward to picking up his winnings tomorrow. He liked women with long, black hair. Juanita, his girl back in San Juan, had long, black hair. Joe remembered his hands deep in it, when he had her hands and feet tied to the bed. He loved the way she'd tried to fight him off, it excited him even more.

◆ ◆ ◆ ◆

The next day, Sam's head was killing him. He'd walked beside Ele to the saddling enclosure and watched as Mike put on her number cloth and saddle. Then Mike led Ele to the walking ring.

"Rider's up!" the call came from the paddock, the voice on the loud speaker making Sam flinch.

"Joe," Sam said as Mike gave Joe a leg up into the saddle, the gold stripes on his dark blue jersey shimmering in the sunlight. Sam had chosen those silk colors from his years in the service. "Make sure she gets a clean start from the gate, but hold her back a couple of horses from the lead. Then, on the last turn, give her the rein. She'll take over from there."

"You all right Sam?" Joe asked, seeing the dark circles under Sam's eyes.

"Sure," Sam said, sweat starting to bead on his forehead. "Just make sure she wins."

I'm gonna win, Joe thought to himself as Mike led the horse and rider to the track. He pulled on his gloves, knowing it was for the last time. Early that morning, while Mike was getting coffee, Joe had quickly given Ele the drug, hiding the syringe deep in a large garbage can at the back of the next shedrow.

Maria, here I come, Joe thought as he smiled to himself.

◆ ◆ ◆ ◆

The horses were loaded into the gate, the tension heavy in the air, waiting as a reluctant bay was guided into his stall. When all were loaded, there was a pause before the bell sounded and the horses were off. Sam watched as Ele lunged out of the gate, but bobbled for a moment. She caught herself and began to run as if she was on fire. Koenig's Pride was back three horses from Percy's Choice in the lead. Ele was three behind Koenig's Pride. Percy's Choice was a newcomer out of Kildaire Ranch. Sam had seen his stats, but knew Ele could beat him. *She has to beat him*, he thought.

"Come on, girl. Get moving," Sam yelled. Out of the corner of his eye, he saw George Mason sitting calmly in his box seat, watching Sam with a smile on his face.

Ele was now fourth as the horses rounded the back stretch, Koenig's Pride was still in the same position. Sam saw Joe let up on the rein and Ele began her move, just as she always did. Sam got to his feet. He knew she liked to come up from behind and rush past the lead just at the wire. She started to pass the other horses, coming up on the lead. Sam's heart was thundering with the sound of the hooves as the horses came around the last turn. The black colt began his move. Koenig's Pride pulled out around to the outside and began knocking off each horse with speed Sam had never seen before. The black's shoulder was now even with Ele's as they approached the grandstand, neck and neck, with Percy's Choice still in the lead. Suddenly, Ele faltered in her stride and began to fall back. By the time Koenig's Pride crossed under the wire a nose behind Percy's Choice, Ele was back by two horses. Sam stood in disbelief, staring as the blur of horses raced past his eyes to finish the race.

Someone bumped Sam as they were leaving the grandstand. He watched Ele as she slowly began the last turn before leaving the track. She looked beaten. He'd never seen that in her before. He looked up and saw the board, confirming that Koenig's Pride placed second and Percy's Choice had won the race. He looked over at Mason's box and saw it was empty.

◆ ◆ ◆ ◆

"What the hell happened?" Sam yelled at Joe in the backside, after Joe had weighed in and Ele was returned from the testing barn to cool down by her groom. The results of her urine test wouldn't arrive until the following Monday, but Sam's heart had stopped when he saw the red tag on her halter. Someone had claimed her!

"I don't know," Joe said, not looking at Sam. Sweat was running down his back as he watched out of the corner of his eyes for Carlos. "She seemed to have it to give when I told her to run, but then she was tripping all over her feet."

"Do you have any idea what you've done?" Sam was irate now, pushing Joe up against the barn, taking his frustration out on the small man.

Mike pulled Sam back as Ele whinnied loudly.

"Stop this, Sam. Look at Ele. She was cut down during the race."

Sam stopped and looked down at Ele's legs. Her left front fetlock was bleeding.

"Oh, Mike. Get the vet." Sam went down on his knees with a towel in his hand and wiped away the blood to see the severity of the damage. The cut wasn't bad, but it would take some time to heal. He cleaned it, and liberally rubbed in nitrofurazone before bandaging the leg. He began slowly walking her in a small circle to cool her down until the vet could arrive.

Joe saw this as a good time to leave and he walked quickly around the backside of the shedrow.

"That was a good race, Sam," George Mason said behind him.

Sam turned and saw George standing with a claiming slip in his hand with Ele's name on it. Not only had he lost the bet to George, but he'd lost his horse to the man.

"You're the one?" Sam asked.

George nodded. "If it's any consolation, I lost Koenig's Pride, as well, today. A man named Reichmann had placed a claim on him just before the race." Then George saw the wrap on Ele's leg.

"What has happened to her?" George demanded and looked for himself, unwrapping the bandage.

He could see that she had either cut herself or another horse had kicked her during the race. He stood up and immediately walked to the phone at the end of the shedrow.

"Fred, send Eric over to Barn G. Now," he yelled into the phone and then hung up.

Mike and the track vet came running, but stopped and stared as George Mason bent over Ele's leg.

"What are you doing?" Mike demanded.

"I'm tending to my horse," George answered, handing the claiming slip over to Mike. Mike read the paper, then looked at Sam with shock on his face. He hadn't seen the tag, only the injury to Ele's leg.

"Oh, Sam..." Mike began, but Sam held up his hand to stop him.

All three men stared at each other as the vet checked Ele. Sam ran his hand through his tousled hair, then he looked at Ele. He walked over to her and put his forehead onto hers.

"Bye, lady," he said softly, rubbing her sweaty neck. After a moment, he sighed and turned back to Mike.

"I've got some business to take care of, Mike. Please see that she is taken care of and make the arrangements for her to go to her new owner. Also, would you see that a check for one thousand dollars is sent to George Mason at Essen Farms. I owe it to him."

"Sam..." George began. He had watched Sam and the chestnut during the race. At one point, he thought she was going to win. She was strong and had the heart of a winner. "I know what this means to you. I was foolish last night and took advantage of you. I want you to—"

"No," Sam said sharply, shaking his head. "You got her fairly, and I never go back on my word."

Sam left the track, his entire life's dream taken from him through his own stupidity. His heart ached, knowing he could never face his dad. He needed to leave, go somewhere where no one would find him. As he left the Del Mar grounds, he vowed to himself to never set foot on another race track in his life. He had no idea how one day he would break that vow.

◆ ◆ ◆ ◆

Fall, 1966

Emma and Jennifer entered a jazz club in Portland, near the university. It was warm inside, after the cool, autumn night air, but a haze of cigarette smoke hung above the heads of the young students standing near the bar yelling at each other over the loud music. The club was not very large. There were a few tables in front of the musicians, a tiny dance floor, and pool tables that stood in the back behind the long bar. Jennifer had insisted that Emma go out with her to-night. Emma hated these places, mostly because of the smoke, but she did love the jazz.

"Tell me again why we're here?" Emma yelled over the music as they sat down at a recently vacated table.

"Because you need to get out more," Jennifer said. They ordered drinks just as the musicians took a break. "Jason's going to meet us here."

Emma had met Jennifer's boyfriend many years ago in Chicago, during one Spring Break, when she and Jennifer'd stayed in the city. Emma had liked Jason instantly.

"But, we could have gone to the art museum. I like it much better than this."

Jennifer wrinkled her nose. "There's no action there."

"Action?" Emma snorted softly to herself, looking around the room at the people, both young and old, who were obviously hoping to meet someone that night. She had been hopeful before, but now had closed her heart.

"Em, I'm worried about you," Jennifer said, looking deeply into her friend's eyes.

"What do you mean?" Emma asked, then looked away. She knew exactly what Jennifer meant, but she hadn't been able to talk to her about her trip to Eugene. It was the first time she'd ever kept anything from Jennifer, but she was too embarrassed. The waitress brought drinks to their table, took their money, and left.

"For the last six months, you've been acting like a mad woman. I've sat back and watched you dive into your work with such a fury, up early, working until late at night. You've built that arena, added more students, and you judge those shows every weekend. You can't possibly have a spare moment in a day. What are you afraid of, Em?"

Emma was quiet for a moment as she looked at her friend.

"I don't know what you're talking about?" she finally said as she looked around the club. "I've just been very busy lately."

Emma saw a tall, thin man standing at the bar in a white shirt and dark jeans. She quickly looked away when she saw that he was watching her.

"I think you miss your parents so much that you're keeping yourself busy so you don't have time to think about them," Jennifer said, placing her hand on Emma's.

Emma looked at her friend, then gazed at her drink.

It was true, she'd become restless and used her work to hide her feelings. At first, she'd been happy in her new home, turning it into exactly what she wanted. But, after awhile she'd found that what she'd run away from when she left Indiana was still with her, her feelings of abandonment, both of her parents leaving her, and then to learn that her last hope of happiness was gone. Now, she was afraid that she would never meet a man that she could love, one she could have children with, a family. Her mother's words kept haunting her. Now, her home was large and empty. She would work late into the night, then go to her house and fall asleep in the large chair before the fireplace in the den, too tired to go upstairs to her empty bed. A small tear fell onto the table as the band returned, and a beautiful woman began singing *"Someone to Watch Over Me."*

"It's okay, Em. I understand. I just don't like you pushing yourself so hard. I love you."

Emma wiped her tears away and smiled at her friend.

"Thanks, Jenn. I love you, too. You're all the family I've got now." Emma remembered how they had vowed in college that they would be sisters till the end.

"There's something..." Emma began, about to explain her trip to Eugene, when she saw the man at the bar walking toward their table. He was a tall, wiry man, with sandy, wavy hair, his white shirt sleeves rolled up to his elbows, revealing tight muscles in his arms. He smiled as he stopped in front of her.

"Would you care to dance?" he asked Emma, his eyes locking onto hers.

"I don't think so," she said, remembering the last time she'd danced was at one of the church socials back in Indiana with the local veterinarian.

"Go on, Em," Jennifer encouraged her. "It'd do you some good." She eyed the tall man up and down.

"Well, all right."

"I've been watching you," the man said to Emma as he walked her to the dance floor. He smiled and took her gently in his arms and began to dance slowly in one area of the small, wooden floor. Other couples danced around them in the dim light.

"I know," she said, daring to look into his eyes for a moment. She liked his blue eyes and his smile. She had allowed herself to be taken in once before by a man with eyes like his, but she felt she knew what she was doing this time. The shield she had built around her heart had grown stronger every day.

"My name is Ted Jacobs. I've just moved here from California."

"I'm Emma Maseman." She allowed herself to relax a little in his arms. "What brought you to Oregon, Ted?"

"California was getting too busy, and I heard about the open spaces up here. I work with horses."

"Oh, what type of work?"

"I'm a farrier. I shoe horses."

"I know what a farrier is," Emma said.

"How do you know?" He was used to having to explain his work to girls.

"I own a riding school west of Portland."

"Do you need a farrier?" Ted asked, still smiling down at her. He was hoping she'd say yes to give him a reason to see more of her.

"Well, not at the moment."

"I worked mostly around the race tracks down south. Are you married, Emma?"

Emma was surprised by his question and tightened up for a moment, then she saw his smile. She smiled. "No, I never got around to it."

"Good," Ted said, laughing as the song ended. They stood on the floor, staring at each other.

"You have the prettiest hair I've ever seen," he said, his fingers toying with a strand that hung over her shoulder. It was like the mane of a horse, thick and long. He wanted to get his hands deep in it and pull her hard against him. He'd watched her walk into the club, swaying her slim hips and firm breasts. Her red lips were so inviting. His body ached. He hadn't been with a woman since his divorce from Sharon, and he was hungry.

Just as Emma was about to turn and walk back to her table, the next song began.

"Want to dance again?" Ted asked.

"No, thank you, Ted. I'd better get back to my friend..." When Emma saw that Jennifer wasn't at their table, she skimmed the room. Jennifer was playing pool with Jason in the back of the club. Jennifer waved at her from the pool table.

Emma turned back to Ted. "I guess I've changed my mind. It seems my friend is busy."

The saxophonist was playing "*Detour Ahead*," while the jazz combo accompanied on bass and piano. Ted took her into his arms again, and this time, he pulled her closer to him. He felt her tighten at first, but he kept his hold and smiled into her hair as she began to relax. He turned her around on the floor, feeling her soft body against his, wanting her. He knew how to work a woman to get them to do what he wanted, just like when he worked with a horse. Some of them needed a little prompting, others needed to be held firmly. This one, he decided, liked a firm hand.

He knew that he would have to stay off the booze, because it had ruined his marriage with Sharon. But, he'd been dry now for over six months and knew he could do it. That was why he'd really left California, for a new start. He liked Emma, the smell and feel of her. He hoped his fears wouldn't get in his way with her. He didn't want to make the same mistakes he'd made with Sharon.

CHAPTER NINE

Summer, 1967

It was a clear summer day with three mountains, Hood, Adams, and St. Helens, visible in the distance as a backdrop for Emma's wedding. She walked down the pathway through the roses in the garden, the heavy aroma thick in the air, skyscrapers of Portland visible just over the cliff to her left. Her bare shoulders shone in the sunlight above the snug, white dress. A small ring of tiny, yellow roses nested on her dark hair, which she had pulled up on top of her head. The cascading bouquet of the same color of roses shook slightly in her hands in front of her.

Ted waited, uncomfortable in his dark tuxedo. He was more at home in jeans and boots. His face looked tight and nervous as he stood next to Jason Carter, Jennifer's friend. Jason was a tall blond with long legs and looked quite at home in his tuxedo. When Ted saw Emma, he smiled and relaxed a little.

Jennifer stood on the other side of Ted, her yellow, chiffon dress floating in the soft, warm breeze. She was glad that Emma and Ted had asked Jason to stand with them, even though he really wasn't Ted's friend. He had simply been the one person that Ted knew the most since he'd moved to Oregon. She was concerned that Ted didn't have any friends of his own, but when she saw the joy in Emma's eyes, she decided to keep her own fears to herself.

Ted thought he loved Emma and wanted to make her happy. She was so beautiful and innocent. Every day since they had started dating, he vowed to himself not to touch any alcohol. At last, he thought he had finally found happiness.

He hadn't told Emma of his marriage to Sharon. He was too embarrassed, and he figured what she didn't know wouldn't hurt her. Sharon had divorced him when his alcohol took over for the third time and he'd lost everything with his gambling. He had tried to quit again. He really hadn't wanted to hurt her, but it was what he knew. After she had left and he'd been dry for about three months, he'd moved to Oregon, thinking a change in location would allow him also to change. It seemed to have worked so far.

Emma looked around at her few friends that she had acquired since her move to Oregon. Most of them were students, except for Jennifer and Jason. She had wished Jennifer and Oliver Stenson would have been able to come, but they were in Switzerland.

Emma stepped in next to Ted and put her hand on his arm, handing her bouquet to Jennifer. It had taken Emma years to get here, but she was happy. At least, that's what she kept telling herself.

The couple turned toward Judge Thomas Blake, who was officiating. He was a tall man with square shoulders in his dark suit. His hair was beginning to gray at the temples, and his gentle, blue eyes smiled at Emma and Ted. His strong voice carried over them and out through the rose garden.

"We are here today to join Emma Maseman and Ted Jacobs in holy matrimony..."

Emma heard the rest and responded when it was her cue, but she was in a dream through the entire ceremony. She thought of her parents and the love they'd had between them. She had watched their love grow over the years, caring and helping each other through anything life brought. Wishing that they could have been here today, she smiled and prayed that she had also found that same love.

"I now pronounce you man and wife," the judge said. Then, he looked at Ted and added, "You may kiss the bride."

Ted turned Emma to him and gently kissed her at first, then a heat rose in him and he wanted more. His lips were hot on hers and his hands pulled her closer against him.

"Come on, you two," Jason finally said, nudging Ted on the back. "You can finish this later."

Emma was blushing when Ted released her. She reached up to straighten her hair and saw Jennifer wink at her as she handed back her bouquet.

"Thank you, Judge Blake," Emma said, shaking hands with the older man. She liked the way his eyes seemed to twinkle at the joy he saw in her face.

"It was my pleasure," the judge said, also shaking hands with Ted. He had performed over a hundred weddings since he took the bench, and he felt he was a fairly good judge of character by now. He wasn't quite able to put his finger on why the hair on his arm had tickled when he'd taken Ted's hand to congratulate him.

"Be good to each other," he said.

◆ ◆ ◆

After pictures were taken and the other guests had left, they left the garden. Jennifer and Jason took the newlyweds to the Benson Hotel for a small, intimate reception. They had arranged for Emma and Ted to spend the night in the Honeymoon Suite at the hotel as their wedding present. The large sitting room opened with an arch of dark mahogany. Heavy, gold velvet drapes framed the tall windows, as a soft sunlight came through the soft sheer curtains between the heavier fabric. The deep, maroon carpet and rich, dark furniture reminded Emma of the lobby of the Drake Hotel in Chicago.

A tall table behind the love seat had a tray with chilled champagne and tall, crystal flutes. On each side were smaller trays of appetizers of different types of cheeses, fruit, and sliced French bread.

Jason filled the glasses and handed one to each of the party. He noticed that Ted's hand shook slightly as he handed him a glass.

"Here's to you two as you begin your life together. May you always be as happy as you are today."

"I can't wait to get you alone," Ted whispered into Emma's ear, making Emma blush.

Jennifer noticed that Ted only pretended to drink the champagne after Jason's toast. She didn't know that he wanted to start this marriage right. He didn't want to give in to his habit, because he knew it would take control of him if he took even one drink, and then it would all start again.

"Thank you," Emma said to her friends. "This is a happy day."

"When do you two plan on doing this?" Ted asked, setting his glass down next to the cheese tray to shrug out of his jacket.

Jennifer blushed and smiled at Jason, leaning into his side as he put his arm around her. "Should we tell them?" she asked.

"Sure," Jason smiled.

Jennifer took a deep breath and smiled back. "Jason's asked me to marry him."

"Oh, I'm so glad for you," Emma said, hugging her friend. She remembered that on the day she and Jennifer had met that Jennifer knew she was going to marry Jason.

"Have you set a date yet?" she asked.

"No. He only asked me today, when you two were getting some pictures taken." Jennifer brought up her hand and showed Emma her ring. The diamond shone in the light from the overhead chandelier.

"Oh, how beautiful," Emma said, tears very close to spilling over in her eyes.

"Well, then, another toast." Emma raised her glass. "To my best friend, and her fiancé on their engagement." Emma sipped with the others, all except Ted. Her heart was bursting with joy and the tears finally fell.

"Excuse me," Emma said to Ted. "I'll be right back."

"Where 'ya going, Hon?" Ted held Emma's hand tightly.

"To the ladies' room."

"Wait, Em," Jennifer said, setting her glass down. "I'll come with you."

The bathroom in the suite was very large and was the color of the sea. The surface of the jade green tile reflected the lights around the large mirror. Emma swung her dress through the door and sat down on a large, maroon wing-backed chair, tossing off her heels and rubbing her feet.

"Oh, that feels good," she sighed, checking her face in the small mirror on the table near where she sat. Looking up at her friend, Emma smiled. "Jenn, I'm so happy."

"I can see that, Em." Jennifer looked away as she said this. In her heart, she hoped that this was true, but she had seen the shadow on Ted's face when he repeated his vows in the garden. Ted was hiding something, she was certain of it.

She thought back to the day she and Emma had gone shopping for her wedding dress and she'd asked Emma about Sam Parker. 'He's in the past,' Emma had said too quickly. 'He doesn't want anything to do with me. Besides, he's married to someone else.' That was when Emma had told her about her visit to Eugene.

"I'm so happy for you, too," Emma said, bringing Jennifer's thoughts back into the room. She was looking at her ring again.

"Thanks, Em. We'll always be friends, no matter what," Jennifer said, looking into Emma's eyes. "Remember, we're sisters."

"Yes. Forever."

Emma rose and looked at her reflection in the mirror. She noticed the sequins on the bodice of her wedding dress sparkle in the light as she tucked in a stray hair

"I'm glad I met Ted," she said. "He's so right for me."

Jennifer noticed that Emma was looking down when she had said this, not at her own reflection. She smiled at her friend and touched Emma's hand. "We'd better get back."

◆ ◆ ◆ ◆

After the two women returned to the sitting room, Emma picked up her glass and took a long sip. Ted smiled, walked over to her, and slipped his hand around her slim waist, pulling her closer to him. He liked the feel of her in his arm.

Jennifer walked up to Jason and put her arm through his. He looked at her and winked. She didn't want to tell Emma all of their plans just yet, but she had no choice.

"Emma," Jennifer said, after taking a deep breath. "Jason and I have decided to move to Montana."

Emma put her glass down and stared at her friend. Jennifer had been with her through so much in her life, she knew everything about her. She thought of the day Jennifer had taken her to see her ranch for the first time. Emma became afraid that the distance would separate them more than the miles. She didn't want to lose Jennifer.

"When?" Emma finally asked.

"Actually," Jason said, clearing his throat, "we're leaving tonight." He thought that Jennifer had told Emma about their move while they were in the bathroom. He and Jennifer had been planning it for a few months now. He looked at his fiancé, hoping she'd say something to break the silence.

Jennifer's eyes were filled with tears, but she brushed them aside and smiled, holding tighter onto Jason's arm. "Yes, I didn't know how to tell you, Em."

Emma stood in shock, her face pale against the white dress. She looked away for a moment, then turned to look at Jennifer, smiling. "You always wanted to move away from here. You've been talking about it for some time now. I'm happy for you." She reached over and hugged Jennifer. "I'll miss you terribly," she whispered in Jennifer's ear.

"I'll be back a few times on assignment," Jennifer assured her friend. "We'll keep in touch. I'll send you our new address as soon as we are moved in."

Ted had stood and watched Emma and Jennifer. He'd never had any friends. Most of the people he knew were on the same alcoholic road, the one he'd turned away from.

"Well, we'd best be going," Jason said. He shook hands with Ted and gave Emma a slight hug.

"Take care of this lady," Jennifer said to Ted as she gave him a hug. "She's very special."

"I'll do my best."

Emma walked with them to the door of the suite and waved. "Goodbye, Jenn." She fought to keep the tears back.

"Bye, Em."

◆ ◆ ◆ ◆

Emma looked out of the East window of her studio. She had an hour before her first student of the day arrived, and she'd decided to start a new watercolor painting of the valley from the hill on their property. The vivid fall colors in the photograph on her easel guided her as she began the blue backwash. She was hoping to capture the softness of the early morning light as the sun began to rise in the hills to her left. An unfinished painting leaned against the wall; the one of her father she had started, but could never complete.

She saw a black truck pull into the lane of the property across the road from their ranch. She'd known the property had recently sold, but they hadn't heard yet who had purchased it.

"Ted," she called out to her husband in the next room. She knew he was awake and reading in their bedroom. "Someone's moving in across the road."

She heard him get up and walk toward her studio. She smiled as he came up to her in his bathrobe and hugged her. Ted wasn't an early riser. He liked to sit in bed, drink his first cup of coffee, and read the newspaper before he began his day. He always found Emma working in her studio. He kissed her on the top of her head, then went to look out of the upper-story window.

"Yeah, it's a guy I met at Portland Meadows last month," he said. "He was asking about ranches for sale in this area. I'll go down later and see if I can give him a hand."

"That'd be nice. Mary's coming at nine for her lesson. Maybe after she leaves, I'll get a chance to meet him, too." She rinsed her brush, wiped it carefully, and placed it in the jar with the others.

She looked at her husband and walked over, wrapping her arms around him. She kissed him and thought how lucky she was. Ted was a good man. He wasn't overly affectionate - she was the one who usually approached first. She felt that he always seemed to be holding back and attributed it to his being shy. He was usually gone most of the day, shoeing horses with his new mobile farrier van, but he would help her around the ranch after he returned from his appointments. She liked the way they cared for each other. Since they were married, they kept mostly to themselves, rarely leaving the ranch, unless it was for business or supplies. She felt content, but always had a nagging feeling that it wouldn't last, that someday something would happen to change it all.

◆ ◆ ◆ ◆

"Try gently using more pressure with your right leg to signal the next turn," Emma said to Mary, who was riding the tall bay gelding. The horse was now sixteen hands.

She had been working with Mary now for six months and her progress was tremendous. The young girl had the same drive and perfectionism that Emma had when she was first learning to ride from her father. Emma had paid attention to the subtle directions he had given her and carried this same guidance in her own training.

When the horse responded to Mary's new command, Mary's face lit up in a wide grin. "It worked!" she exclaimed.

"Very good. I think that's all for today, Mary."

Emma saw the young girl's eyes sadden and understood all too well how the length of a successful lesson came too early. She reached up and grabbed the horse's reins while Mary dismounted.

"He's a great horse," Emma praised, watching the pride jump into the young girl's face. "He's very light on his feet and will do well for you in the arena."

"Thank you, Emma," Mary said beaming.

On their first lesson, Emma asked all of her students to call her Emma - not Mrs. Jacobs. She felt the informality helped to put her students at ease.

After her student left, Emma was in the stable putting the tack away when Ted walked in. She saw the change in Ted's face as he walked up to the tack room door, but didn't have a chance to ask him about it.

"Hey, Em," he said, grabbing her shoulder and turning her around. "I brought our new neighbor over to meet you."

Emma saw the small, sandy-haired man with dark, gray eyes. The sleeves of his shirt were pushed up to his elbows, and she could see the strength in his forearms as he stood with his hands on his hips staring at her. There was a gleam in his eyes that she didn't understand, but she smiled and reached out a hand to him in a neighborly fashion.

"Hello, I'm Emma Jacobs."

"Joe Remsky. I'm real glad to meet you, Mrs. Jacobs." He tightened his hold on her soft hand when she first tried to pull it away. He liked the feel of it and was becoming jealous of Ted for having such a treasure. His mind began working on ways to spend more time at the Jacobs' ranch.

"Ted," Joe said, still holding Emma's hand and looking into her deep eyes. "You didn't tell me your wife was so beautiful."

Emma pulled her hand away and reached up to straighten her hair. He was making her feel self-conscious and she had to look away from his gaze.

"Where did you come from, Mr. Remsky?" Emma wanted to change the conversation from her.

"California, Mrs. Jacobs. Ted and I knew each other there. I was telling your husband that it was luck that he was a farrier and lives so close." He looked over at Ted and smiled. "I'll be needing one soon, when my horse arrives a few days from now."

"Only one? What type of horse do you have, Mr. Remsky?" Emma asked, looking over at Ted, who looked nervous and scuffed the ground with his boot, his hands deep in his pockets.

"Please, Mrs. Jacobs. Call me Joe. I hear you run a riding school here," Joe said, sidestepping her question. All he knew was that he was to purchase that ranch and get to know the people across from him. Luck had been with him when he learned that Ted Jacobs owned that ranch. He'd seen Ted around some of the tracks in California.

Joe's visitors coming tomorrow would explain everything to him, the letter had said. Joe was enjoying getting to know his neighbors and was looking forward to knowing Ted's wife much better. This lady was a beauty. He couldn't take his eyes off of her.

"Yes, a dressage riding school, like my father's." Emma was becoming nervous and felt the tack room closing in on her. She looked at Ted with a plea in her eyes that she hoped he understood.

Ted didn't like what he saw in Joe's face as he stared at Emma. He put his arm on Joe's shoulder and steered him out of the room.

"Come on, Joe, I'll show you the rest of the place. I'm sure Emma's got more work to do." He winked at Emma and began walking toward the stall where he kept his mustang. He knew he'd have to explain to Emma later about knowing Remsky and wasn't looking forward to it at all.

◆ ◆ ◆ ◆

Joe opened the door of his long ranch house as the black truck and trailer drove up the lane, the blood red streak running across the door and down the side of both the truck and trailer. He'd been expecting them, but they were late. He didn't like people who were not on time, but he had no choice. This whole business was beginning to bug him.

He'd stayed in California after his race on Classy Elegance at Del Mar, but could never hire on as a jockey - he'd been suspended. Mason had been charged with providing the drug. During the investigation after the race, Joe testified that it was Carlos, Mason's jockey that had given him the drug. Joe remembered Carlos talking about 'his man' that night, so he'd made the assumption it was Mason behind it. But, Carlos had denied knowing anything about it, making Joe look like a fool and taking the wrap for it. Mason was later cleared of the charges.

Joe had used his twenty thousand to live on and for bets at the track. At Del Mar, Carlos had pointed Maria, his girlfriend, out to Joe when they were in the paddock area before the race. She was a beauty. Joe had been pissed he'd lost his bet money when Ele had lost, but he still liked to think about the time he'd enjoyed with Maria before he left town.

A few months later, Carlos had cornered Joe at Santa Anita Park and offered him this job in Oregon. Joe knew he had nowhere else to go. He was finished now as a jockey, and his money was running out.

The truck stopped and Carlos got out with a tall, thin man in a tan overcoat, wearing dark glasses and black, leather gloves. They stood next to the dark vehicle as Joe walked over to them. The tall man looked over at the direction of the Jacobs' ranch and stared for a moment.

"Mr. Reichmann," Carlos said to get the man to turn around. "This is Joe Remsky, the man I told you about."

"Hello, Mr. Remsky," the man said in a heavy German accent. "I see that you have fulfilled the second phase of our project." The man looked at the stable and corral behind Joe. "This is a wonderful location. It is a pity that Koenig's Pride did not prove to be the horse I thought he was."

Joe just stared at the man with the icy voice. He remembered that horse's name from Del Mar.

"Have you met your neighbors yet, across the road?" Reichmann asked, looking again in that direction.

"Yes, I have. Ted and Emma Jacobs make a very nice couple. I knew Ted in California at the tracks," he said with a wink at Carlos. "Emma's a real beauty," Joe added. He was beginning to enjoy this job.

"Yes, I know," the man said as he came closer to Joe and took off his glasses. His blue eyes were like ice, cutting into Joe's face. "And, I trust, that you will keep your mind and other things on your business, Mr. Remsky."

Joe's knees weakened and he smiled to cover his fear. He'd never been afraid of any man in his life, but Joe was sure this one was the devil himself. "Sssure, Mr. Reichmann," Joe stammered. "Just like you want it."

"Good. Now, kindly assist Carlos in removing Frank's Revenge from the trailer. He has had a long ride." He walked over next to the fence around the corral. "This will do nicely."

Joe and Carlos walked back to the end of the trailer and opened the door. A high-piercing whinny came from the darkness within. Joe took a step back as Carlos entered the trailer, talking softly to the animal inside. As the light hit the hind quarters of the tall beast, Joe whistled, then went to open the corral gate. He'd never seen anything like it - black as midnight, no markings anywhere on the sleek coat, the strong legs eager to move. Carlos held the halter with both hands and led the tall colt through the gate. Once released, the animal circled the perimeter of the corral, testing the new territory, his head held high and dark mane like ribbons in the light, eyes wild and searching, thundering hooves flying through the air.

"He's a fine animal, don't you agree, Mr. Remsky?" Reichmann asked with pride in his voice. He had waited a long time to reach this point in his plan.

"Yyyes," Joe stammered, his mouth hanging open as he watched the strong animal in awe.

"Good." Reichmann slapped his gloved hands together. "Now, let us go inside and talk about our project."

Reichmann sat back in the large armchair opposite Joe, his arms stretched out over the arms of the heavy chair. Carlos stood near the door, facing the two other men, his hands behind his back.

Joe looked nervously from one to the other.

"Carlos will be waiting for you, Mr. Remsky, at Churchill Downs when you arrive with Frank's Revenge. The horse has been entered to run in the Kentucky Derby. You will go under an assumed name as his jockey, and Mr. Jacobs will be listed as his trainer."

Joe began to object, but Reichmann cut him off with a raise of one gloved hand.

"This is only a formality, Mr. Remsky. I am sure you understand," Reichmann said.

Reichmann didn't add that the foal certificate copy that was to be sent to the racing secretary's office would be altered, since the horse had just arrived from Venezuela and was not registered with the American Jockey Club. It still burned that Koenig's Pride did not win for him and he'd had the horse put down. Soon, he knew he would fulfill his need for revenge. Then, his life's work would be finished and he would once again have the painting.

Reichmann smiled at Carlos, "I have a buyer who will be waiting with another colt, which is the payment." He turned and looked intently at Joe again. "You are to make the exchange, bring the other colt back here to the ranch, and wait until further notice."

"Let me get this straight. You're going to race your colt in the Derby, then sell him in Kentucky for another horse, which I will bring back here?"

"That is correct." *Almost correct*, the man thought to himself.

"And, for this, you will pay me fifty thousand dollars?"

"That is correct."

"How do you plan for me to transport him? I don't have a trailer."

"You will have my truck and trailer at your disposal, after you return Carlos and I to the city today. Have you made the arrangements for the training track on this property? It is most important that you continue the horse's training until the Derby."

"Yeah, sure. The contractor is coming out later this week to finish the track. It's just as you ordered."

Reichmann looked over at Carlos. Simply with a look, Carlos knew to leave and check the status of the track.

Joe hesitated when he was alone with the man, and knew he had to ask the question. "After the Derby, after I bring this other horse back here, then what?"

Reichmann slowly took off his gloves and pulled himself forward in his chair. Joe saw the scars; thick, jagged lines covering the backs of both of his hands. The heat rose around Joe's shirt collar and sweat beaded on his forehead.

"When it is necessary, you will be contacted with the remainder of your instructions. Is that clear, Mr. Remsky?" Reichmann said in a soft whisper, then waited until Joe nodded.

Reichmann sat back into the large seat, the man much larger now than the chair. His eyes carved through Joe, as if he wasn't even there, and his face became gray. After a long silence, he said, "I also want you to fabricate a reason to get Mr. Jacobs to accompany you to Kentucky - without his knowing our purpose. As I said, he will be listed as the horse's trainer on the papers. It is important that he be involved. Can you do that, Mr. Remsky?"

Joe was about to ask why, then the prospect of spending time with Jacobs appealed to him. It meant that he'd get the chance to be around Emma Jacobs. He licked his lips and swallowed. Then, he smiled, wiping his brow. "Sure, Mr. Reichmann. I'll find a way."

Carlos re-entered the room and nodded his approval to Reichmann.

Reichmann stood up to indicate the interview was over. Carlos brought the tall man's coat and held it for him. Reichmann slid his long arms into the sleeves; then, he placed the gloves again over his hands.

"I'll take good care of Frank's Revenge. You can count on me." Joe's voice shook, but he held his body still. He wasn't going to show his fear, not to this man, nor any man.

"You don't want to disappoint me, Mr. Remsky," Reichmann said, then walked out.

◆ ◆ ◆ ◆

Joe returned to his ranch after taking Carlos and Reichmann to the Portland airport. He sat down on the couch in the den. When he looked at the large arm chair, he shuddered, thinking about the gruesome man who had just sat there. He placed his head in his hands. *How'd I get myself in this mess*? he thought. Then, he thought of the first time he'd met Carlos at Del Mar. That was when all of his nightmares had begun.

When his thoughts turned to Emma Jacobs, he smiled. He felt it was a stroke of luck that Reichmann wanted Ted involved in this Derby thing. Now, he only needed to find some weakness in Jacobs to get him to play along. Then, afterwards, he'd find a way to ditch Ted and have Emma all to himself. His body stirred when he thought of her face and body. Oh, he wanted to get his hands in her long, black hair and pull her hard against him. He sat upright and slapped his knee. "And, by god, I'll have her," he said out loud.

◆ ◆ ◆ ◆

"Ted," Joe said, as he placed his arm around Ted's shoulders. "I'm glad you came over to help me work on this track of mine. The contractor's trying to tell me it's going to take weeks, and I don't have that long. Besides, you haven't seen my new horse, yet."

Joe was leading the way to his stable. He'd decided that the colt was too much of an attraction and would create a commotion if he was left out in the corral, so he'd put him up in a stall inside to keep him out of sight.

Once inside, Ted's eyes adjusted to the darkness and stood before the gate on the stall. He'd never seen such a beautiful animal in his life, even when he'd worked at the tracks in California. He could tell this horse was special.

"My god, Joe. Where'd you get him?"

"The owner's got plans to sell him next spring. I'm just boarding him till then. His name's Frankie." Joe was pleased to see Ted so interested in the colt. He knew about Ted's work at the tracks. He also knew about the abuse cases with his first wife, but he wasn't going to let Ted know. He might have to use it later.

"Come on," Joe said. "I'll take you to the track."

Ted followed Joe as he walked out to the back of the stable and down a wide trail through the woods. Eventually, they came to a large clearing, which was surrounded by the evergreen forest. A small brush pile still smoldered in the center. Ted could see the tracks of the heavy equipment, leading down a road that had been cut out of the trees, which had created this oval gap.

"What're you going to do with this?" Ted asked. It looked like a mile-long track.

"You have to keep this a secret," Joe said in a whisper next to Ted, his eyes smiling with mischief. "You can't even tell Emma about this."

"Why?"

"I can't tell you now. You just have to swear to me that you won't tell a soul about this."

Ted was intrigued. His life had become too quiet and comfortable lately and he was becoming bored. He missed the action around the track. He loved Emma, but he figured it couldn't hurt if she didn't know about this little secret with Joe.

"Promise. Now, what's this for?"

"I'm going to use this track to exercise Frankie. I'm taking him to the Derby next May."

"To the what?"

"The Kentucky Derby. I need your help, pal. I have to get the fencing around this track finished as soon as possible. So, will you help me? I'll make it worth your while."

"How much?" Ted asked.

"Five hundred dollars," Joe said, as he watched Ted's face. He could see the twitch around Ted's mouth. Joe had seen that look before, around the betting areas of every track he'd been to - he'd called it 'the hope of money.'

He smiled and put his arm around Ted, pulling him closer. "You could come with me to the Derby," Joe whispered, knowing he now held a small secret about Ted Jacobs in his hands. He could see Ted's mind working, the idea of going to the largest race in the country, the betting, the racing, and the connections. He saw the moment Ted turned the dream off.

"Naw," Ted finally said. "I won't go there, but I'll help you get this done."

"Great." Joe knew he had time to keep working on Ted.

The two men shook hands and began to get to work. While one dug the holes, the other dropped the main posts in. Then, they cemented them in place. It took them only a few days to have the last of the posts ready to begin adding the cross pieces.

Ted told Emma that he was going to be working on a big job on a new horse ranch near McMinnville, a few miles south of their ranch. He left before sunrise each day and didn't return until after sunset, always using the darkness to hide his journey down the back road that took him to the track on Joe's ranch. He hated lying to her, but he wanted to surprise her with the extra money he was bringing in. Besides, he felt Joe was his first friend in Oregon - his first real friend anywhere.

◆ ◆ ◆ ◆

One night, Emma invited Joe over for dinner, saying it was the neighborly thing to do. At first, Ted had liked the idea, but then as other dinners turned into late nights, Joe insisted on staying, talking of days as a jockey, weaving stories about races, the horses and excitement at the track. Emma had held onto Joe's every word about the races, laughing with him as he talked of driving each horse home to the finish line.

"But, I've given that all up," Joe said.

"Why?" Emma asked.

"I've got better things to do with my time, now."

Ted didn't like the way Joe looked at Emma. Joe would touch his wife as he talked, and Ted's jealousy began to surface. Other men had touched his ex-wife, Sharon.

Joe also watched Ted. He'd seen how Ted always refused a beer when it was offered with the dinner. Now, he had what he was looking for - the final secret to Ted Jacobs.

◆ ◆ ◆ ◆

The first day Joe took the colt around the track in the woods behind his stable, Ted saw the speed in this animal. They had just finished laying the last of the fence, and Joe couldn't wait to get the colt out. Joe slowly rode him around the first time, letting the horse test the feel of the track. Then, he let him have his head and the horse raced as if his life depended on it. Excited by the potential of this sleek animal, the two men walked the sweaty colt back toward the stable to be cooled and dressed down. By then, it was dark outside.

"I'm going to bet a bunch of money on this animal at the Derby," Joe said on the way back up the path. "I know he's going to win. Sure wish you were going with me."

He looked sideways at Ted, and could see he was thinking about that dream.

After the colt was back in his stall, Joe went to the tack room. When he walked back to Ted, he held a bottle of Jack Daniels. He took a deep swig of the golden liquor, then wiped off the neck of the bottle before holding it out to Ted.

"Here you go, pal, for all of your hard work and friendship."

Ted's gut knotted in fear, but the smell was overwhelming. "I can't..." he started, then turned away. "No. Thanks, Joe, but, no."

"Oh, come on, man. You've earned this one. Besides, didn't our boy do great out there today? He's going to do that and more for us in Kentucky."

Ted, tired and excited, threw away his vows and took the drink, slugging it down like a pro, a habit that had been a part of him just as combing his hair with the part on the left. Joe watched Ted, seeing the weakness he had been looking for.

◆ ◆ ◆ ◆

A few days later, Joe took Ted into McMinnville with him in the late afternoon for a friendly game of cards in the back room of the Western Inn, plying Ted with booze until it was dark outside. After a few months of this, he and Ted began making it an every Friday night event, drinking and gambling at the tavern. Ted was beginning to see himself at the Derby. Joe knew this and kept pushing, keeping Ted under his control.

Ted hadn't liked it at first. He'd seen that his right hand was beginning to shake from the whiskey Joe kept offering him. Ted knew that if he didn't stop soon, it would take over his life again.

◆ ◆ ◆ ◆

In the fall, Joe took Ted hunting for deer on his property. Well, it wasn't really his property. It belonged to Reichmann. But, while he was here, Joe had decided to enjoy himself with all the acres surrounding the ranch. There was a wooded area with a stream that ran through it where the deer frequented.

"What kind of money does a farrier make?" Joe asked, while he and Ted sat on a hillside across a meadow watching for deer. The leaves on the trees were turning colors, and he could see his breath in the crisp, early morning air.

"It depends on how many jobs I have."

"Do you have many clients?" Joe asked, trying to get Ted to talk more about himself.

"Sometimes I have six or seven a day." Ted leaned back on his elbows against the hill behind him, keeping his eyes peeled to the stream yards below. "When I was younger, I could do twelve to fourteen. It's an amazing job. Every six to eight weeks, I have to go back around to redo the shoes. Talk about supply and demand."

Joe nodded. "It's a great racket," he said laughing. He knew that most tracks had a farrier barn available in case a horse threw a shoe, but he wanted Ted to continue. "Did you work mostly at tracks in California?"

A shadow came over Ted's face. He'd told Joe more than he had to anyone since he left there. The booze always loosened his tongue. Joe knew about his marriage to Sharon, but he'd vowed not to say anything to Emma about her. Ted didn't want his friend to know that he'd been fired from the Santa Anita track because of his drinking. Before he had to answer, Ted saw a six-point buck walk out of the grove and stop near the stream below. He raised his rifle, took a deep breath and held it while he brought the buck into focus through his scope. He fired and the buck went down.

CHAPTER TEN

Winter, 1967

T he air was bitter cold when Jim Barolio arrived in New York. The foot of snow on the ground was frozen solid, and there was a thick layer of ice on the roads from the storm that had blown through the night before. He wished he was back in the Willamette Valley in the Northwest, where the winters were not so severe. But, Jim knew he couldn't go back until he'd found Sam Parker.

When Mike McKeegan had returned from Del Mar Park without Sam and Classy Elegance, Jim had convinced Sam's dad to patiently wait for one week to see if Sam would come home on his own, but he never did. Then, one day, Sam had called Jim at his office to say he was taking a flying job overseas. That was almost a year ago. Last weekend, Sam's dad had called Jim and asked him to find Sam. Harold knew that if Sam didn't want to be found, it would take a miracle to ferret him out. Jim was the only one who could do it.

Jim had sent word around to the small airfields all across the country, asking for any information about Sam. It wasn't until a few days ago that a mechanic in upstate New York had called him. Sam had been working there as a hired pilot for the last couple of months. The mechanic had told Jim where to find Sam.

Walking into the club, Jim saw Sam sitting at the bar. His heart ached when he saw his friend slumped over his beer, beaten by his mistakes. This was not the Sam Parker he knew. This was a man who had let life get to him. Jim thought how far they had come from those early years of innocence and wonder in Oregon to The Iron Horse Bar and Grill of New York City.

They both grew up at the small airstrip outside of Eugene, learning to fly before they could walk from Jim's dad, who was an airplane mechanic there. The need to fly had been ingrained in them since they were young. The two youths had first learned that being airborne was a privilege of this divine accomplishment and ability of man. In their spare time, they had eagerly taken odd jobs at the airstrip, just to be near the planes and the chance to fly.

Jim had been with Sam when he'd bought the Reliant V-77 "gull" wing shortly after high school graduation. Sam had gotten it for a song because it needed a ton of work. The hulk was intact when they found it, but the rest of it was in burlap sacks. For two years, Jim and his dad helped Sam restore the plane to its original, beautiful self. Piece by piece, in a most orderly fashion, those bags of bolts, metals, cables, and parts was lovingly reassembled until it could safely leave the confines of the ground that had held it captive for all those years.

When finished, the 1942 plane was the same type that had been used for VIP transport in WWII, with a diamond-tuck, velour interior they had found in a guy's barn near Portland. The plane was reliable and smooth, and had an exceptionally quiet ride, with large windows for excellent visibility and gull-type, overhead wings. The 300 horse-powered radial, air-cooled engine was a gas guzzler. Sam loved that plane.

After its initial test, Jim and Sam had decided to fly to Eastern Oregon, where the skyway was wide open. Jim knew a guy who had a restored P51 Mustang. Jim flew the Mustang and Sam, the Stinson Reliant. For practice, they flew over the desert throwing rolls of toilet paper out the hatch to see if the other one could maneuver fast and cleanly enough to cut the paper from the falling roll. That's when they knew they wanted to fly jets.

Jim knew that Sam had stored the Reliant at the airstrip while they were in the service. That was the first place Jim had looked, but he'd known the plane was gone. He'd somehow felt the void, even before he'd called. Looking at Sam now, Jim's heart ached. He took a deep breath and sat on the stool next to Sam.

"What'll you have?" the bartender asked Jim.

"I'll have what he's having," Jim said, pointing his thumb at Sam.

Disheveled, unshaven, and trembling as he lifted his glass to take yet another drink, Sam looked up blankly at the mirror to see the unexpected face of his friend staring back at him. A small glint of hope came into his heart. Oh, how he had missed Jim and his home. But, when Sam thought of his parents, the guilt grabbed him again. He was too afraid to go back, afraid to face his father. He let himself slide back into his drunken stupor, ashamed to look Jim in the eye.

"What're you doing here?" Sam asked into his beer.

"I'm here for a meeting with the Racing Bureau. What're you doing in New York?"

Sam continued to look into his beer. "Not much," he grunted.

"Have you been working?" Jim asked, testing the ground to see what steps he should take next with Sam. He could see Sam's clothes were wrinkled and stained with grease, as if he'd been sleeping in them in a hangar. The last time he'd seen Sam was at the Portland track. He remembered the pride in Sam's face as they watched Sam's mare race around the track.

"Oh, I've been flying - when I can get a job." Sam looked sideways at Jim. "I ran some cargo, over in Africa."

Through the fog, Sam thought of when he'd converted the Reliant into a flying gas can, stripping it down inside for hauling extra fuel. He'd taken the polar route up through Europe and back down, until he'd arrived in Casablanca, making as few stops as possible along the way. For two years, he'd flown all over eastern Africa, taking on every type of cargo imaginable that the Reliant could hold, including human beings, packed in like sardines.

Sam looked at Jim again in the mirror; he saw his own reflection and quickly dropped his eyes. This was killing him inside, having his best friend see him like this. He tried to straighten his dirty tan shirt and tuck it in, then stopped. His arms felt like they were made of lead. He was exhausted.

"Why don't you come back with me?" Jim asked. "Your dad thinks—"

"I don't give a damn what anybody thinks anymore," Sam yelled, trying to convince himself. This was the same old thing Sam had played back in his mind for the past year, whenever he began to think about going back. He knew he couldn't go back. He'd let his father down.

When he saw Jim staring back at him with clear eyes, Sam knew what his friend was going to ask. He took one more, long tug, thinking it might help erase the pain of having to answer the inevitable question.

"Do you still have the Reliant?" Jim asked, knowing the answer in his heart.

"No, I..." Sam began, then stopped and looked at himself in the mirror behind the bar. "No," he said into the mirror. He couldn't tell his friend he'd sold the plane when his money had run out and he was too drunk to fly.

Jim looked into Sam's eyes in the mirror. He'd been down like this once, after his dad had died in a plane crash, just after Jim had entered the Air Force. He'd been very close to his dad and had wanted to die along with him. Sam was the one who'd found him and pulled him back among the living. Jim knew Sam Parker. He knew that Sam wouldn't stay down very long. Sam just needed a reason to get up and find himself again.

"Did you know that the California Commission ruled that Ele had been drugged before the race?" Jim waited for a moment, watching Sam's eyes. "Your jockey, Joe Remsky, did it. The hypodermic was found later with his prints all over it. He was suspended from racing." Jim saw the reaction he was looking for in Sam's eyes.

Sam slowly awoke from his drunken stupor, his eyes beginning to clear as his mind absorbed Jim's words. Ele would have won! He knew she could do it, but he'd never thought she'd been drugged – all because of Joe Remsky. 'There's something about him I can't put my finger on,' Sam remembered his dad saying at Portland Meadows, when he'd first met Joe. Sam thought now that he should have paid more attention to those words. Entering her in the Claiming Race was history, but maybe someday he'd get a chance to get even with Remsky.

Jim saw the anger building in Sam's eyes and smiled. He knew he had his friend back.

"Where's Remsky now?" Sam growled.

"No one knows. He disappeared from the circuit and hasn't been seen since. So, are you going to just sit here and cry in your beer?" Jim asked Sam, spurring him on.

Sam looked at Jim and saw he was smiling.

"Well, do you have anything better for me to do?" Sam asked. The fog in his mind was beginning to lift and he thought he saw a light shining in the back of it.

"Yes, I've got a job for you, if you'll take it. A guy here in New York told me the Racing Bureau in Baltimore needs a good pilot to fly their investigators around the country. They've got a Shrike Commander, a 500U, just waiting for you if you want it. That baby has twin, fuel-injected, two hundred-ninety horse powered engines, a maximum cruise speed over two hundred miles per hour, dual controls, and a sweet interior that can quickly change to accommodate freight or up to seven passengers."

Jim knew how much bait to put in front of Sam and hoped now that his friend would take it. "You might even decide to move into an investigator position down the road," he added.

Jim waited patiently, watching Sam. He could see Sam's jaw working as his mind digested the new possibilities for the future.

"Are you interested?" Jim finally asked, taking another sip of his beer.

Sam knew of the Thoroughbred Racing Protective Bureau. His first dream, to have a large racing farm, was now history. Working for the Bureau was now possibly a way of stopping what had happened to his mare. Then, Sam thought of his dad and looked into Jim's eyes. "I don't want to let you down, buddy."

"You won't," Jim smiled and put his arm around Sam's shoulders. "I know you, Sam."

Sam smiled for the first time. Maybe he could do this. Maybe his life could be different. Maybe he could make a difference in the racing world. Maybe, someday, he'd get the courage to talk to his dad again.

"When do I start?" Sam asked. He hoped his life was beginning to take a turn in the direction that would lead him to his true heart's desire.

◆ ◆ ◆ ◆

Sam loved his job. At first, he'd flown the Shrike from coast to coast across the country, taking the Bureau's investigators wherever the job took them. He'd learned a lot on those trips. One night, at a hotel in Elmont, New York, he was with two investigators, following up on a complaint of Bute that had been used on a million-dollar horse just before a race. Sam had listened to the two men talking over dinner at the hotel's restaurant.

"Sam, why don't you join us?" Simon had asked. "Become an investigator?"

Sam had thought then back to the first day he'd met Simon. It was at Churchill Downs, when Bute had been found in a post-race test.

"Maybe I should, just to keep an eye on you," Sam said with a laugh.

"No, I'm serious. You'd make a great investigator." Simon was not smiling.

"To tell you the truth, I've been thinking about it. I like what you do for the horses."

"That's why I switched over to the Bureau. Give it some thought."

Sam was glad he'd taken the job. It was exactly what he'd wanted. It kept him around horses. He'd heard about some of the abuse cases, but this job had opened his eyes. He still flew the Commander, but mostly for his own investigations now. The Bureau had retired the plane, and Sam's bid had been accepted.

Now, while sitting at his desk in Baltimore, Sam was looking over the Henry Morris file. Morris' horse was found with Lasix in his system after a race. As Sam read the evidence, his skin began to crawl. So far, the investigation had revealed that the amount of Lasix and overall length of time it'd been used on the horse had caused kidney failure. This horse was going to have to be put down.

Sam sat back in his chair and thought about Ele. He'd seen the California Commission file on Joe Remsky. Now, he knew what kind of man Joe truly was. Sam was still angry at himself for not listening to his dad's warning, but he'd been young and stupid then. *But*, he thought now, *that was in the past.*

Once, when he'd been at the track in Portland, Oregon, he'd come very close to flying to Eugene to see his parents. He'd called his mom, at a time when he knew his dad was at a race. Sam still hadn't been able to bring himself to see his dad, but he knew he couldn't put it off much longer.

Sam picked up the phone and started to dial the familiar Eugene number, when there was a knock on his door.

"Come in," Sam said, replacing the receiver. He was a little annoyed that his secretary hadn't buzzed him on the intercom to announce the visitor.

The door opened and Sam's father stood with his hat in his hand. His hair was grayer now, and his lean body seemed thinner. Sam's heart swelled at the sight of him. His father had always been a tower of strength that Sam had strived to achieve, but somehow he felt like he always fell short of it. The old fear grabbed him, making him stiffen his shoulders. He could hardly breathe, the air seemed so thick.

"I figured if you weren't going to come to me, I'd better make the first move," Harold said, watching his son. He'd seen Sam stiffen and knew this wasn't going to be easy.

"Hi, Dad."

"So, are you going to ask me in, son?"

"Sure, have a seat." Sam motioned to one of the chairs in front of his desk and noticed that his hand shook. His insides were quaking with fear. He never feared his father – he feared that he had disappointed him.

Harold sat in one of the red leather chairs across from Sam and looked around the room. The large, oak desk looked worn from years of use, but was highly polished. Shelves of books climbed up the wall behind Sam. Harold was now sure he'd done the right thing by coming here today. He knew what he was going to say, but he waited for Sam to speak first.

"How've you been?" Sam asked, to end the uncomfortable silence.

"I've been better. Your mother sends her love."

Sam winced. He hadn't called his mother for some time, afraid his father would answer.

"Dad, I—"

Harold held up his hand.

"No, Sam. Let me get what I came to say off my chest; then I'll be going."

Sam waited, holding his breath, his palms sweaty. He wished at that moment that he was somewhere else, anywhere else. Flying in Vietnam was easier than this.

"I know it's been hard for you..." Harold began. "It's been hard on all of us. Mike took a lot of heat for Ele's test results, until the Commission investigation turned up the evidence on Remsky—"

"Dad, there's no excuse..." Sam began, but the look in his father's eyes stopped him.

"I want you to know that your mother and I love you. We know you did what you thought was right at the time."

Sam shook his head, about to say something. But, his dad interrupted him again.

"No, son. I've thought this over carefully. I think I would have done the same thing if Ele had been my horse." He saw Sam's eyes widen in surprise. "A claiming race is the best way to classify a horse, but it's always a risk. I know she would have won. That damned Remsky just got in her way."

Harold stopped for a moment, watching Sam's face. It was going to kill him to say it, but he went on. "Maybe you weren't destined for racing."

He had always dreamt of Sam taking over the farm someday, continuing the racing stable. At that moment, he knew that Sam had to do what called to him, not what he wanted for his son. He'd learned a long time ago that life sometimes had a way of setting up barriers to his best laid plans.

Sam was quiet. His dad's words circled in his mind and finally reached his heart. He got up and walked around his desk, leaning against it, hands on the edge, facing his dad.

"It means a lot to me to hear you say that," Sam said. "I've been afraid all this time, afraid to face you. I felt like such a fool – a failure."

Harold stood up and put both of his hands on his son's shoulders.

"Look at what you've done because of it. I believe in destiny, but I also believe that there are times that life gives us choices. Which path we choose is based on where our heart lies. And you, Sam, have a good heart."

Tears came to Sam's eyes and he hugged his dad.

"You're mother and I are proud of you, Sam," Harold said, holding his son.

"Thanks, Dad," Sam said, looking into his dad's eyes. "That means a lot to me." He looked down at the floor for a moment. He thought of the words he'd wanted to say to his dad for a long time, but had never seemed to find the courage. Sam looked up at his dad.

"I'm sorry I lost Ele for you," Sam finally said.

Tears came to Harold's eyes, but he tamped them back. "You didn't lose her for me. Classy Elegance was yours. Your mother and I knew it wasn't totally your fault. Ele's a horse with heart, she should have won that race. Oh, the bet was a stupid thing to do, I'll admit."

Sam flinched at the thought of the money he'd lost to George Mason, but he saw the gleam in his dad's eyes.

"But," his dad continued, "when Jim told us about Remsky, I got so mad. If that jerk ever comes near me, he's going to be wearing his nose somewhere else." Harold laughed.

Sam laughed with him. It was good to hear his dad laugh.

"I asked Jim to find you," Harold added. "You needed to know the truth."

"I know."

Father and son sat down, the air in the room seemed lighter now.

"You've got a great office here," Harold said, looking around again.

"Thanks," Sam said. "I like what I do."

"It shows," his dad replied, smiling.

"Dad, Grandpa worked on the Commission when you were young," Sam said, leaning forward with his elbows on his knees. "And, you know more about racing than I do. We've got a couple of guys retiring soon. We're going to need to hire some new fellows on our staff. They've asked me to be a part of the interview team, but I'm not sure what I'm looking for."

"Sam, I've seen trainers and owners on the racing circuit who would do anything to win a race. They'd use different methods to make a horse run harder or longer than it was capable of, sometimes killing the horse in the process. They'd even change another horse's markings to slip a better horse into a race, dying hair to make it look like the registered horse. Recently, Mike McKeegan was talking about something he'd heard about freeze-branding at Portland Meadows. Some guy used freon on a horse and blasted a blaze-like stencil with gas, which immediately destroyed the color of the hair. The skin underneath wasn't harmed and its color didn't change, but Mike wondered what it was like trying to keep a horse still while using an aerosol near his face."

The two men laughed, thinking it would be almost impossible, knowing horses and aerosols.

"Yet," Sam's dad continued, "it was always the lip tattoo that tripped them up in the end - the one identifier they couldn't hide."

"The Bureau's been doing lip-tattoo dye branding on Thoroughbreds for years, whenever a horse is registered to race with the Jockey Club," Sam said and saw his dad nod.

"I'm surprised that some crook hasn't figured out how to alter the tattoo, yet," Harold said.

"Yeah, that's the one thing they can't alter without being detected. The tattoo on the upper lip of every horse is always checked before each race. Any other advice you have before I go into those interviews?" Sam asked.

"Sam, just remember. There's one thing your grandfather always said. 'You need to hire crooks to catch crooks.'"

CHAPTER ELEVEN

Spring, 1968

"Today's the day of the Race for the Roses," the voice on the radio said. Emma quickly turned it off as she drove back to her ranch. She didn't need to hear about the Kentucky Derby now, not in the mood she was in. She'd just left the bank, after having been forced to sell more of her property to pay for her husband's gambling debts. She felt humiliated.

It wasn't just the loss of the property that bothered her. It was the mistake she'd made in marrying Ted. Emma wished there was something she could have done to avoid this, something that she could have seen before it had gotten out of hand. She looked into the rear-view mirror and saw her face; the makeup she had used to cover the bruise under her eye was beginning to fade.

Tears began to stream down her cheeks.

She knew Ted was at the Derby with Joe. She had been in the den the night before, going over the figures again. Ted had cut back on the number of his clients and wasn't bringing in as much money with his farrier business as he had when they were first married. No matter how many times she looked at the numbers, they never came up with the right answer.

Their problems had begun ever since Joe Remsky had moved in across the road from their ranch. He would take Ted into McMinnville most nights, and Ted would come home, smelling of alcohol and smoke, which revolted Emma. She didn't want him near her then. Later, she'd learned about the gambling, when the money began to disappear from their account. She remembered now the night before Ted had left for Kentucky.

"How much did you lose tonight," she'd asked as he'd walked into the den.

"I won some," Ted had lied, pulling the few bills he had left out of his pocket and tossing them on the desk.

He didn't want another scene. He was tired and just wanted to go to bed. Joe wanted to leave before dawn the next morning for Kentucky, and Ted planned to bring back a lot more money after this trip. At first, Ted hated how he'd let Joe push the whiskey at him, but now he felt more like himself again. He felt more like a man.

"Joe and I are leaving early tomorrow—"

"You're not going to the Derby," Emma said, cutting him off. Her voice was stern, as if she was talking to a child. She could feel a headache coming on.

Ted stared at her for a moment. Then, he pulled himself up to his full height. "I damned well am going," he said, weaving slightly.

"Ted, we don't have the money—" she began.

"I don't care about the money. I'm going to bring a bundle back from this trip. You'll see."

Joe had promised Ted that he had some inside information on which horse would win this year. Ted had a stash of money he planned to put on it. He'd bring back enough to pay everything off and take Emma on a vacation.

Before she could ask where he was going to get the money to bet with, he leaned over to kiss her. She turned her head away.

"You think you're too good for me, don't you, Miss High and Mighty?" Ted said between his teeth, pulling her head back with her hair and bruising her lips with his.

"Ted, stop it," she yelled, pulling away from him and standing with her hands fisted at her sides. "Don't you see what you're doing to us?"

"To us?" Ted yelled as he quickly moved toward her, pinning her against the wall. He ran his hands roughly over her body, pressing his body hard against her. She turned her head so she didn't have to smell the stench from his breath, but he took her face in his hands, his eyes were red and wild.

"I'm just trying to get a little kiss from my wife," he hissed. He kissed her again, this time holding her as she struggled against him. He was becoming excited by her resistance. He thought of his ex-wife, Sharon.

Emma surprised him as she pushed him, sending him back a step. She wiped her mouth with the back of her hand.

"Don't you ever touch me like that again, Ted Jacobs," she yelled. Then, she saw the fury in his eyes.

Ted reached back and slapped her, causing her head to snap back, slamming it against the wall. It wasn't the first time he'd hit her, but never with such force. Then, he pushed her back against the wall, pinning her arms with his own. Sweat and fear ran down her spine.

"Don't tell me what I can and can't do with my own property," he yelled back at her.

"I am not your property," Emma spat into his face. She brought her knee up, catching him in the crotch. When Ted doubled over, she ran out of the den and into the spare bedroom, locking the door behind her. Without even thinking, she rushed to the closet and turned on the light. With shaking hands, she pulled down a box from the shelf, frantically digging in it until she found her father's pistol and clip. She fumbled as she pushed the clip into the gun and advanced a bullet.

Ted began pounding on the door, after he'd found it locked.

"Come on, Emma, open up. I'm entitled to a kiss from my wife." He pounded again, twisting the door handle.

"Don't shut me out, doll. You know I love you," he slurred.

His voice had turned into a whine, which turned Emma's stomach. *Love*, she thought. *If this is love, I don't want any part of it.* She tightened her hand on the gun, which was aimed at the door. She didn't know if she would be able to pull the trigger.

Ted rattled the handle again, and shoved his shoulder into the door, but it held. Finally, he gave up and she heard him walk up the stairs to their bedroom.

Emma walked to the dresser and looked into the mirror. The soft light from the closet framed her face in the glass. She didn't recognize herself. She looked like a woman who had gone mad, her hair was tangled and clung in stands from the sweat, her left eye and lips were red and swollen. Tears silently poured down her cheeks as she had realized what kind of man she had married.

When she opened the top drawer in search of a handkerchief, her hand touched a cold metal. She grasped it and picked it up, holding it up to the light behind her. It was the necklace that Sam had given her. With trembling fingers, she put it around her neck. As she had gazed in the mirror at the oval locket hanging between her breasts, she felt it was like a shield and had vowed to keep it there for the rest of her life.

♦ ♦ ♦ ♦

Ted's last words flooded back to her now, as she drove down the road to her home. Maybe she didn't know what love really was. She thought she had seen it with her parents, and had felt it once before, with Sam. She brought her hand to her heart and felt the gold locket. At the beginning, that's what she thought she'd had with Ted. Now she knew she'd been wrong. She sighed heavily as she realized it was too late for her now. Love just wasn't in life's design for her.

When she turned her car into the lane to her ranch, she was startled to see Jennifer's car parked in her driveway. Emma quickly looked in her rear-view mirror, wiping the tears away and reapplying some powder around her eyes. She could see the bruise under her eye, but hoped Jennifer wouldn't. She took a deep breath and got out of the car.

Jennifer was running out of the stable toward her. They hugged each other next to Emma's car.

Noticing that Emma didn't seem to want to let go, Jennifer pulled back and looked at her friend. She saw the faint color under Emma's eye and narrowed her eyes.

"Oh, Em, what happened?" she asked, placing her hand on Emma's cheek.

"Nothing," Emma lied, placing her arm in Jennifer's and steering her toward the house. "I got bucked off by a wild mustang, that's all."

"You've never let a horse throw you before," Jennifer laughed, the tension in her shoulders relaxing a little.

"There's always a first time," Emma said, looking away. She hated lying to her friend, but she knew she couldn't tell her the truth. That would mean she'd have to admit her own failure.

"I've missed you terribly," Jennifer said, reaching down and holding Emma's hand. She could feel Emma was trembling.

"Jenn, you look wonderful. Come inside and I'll make some coffee." Emma quickly walked toward the front door, with Jennifer following alongside.

"Why didn't you call to tell me you were coming?" Emma asked, as they walked past the rows of daffodils along the walkway to the house.

"I had to leave without much notice. My agent called this morning about an assignment to take some promotional photographs of a new inn at the Pacific Coast, so I flew down right away. I just had to stop and see you before driving west. I'm thinking of using a family setting, maybe with a dog, and the view of the ocean in the background. What do you think?"

"That's a great idea," Emma replied, trying to smile. The thought of a family setting turned her stomach now. She opened the large oak door and led the way to her kitchen.

"Em, is anything wrong?" Jennifer asked, once they were inside.

"No, everything's just fine." Emma busied herself with making the coffee to keep her hands from shaking.

"Where's Ted?" Jennifer had noticed that his hat was gone from the rack by the front door, but there was no sign of him in the stable and his truck was still parked by the barn.

Emma's hand paused in mid-air as she was about to get another spoonful of coffee. "He's gone for a few days," she finally said. "On a hunting trip," she added quickly. She'd had to admit that she had been glad when she'd found the note from Ted in the den that morning, saying that he'd left for the Kentucky Derby.

"Well, that gives us some time to catch up," Jennifer said, a little puzzled. She had seen Ted's rifle still in the rack by the door.

"Oh dear," Emma said. "I'm sorry, but I have a show to judge today." She turned to the sink to fill the coffee pot with water. She couldn't look her friend in the eye. She really wanted to tell her everything and was just about to, when Jennifer spoke first.

"Jason and I have set a date. Emma, I'm so happy. I want our marriage to be as happy as yours." She didn't see Emma flinch, since her back was to her.

Emma took a deep breath, then turned and smiled. "I'm so glad for you. When is the date?" She was actually glad to think about something besides her own problems.

"Next June. June 5th. You and Ted will come, won't you? We're going to be married on the hillside behind our home. It is so beautiful there."

Emma thought of the large bungalow Jennifer and Jason had built on their hundred-acre property in northern Montana. The view of the glaciers from the house was breathtaking.

"Of course," Emma replied, hugging Jennifer. "I wouldn't miss it for the world."

Emma prayed in her heart that her friend's marriage would be more like the marriage she had wanted, instead of the one she had.

◆ ◆ ◆ ◆

Sam settled in to watch the ninety-fourth Kentucky Derby, the race that revealed the year's best three-year-old Thoroughbreds. The race only took two minutes around the mile and a quarter track, but when the horses left the gate at the twin towers of Churchill Downs each first Saturday of May, most of America stopped to watch. It was just a few minutes till post-time, and the horses were being led toward the gate.

In the gray, drizzly day, Sam watched as the mixed crowd of people bustled to their seats, dressed in every style from casual to the most elegant dress. Some of the women wore wide hats and were holding tall glasses of the traditional mint julep in their hands as they talked loudly to their neighbors. The sound was deafening and exhilarating.

Sam looked at the board and saw that Frank's Revenge had been scratched. It was a horse he was unfamiliar with. A note in *The Racing Form* showed that the owner was from Venezuela.

He also saw on the *Form* that Koenig's Wonder, one of George Mason's horses, was running. Sam remembered watching the young colt's birth at Essen Farms. George had said then that this colt was going to win the Triple Crown.

Earlier today, Sam had run into George in the backside before the horses were called to the paddock area. He'd been avoiding George since the last time they'd seen each other at Del Mar Park. Sam still held some of the shame of losing Ele to George in that claiming race.

In the backside, Sam had seen the grooms going about their chores. A few were rolling clean bandages and placing them in a tub next to the stalls. These were sometimes used on the tall animals' legs during or after a race. The air was electrified with tension.

"Sam Parker," a voice Sam knew had said to his back. When he'd turned, he'd seen George standing next to one of the stalls in the shedrow. George had aged well, the threads of silver filtered through his dark hair at the temples and his brown eyes shown with the excitement of the day.

"Hello, Mr. Mason," Sam said, shaking the older man's hand. Sam looked over at the horse standing outside of his stall, his muscles rippling with anticipation.

George had winced at the formal name Sam had used, but his spirits were too high to let that bother him. His colt was going to win the Derby today; he knew it in his heart.

"I understand that you are working for the Racing Bureau now." George had been somewhat surprised when he'd learned this. He knew of Sam's desire for a racing farm.

"That's right. I saw that you have Carlos Madera riding for you. Isn't he different than the jockey you usually use?"

"Yes, Juan Martinez disappeared three days ago - very unlike him. I've used Carlos before, at Del Mar on Koenig's Pride..." He stopped when he saw Sam's eyes.

"I recognize the name," Sam said, looking down the shedrow of stalls. Since he'd started his new job as an investigator, Sam had seen that George had been cleared of any charges for providing the drug to Joe that had been given to Ele.

Just then, Fred Jamison walked up and stood next to George. He couldn't place where he knew this young man from.

"Hello, Mr. Jamison," Sam said, shaking his hand. He'd met Fred at Essen Farms years ago. "Well, good luck, sir," Sam said to George with a wave and turned to go to the grandstand.

"Wait, Sam," George said, placing his hand on Sam's arm. Sam saw Jamison turn toward the colt, seeming to busy himself with the horse's bridle.

"I wanted to talk to you about Classy Elegance..." George began in a low voice.

"Sure, Mr. Mason," Sam interrupted, looking into George's dark eyes. Ele was a chapter in Sam's life that he had closed. "But, not now," Sam added. "You've got better things on your mind." He nodded toward the dancing tall, black colt, the white star on his forehead shining brightly. Sam could see the need to run in the horse's eyes.

"Let's get together sometime, after the race," George suggested. "Please come by the house later."

"Sure thing, Mr. Mason." Sam had saluted and walked away, knowing that he had no intention of going to Essen Farms.

On his way back to the grandstand, Sam thought he had seen Joe Remsky out of the corner of his eye, leading a black horse near one of the shedrows. Across the horse's back was a red blanket, with the name "Frank's Revenge" written across it. When Sam turned to get a closer look, the man and horse had turned the corner of the building. Sam tried to follow, but they were nowhere in sight. He'd decided he must have imagined seeing Joe.

◆ ◆ ◆ ◆

Now, seated in the grandstand, Sam thought of being face to face with Remsky. Sam knew that someday he'd get his chance. His dad's words returned to him, about Ele having the heart to win. He wished now that he could have that day all over again.

Sam saw that the horses were loaded into the gate. The bell rang as the gates swung open, and in a flurry the horses were off. One gray stumbled, but the rest of the field went around him. As they passed the grandstand the first time, Sam saw that Koenig's Wonder was five horses back from the lead. He had watched Carlos do the same at Del Mar on Koenig's Pride. A tall sorrel and a bay volleyed for the lead for most of the race. Sam watched closely as the black horse came up just outside near the middle of the field until the last turn for home, then rallied with a burst of speed around the first four leaders, mud flying up from his hooves pounding the track as he rushed past, coming up on the lead horse. The two ran neck and neck until they were almost to the finish line. Then, Sam saw Koenig's Wonder pull forward by a head just as they crossed under the wire. He thought that maybe George had a good chance at that Triple Crown, after all. With the roar of the crowd around him, Sam stood up and stretched the tension from his shoulders. Then, he went down to the Winner's Circle.

The photographers, reporters, and spectators crowded around the tall black colt in the famed circle at Churchill Downs. The sleek horse stood with his head held high in the fine drizzle, the white star on his forehead bright against his black, shiny hair, a blood-red blanket of roses draped over his back. George stood proudly with a big smile on his face in a dark suit and a tan fedora, holding the bridle of his horse as the flashes from the photographers' cameras lit around them like fireflies. Fred Jamison stood next to George. The small jockey patiently sat on the horse's back, holding the traditional bouquet of roses, his goggles shoved on top of his helmet, his face and the red and gold colors on his silks barely visible through the thickly splattered mud.

"What do you think of your boy here, Mr. Mason?" Sam heard one of the reporters ask, nodding to the horse.

"Koenig's Wonder has made me very proud today," George answered with his heavy German accent as he looked first at the horse, then at Fred. "We have all worked very hard for this moment."

After the clamor of questions and applause began to slow, George handed the horse's bridle over to the groom, a black man with a large smile, who had just entered the circle carrying a blanket. The groom attached a lead rein to the horse's bridle, then led the horse and jockey to the judge's stand. The jockey waved his hand in the air, signaling for permission to dismount. After the jockey had hopped down from the colt to be weighed in, the groom removed the roses, the saddle and cloth, then placed the soft, red blanket with the colt's name in gold letters on the tall animal's back, gently replacing the well-deserved drape of roses. Fred Jamison led the winner to the detention barn to be tested and watered, Carlos and the groom walking beside, smiling, and talking about their victory. When the test was finished, Fred and the groom escorted their winner to the end of their shedrow to cool down. Carlos returned to the jockeys' barn to clean up.

Later, Sam arrived at the winner's stall. Koenig's Wonder stood proudly in his stall as a small handful of people still hovered around to get a glimpse of the champion and take pictures.

"Congratulations, Mr. Jamison," Sam said, shaking his hand. "Koenig's Wonder ran a good race."

"Thanks, Sam." Fred then remembered the young Air Force pilot who had watched Koenig's Wonder's birth. "He's not finished yet."

"So, George is taking him to the Triple Crown?"

"You bet," Fred beamed. Sam watched as Fred went into the stall and put his hands down the legs of the tall animal, looking for any sign of heat. Sam had done the same thing to Ele after every race.

"Johnny," Fred said to the groom. "Watch his right foreleg. There's a bit of heat there. You may want to get the icing tub ready."

"Sure thing, Mr. Jamison," Johnny nodded and took a bucket with him to the nearest ice machine.

"George will be wondering where I am," Fred said to no one in particular, looking at his watch.

"I'll stay here with the horse until your groom returns," Sam offered. He knew the celebration party was an event that no owner or trainer liked to miss after a Derby win.

"Well, I don't know..." he began until out of the corner of his eye, he saw Johnny walking back down the row of stalls. Fred usually wouldn't leave his colt with anyone but his groom, but he knew Sam worked for the Bureau. "If you don't mind, Sam."

"No problem."

"Well, then, thanks." Fred picked up his tweed jacket and turned to leave.

"Tell George congratulations for me," Sam called after Fred, as he walked out of the shedrow toward the track's private dining room.

Sam stepped up to the tall animal and scratched his long, black neck.

"You've done a great thing here today, boy," Sam said softly to the horse. "But, then, you were born for this, weren't you?"

Koenig's Wonder nodded his head and whinnied, as if in agreement.

♦ ♦ ♦ ♦

Later, deep into the night, when all was dark and quiet again in the backside at Churchill Downs, a short man in black slowly led a black colt around the backside of the shedrow where Koenig's Wonder stood. The man let out a soft whistle, then waited until the bare light bulb in front of the champion's stall went out. Out of the darkness, Carlos Madera appeared, leading the champion to where the man in black stood.

"The groom and the guard will be back any minute," Carlos whispered softly, handing the lead rope to Joe. "Did Jacobs give you any trouble?"

"Nah, I just told him I needed to take the horse for a walk to settle him down before we take off. Jacobs has no clue what's going on." Joe had been instructed to keep the imposter in his stall with the gate closed to avoid prying eyes, until now.

"Keep it that way," Carlos hissed.

"I'll take him from here," Joe whispered, nodding toward the tall horse. "The trailer's waiting and the security guard at the gate knows that 'Frank's Revenge' is leaving tonight," Joe winked at the jockey. He smiled at the thought of the money he was going to get.

Carlos grabbed the lead of the other colt, noticing that the white star on the animal's forehead matched that of the winner's. The dark hair on Frank's Revenge had been freeze-branded just six months prior to the race, to give the hair a chance to grow completely back – except now it was white. Carlos had been instructed to take a close-up photo of Koenig's Wonder's forehead, so the branding iron could be made in the same shape as the winner's natural star. The brand was now permanent - like a tattoo. He was glad that it would take some time before the swap was detected, if the horse performed as he had been trained. Now that Carlos was George Mason's jockey, he'd handle that.

"Make sure you do your job," Carlos added softly. He had quickly colored Koenig's Wonder's forehead after the groom had left. "I'll see you in a few months."

Carlos walked back around the corner of the barn with the imposter and placed him in the winner's stall, quietly closing the gate. Just after the light bulb lit again, the guard turned the far corner of the shedrow of stalls for his routine check on the area.

At that same moment, the champion was being led into a trailer waiting to take him out of Churchill Downs.

CHAPTER TWELVE

Fall, 1968

"Welcome to my humble abode, Amigo," Joe said to Carlos with a smirk.

"I'm not your 'Amigo'," Carlos snapped as he stepped from the black Jeep.

"Sorry, Carlos. I was just trying to be friendly."

"Mr. Reichmann wants me to change my name while I'm here. So, call me Casey Morales."

"Sure, Casey," Joe snickered and slowly lit a cigarette to drag out the moment. Then, he saw Carlos' glare. Joe hoped it wasn't going to be a long wait until they heard from Reichmann again.

This man has messed up my life, Joe thought to himself, trying to keep a smile on his lips. He knew that he was going to be the one to walk out of this deal with a lot more than Carlos. He had some plans of his own.

"When did you start smoking?" Carlos asked as he looked around the ranch. He saw the empty corral next to the stable.

"When I stopped riding," Joe said, wishing he'd never met Carlos Madera.

"How's the colt doing?" Carlos asked, nodding toward the stable. "Have you been keeping his hair covered, like you were told?"

"Sure. He's in good hands. I'll go over to Jacobs' ranch tomorrow to do the touch-up."

The small man whirled around. "What are you talking about?" he said, an edge of steel in his voice.

"I took the colt over to Jacobs' ranch."

Carlos grabbed Joe's shirt collar with both hands. "You did what?" he yelled, then moved his hands to Joe's throat. Fear had grabbed him at the thought of what Reichmann was going to do when he found out.

"When I saw the news in the papers, I thought it'd be a great place to hide a stolen Thoroughbred. No one will think to look there," Joe said quickly. He saw Carlos' eyes darken and felt the fingers tighten around his neck.

"Jacobs' a nobody," Joe continued. "Besides, he has a dressage stable. They use retired Thoroughbreds for dressage. Frankie, that's what I call him, won't stand out like a sore thumb like he would at my place."

Joe didn't want to admit that he'd gotten nervous when the newspaper headlines announced the swap of Mason's colt with an imposter sometime after the Kentucky Derby. It had surprised him that it hadn't been discovered until the Belmont race. But, now the police and investigators for the Racing Bureau were combing the country for the missing colt. He'd gotten the idea when he'd remembered that Ted's name had been used as the trainer on the foal certificate for Frank's Revenge. Joe was on to the game, but Carlos didn't know it yet.

"Besides, Casey" Joe continued, as he felt Carlos' hands relax. "You *will* stick out like a sore thumb. You'd better stay near the ranch."

"Mr. Reichmann's not going to like this," Carlos said, a strange look on his dark face. He dropped his hands and stepped back. He knew that Reichmann was a man to be feared. He'd seen him kill before.

"Well, he doesn't have to know about it, does he?" Joe said, looking sideways at Carlos with a sly smile on his face. "So, leave it for now. I'll take care of the hair, and we'll bring him back here when we need to."

"What'd you tell Jacobs?" Carlos asked. He was glad that this job was about to end.

"I used the excuse that I needed to do some repairs in my stable. Yesterday, I told him the contractor that I'd hired was called out of town, so there'd be a delay in getting it done."

"You hired a contractor?"

"No, Casey," Joe said, drawling out Carlos' new name, tickled with himself. "I just told Jacobs that."

"I want to see the colt," Carlos said, looking across the road toward the house with the long, white fence.

"We'll have to wait until both of them are gone. I'd rather no one knows you're here."

◆ ◆ ◆ ◆

The yellows and oranges of fall painted the landscape as Ted drove to Portland for supplies. The earlier cold front had brought out the colors sooner than usual, but today was a warm and sunny day.

When he'd returned from the Derby, Ted had found Emma sleeping in the small bedroom downstairs. He'd begged her to forgive him, showing her the money he'd brought back from the races. He didn't tell her it was less than he'd taken to Kentucky, but he'd promised he'd stay off the booze and make it up to her. He was thankful that she had believed him.

Ted had stayed away from Joe's, but the pain in his gut was killing him. Emma didn't know about the small bottle of whiskey he had stashed in his truck for emergencies. He was very careful, so she wouldn't find out. He figured what she didn't know wouldn't hurt her.

After he'd finished with his supplies, Ted walked into the bookstore that was holding some art books Emma had ordered. Once he was in the checkout line, he could see that the guy in front of him was going to take awhile with only one checker and a huge stack of books. Ted rolled his eyes while he waited, then looked down at the long table next to him of new releases. He saw a book on famous race horses. It was the kind that some people liked to put on a table to impress their friends.

Since he had time to kill, he picked up the book and thumbed through it. On the last page, he stopped and stared at the photo of the horse in the Winner's Circle in this year's Kentucky Derby. He read the horse's name in the caption:

'Koenig's Wonder.' Then, he remembered seeing the newspaper reports on the horse that had been switched with this winner.

Sweat began to run down his back. Finally, the man in front was finished and it was Ted's turn. He put the book on the counter in front of the clerk and asked about Emma's order. He hurriedly paid and left, beads of sweat now forming on his forehead.

♦ ♦ ♦ ♦

After he returned to their ranch, Ted tossed the books down onto the desk in the den. He needed a drink, but this time he needed to see Joe first. He located one of the newspapers with the headlines of Koenig's Wonder's theft in large letters across the top and left the house. He found Emma working with a young gelding in the covered arena. She stood in her dark jeans and flannel shirt, her dark hair flowing in the cool breeze, the reins to the horse held gently in her hands as he pranced around the ring. Ted was struck by her beauty. He didn't think he'd ever get used to it, but he was beginning to shake from fear.

"I'm going to Joe's," Ted yelled across the large arena.

She turned and looked at Ted with disappointment in her eyes. She could see he was nervous, and a knot formed in the pit of her stomach. It was the same look he'd had before, when he used to spend so much time at Joe's. She brought the horse to a halt and put her hands on her hips.

"I thought you were staying home tonight," she said. She knew her voice was sharp, but she knew what condition he would be in when he returned.

"Well, I've changed my mind. There's some business I've got to talk to Joe about."

"Be back by dinner," she said with a fire in her eyes.

"What are you, my warden?" he yelled back at her. His fear was beginning to eat at him.

"Ted, don't go. I thought we were going to—"

"Things have changed," he said, over his shoulder as he walked away. "Don't wait up for me."

♦ ♦ ♦ ♦

"What's up, Ted?" Joe asked, looking nervously at Carlos across the stall. When Ted had walked in, he and Carlos were working in the stable, resizing the stall they planned to use when they went to get Koenig's Wonder.

"Who's he?" Ted asked, nodding his head toward Carlos.

"Uh, this is my friend, Car..Casey. He and I, uh, worked together in California." Joe turned to Carlos. "Casey, this is Ted Jacobs."

Carlos only nodded at Ted, turned his back to him, and walked out of the stable. He stopped just outside of the stable door to listen. He'd seen the fear in Ted's eyes.

Joe watched Ted wipe the back of his hand across his mouth as he paced back and forth. He knew something was eating at the man and could see he needed a drink. He walked to the tack room, then returned to where Ted stood.

"Here," Joe said as he handed the bottle of Jack Daniels from the tack room to Ted. "Drink this."

"You conned me into helping you steal that damned horse at the Derby, didn't you?" Ted said, after slugging down the warm liquor. The burning was a familiar feeling as it traveled down until it hit the pit of his stomach and he felt the fire. *God, I've missed this*, Ted thought.

"What the hell are you talking about?" Joe asked, quickly prodding Ted to take another drink.

"That black you brought to our stable. That's Koenig's Wonder, ain't it?"

Joe stared at Ted, hoping his face didn't give him away. He reached out for the bottle, stalling for time, waiting for his pulse to settle.

"You're nuts," Joe finally said, after taking a swig of the liquor and passing it back to Ted. "Don't you remember that the winner had a white star on his forehead? This animal doesn't have a mark on him."

Ted thought for a minute, then downed a third gulp. He wasn't shaking quite so badly now, and was glad when Joe offered it back again after taking a short sip. Ted was downing the whiskey like a man dying of thirst.

"You're right," Ted said, coming up for air, wiping his mouth with the back of his hand. He was beginning to feel the buzz in his head. "I didn't think of that."

Joe knew it was going to be one of those long nights and he'd have to stay ahead of Ted all the way. Ted began to pace, like he was trying to gain control of himself again. Since they'd returned from the Derby, Ted had kept to his own ranch, saying he was busy. Joe knew Emma was the reason. *Women*, he thought to himself. He'd take care of her another time. Now, he needed to get Ted back where he wanted him, and he knew the way to do it.

"Frankie's owner called today," Joe said. It wasn't a lie. Reichmann had called to say it would be soon when they would be moving the colt. "He said he's got a buyer for the horse. We're talking big bucks, pal. Twenty grand. And, I'll split it with you."

Joe eyed Ted, watching as his pace slowed and his eyes relaxed. *He's such a fool*, Joe thought. *So gullible*. He could see that with just a few drinks and the promise of money, he would have Ted again.

"Why're you going to split it with me?" Ted asked.

"Because you're my friend," Joe lied, placing his arm around Ted's shoulders. "And, besides, you've helped me around here on my ranch. Just think of it as part of your wages."

Ted stood and looked into space, his eyes shining. Joe could almost see the pile of money Ted was thinking about.

"Come on, buddy," Joe said as he slapped Ted on the back, offering another drink of the whiskey. "I feel like celebrating tonight. My treat."

"Yeah, sure Joe. I was hoping you'd say that." Ted took three long pulls on the bottle.

"Why don't you have a seat there on that bale and I'll go in and get my keys."

◆ ◆ ◆ ◆

As soon as Joe stepped into the house, Carlos whirled him around. Carlos had gone back to the house after he'd heard Ted agree with Joe's explanation about the horse's markings.

"You idiot," Carlos hissed. "You've trusted a fool."

"Hey, buddy," Joe said, pulling free of Carlos' grip. "He may be a fool, but I've got him back where I want him. He'll be no trouble."

Joe opened a drawer and pulled out his keys.

"Where are you going?" Carlos asked, watching Joe.

"I'm taking our patsy into town to get him dead drunk. He'll forget everything by morning. It's his pattern."

Carlos thought for a moment. "Okay, but be careful what you say." Then, with a strange look on his face, Carlos added, "I want you to get him to come back here tomorrow, before dawn."

When Carlos placed his hand on Joe's arm, it was cold. Fear stirred in Joe's gut.

"Why?" Joe asked.

"We're going hunting - the three of us," Carlos said with a smile.

"What?"

"Just do as you're told."

◆ ◆ ◆ ◆

Joe drove Ted into McMinnville where he bought him a continuous flow of drinks while he nursed one or two himself all night long. It was midnight when Joe drove Ted home.

"Joe, you're a true friend," Ted slurred. He looked like he could barely focus on Joe's face. "I'm so lucky to have a friend like you. I never had any friends."

Joe smiled. "Sure, pal."

As his headlights caught the white fence around Ted and Emma's ranch, he saw the light in the upstairs window and wished he was the one going in to see that lovely woman.

"You're the lucky one, Ted, having a lady like yours. I wish I was going in there to see her tonight, to get my hands in that dark hair of hers. I bet she likes it rough, doesn't she?"

"Like what?"

"You know..." Joe smiled. Ted didn't like the look on Joe's face. It looked like a man who had already tasted another man's goods. A burning started deep inside of him in spite of the cool night air flowing through the open window and the fog in his brain.

"Oh, yeah. She likes it when I come home and be the man," Ted lied. That was what his dad had taught him about women. He'd said they liked it better when he was rough with them and held them down, making them feel helpless. He knew it excited them. Sharon, his first wife, had liked it - at first.

"She's been pretty high and mighty lately," Ted said, turning his face toward the light, which he knew was their bedroom. She had started sleeping with him again, since he'd stopped drinking. He was going to have a little talk with her tonight about Joe.

"You lucky dog." Joe licked his lips, a hungry look in his eyes. Ted could see Joe was enjoying himself with what he was conjuring up in his own mind about his wife. He watched Joe now, a sobering fire building deep in his stomach. He'd seen the same look on other men who used to hang around his first wife.

"You OK, pal?" Joe asked as he stopped the car.

"Yeah, sure." Ted opened the door and stumbled out, then closed the door.

"Say, Ted," Joe said through the open window. "Come on over to my place tomorrow, just before dawn. We'll go hunting. I feel the urge to shoot something."

Ted stood for a moment, swaying slightly. Joe was surprised the man was still standing, with the amount of alcohol he'd bought Ted tonight.

"Sure," Ted said. He was now beginning to feel like shooting something himself. "See you in a few hours."

Ted watched Joe drive away and turn into his own driveway, Then, he turned and walked down to where his truck was parked, carefully taking every step in the moonlight. He needed one more drink before he went into the house. When he thought of Joe's words, he felt his strength returning as his anger grew. He'd married another whore.

Just as he put the bottle away, he heard a high whinny. He went into the stable and turned on the light. Frankie's head came out of the top of the gate to his stall. The horse bobbed his head up and down, as Ted walked up to the black horse. Looking directly at him, Ted couldn't see anything different about the horse. But, when the horse bobbed his head again, Ted saw a flash of white. He placed his hand on the horse's nose, holding his head still. With his other hand, he reached up and pushed the hair back up.

Fear gripped his heart.

The hair was black, but the skin underneath was white. He'd heard about this being done for races, a temporary dye in order to use a different horse for a race.

He now realized that this horse wasn't Frankie. He was the winning race horse, Koenig's Wonder. Ted was sure of it. His mind began to clear a little, and he looked back over the past few months. He knew now what Joe had done to him - what he had let happen to himself. On some occasions, when he and Joe had gone out, he'd only played dumb. It'd all been an act to him. Ted knew he could out-drink any man.

It'd been something Joe had said earlier at the black-jack table. He called this horse 'Frank's Revenge.' Ted remembered seeing that horse's name on the *Racing Form* at the Derby. Ted only knew Joe's horse as Frankie, until now. It all fit now.

Anger replaced his fear.

What an idiot I've been, Ted thought, shaking his head. Seething with disgust at how he'd thought Joe was his friend, he walked to the door of the stable and slammed off the light. As he walked up to his house, his stride much steadier now, he saw the bedroom light again. Visions of Emma with Joe flooded his mind.

What a slut, he thought to himself. She'd give herself to any man, just like Sharon had done, after he'd started drinking. It didn't matter to her who she went with. His anger at Joe was now turned toward Emma as he walked up the stairs.

Emma was lying in their bed reading a book, wearing a short, cotton nightshirt when Ted walked in.

"It's about time you got home," Emma said. She could smell the alcohol and smoke on him again and hated him for it. He was beginning to disgust her with his weakness.

"I'll come home when I'm damned well ready," he hissed at her. "And, no bitch is going to tell me when, you see?" Ted's voice boomed across the room at her, just like he'd heard his dad's voice in his past. He needed to control something in his life right now. "This is my home, an' I'll do as I damned well please, do you hear me?"

"Yes, Ted. I can hear you," Emma said, the anger in his eyes stirring her on. She'd vowed to herself to never be frightened by him again. "Joe probably can, too. When are you going to stop, Ted? We're losing the ranch because of your drinking and gambling."

"All you think of is this damned ranch. I'm tired of you acting like you're better than me. You've always been that way. Maybe you think Joe is better?"

"Joe?"

"Oh, don't act innocent with me. I heard him tonight, talking about you. He knows you, you whore."

"What are you talking about?"

"You probably go sneaking over to his place every time I leave, don't you?"

"You're crazy," she said, sitting up in bed.

"Yeah, I'm crazy to have married a slut like you." He began taking off his clothes. "Joe told me how you like it."

"What are you doing?" she said, seeing the hatred and anger in his eyes. She started to get out of bed.

Ted slapped her with all of his strength, the force of it throwing her back against the mattress. She was stunned for an instant. The fear grabbed at her as Ted held her arms over her head, pinning her to the bed, lying over her with his hard body.

"You tease. What kind of games did you play with him?"

Ted saw the glint of gold around her neck. He yanked on it, the chain breaking in his hand, and held it up in her face. He couldn't think straight, the red rage bursting inside of him.

"Did Joe give this to you?" he spat at her.

"No, I've had it for years. You've known—" She turned her face and tried to bring her knee up, but he spread her legs with his.

"You're lying to me, you bitch," he growled, throwing the necklace across the room. "He told me tonight. He told me how you liked it rough," he yelled into her face, hurting her, forcing himself into her. "I'll show you rough."

"Ted, stop," she pleaded, twisting her body, trying to free herself of him. "I've never been with Joe."

"Don't lie to me. You're mine to do with as I please, you bitch. And no other man is ever going to touch you again."

Emma tried to scream, but he bruised her lips with his own, causing them to split. She could taste the blood in her throat.

Quickly, he filled her and then passed out, the heavy weight of his body locking her where she was. Tears streamed down her face and into her hair and ears as she silently sobbed, the pain still ripping through her.

◆ ◆ ◆ ◆

What seemed an eternity, Emma felt Ted relax. She silently pulled herself free of him, being careful not to wake him. She grabbed the clothes she'd worn that day, crept down the stairs, and into the bathroom near the small bedroom, locking the door behind her. Sobbing and shaking uncontrollably, she quietly tried to clean him from her body. She sat on the cold, tile floor, hugging herself and rocking.

When she looked in the mirror, she saw the bruises starting around her mouth and across her eye. She looked into her dark eyes and promised herself she would never let any man hurt her again.

She listened at the door before unlocking it. As she entered the hall, she could hear Ted's snoring upstairs. She went softly to the small bedroom and locked the door. She felt lost and frightened, pacing the room like a caged animal, not sure what to do next.

All she could think of was she needed help. Picking up the phone, she dialed Jennifer's number in Montana.

"Spencer Studio," a strange voice said on the other end.

"Is Jennifer there?" Emma whispered into the phone, her voice shaking.

"I can hardly hear you. Can you please speak up?"

"Is Jennifer there?"

"No, I'm sorry. This is her answering service. May I take a message?"

"When will she return?" Emma asked, numb and frightened.

"Not until next Tuesday. Would you like to leave your name and number?"

Emma quickly hung up the phone. She was beginning to shake uncontrollably. She went to the night stand and pulled out her father's pistol. She had placed it there the last time she'd felt she needed it. Tonight, she knew that if he tried to come through the locked door, she would kill him. She wanted Ted dead.

◆ ◆ ◆ ◆

It was still dark outside when Ted awoke. His head began to pound as he got up. Then, he remembered what he'd done the night before. His mind clearer now, he knew that Emma had told him the truth. He looked around the room and saw that she wasn't anywhere. He dressed and ran down the stairs, seeing the spare bedroom door shut. He tried the handle and found it locked.

"Emma," he called. "Emma, honey, I'm sorry. I didn't know what I was doing last night. Please open up."

Emma, frightened and in pain, sat in silence with the gun aimed now at the door. She hadn't slept all night.

"Come on, Emma. I'll never do it again. I promise. I know now that I can't handle the booze. I'm sorry, Em." He knew he'd said the same words before.

She still didn't answer.

Finally, Ted went down the hall and into the den.

He sat down at the desk and pulled out a sheet of paper and began to write quickly. Suddenly, he stopped and shuddered as he thought of the nights long ago, when he'd lain in his bedroom in his parents' house. He would hear his mom screaming when his dad was hurting her, helpless to do anything to stop it. Ted had tried once, when he was twelve years old and his dad was beating on his mom in the kitchen for something she'd said. Ted's dad had thrown him across the kitchen, slamming him into the wall, telling him it was none of his damned business. That was the night his dad introduced him to whiskey, telling him that if he was going to try to act like a man, it was time he started drinking like one. His dad had told Ted he'd understand how women liked to be handled, how being the strong man in charge excited them. Here he was, following in the footsteps of the man he hated the most. Ted hated himself now for what he'd done to Emma.

When he'd finished writing, he slowly folded the paper, placed it in an envelope and sealed it. He wrote "Emma" on the front of the envelope. Then, as he stood up, he saw the horse book he'd just purchased and inserted the letter at the page where Koenig's Wonder stood in the Winner's Circle. Looking at the photo, his anger began to burn again, but this time it was aimed in the right direction.

Ted left the book on the desk, and went to put on his jacket. He picked up his rifle and hat, and opened the door. A feeling came over him that he might not return, but if he did, he promised to himself he'd make it up to Emma.

Someone has a real surprise coming, he thought as he left.

◆ ◆ ◆

Emma heard Ted leave. She watched from the dark window as Ted walked up their lane and turned into Joe's. He was dressed for hunting and was carrying his rifle. She went to the front door and locked it. She was surprised, but relieved to see Ted's keys hanging on the peg where his hat had been. She quickly ran and also locked the deadbolt on the back door, even knowing that if Ted wanted to get in, the locks were useless. Yet, it made her feel a little more secure. Taking the pistol with her, she went upstairs.

When she walked into the upstairs bedroom, she became sick to her stomach. Her nightshirt lay torn and bloody on the floor. She locked the door for the first time and went into the bathroom to fully shower in an attempt to wash the night from her, knowing it would never leave her.

After dressing, she picked up her nightgown and threw it into the waste basket. On the floor, she saw the necklace Sam had given her. Her fingers trembled as she reached for it. Her heart sank when she saw that one of the links in the chain had been broken. She used her teeth and broke a fingernail trying to pry open one of the undamaged links to mend the chain, tears streaming down her face. Then, she placed the necklace back around her neck.

She looked through the upstairs window and could see the first light of day opening above the trees on Joe's ranch. Slowly, she walked down the stairs, sore and bruised.

In the den, she saw the book Ted had bought on the desk. Angrily, she tossed it into a box of other books that she planned to donate to the public library. Emma laid the pistol on the desk, then looked in the middle drawer and found the phone number that Chris Schmidt had given her years ago. It was stuck inside of an old address book her mother had kept. Chris' face had come to her mind late the night before, when she couldn't reach Jennifer, but it had been too late to call him then. He had always been there for her in the past. She now said a little prayer that he would still be at his sister's in Kentucky and dialed the number.

"Essen Farms," a man said on the other end of the line.

"I'm sorry. I must have dialed a wrong number." Confused, Emma hung up. Her head was beginning to hurt. She didn't know of an Essen Farms. She dialed again, more carefully.

"Essen Farms," the same voice repeated.

"I'm trying to reach Chris Schmidt. Do you know where I can reach him?" Her own voice sounded hollow, like she was in a tunnel.

"May I ask who's calling?"

"This is Emma Jacobs."

"Who?"

She remembered that Chris didn't know she had married. "Emma Maseman," she said. "Chris used to work on our farm in Indiana."

There was a long pause on the other end. Then the man said, "One moment please."

Emma heard nothing for some time. She began to wonder what she was going to say. She knew why she had called Chris. He was the only link she had left now to her past - to her life before she'd met Ted. After waiting for what seemed a lifetime, but in reality had only been seconds, she was beginning to change her mind and was about to hang up when she heard a slight click, then a familiar voice on the other end. She clung to the phone as if it was a lifeline.

"Emma? Is that you?" Chris' voice sounded tired. He hated the fact that George Mason was listening in on the house phone.

Tears came to her eyes as she tried to swallow back the fear still inside of her.

"Chris? Oh, Chris. How are you?"

"I'm fine."

"How's your sister?" She didn't know where that had come from. It was like she was on auto-pilot and something inside of her had taken over. She began to shake, and realized she was still in shock. She leaned her elbows on the desk for support as tears silently began to fall down her face.

"She's much better now." Chris could hear something in Emma's voice that he'd only heard once before. It was the panic he'd heard when he'd found her after the Indiana house had been ransacked.

"Are you OK, Emma?" he asked.

She was quiet for a moment, wiping her tears away. She was feeling foolish now, calling this poor man and getting him upset. She knew that there really wasn't anything he could do. She would have to handle this herself. She quietly took some deep breaths to calm down, and winced when her ribs hurt.

"Emma, honey, is everything all right?" Chris asked again.

"Yes," she lied. "I just needed to hear your voice again. It's been a long time - too long." It was all she could think of.

"Where are you?" Chris asked.

"I live in Oregon, on Chehalem Mountain, just outside of a small town called Scholls. I've missed you, Chris." She was glad her voice sounded calm and in control now, in spite of her body shaking.

"I've missed you, too," Chris said with a sigh. "Why don't you give me your address and phone number. Maybe I'll get a chance to come out and see you soon."

She gave him the information, not knowing that George was writing it all down for Chris.

"Emma, Fred said your name is Jacobs. Did you get married?"

"Yes."

"Is he a good man?"

Emma was silent. What could she say? How could she tell Chris that her husband had just raped her and that she wanted him dead?

"Yes," she lied again.

"That's good," Chris said.

"Well, I'd better be going now." Emma wanted to get off the phone. She was now beginning to see that this phone call was pointless. She needed to take care of herself, to be on her own. That was what she'd wanted when she left Indiana. *You can't go back*, she thought to herself. She straightened her shoulders, finding her own strength again. She took a deep breath, ignoring the pain in her chest.

"I'll call again sometime," she said, not sure if she ever would.

"OK, Emma. It's good to hear your voice. Thanks for calling."

"Goodbye, Chris."

She sighed and replaced the receiver. Sitting quietly, the only sound was the ticking of the clock on the mantel above the fireplace. She felt numb and alone. She knew her life would go on, but she would never be the same again.

She went back to the small room on the first floor and locked the door. Wrapping herself in a large afghan, she sat in the dark in a rocking chair near the window and hugged herself, letting the tears fall as the sun began to rise.

After awhile, she heard a shot.

◆ ◆ ◆ ◆

Joe stood next to Carlos in shock, looking down at Ted lying on the ground across the narrow meadow from them. They were standing in the same place Ted had been when he'd bagged that big buck almost a year ago.

"What the hell did you do that for?" Joe yelled, turning to Carlos. He didn't know this was what Carlos had planned when he'd suggested going hunting.

"Because you didn't, and we needed to get rid of him. He was getting too nervous for us. Mr. Reichmann wouldn't like it if we were to let some cowboy mess up his plans." Carlos' eyes were cold as he expelled the casing from his gun and picked it up, placing it calmly in his pocket. He would dispose of it later.

Joe's knees began to shake. He'd never seen a man shot before. In the service, he'd been stationed at different bases across the country. He'd never been involved in any real fighting.

"You're going to have to tell his widow," Carlos said calmly.

"Me?"

"Otherwise, she'll suspect something. Tell her it was an accident - that someone else must have been hunting on your property and shot Ted. It's almost the truth." Carlos smiled coolly, as he walked toward where Ted lay.

"What do you mean?" Joe asked, following closely. His stomach turned as they came near the body. He could see Ted's blood seeping through his clothes, his eyes staring up at the pale sky as the sun flashed through the trees.

"I've heard that other hunters will see something move in the woods and shoot, thinking it's a deer. It happens all the time out here, right? Poachers are always ignoring the useless 'No Trespassing' signs people post here. It could have been anyone. We just didn't see anything, got it?"

Joe stood in shock, his stomach beginning to roil.

Carlos looked at Joe and shook him. "Snap out of it, you idiot," he said, slapping Joe across the face.

Joe staggered back a few steps, wiping the back of his hand across his mouth. He looked down again at the body. *Ted was a loser*, he thought to himself. *He had no spine, but he never deserved this.*

Carlos began walking out of the woods. A few paces behind, Joe followed.

When Joe came into the clearing near his house, he saw Carlos walk out of the stable without his rifle in his hand. Joe stood and waited, wondering what to do next. Maybe Carlos had put the rifle in his stable. Joe began to plan how he could get rid of the gun. He didn't want it anywhere on his property.

Carlos first looked over at Joe, then went to his Jeep.

"Get a grip on yourself," Carlos snapped. "Go over to her house in a few minutes and tell her. You hear?"

"Where are you going?" Joe asked as Carlos started the Jeep.

"To get a drink." Then, Carlos drove away in a cloud of dust.

Joe was still numb with shock. Slowly, he walked into the stable and looked around. He went to the tack room and took several swigs from the bottle stashed there. If Carlos had brought his rifle in here, Joe knew now what he had to do to get rid of it and create a diversion in an attempt to minimize the publicity of Ted's death. The whiskey was giving him courage and snapped him back to life. He put the bottle in his back pocket.

He went to the backside of the stable, where he kept a couple of cans of gas for emergency, in case he forgot to gas up his truck when he was in town. He began splashing the liquid over the straw and up the walls of the stalls. Then, he lit a cigarette and tossed the match down next to the straw. The blaze caught quickly and began to spread. He closed the doors to his stable.

As he walked toward his truck, he began to think about how he was going to tell Emma about Ted. His stomach felt warm now, but his hands still shook. He took a long drag off the bottle he still carried to steady not only his hands, but his heart. When Joe thought of Emma, he realized that she was now a free woman. He forgot his fear as he saw himself spending lots of time with her, to help her through her grief. A smile slowly slid across his face as the sun rose over the tree tops and he began to see a small amount of smoke coming from the doors of his stable.

◆ ◆ ◆ ◆

Spring, 1969

Sam stood and looked out of his office window in Baltimore, where an Eastern Redbud was in full bloom. Spring on the east coast was beautiful, but it came much later than Oregon's. He picked up the telephone as it rang.

"Sam Parker here."

"Sam, this is Jim."

Sam hadn't heard from Jim Barolio in months. "Hey, how've you been? How's the family?"

"Great. Nancy and the kids are great," Jim said.

"You still working for the Racing Commission?"

"Yeah, but since Nancy and I took over the airport in McMinnville, I've been thinking it's about time to start looking at retiring from it." Jim was quiet for a moment.

"What's up, buddy?" Sam could tell by Jim's voice that something was on his mind.

"You know about George Mason's missing Derby winner?"

"Yeah, I've been working on that case ever since last June. Why?"

"Can you tell me about the evidence that made Mason's trainer suspicious?" Jim asked.

"Fred Jamison thinks the horse was swapped with a good look alike sometime after the Derby, probably that same night, in the shedrow at Churchill Downs. They didn't detect it until the Belmont race. We've been looking into every horse that was registered to race that day. There's one that has simply disappeared - Frank's Revenge from Venezuela."

"But, wasn't the lip tattoo on the imposter correct?" Jim asked.

"Yeah, the tattoo was right. That's what's so screwy. Jamison had said the horse ran the Preakness and won, but a groom said he wasn't running the same way. Jamison and Mason had gotten so wrapped up in the possibility of winning the Triple Crown, they blew it off."

"What triggered them at Belmont before the race?"

"Mason finally listened to the groom who still insisted there was something different with the horse. A blood test was ordered."

"What were the results?" Jim asked, but he figured he already knew the answer.

"The test showed that the imposter they had was sired by Koenig, the same sire as Koenig's Wonder, but from a different mare - one that belonged to some guy in Venezuela..." Sam stopped. He took a long, slow breath, then said, "Oh, my god."

"Sam, what is it?"

"I just remembered something. I was at Mason's when Koenig's Wonder was born. There was a new colt in the next foaling stall that was owned by a Venezuelan, but that colt had no white star. He had no markings on him."

"Can you check on it?" Jim asked.

"I'll call Jamison right away. Oh, and one more thing. When I asked Jamison to check the forehead of the imposter, he found that the hair had been bleached using something like freeze-branding - a process that destroys the color producing pigment within the hair follicle, resulting in white hair growing at the brand site. Because the brand was just like Koenig's Wonder's star on his forehead, Fred thought they'd probably had someone inside to be able to get the brand so exact and had used liquid nitrogen. What's this all about Jim?"

"Yesterday, our office in Portland received a tip from a vet out here near Newberg who thinks he's seen Koenig's Wonder at a riding school."

"Who's the vet?" Sam asked.

"Emerson White."

"Jim, I know him. He knows his horses. Remember, he was my dad's vet up until a few years ago. Where's this riding school?"

"In the Chehalem hills, outside of Scholls. I thought you might want to come out here and help us on this one, since you know so much about the case already."

"What kind of school is it?"

"Dressage."

Jim was quiet for a moment. He knew that Sam was thinking the same thing he was. "What a great place to hide a stolen Thoroughbred race horse, huh?" Jim said.

"None better that I know of."

"What're you flying these days?" Jim asked.

"I bought the Shrike Commander from the Bureau when they were talking about retiring her. I've logged so many miles in it, I hated to part with her. I'll clear everything and fly out tomorrow."

"Good. It'll be great to see you. Let me know your arrival time, and I'll meet you at the airport."

"Jim," Sam said, before hanging up. "Who owns the riding school?"

"Emma Jacobs."

PART THREE

CHAPTER THIRTEEN

Spring, 1969

Music filtered through the hallway of the Portland tower building as Emma approached the club. Being with her friends for dinner at the Beaumont Hotel only reminded her how lonely her house would be when she returned. It had been six months since Ted's hunting accident, but she'd grown used to being alone. Her husband had been dead to her long before he was killed, but for some reason she was restless tonight. She hadn't felt like this in a long time.

The club was warm and crowded with various people sitting at the tables after finishing their dinner, watching the musicians, talking amongst themselves, laughing, drinking, sharing. The bar and stools were polished, dark mahogany wood. Emma knew the designer of the club. He had found these magnificent pieces in an old building downtown and salvaged them before the building was demolished to make space for a new office complex. A large mirror on the wall behind the bar, framed in the same dark wood, reflected a copy of Emma back to her. The familiar face reminded her of her mother, her long hair pulled up onto her head, a few strands curling around her face, the same large eyes and long, white neck in a photograph which hung by the door of Emma's bedroom, encased in an oval, beveled-mirror frame. Emma's skin looked like alabaster against the black silk suit. In the mirror, she saw a tall, older man walk into the club behind her and pull out a stool at the other end of the bar. He looked vaguely familiar, but she couldn't recall why.

She sat on a tall stool as the bartender came up to her. He was tall and dark, with broad shoulders and striking gray eyes in his rugged Indian face. He was of the Nez Percé tribe.

"Hi, Emma," the bartender said, placing a napkin on the bar in front of her. "What can I get for you?"

"Hi, Skip. I'd like one of your famous Nudges."

"Great," Skip winked, flashing a bright smile. "I'll make it special, just the way you like it."

"Thanks."

Emma had gotten to know Skip since last Christmas, when she and her friends, Jennifer and Jason Carter, had followed a pianist here after a concert at the Paramount. Jennifer had been visiting her aunt in Portland for the holidays. Since then, Emma came to this club almost every Friday. She remembered her father's ritual of playing cards at Henry Miller's house. She hadn't thought of her father's death for quite some time, until now. Something about the man at the end of the bar reminded her of her father.

She looked around the busy room. Waiters and waitresses, dressed in crisply starched white shirts and black trousers or skirts, bustled in and out of the swinging doors leading to the kitchen, carrying large trays. The luscious smells of grilled salmon, garlic, and wine filled the air as they passed. In the lower level of the room, numerous tables were covered in white linen cloths, with flowers in tall crystal vases and small candles on golden trays. Tall booths, in the same dark wood as the bar, stood on one side of the lower area, where couples were hidden from view. The lighting was soft and warm. A large dais, where the musicians performed, stood next to the tall glass windows. Behind them, colored lights twinkled through the windows, the city just outside.

Tonight was Jam Night. Professional performers passing through the city would occasionally sit in with the local musicians. A flutist was performing a slow jazz melody, the sweet notes weaving through the air like colorful threads of a tapestry, carrying Emma back to when she was young and in love for the first time. That was when Emma had first become aware of her life's dream. The gentle love she felt when she was eighteen for a man she hardly knew had been lost when life separated them, each of them going in different directions.

The music transported her to another time and place, helping her to distance herself from the pain - the result of the choices she had made in her life. The club gave her a place where she could escape into her memories. Chicago was far from Oregon, yet it always remained in the back of her mind to recall whenever she needed an escape from her own reality.

"Here you are," Skip said, his words breaking the spell and drawing her back inside the club. He placed a tall glass coffee mug with a thick crust of caramelized sugar around the rim before her. The blue blaze was still dancing on the dark liqueur's surface.

"Who's playing?" Emma asked Skip, shaking herself from the dream of long ago. She now believed this would never become a reality.

"It's Peter Harrison. He's in town on tour from Chicago."

"What a treat. I thought I recognized his music. He's changed a lot since I last saw him in concert in Chicago years ago," Emma said, shrugging her shoulders and smiling. *But then, so have I,* she thought.

Skip smiled, then went to wait on a couple who had just sat down. Emma noticed the man she'd seen earlier at the end of the bar looking at her, his dark eyes holding hers for an instant, then he looked away. He slowly got up, placed some money on the bar, then left.

Emma turned her stool so her back was to the bar, took off her jacket, and rolled up the sleeves of her white, silk blouse, crossing her long legs. While she watched the musicians, she noticed a dark-haired man walking her way wearing jeans and a crisp blue shirt that matched his eyes. She thought of a lone, prowling wolf – all muscle and bone. He was carrying a brown, leather flight jacket in one hand and a bottle of Henry's beer in the other. Something inside of her moved at the sight of him. She noticed a flash of something that looked like recognition in his eyes as he looked at her, and then, quickly it was gone. The man smiled at her, hesitated for a second in his stride, then nodded as he walked past her. Emma smiled in return. He reminded her of Sam Parker, the one man she could not forget. She brought her hand to her neck and fingered the chain that held the gold locket. When she had first looked into Sam's eyes at Arlington Park, she had felt the same stirring deep in her stomach as she felt just now.

She'd also had similar feelings when she met Ted. But what she mistook for love, she later realized was fear. By the time she knew the truth, it was too late. It amazed her how similar the body's response was to both of these emotions and how easily they were misread, especially when the need for love was so strong.

Ever since Ted's death, she had been living in a fog, unable to find the energy to deal with life. The bills that had swarmed in after his funeral had forced her to see the trail of destruction that Ted had left for her. She'd been forced to sell even more of her property to pay for his debts. Embarrassed, she had withdrawn and closed her training school, hoping that one day she would find her strength again.

When Casey, Joe's friend, had arrived after Ted's death, offering to help her with the horses, she had been thankful to let him take care of everything, sometimes letting the days go by without even going to the stable.

◆ ◆ ◆ ◆

Just at that moment, someone was roughly hugging her. She turned and saw her neighbor, Joe Remsky. Emma had never liked Joe. He had always been overly friendly to her from the moment she had met him, touching her in a familiar way that made her feel uneasy.

"Hey, Emma," Joe said. She could smell the alcohol on his breath, and his eyes were glazed from what he'd already consumed. She had seen that look before in Ted's eyes when he'd returned home from a night out with Joe. Her stomach tightened as she remembered those nights when she had learned to fear and despise her husband.

"What are you doing here, Joe?" Emma asked, releasing herself from his embrace.

"I just stopped in before heading home," Joe answered. He'd just come from another bar, but had struck out with one dark-haired lady and was still hungry. He thought that perhaps his luck was about to change.

As Emma turned back to the bar, Joe put his arm on Emma's shoulders, looked at her again and smiled.

"What brings you into the city?" Joe asked.

"I had dinner earlier with some friends. They wanted to go somewhere else for dancing, so I came here instead," Emma said as she wriggled free of Joe's arm. She wasn't about to tell him that her friends had been other dressage judges and it had been a business dinner. "What have you been up to, Joe?"

"Busy," he said, lighting a cigarette. He moved to the end of the bar next to her and sat down, making sure his shoulder rested against hers. Skip walked over to Joe.

"Shot of Jack Daniels," Joe said to Skip, then turned to look around the room.

"Skip, could I have a glass of ice water, please?" Emma asked, moving away from Joe.

Skip nodded to Emma and turned away.

"I haven't seen you since the fire," Emma said to Joe. She thought of the night that his stable had burned - the night of Ted's death. Joe had just arrived at her house to tell her about the accident. They were in the den when she'd seen the light of the fire in the sky from her window. By the time the fire trucks had arrived, the building was a total loss. She had been glad that there were no horses in it.

"I've been busy," Joe said. "I was hit pretty hard when that happened, but the insurance just came through," he lied with a grin, thinking of the cash that was about to come his way when this job was finished.

"Are you going to re-build?"

"I thought so - at first." Joe thought of the night he'd set the fire himself. He made the mistake in thinking he was getting rid of the gun that Carlos had used on Ted, but Carlos still had it. Joe had recently seen the rifle in Carlos' room in Emma's stable. Joe sat steaming, looking into his glass. He was still pissed off that Reichmann had insisted that Carlos, not he, go over to Emma's a few days after Ted was shot, using the pretense of helping her with the horses on her ranch. The Venezuelan slime-ball was living in her stable now.

"But, that's all changed now," Joe added, thinking of Reichmann's phone call yesterday. "I'm celebrating tonight!"

"What's the occasion?"

"I made a great deal yesterday." Joe slugged down his whiskey in a big gulp, and motioned to Skip for another.

"What's the deal?" Emma asked.

"It's the craziest thing," Joe continued. "Your man, Casey, came over to my place with some information about an old German fellow from South America. The foreigner had told Car..Casey that he was interested in buying my ranch - sort of a winter hunting spot."

Joe stopped and looked at Emma.

"I'm sorry," he said, placing his hand over hers. Joe had been using Emma's grief to get closer to her. His sincerity was only a mask, but he hoped she'd eventually fall for it.

Emma shook her head and looked away, pulling her hand free. She had learned to harden her heart toward Ted, and she hated the fact that she was glad he was dead.

"Casey is not my man, Joe," she said, looking back at him. "After all, you were the one who sent him to help me on my ranch after Ted died."

"The price was right," Joe said, getting back to his deal. "It's been a real struggle for me, since the fire and all," he said, putting on a hurt face.

"You didn't sell, did you?" Emma thought of her own ranch. It had almost killed her to sell the acres it took to pay off Ted's debts. She couldn't imagine selling her home.

"Yep," Joe said, turning on his stool to face Emma, touching his knee to her thigh. *God, she's beautiful*, he thought. *I'd give anything to get my hands on her.*

"I should get the money in a couple of days," Joe continued. "With the insurance money, and now this deal, I'm going to be sitting pretty again." None of this was true, but he knew Emma would never find out - not until he was ready.

"What are you going to do with your horse?" Emma asked, moving her leg away from Joe's. Frankie was still in her stable.

"I'm taking him with me."

"I thought you had a buyer for him?"

"Nope - that deal fell through. He's mine now, and we're going to be leaving soon."

"Where are you going?" Emma asked.

"Someplace warm." Joe looked at Emma over his glass with a strange grin on his face. "You could come, too," he said.

Joe took a drink, then stopped, his glass held in mid-air. His face turned white as he looked past her. He set down his drink and swiped the back of his hand across his mouth. Emma noticed his hand was shaking. She looked up in the mirror and saw the man that had walked past her earlier. He was walking up behind her, wearing his jacket.

"Sam," Joe said, quickly standing up, looking as if he was about to bolt. "Where the hell did you come from?"

As Emma turned, the man had pulled out the stool next to her and stood looking down at Joe. *Could this be...* she wondered. She noticed Joe was nervous as he sat back down, but the man continued to stand, towering over Emma as he continued to look at Joe. Emma saw the fire in the man's eyes, which had brought a shiver up her spine.

"I just flew in from Kentucky," the man said in a low, husky, voice. Her body stirred deep inside her belly at the sound of it, and she knew. He looked down at Emma and smiled a slow, deep smile that lit his entire face, causing dimples to appear in his square jaw. The light overhead danced off of his dark hair.

"Hello, my name is Sam Parker," he said to Emma, extending his hand to her. Emma Jacobs had been his target tonight. It was a bonus that he'd run into Joe Remsky as well. Sam noticed the smell of lavender perfume coming from her, a smell that he remembered from his past. Then, he saw the necklace she wore.

Taking a deep breath, Emma tried to keep her hand from trembling as she took his hand.

"Hello, Sam," she said, a little breathlessly. "It's been a long time. I'm Emma Jacobs. My name used to be Maseman." Her thoughts and heart raced. She had dreamt of this moment all her life. Now that it was here, all the things she had rehearsed in her dreams disappeared. All she could think of was the feeling of her hand in his again.

"Then we have met before," Sam said, still holding Emma's hand. Jim had told him that Emma Jacobs came to this club on Friday nights, and he'd been waiting for her. When he'd first walked passed her, he'd been stunned. *It can't be*, he'd thought. He was afraid she'd seen the recognition in his eyes, but he'd tried to cover it up. Now, here was the woman he'd fallen in love with twelve years ago, and he was investigating her in connection with the theft of Koenig's Wonder.

"How do you know Emma?" Joe asked Sam nervously and signaled the bartender for another shot. He'd hoped he would never see Sam Parker again. Parker could be trouble, just when he didn't need any.

"It was at Arlington Park - a long time ago," Sam said with a twinkle of secrecy in his eyes for Emma. He released Emma's hand and picked up his beer, holding her eyes with his as he sat down next to her.

Emma quickly looked, but there was no wedding ring on his finger. *That doesn't mean anything*, she thought. *A lot of men didn't wear their wedding bands after the ceremony.* She remembered that Ted had used the excuse that it was dangerous in his line of work.

"Yes, I remember," Emma said, knowing she had never been able to forget it. "How have you been, Sam?" Emma asked, not sure if she really wanted to hear.

"Oh, I've had some highs," Sam said, then he looked at Joe. "And, a few lows." This was the first time Sam had seen Joe face to face since the race at Del Mar. There was a lot of unfinished business between them.

Joe looked away, hoping Emma hadn't noticed the panic in his eyes.

Sam flashed a broad smile toward Emma that lit his entire face, his deep dimples revealing a slight mischief in his nature. Emma remembered that smile – and the mischief.

Questions hung in the air, but Emma didn't want to ask them in front of Joe.

"How do you know Emma, Joe?" Sam asked, looking again at Joe. He was surprised that Joe was in Oregon, since he'd simply disappeared from the racing circuit. Sam was praying that Joe didn't know about his job in Baltimore with the Racing Bureau.

"Her husband and I were friends. Her ranch is across the road from mine." Sam noticed Joe's hands still shook as he lit another cigarette and smiled.

"So, what type of ranch do you have?" Sam asked Emma.

"I own a dressage riding school, but also board horses when necessary. I only have a few now, but it helps to pay the bills."

"Are you into racing Thoroughbreds, like Joe here?"

Emma looked at Joe. She knew he had boarded a Thoroughbred, until he'd brought Frankie to her ranch. She knew that he'd been a jockey before, but realized now that she knew very little about him.

"No," Emma said, turning back to Sam. "I train Lipizzaners and retired Thoroughbred racers in dressage." She stopped and looked away. "I've temporarily closed the riding school."

"Why?" Sam asked.

"Sam. What are you doing now?" Emma quickly changed the subject, beginning to feel uncomfortable and overwhelmed.

Sam knew a side-step when he'd seen one and decided to let it go, for now. He looked over at Joe, smiled, and saluted with his beer. "I'm in business for myself, like you and Joe. Let's say I search for that which is lost."

Then, once again his eyes searched deep into Emma's and held her suspended for an instant. Sam saw a pain in Emma's eyes that had not been there when he'd last seen her. It pulled at his heart to know that somehow she'd been hurt.

Something that Joe said bothered Sam. "Joe, you said Emma's husband and you 'were' friends. What did you mean?"

Joe looked into his glass. "Ted was killed last fall."

"Oh, I'm sorry," Sam said, looking at Emma. He wondered if that was the reason the school had been closed.

"Thanks," Emma said, unsure of what else to say. She had seen the true feeling of sympathy in his eyes. *What do you say when someone you wanted dead is killed?*

There was an uncomfortable pause.

Then, Emma stood up. "If you two will excuse me, I need to powder my nose." Since Sam had touched her, her heart had been racing inside of her chest, and she needed some space to breathe, to step away from him for a moment.

◆ ◆ ◆ ◆

Sam watched as Emma walked away, her broad shoulders swaying slightly with each step, her dark head held high. She had changed since he last saw her and grown into a fine-looking woman. She still had the qualities that first attracted him - the self-assuredness and sweet calmness, but she'd lost the innocence.

"Wow," Sam said, not realizing he'd spoken out loud.

"Yeah," Joe said, watching Sam. "Watch out though," he said to Sam with a look of warning. "I heard she has claws like a cat. Myself, I like 'em that way."

Joe turned to look around the room, as if he was looking for someone. He couldn't figure why Sam seemed so cool. Maybe he didn't know about the drug used on Ele. Joe looked at the door of the club and wanted to bolt.

"What brought you back to the Northwest, Joe?" Sam asked. "Last I heard, you were still racing in California." He enjoyed watching Joe squirm in his seat. Sam wasn't ready to let Joe see that he knew about his suspension from racing. He'd learned since becoming an investigator that his own emotions needed to stay in check. Yet, sitting across from Joe, it became more difficult not to smash in Joe's face.

"I left California a long time ago. Figured it was time to settle down."

"I thought I heard you tell Emma you were selling your ranch." Sam liked to play cat and mouse in his investigations.

"Yeah," Joe slurred a little, the alcohol beginning to take over. "Well, it's time to move on." Joe's palms were beginning to sweat.

Sam noticed Joe kept looking into his drink, avoiding eye contact. "Who did you say was buying it?" Sam asked.

"I didn't," Joe snapped, then he saw Sam's eyes. "Some German. He's not from around here."

Emma returned at that moment and sat on the stool between Sam and Joe.

"Well, Emma," Joe said as he finished his drink in one gulp and stubbed out his cigarette. "Are you ready to go home?"

Sam watched as Joe placed his hand in the small of Emma's back and a fire burned in his stomach. Confused, Sam looked first at Joe, and then, at Emma.

"No, Joe," Emma said sternly, pulling his hand away. "But, I think you should."

"Nah, I'm going to go somewhere else and mingle awhile. Maybe I'll find me a sweet young lady," Joe said in an attempt to make Emma jealous and want to leave with him. But, when he saw her smile at Sam, he knew it hadn't worked.

"Be careful, Sam," Joe said, his voice sounding like a warning. Quickly, he put his arm around Emma and kissed her hard on the mouth before she could realize what he was doing. "See ya later, honey," he added with a wink.

Emma sat stunned. It was the first time Joe had ever kissed her. A sick, metallic taste hung on her lips, like when Ted had kissed her after drinking. She took a big drink of water to wash it away.

"Joe, I'll look you up soon," Sam said as Joe walked past him, fighting the urge to get his hands on the man.

"Yeah, you do that," Joe muttered, then walked out of the bar without looking back.

◆ ◆ ◆ ◆

"How do you know Joe?" Emma asked Sam, now that they were alone.

"We were in the Air Force together," Sam said. He didn't add the part about Joe being his jockey. He was too embarrassed.

Both of them watched Joe as he sauntered out of the bar, swaying a little from side to side. Emma shivered as she remembered the many nights that he had brought Ted home after a long night of drinking and gambling.

Sam turned to look at Emma and asked, "How long have you lived in Oregon?"

"I moved here about five years ago from Indiana. After my parents died, I sold the old homestead."

"What happened to your folks?"

"Dad died the summer after my third year of college." Emma was quiet for awhile, then added, "He was hit by a car, while he was walking home from Henry Miller's after a Friday night poker game. He didn't know what hit him. They never found the driver of the car that hit him. I never really believed it was an accident, but could never prove it."

Sam remembered the man in Indiana saying the same thing, but kept quiet.

"I quit college," Emma continued, "and stayed home to continue Dad's work with the riding school. Mom didn't like it because she was afraid I was repeating what she had done when she quit her music studies to marry Dad. I finally convinced her that I was doing what I truly loved. She died a few years after Dad. I kept the ranch for a while, working with the horses. Then, I finally sold it to a man who had been one of Dad's young students. I brought our horses here with me."

"I'm sorry to hear about your folks," Sam said as he laid his hand on Emma's arm. "I liked your dad."

In the soft light of the club, Emma could see true heart-felt emotion in Sam's eyes. "Thanks, Sam." Emma hadn't realized how much she missed her parents until that moment, with Sam sitting next to her as a reminder of a time she had treasured with them. Her heart ached and she had to look away for awhile, pretending to listen to the music. She wiped away the tear that had fallen.

Sam was silent. He had noticed the change in Emma, so he took away his hand and sipped his beer. Turning to face the musicians, he saw that they had returned from a break and a young trumpeter was playing his slow rendition of "What's New?" Sam thought that Clifford Brown would be proud to hear this kid playing it with similar feeling.

"What made you choose Oregon?" Sam asked when the music had stopped. "Your husband?"

"No. I didn't know Ted then. I guess it really was because of you..." Emma began. She stopped for a moment, watching Sam's reaction as he looked at her. She smiled and quickly added, "You had said in Chicago that I'd like Oregon. And, Jennifer, a friend of mine I met in college, grew up in Portland. She kept telling me how beautiful it was, so I decided to see for myself."

"Does your friend still live here?" Sam asked. He noticed her brown eyes had lost some of the sparkle he had fallen in love with in Chicago. She had done more than grow up in those twelve years since he'd last seen her.

"No, Jennifer moved to northern Montana two years ago." Emma laughed, then added, "She said there were too many people now in Oregon to suit her." Having lived in Chicago where there was little open space left, Emma saw the irony of her friend's words. Exploring the undeveloped land in Oregon was one of the pleasures Emma found after moving here.

◆ ◆ ◆ ◆

Just then, a slim, young woman came up to Sam and hugged him. Her beautiful, blonde hair hung down her back to her hips.

"Hi, Sam, honey. Where have you been?" Her voice was sultry and heavy with a Southern accent.

"How are you doing, Sally?" Sam looked a little awkward for the first time that evening.

"Going crazy without you, darlin'," Sally said as she gave Sam a peck on the cheek. Then, she walked away to join another woman, sitting at a table across the room. The red-head waived at Sam and winked. Sam smiled at the woman, then he looked at Emma.

"I'm sorry, I should have introduced you. That's Sally Bridges. She, um, works for me." Sam took a nervous sip of his beer, then said, "Will you excuse me for a moment?"

Without waiting for a reply, he got up and walked to the blonde. He leaned over to talk to Sally for a moment, while the other woman at the table smiled up at him.

"Sally, what the hell are you doing here?" Sam asked. "You're going to blow my cover."

"Sorry, Sam, but Jim called and wanted me to get in touch with you." Sally took a long fingernail down Sam's arm as she spoke, looking over at Emma.

"How did you know I'd be here?"

"Jim told me where to find you."

God, she thought, *this man is so beautiful.* Sally was Jim Barolio's assistant at the Racing Commission office in the northwest portion of the city. It wasn't the first time Sam had used Jim's office as his motel, since it had a small bath and couch. Sally had hoped to join him on that couch some night, but when she saw the look in Sam's eyes as he turned his head toward Emma Jacobs, she knew she didn't have a chance. This man was off the available list, but she would never stop trying.

"What did Jim want?" Sam asked, irritated when Sally ran her high-healed foot up his calf and looked at him with her green eyes.

"He'd like you to fly to McMinnville tomorrow to see him. He said he has some information for you." Sally smiled her sweetest smile and licked her lips seductively.

"Okay, thanks for telling me. Would you call Jim for me and tell him I'll be there around noon?"

Sally nodded with a pout.

"Are you going back to 'work' now, Sam?" she said, putting on more Southern in her already sultry voice.

Sam only shook his head as Sally and the other woman began to laugh.

◆ ◆ ◆ ◆

Seeing Sam talking to the two women, Emma wondered if Sam spent a lot more time in the Portland area than he had led her to believe. She became upset with herself when she saw that she was feeling a twinge of jealousy. She shook her head, a gesture she had often begun to use to clear her mind of some unpleasant thought and turned once again to watch the performers. Her past with Sam had told her that he could not be trusted where other women were concerned. However, she was an adult now, capable of making her own decisions and coming to her own conclusions. She saw him walking back to where she sat.

"You're still quite the lady's man, aren't you, Sam?" Emma asked when he returned.

"Well, I know a lot of people in town." Sam looked at her very seriously with his keen eyes. He couldn't tell her the number of times he'd been in Oregon to investigate some gaming crime.

"I see that some things never change," Emma said, remembering the woman waiting in the cab for Sam in Chicago.

Sam looked at Emma. "Are you ready to leave?" he asked. Her words had stung, but he wasn't sure why. He wasn't proud of his past, or what he was doing now. He had a horse to find.

Emma thought for a moment. She was afraid to repeat history. But, she was more afraid she'd never see him again.

"Yes."

Sam laid some bills on the bar as Emma retrieved her jacket. Then, he guided her out into the night air.

"Do you feel like a walk?" Sam asked.

Looking at the sky, a few stars faintly winked atop the buildings through the lights of the city. As Sam helped her into her light jacket, Emma nodded in reply. She wasn't quite ready to let Sam go after all of these years. Sam took her arm, leading her through the city like a man with a purpose, walking toward the waterfront.

Weaving through the air was the sound of a solitary saxophone, the melody revealing the soul of the man who gave it life. There was a sadness to the tune, of lost love and beauty.

The sidewalks had recently been washed by rain, leaving a clean smell in the air. The tall buildings towering over them were like a warm blanket of strength, promising safety, yet somehow maintaining a distance with their many eyes closed for the night.

After she'd first arrived in Chicago years ago, Emma had felt a sense of freedom she had never known. Everywhere she looked, there were people of every race and walk of life busy with their own lives, not caring what she was doing. She had then realized this feeling stemmed from growing up on a farm near a small town where everyone knew everything about her.

She'd quickly learned that the city was a double-edged sword - freedom on one side and on the other were people who trusted no one, living in fear. She had seen the blank faces of those who became lost in the city - the vague, blank stare of abandonment, their walk a shuffle from one meaningless place to another in search of survival while a buzzing society danced around them, almost through them, as if they did not exist, except when they stopped a passerby to ask for some change. On rare occasions, Emma had looked into the eyes of these lost souls and saw a flicker of light. She'd found that if she smiled first, she might receive a smile or a nod in return. It was at that moment Emma would see hope, but it never lasted long.

During the summers, when Emma was home in Grandview, people in the little diner would turn to her as she walked in and smile, as if they were glad to see her, saying 'Hello' and asking about her parents. She had missed that when she was in the city. In Scholls, near her ranch in Oregon, she had once again found that same sense of community.

"Penny for your thoughts," Sam said next to her.

"Oh, I was just thinking about the city, and home." Emma freed her arm from Sam's hold, raising her hand to her hair and tucking a loose strand back under a pin.

"Care to share? " Sam asked.

This had been a question he had asked her once before, when they were walking the streets of Chicago. They had shared their dreams then, but that was a long time ago.

"I was thinking about the differences between living in the city and my home town. I've come to the conclusion that our beginnings affect our decisions later in life, when we are ready to make our own choices where we choose to live. Sometimes, we come full circle, returning to what we were raised with. It may not be exactly where we started, but it's similar."

"I know what you mean," Sam said, his pace slowed as they came to a stoplight. Waiting for the signal to change, he added, "I've flown almost everywhere in the world, and I've lived in Baltimore now for about a couple of years, but I miss home." Sam winced as he thought of his 'pilot for hire' days in New York.

"Baltimore? I thought you said you came from Kentucky."

"I had to go to Louisville before coming here, but my office is based in Baltimore." He didn't tell her about the stop at Essen Farms before flying to Oregon. He'd wanted to talk to George Mason and see the imposter horse. He still couldn't believe that colt had the same tattoo as Koenig's Wonder. Sam had been surprised when George wasn't at Essen Farms.

"Are you still in the service?" There was so much more that Emma wanted to ask, but was too afraid.

"No. I retired from active duty in '65."

"Do you still fly?"

"Affirmative. I'll never stop flying. So, do you still paint?" Sam asked, wanting to change the subject. The light changed and they continued walking.

"I do, when I get a chance. Not as often as I'd like, sometimes."

Emma thought how she had let her art slide over the years, but she had returned to it, after she'd begun to see the truth about Ted. It became her escape into the world she really wanted, not the world she was in.

"I'm currently working on a painting of my father and his Lipizzaner stallion from an old photograph. He was the stallion my father brought from Germany." She didn't add that she'd been working on it for years, but couldn't seem to bring herself to finish it.

While the city was still afire with the lights of the night, they walked out to the edge of the dark river. The lamps on the walkway and the full moon shining through an opening in the clouds above were their only light in the damp night air. The warmth of the spring day was being overtaken by the leftover evening winter winds across the water, not yet willing to fully yield to the new season.

Pausing, Emma turned to look at Sam's face. His hair was full and curled just above his collar, and brushed back on the sides above his ears. A dark curl fell over his high forehead and gently brushed across his large, blue eyes. His high cheekbones and the long slant of his nose, gave his face a long, lean look. His soft lips in the square jaw were pulled in a straight line, as if he was deep in thought. He was leaning on the railing on his elbows, looking out over the water to the lights on the east side of the river. She decided it was the time and place.

"What happened to you after Chicago, Sam?"

"Well, some of it you already know. After college, I learned to fly jets in Arizona."

Emma nodded.

"I went to Texas for my first commission. Then, I was sent to Vietnam." He didn't mention Susan or the long hours of waiting for the call to man their planes, the fear in each man in his unit, the ugliness of war he'd witnessed.

Emma saw Sam's jaw tighten, but she remained silent.

"Then, I grew up," Sam continued, with a long sigh. "I returned to help my folks on their ranch near Eugene for a while. Dad had bought a filly for me and we trained her to race. I began racing her at Portland Meadows, and she was very good. She won a lot of races - while I had her." He didn't want to mention his last race with Ele, and he changed the subject. "When I was younger, Dad used to work as a trainer for a doctor from Seattle with more money than sense. The man bought horses at auctions and expected Dad to train them to race. I went with Dad on the racing circuit through the Northwest. He's an incredible man."

Sam was quiet for a while, looking out over the black water. He could see the small boats in the harbor on his right. A large stern-wheeler was beginning its evening journey down the river in front of them.

"Are your folks still living in Eugene?" Emma asked.

"Yes."

Her mind quickly switched back to her silly impulsiveness that had caused her to drive to Eugene in search of Sam, only to learn that he was getting married. She wasn't ready to ask that question just yet.

"What happened to your horse, Sam?" she finally asked.

It took Sam a long time to answer. He still wasn't used to hearing himself say it after all this time. "I lost her - in a claiming race."

They stood for a moment in silence, leaning with their elbows on the railing, both within their own thoughts of home and life and their mistakes.

"Are you married, Sam?" Emma finally asked.

"No," he said. Emma watched him as he looked out over the water. In the faint light, Emma could see the muscles in his jaw twitch again as his mind worked on something in his past. Highlights in his dark hair were caught by the lamp overhead.

Sam wouldn't tell Emma that every girl he had ever met never compared to her. He looked over at Emma and saw her shiver, wrapping her arms around herself.

"You're cold," he said, taking off his jacket and wrapping it around her shoulders.

"A little," she replied. She loved the smell of the leather and the weight of the heavy jacket. Then, she was glad when Sam left his arm around her shoulders.

"Did you ever think about getting married, Sam?" Emma felt brave enough now to ask. She felt him stiffen next to her, but she watched his face in silence.

Sam thought for a moment, then said, "I came close once. But, at the last minute, I knew that I was really looking for someone else, and it wouldn't have been fair to her if we had married and discovered our mistake later."

Emma stared out over the water. "Unfortunately, I made that mistake."

"We all make mistakes," Sam said, looking at her. "That's part of life." He was quiet, then added, "It's what we do with those mistakes that's important."

He tightened his arm gently to turn her to him. "I see you're still wearing my necklace," he said, his fingers toying with the chain.

"Yes, it's become…" *my shield*, she almost said. "It's one of my treasures."

His eyes pierced hers and held her. She felt her heart turning over in her breast as he seemed to stare deeply inside of her. She wanted to look away, but was unable. Her breath quickened when he placed his hand under her chin, his face slowly moving closer to hers. His arm tightened now around her waist, and she could feel the warmth and strength of his body. She hadn't noticed that her arms went around his neck, holding him closer to her as if she was sinking in quicksand. When their lips touched, she closed her eyes. Her breath was taken away, and her head began to swim as a wave of emotion flowed over her. If his arms had not been around her, she would certainly have fallen. She heard a loud roar, like the crashing force of a waterfall. The wall she'd hidden behind in her mind crumbled at her feet and she was carried by a ribbon of time, penetrated by the gentle, silent rainbow of colors encircling them. After what seemed an eternity, Sam lifted his lips from hers. When she opened her eyes, he was smiling down at her.

"Are you all right?" he asked, his eyes twinkling.

"I-I think so," she stammered, placing her hand to her head. The kisses she remembered from Chicago did not have this overwhelming effect over her.

He grinned even broader, deepening the dimples in his cheeks. He held her close. Then, he reached up with one hand and stroked her long, dark hair.

"I've wanted to do that for a long, long time," he said on a sigh, his voice a little hoarse. "I remember it from Chicago."

Emma leaned back away from him and looked into his blue eyes. She was suddenly feeling the wall that she had learned to carefully create beginning to emerge again, her protection for when she became unsure of her own feelings.

"Sam, why are you here with me tonight, after all this time?"

He started for a moment and his arm stiffened around her. His face shadowed, and he stopped stroking her hair. He was afraid that somehow she'd figured out about his investigation. He tried to relax and smiled.

"When I first saw you walk into the club tonight, you reminded me of when I'd first met you in Chicago - a young woman with an independent flair and unshakable confidence. All eyes turned to watch you. That's what had attracted me to you in the first place at Arlington."

Emma thought for a moment. The lessons life gave us are meant to help us to grow. If we didn't learn it the first time, another one would come to take its place. Her lesson with Ted was one she had vowed to never repeat. Maybe it was time to repeat a different one from her past. She felt part of the wall slipping away again when she smiled.

Sam pulled her back against him. Her head leaned into his neck, just under his chin, her arms wrapped around him.

"Aren't you cold?" she asked.

"No, I'm fine." The air was cool on his arms, but right now he didn't even care. He'd dreamt of this moment for too long.

They stood quietly in each other's arms and looked out over the water. They watched the lights of the large boat now passing under the bridge that connected the west and the east sides of the city, music coming from the band onboard as the large paddles turned. Fleeting diamonds sparkled on the water's surface from the city's lights in the wake of the boat, while a distant motor from some unseen cruiser drummed in the darkness, like a slow, pulsating, heartbeat. A wind began to blow across the river, stirring the diamonds into a blurry sheen, and the air became colder as the stars disappeared behind a layer of clouds.

"I should be going home," she finally said.

"Yes, it's getting late. I'd better take you to your car. Where did you park?"

"Under the tower - where the club is. Where's your car?" Emma asked.

"I'm staying near here, so I walked. I'm only here for a short while on business." He was now beginning to hate the job he was here to do.

She placed her arm in his and they began to walk in silence. Emma looked inside herself and found her emotions jumbled and confused. People passed by them, jostling them on their way, talking and giggling as they went from one bar to another in search of music and love. *Don't these people realize that a bar is the last place to find true love*? Emma thought to herself, remembering that was where she had met Ted.

◆ ◆ ◆ ◆

After she and Sam arrived at her car, Emma unlocked her door and turned to Sam.

"Can I give you a lift?" she asked.

"No, thanks. I like to walk."

"Thank you for a great time," Emma said

"My pleasure," Sam said with a smile, placing his hand on the roof of the silver Skylark, keeping her from opening the car door. He didn't want this night to end just yet.

"I have to fly to McMinnville tomorrow to meet some friends," he said. "Would you like to join me?"

Emma thought for a moment. She felt that she was making the same mistake she had when she was eighteen, but then a part of her was afraid she'd never see Sam again.

"Yes," she said. "I'd like that."

"I could fly down from Portland and meet you at the Newberg airport around ten o'clock. How does that sound?"

"I think that would be alright. It would give me time to do some work."

Sam pulled open the door. A small light came on inside to light the red interior. Emma turned and handed Sam's coat to him.

"Thanks," she said, looking into his eyes.

"For what?"

"For being you."

"My pleasure." Sam smiled. Then, he took out a pen and a small piece of paper and wrote a phone number on it. "Here's my number in town. Call me if anything comes up." Sam handed her the paper, their fingers touching lightly. Emma remembered another phone number he had given her once before.

Sam looked into her eyes, smiled, then said, "See you tomorrow, Emma."

"Yes, tomorrow."

◆ ◆ ◆ ◆

On the way home, Emma chased the full moon, the open windows of her car letting the cool wind whip through her loose hair. She hadn't left it bound up very long. She looked in the mirror and saw a smile on her face, her eyes glowing in the light from the car's console. She remembered seeing that same look in her eyes when she had returned to her hotel in Chicago, after her first date with Sam. Then, she smiled as she heard her father's voice in her mind saying, '*Tomorrow is another day in paradise.*'

CHAPTER FOURTEEN

The next day, Emma awoke early to a sunny day. Looking out of her window facing east, she could see the pale morning light washing over the hills in the distance. Shadow, her black cat, was curled next to her on the bed. Emma stroked the cat's silky fur, and Shadow mewed softly and began to purr deeply within her warm, soft body. Emma and Shadow had found each other in the back of a bookshop the previous Christmas.

Emma stretched her arms up over her head and sighed. This dreamy feeling had not swept over her in many years and she knew it was because of meeting Sam again. He'd stirred a part of her that she had feared was dead.

She swung her legs over the side of the bed, stood up, and stretched before taking a step. Shadow, stretching along with her, yawned deeply, and jumped off the bed in search of breakfast.

Emma looked at herself in the mirror on her bureau. Looking into her brown eyes, an inner voice began to warn her to learn from her past and not fall so carelessly and easily as she did before with Sam. "Watch out, girl," she told her reflection. "This man hurt you before and he can do it again. Remember your promise!"

While she showered, she imagined herself staying on her guard, watching everything Sam did today. She wasn't going to openly and foolishly trust him as easily as she had when she was young. She'd finally learned that actions were the true meaning behind everything a person did, not what they said. She had fallen once on words alone. *Never again!*

As she dressed before the full-length Bentwood mirror that had been her mother's, Emma saw something in herself she hadn't seen in years - a spark, a light in her eyes and a slight curl on her lips from some hidden happiness buried long ago. She stepped into her work jeans and tucked in a clean, tan shirt. She was proud of her slim hips and knew it was due to her work. After tugging at her boots, she placed her hand in her long, wet hair and tied it back, a gesture she had done automatically for years. Yet, today, somehow it felt different. It was as if someone was watching her this time. Maybe that was what she truly wanted - not to be alone.

She went down to the kitchen to make coffee. Shadow greeted her and curled herself around Emma's legs, purring and rubbing her face against the material of her jeans in a morning ritual. While the coffee brewed, Emma turned and leaned against the counter, her arms crossed in front of her as she gazed out of the window toward the stable. The bright sunlight filled the world outside. The sky was a blue that only appeared rarely in the spring. White, puffy clouds danced in the light breeze and changed their shapes ever so slowly over the green hills in the distance. The young leaves of the dogwoods outside the window shimmered in the sunlight as they waved with the wind. She was looking forward to seeing Sam today.

"Hello. Anybody home?"

Emma groaned as she heard Joe Remsky's voice. It annoyed her that he was so bold to walk into her home without knocking, but he'd done that ever since he and Ted had become friends, even though she'd repeatedly explained to him that she didn't like it.

"In here, Joe," she answered as she poured coffee for herself.

Joe came into the kitchen and gave her a hug, then sat down at the table.

She noticed he was wearing his boots with big heels. She guessed this helped him to feel taller and more of a man. She just shook her head.

"Would you like some coffee?" she asked.

"Thanks," Joe said. "Don't mind if I do."

He smiled at Emma, then slowly licked his lips as he looked her up and down. "You look great today," he said.

As Joe watched her reach for the coffee cup in the cupboard, his body stirred. He'd wanted her from the moment Ted had introduced her to him. He knew she had a fire inside of her, from what Ted had told him, and he wanted to be the man to put it out. Her black hair reminded him of Maria, Carlos Madera's woman.

Joe's gaze made Emma uncomfortable as she sat down at the table across from him. She turned to look out the window.

"What are you doing here, Joe?" she asked, still gazing out the window.

"Well, I came to talk to you about Sam Parker," Joe said, trying to tamp down the ache in his body as he sipped his coffee.

"What about Sam?" Emma said, looking at him now.

"You don't really know Sam like I do. He's a real lady killer, picks them up, uses them, then brushes them aside to turn to the next one - sort of a Don Juan kind of guy, if you know what I mean." He looked at her hand lying on the table and placed his hand on it.

"How do you know Sam so well?" Emma asked, pulling her hand away and placing it in her lap.

"I knew him in the service. Then, three years ago, we worked together for a while. After that, I lost track of him. Emma, he's a drifter and a gambler, lost a horse once - in a bet," Joe lied. "I heard he began drinking, and he was always getting into trouble with a woman somewhere." Joe didn't tell Emma that most of what he was saying was more about himself, and not Sam.

"Why are you telling me all of this?" Emma asked, annoyed with the emotions stirring inside of her. Every red flag that was a warning signal had shown its ugly head, and she clasped both her hands around her cup for stability.

"I just don't want you to get mixed up with him. He's the kind of guy that could hurt you. Besides," Joe continued, taking one of her hands in his hand again, "I feel I have an obligation to take care of you, now that Ted isn't here." Joe had a look on his face she had seen before, the same look when he'd told her Ted had been shot.

Emma's stomach tightened. She pulled her hand away to pick up her coffee cup and take a sip, but she found her throat had tightened. Joe was beginning to make her nervous, but she was determined to get to know more about this small man.

"Didn't you move to Oregon about three years ago?" Emma asked, trying to ignore the ache in her heart at Joe's words about Sam. The wound Sam had left years ago was scarred over, but she was surprised to feel that it was still sensitive.

"Yeah, I got some money...on a race that year and bought my ranch with the winnings," Joe lied again. That, at least, was what he'd told Ted when they'd first met. Reichmann was financing this gig, but Emma didn't need to know that.

"You seemed a little nervous last night when you first saw Sam."

"Me? Nervous?" Joe looked down at his cup and wrapped both hands tightly around it. "I was just excited about the sale of the ranch. I'm glad to be rid of it."

Emma saw his knuckles growing white around the cup.

"Well, I would find it very hard to sell my ranch so easily."

Joe's eyes were bright as he looked up at Emma. "Even if it meant going somewhere new and exotic, with a lot of cash in your pocket?"

"I wouldn't sell for any reason," she said. "I can't imagine leaving the ranch. It's home."

Joe got up and stood next to Emma, looking down at her and touching her shoulder. Chills danced on her skin at his touch.

"You could come with me," he said, smiling at her.

Emma pulled away from Joe and got up. She picked up their cups and walked past him to place them in the sink.

"I've got work to do, Joe..." Emma caught herself, just as she was about to say, *before I meet Sam.*

She led the way to the front door, and Joe followed her. He grabbed his hat from the rack next to the door and put it on. Emma noticed Ted's rifle still standing in the gun rack. The sheriff's deputy had put it there when he'd returned it after Ted's accident. She decided then it was time to get rid of Ted's things.

"Maybe you'll change your mind and come with me," Joe said, running his fingers up her arm.

"Never," Emma said as she pulled away from him, a chill running up her arm where his fingers had been.

Joe's eyes narrowed and his mouth tightened.

"By the way, Joe," Emma said, opening the door. "I didn't know you still raced Thoroughbreds. I thought you gave that up—"

Joe grabbed both her arms and pulled her to him with a wild look in his eyes Emma had never seen before.

"Where did you get the idea I have anything to do with racehorses now?" he whispered in a harsh voice.

"Welll..." she stammered, taken off guard by his anger and his strength. "Sam mentioned it last night."

Joe stood, shaking with fire in his eyes, his grip on Emma's arms began to sting. She tried to pull free, but he only held her tighter and backed her against a wall, his face close to hers.

"Just remember what I said about Sam Parker," Joe hissed, looking deep into her eyes.

He pulled her roughly against him and kissed her. She struggled to pull away from him, but he held her firmly. Panic grabbed her. She didn't close her eyes. She watched his face close to hers and felt her stomach pull into knots. She could see the lust in his eyes as he stared back at her, his tongue forcing her teeth apart.

"Remember that, too" Joe said in a husky voice before he released her. Then, he stomped out, slamming the door behind him.

Stunned, Emma wiped the back of her hand over her mouth trying to erase the sickening taste of the man. She rubbed her arms, which still stung from his surprisingly strong grip. As she walked back into the kitchen, she noticed that her knees were shaking. Joe had scared her, shattering the protective box she'd created around herself.

Emma sat down at the kitchen table, dazed and immobile. Joe's words and actions had thrown her back into another time when a man had come home after drinking. The anger inside of her now stopped her cold, fed by her feeling of helplessness and the need to survive. Ted had died, shot like a deer in the woods, but Emma had found it hard to feel sorry then. She remembered now that she had wished she'd been the one who had pulled the trigger. That same anger was near the surface again. She was afraid now - of herself and what she would do. Was she capable of killing a man? Emma wondered. Could she really pull the trigger?

◆ ◆ ◆ ◆

"Stop this," she said to herself. "Joe's nothing. He can't hurt me now - I won't let him."

Sighing heavily, Emma pulled herself up straight in her chair. She glanced down at an article in the local paper lying on the table. A state policewoman was offering night classes on self protection. Emma decided to sign up. *No one will ever hurt me again*, she vowed silently. Men like Ted and Joe are why those classes were designed. She didn't need a gun to protect herself.

She looked at the clock and realized she needed to shake this from her. *Work*, she thought. *I need to work...to forget.* She stood up and walked to the back door, looking out at the stable and riding arena.

"Stop feeling sorry for yourself, Emma, and get on with it," she said out loud. She heard her mother's voice in her own at that moment. Realizing that everything she now owned was because of her hard work and character. It was as if she had just awakened from a deep sleep. Everything around her seemed crystal clear now. Today, for the first time since Ted's death, she felt ready to get on with her work.

She walked into the den, sat down at her desk, and pulled out the training journal for Conversano Sophia, Gandolf's young colt. She'd bred Gandolf to a Lipizzan mare from a breeding farm in Salem, Oregon, and had nick-named the colt "Sonny." She glanced over her notes she had made the last time she'd exercised the colt, surprised to see the time that had passed. She'd been working on strengthening his hind legs and shoulders, preparing him for his formal training as a dressage performer, as her father had taught her. Her last note showed that Sonny had the same high gait as his sire, but still needed work with his timing. She entered today's date on a clean page and began writing her plans.

When she was finished making her notes, she walked back into the kitchen and grabbed treats for the horses, then walked down to the stable.

♦ ♦ ♦ ♦

As she entered the large building, she was thankful that Casey was nowhere in sight. She was in no mood to talk with him now.

She walked to Gandolf's stall and scratched the white stallion behind his ear. "Hello, dear friend," Emma said. "I've missed you."

He nuzzled her hand as she offered the apple. Emma had learned that her horses were understanding creatures. She'd found them to be patient friends. They would listen to her with their sad eyes, sometimes nodding their heads as if in agreement with whatever she said.

Emma walked down the aisle and past an empty stall. She reminded herself that it was about time she started looking for a new broodmare. She had recently heard of a new Lipizzaner breeding farm near Tualatin. Emma stopped where a chestnut mare stood. She handed the carrot to the mare, which the horse took greedily, while Emma stroked her long neck. Emma had found by accident that the mare liked carrots better than apples.

"Hello, Miss Ele," Emma said softly. "You're looking very fit today."

Emma still wondered why the owner had not come to see his mare. Ele had arrived last January by transport with only a very generous check and a letter, explaining that she would need boarding until the following spring. The letter had said her name was Classy Elegance, but that they called her 'Ele.'

A high-pitched whinny rang out from one of the stalls across the aisle. The mare whinnied back in response. Emma walked over to the stall and saw Frankie, Joe's black colt, standing cautiously at the back of his stall. He was a big animal, with strong legs and shoulders. His sleek coat shone in the light from the window behind him. Emma could see that Casey had already groomed him and replaced his bedding. She had noticed, on the few days she'd gone to the stable that Casey always worked with this colt before the other horses and had wondered why.

"What's up, boy?" Emma asked the dark horse. She could see his muscles relax as he walked up toward the front of his stall. He stopped midway, looking at her, nodding his head up and down, his dark mane flowing with the movement. He pawed at the straw with his right front hoof. When she reached out her hand, he slowly walked up to the gate and ate the carrot she offered him. *He is a cautious one*, she thought.

She turned and stopped at the stall next to Frankie's. Deep in the darkness, at the back of the stall, stood a golden mustang. He raised his head slightly as

Emma placed her hand and the apple slowly over the top opening of the gate. His nostrils sniffed the air, and then he started to walk toward her. He came just within reach of her hands, stretching his neck as far as he could without taking another step closer. His soft lips gently reached to take the extended apple as Emma slowly pulled her hand back a little.

"Dear Flash," Emma said in a soft voice. "Come here, boy. You have to come closer if you want this." She and Flash had been playing this same game since last summer. The mustang was Ted's, and was sometimes very unpredictable. One day he could be gentle as a lamb; another time he'd have fire in his eyes, looking as if he wanted to trample everything in his path. She loved to ride him when he showed the fire; he had so much speed inside of him.

The horse finally took one step, then another, until he was almost up to the gate. Emma let him take the apple, slowly rubbing under his extended chin with her other hand.

"We'll go for a ride later," she promised the horse.

Just then, the young colt across from Gandolf whinnied. Emma walked back up the aisle as he brought his head out over the gate.

"Hello, Sonny," she laughed, rubbing his soft, gray muzzle. His dark coat was beginning to lighten, and he was tall, like his sire.

"Are you ready to get to work?" she asked, scratching the young colt behind his ears. He nodded his head, as if in response to her words. His nose searched both her hands for his treat. When he found them empty, he stepped back and looked at Emma with sadness in his eyes. She laughed and pulled out a carrot from her back pocket. He took the carrot and chewed contentedly.

Emma walked to the tack room and gathered Sonny's training equipment. She picked up the small saddle pad and dressage saddle her father had given her when she began showing an interest in learning to ride.

Walking into Sonny's stall, she placed the old pad and saddle on the horse's back, as if she was going to ride him. She felt him stiffen with the unfamiliar gear. Emma waited for a moment; patiently stroking his neck until she felt him begin to relax. Then, she placed the lungeing cavesson on his head, making sure the throat latch was not too tight. Attaching the lunge line to the cavesson, she let him stand for a moment, caressing his neck as she talked softly to him.

When she felt he was ready, she led Sonny to the outside arena and let him trot at his own pace while she held onto the lunge line loosely. He ran freely, playfully bucking his long legs out behind him as he warmed up, adjusting to the new sensations of the saddle. When he began to slow down, Emma began his work.

The young horse responded easily to her commands and gentle pressure on the line, while she walked farther from him to let out more line as he circled her. Emma pulled her long whip gently on the ground like a snake, encouraging the animal to continue his pace.

Eventually, she said, "Halt," in a commanding voice. The horse stopped. Then Emma walked up to him and praised him. She slowly walked to his other side and started again, walking him in the opposite direction. She noticed he needed more work on this side and watched his feet as she moved him from a walk to a trot to a canter, working toward a cadence in each of the horse's gaits.

After awhile, Emma became lost in her thoughts. Sam's face flashed in her mind and she was eighteen again, back in Chicago and in love. Visions of that time long ago flipped through her mind like pages in a book, each page reminding her of the moments treasured in her heart. Then, she saw visions of her parents' farm in Indiana, her father's face, and heard her mother's music in her mind. She wished she could go back there and hold them again, be held by them again. She wasn't aware of the small tear that had escaped down her cheek.

A warm feeling swept over her as she thought of last night with Sam's arms around her, of his kiss. Then, the image of a yellow taxi jumped into her mind and she began to think about the things Joe had said about Sam. She wondered if they were true. *Had Sam changed that much since she had known him in Chicago? Could she trust him now?* A lot of time had passed since she'd last seen Sam. She had felt at ease with him last night, but there was a lot about Sam she didn't know. Maybe it was time to find out.

Just then, she heard a snort from the young horse. Slowing Sonny down, she walked up to him and praised him again.

"Sorry, boy," she said as she patted his long neck. "I got side-tracked, didn't I?"

She glanced at her watch and noticed it was time for her to change before she drove to meet Sam. She led Sonny back to the stable as a gentle rain fell on them when they walked between the buildings.

"Good Morning, Mrs.," Carlos said, raising his hand out to take the horse from Emma.

Emma jumped. She hadn't seen him come out of his room near the tack room. She had asked him to call her Emma, but he insisted on using 'Mrs.'

"Hello, Casey," Emma said. "Would you mind stripping Sonny down and grooming him? Then, put him and Gandolf in the corral for a while. I have to go meet a friend."

"No problem," he said, his smile crinkling his dark eyes. Carlos liked the way she called him by his alias name. She had no idea who he really was, and he wanted to keep it that way. "How long will you be gone, Mrs.?"

"I'm not sure," she said. "At least a couple of hours."

Emma turned and walked out of the stable, placing her hand up into her hair. She always felt a little awkward around him and wondered if it was his Latin blood that caused it.

◆ ◆ ◆ ◆

Carlos watched Emma leave. He thought she was a beautiful woman, and when she put her hand to her hair like that, his blood rose. He missed his Maria, who was now in Venezuela. Shortly after the race at the Derby, she had left America to return to their home land. He never understood why she needed to go back without him, but she had insisted that her sister needed her. He'd written to her often, but only received her silence. Finally, he'd contacted her sister, but she didn't know where Maria was, either. *Soon*, he thought to himself as he led the two horses to the corral, *I will find my Maria soon.*

After Carlos finished with the horses, he went to his room and picked up the receiver on the phone, dialing a number on a piece of paper next to it.

"Joe," Carlos said into the mouthpiece. "The Mrs. is going to be gone for a couple of hours. I think we need to exercise the colt."

"Sure, Casey," Joe said on the other end with a chuckle. Joe liked egging Carlos on about his alias name. "As soon as Emma's gone, load Frankie up and bring him over. The track may be a little wet, but I don't think it'll be a problem."

Carlos hung up without an answer.

◆ ◆ ◆ ◆

The sun broke through the light cloud cover and was now high as Emma drove west up Chehalem Mountain. The road wound in hairpin curves through the trees, the color of the soft greens brilliant with raindrops against the dark, wet bark, and she noticed the air was cooler under the trees. As she neared the top of the mountain, a grove of apple trees in bloom on both sides of the road burst into view. When Emma came out of the orchard, the valley floor opened below, the air was warm now in the bright sunlight. She saw the steam from the paper mill rolling upwards over the patchwork of farmland below, the blue hills of the Coastal Range in the distance pointing the way to the ocean.

When Emma pulled into the small airport, she saw Sam in his leather jacket, standing outside of a white plane, talking to a short, red-headed man. The man was dressed in greasy overalls and had a short stub of a cigar poking out of one corner of his mouth. The plane behind them stood low to the ground, with wings high overhead, an engine mounted under each wing. A gold and blue streak was painted down the side of the plane, the same colors as Emma's riding school's logo.

Sam waved to her as she parked her car near an office building, a wind sock near the building blowing toward the east. An old golden lab came rambling out of the building to greet her, wagging his tail. She reached down to scratch the dog's ears, then walked to where the two men stood.

He was stunned by Emma's beauty. Her dark hair hung loosely down her back, billowing in the wind against the red silk shirt that was tucked into her black jeans. She carried a short, black leather jacket across her arm.

"Hello, Emma," Sam said.

"Hi, Sam," she smiled.

A yellow single-engine plane flew low overhead. Emma watched as the plane circled and came in low, as if to land. The plane flared over the runway and touched down lightly. Then, the engine roared, and the plane started climbing back into the air.

"What is he doing?" Emma asked Sam, pointing to the ascending plane.

"It's a training flight. He's a student pilot learning to land."

Emma turned to look at the plane circling again to approach for landing, shading her eyes with one hand while placing her other hand on her hip. Sam sucked in a deep breath between his teeth as he watched her. He ached to touch her again, to feel the softness of her lips.

The man standing next to Sam poked him playfully in the ribs and winked at him as he motioned toward Emma.

"Emma," Sam said, after the plane had begun to climb again. "This is Smitty. He's one of the best mechanics around here."

Smitty rolled his eyes and shuffled his feet on the asphalt.

"Hello, Smitty," Emma said, extending her hand to the short man. His hazel eyes looked sharp as a hawk's. A day or two's stubble was on his leathered, tanned face, but his smile was genuine.

"Nice to meet you, ma'am," Smitty said, wiping his hand first on his overalls before placing it in Emma's.

"Please, call me Emma," she said with a smile. "I always think of my mother when someone calls me that."

"Okay, Emma."

"Are you ready?" Sam asked Emma, placing his hand gently on the small of her back. He could feel her muscles tense.

"Yes," she answered, taking a deep breath. "I've flown commercially a few times, but it's been a lot of years since I was in a small plane."

"No problem, Emma," Smitty said, nodding toward Sam. "You're with an ace."

Sam led the way, opening the door for Emma. When he placed his hand on her arm to help her in the plane, a jolt went through his system. The smell of lavender and soap rose up to him as she passed into the interior of the plane. He winked and waved to Smitty, then climbed in himself, closing the door behind him.

Emma was surprised to see how large the plane was inside. There were two seats on each side, curtains in the windows, a long bench seat in the rear, and wooden storage cabinets. She stepped aside to let Sam lead the way to the front. Controls sat before each seat in the cockpit. This was a long cry from the small Cessna she'd been in when she was a child.

"Will there be a beverage service on this flight, sir?" she giggled, as she sat in the seat Sam offered next to him.

"Maybe," he winked with a grin, then checked his instruments. Emma watched as he opened a small window at his side.

"Clear!" he yelled, then waited a few seconds.

"What'd you do that for?" Emma asked.

"To warn anyone walking near the plane, that I'm going to start the engines."

Sam turned the starter switch and the right propeller blades began to slowly turn. The engine caught with a roar, then settled down to a smooth idle. After both engines were running, Sam slowly taxied to the end of the runway in use, then pulled out a clipboard with a printed check list and did a quick check of the engines and instruments.

"Is this your plane, Sam?" Emma asked, a little nervously, holding tightly to the armrests of her seat.

"Affirmative."

"How long will it take us to get to McMinnville?"

"About six minutes, if we go straight there. It takes longer to run up than it does to get there, but it's a ritual we all go through before takeoff," Sam laughed as he replaced the clipboard.

He could see her white knuckles and gently placed his hand on hers.

"Relax," Sam said, smiling before he put on his sunglasses. "I've done this a thousand times. I think you're going to like this ride."

Emma caught her breath. She could feel the tingle of her skin where his hand had been, and his blue eyes had reached deep inside of her, touching her heart. *Oh, dear*, she thought. *I'm in trouble.*

She watched as Sam aligned the plane with the center line of the runway, pointed into the wind and pushed both throttles to full power. The plane responded, running down the pavement until it was airborne, climbing above the trees and into the blue sky. Emma's stomach jolted with the lift, but she loved it. She looked out at the panoramic view of the world in front of her, watching the houses below grow smaller as they climbed. She heard a whirring noise and then felt a bump and looked at Sam.

"Landing gear," he said, grinning.

She had just begun to relax when Sam turned the plane back to the north.

"Where are you going, Sam?" Emma asked, surprised how quiet the engines were. "I thought McMinnville was to the south."

"It is, but I thought I'd take you on a small detour on the way," he grinned, his eyes hidden behind his dark Ray Bans.

Emma looked below them and saw the highway weaving its way toward Portland. Then, she realized where they were headed.

"Sam, are you going to fly over my ranch?" she asked excitedly, forgetting to be nervous.

"Yes."

"Oh, I wish I had thought to bring a camera," she said.

Sam reached under his seat and pulled out a Nikon with a zoom lens. "I always have this with me when I fly," he said with a smile. He liked the anticipation and excitement he saw in her eyes. She was no longer holding so tightly onto her seat, and the sunlight danced in her hair as he circled the plane.

"Now, it's time for your first flight lesson," he said.

Emma's eyes went wide. "Me?" she asked.

"Well, you're the only other one here," he laughed. "I'll control the speed; you just keep us flying level."

"I...don't think I..," her voice quivered. He saw she was holding onto the seat again.

"I'm willing to take the risk," he said.

"I've only done this once before."

"When?"

"I was about ten, in Indiana. Sunday afternoons were usually very lazy, with not much to do. For entertainment, Dad would take me to the small airstrip near our home and pay for rides in the airplanes. Once, a pilot let me take the wheel. I was so excited and frightened at the same time, but loved every minute of it. I do have to tell you we did a nose dive as soon as I took over," she laughed nervously. She knew she was chatting, hoping she'd talk Sam out of it. But, here was another chance for her to fly and she felt as if she was ten again. Her stomach was in knots.

Sam loved to hear her laugh. He smiled and reached over, taking one of her hands and placing it on the wheel in front of her. She felt the movement of the plane through the metal.

"Both hands now," Sam said, placing her other hand on the wheel.

"Watch this dial," he instructed, tapping on the control panel, "and keep that line straight across."

She saw Sam let go of his wheel and hold up his hands, surrendering the plane to her. At first, the nose of the plane began to dive down through the air.

"Pull the wheel gently back toward you," Sam said softly, just as she was beginning to correct the plane herself. "You must have been paying attention when you were ten," he smiled. "I'll make a pilot out of you yet."

She smiled as the plane leveled. After awhile, she began to relax and quickly glanced out the window. She could see the woods west of Joe's ranch on the horizon, with a tall tower poking up through the treetops. Sam began taking pictures out of his side window of an oval clearing that had been cut into the trees.

"What's that?" Emma asked, as she saw the curious clearing in the woods below. Then she quickly looked back at the dial.

"It looks to me like a training track," Sam said. The shutter of his camera rapidly fired as he captured the action below him. The small man and black horse sped around the track, while another man watched from the side rail.

"That's Joe's ranch," she said.

"I know."

"Why do you want photos of Joe's ranch?" she asked.

He thought for a moment. *Be careful, Parker*, he warned himself.

"I figured he might like some snapshots before he sells. Keep her steady," he said, to make her look again at the control panel as he zoomed the lens in closer.

Emma saw the rooftop of her home. Her heart grew with pride as she gazed at the enormous size of the property around it, knowing that it was hers. From the air, it seemed much larger. The bright sunlight glanced off the metal roof of the covered arena and the side of the white stable. When the plane passed over the corral outside of the stable, she saw Sonny and Gandolf look up curiously.

Sam began taking pictures of Emma's ranch, liking what he saw. He had always wanted a ranch of his own, but somehow, life always seemed to get in the way. He knew that his father wanted him to take over the ranch in Eugene, but

Sam was through with racing. Besides, the Bureau kept him moving all over the country. He'd enjoyed it over the years, but this was the first time in his life he wished he was based in Oregon.

The plane continued, it's shadow crossing the land below as they approached the grove of fir trees to the north.

Sam put his camera away, then said, "Okay, I'll take over now."

He took the wheel in front of him and looked over at Emma. She was still looking down at the ranch below. He turned the plane and flew back over it for her to enjoy one more time. Sam never forgot how he'd felt the first time he and Jim had flown over Sam's parents' ranch. He smiled to himself and let her enjoy the view, watching the sunlight on her face.

When Emma finally looked at Sam, her eyes welled with tears.

"Oh, thank you, Sam," she said, wiping her eyes. She smiled and held out her hand to him. He took it gently in his and lightly kissed her palm, tasting the salt from her tears. His heart rolled over in his chest.

"It's my pleasure," Sam said, smiling back at her.

They were quiet for a while. Emma looked all around her as they flew toward McMinnville. Her hand still tingled where Sam's lips had been, and she had clenched her hand into a fist, as if to keep the feeling alive.

She liked the contrast of the bright green fields of winter wheat, against the brown cornfields from last year's harvest, which one farmer had begun to plow under. They seemed to be standing still, as the homesteads and buildings passed beneath them. Emma saw neat rows carved out of the southern hillside.

"What is that, Sam?" she asked, pointing to the rows of plants.

"That's Oregon's largest vineyard," Sam said, as he circled the plane over the grapevines. "About three years ago, a man came up here from California's Napa Valley and started to grow wine grapes on the southern slope of the red hills of Dundee. I understand he lived in France for a while, where he learned that their climate was very much like ours in the Willamette Valley for growing Pinot Noir, a grape that is the same as a Burgundy."

"How do you know so much about wine?" Emma asked.

"A friend of mine back on the East Coast got me started on wines. He's a chef in a great French restaurant. When I was flying over this area a few years ago, I saw what they were doing, so I started asking around. I hear the owner, which is also the wine maker, is about ready to bring out his first bottle. He's going to use a red-tailed hawk on his label, 'for luck' he said in an interview I recently read. I can't wait to try it."

Sam looked over at Emma with a smile and added, "I'm as curious as you are." They both laughed as Sam turned the plane west, the blue coastal range once again in the distance.

"What type of plane is this, Sam?" Emma asked, looking around her inside the cockpit.

"It's a Shrike Commander. I've flown her now for about two years." He was proud of his plane, which was used mostly for his work now, but he loved to take her up and let her cruise. He could get from Eugene to New York with only four re-fuels.

"You said you and Joe were in the service together," Emma said, deciding it was time to get to know more about Sam - especially after this morning.

"When did I say that?"

"In the club. Last night."

"I met Joe in pilot's training at Marana air base in Arizona."

"Joe said that you and he worked together," she continued.

Sam was silent for a moment.

"Yes, he helped me with a horse once."

Emma could tell he was evading her question, but decided to let it go for now.

"Do you fly often?" she asked.

"My job takes me all over the country. It's a good thing I fly myself, because I can't stand commercial planes."

"Just what is your job?" Emma asked.

Sam thought for a few seconds, then said, "I work for an agency based in Baltimore, I fly their staff around the states. It's a company that works on claims." It was close to the truth, but he didn't add that he was one of the investigators, working on a case at this very moment.

"Like an insurance company?" Emma asked.

"Somewhat."

"Is that what you meant earlier by 'finding that which is lost'?"

"Well, sort of," he replied. Emma noticed his manner had become more guarded.

He would not look at her, and he began fidgeting with the instruments. Sam explained to Emma that he was obtaining the local weather and altitude settings by selecting a frequency on his radio, an automated recording that was continuously broadcast. He made the needed corrections, using the plane as a diversion away from his work.

"We'll be landing in just a few minutes now," Sam told Emma. He lowered the landing gear and announced on a common frequency his position and intention to land.

"How long will we be here?" Emma asked.

"I have to meet a friend...about a plane." He couldn't lie to her, but he could hardly tell her the whole truth – not yet.

Emma looked out at the town spreading out from its center, a few buildings jutting above the other rooftops of different colors. Ahead of them was the airport. Emma saw that there was no tower, but there were various runways, one that was very long. A small grove of trees stood near the end of it toward the southwest, like a little island amidst the farmland surrounding it.

Sam banked the plane as he turned to prepare for landing. The runway lights were faint in the daylight, but still visible from the air. Sam came in low, flaring over the runway, then gently set the wheels down. The engines dropped to an

idle as Sam taxied off the runway. Then, he slowly taxied toward a large, flat
building and stopped the plane, shutting down both engines.

Sam helped Emma step out of the plane, and led the way into the airport office.

"Emma," Sam said, "this is Nancy Barolio, my best friend's wife."

The woman's face behind the desk lit up and she looked genuinely glad to
see Emma. She stood, reached out, and shook Emma's hand with a strong,
friendly grasp.

"Hello, Emma," Nancy said, her green eyes shining in her pale face, framed
with curly, blonde hair. The flowing dress that brushed her tanned calves
matched her eyes. "Glad to meet you."

"Thank you, Nancy. I'm pleased, too." Emma immediately felt as if she had
known Nancy all her life.

"Sam, why don't you go out to the hangar and get Jim. He's been working
on a stubborn engine all morning, and I'm getting hungry." Sam nodded, looked
Emma's way to make sure she was okay, then walked out through a side door.

"Well, Emma," Nancy said, as she sat down behind the desk again and motioned to another chair for Emma. "Have a seat. Those two will be awhile."

"What a fascinating job," Emma said, looking at the array of machines and
gadgets around Nancy. "How many planes do you get in here in a day?"

"Oh, it could be anywhere between two and ten. Some of them just stop off
to refuel; others come in on business, or to see what McMinnville has to offer for
fun."

"You mean people fly their planes in search of fun?"

"Oh, sure," Nancy replied, with a smile. "They will fly their planes for almost any reason. Jim says that being a pilot is like a drug. Once you start, you
can't get out of it, you love it so much." She laughed, then added, "When Jim
and I were dating ages ago, he flew me down to Calistoga, California for cheese-
cake. That was a fun date."

The phone rang and Nancy answered it, telling the caller that the office was
only open until six o'clock. While she talked, Emma looked around the office,
seeing a bulletin board with advertisements for motels, restaurants, real estate
agents in the area, and planes for sale. Old photographs of planes that Emma
didn't recognize hung everywhere. One photograph caught her eye, and she
walked over to look at it more closely. She saw Sam's young face smiling back
at the camera. His arm was wrapped around another tall, slim man, both wearing
dark, green flight suits and baseball caps with some insignia on them. They
looked like they were soaking wet and were standing in front of a tall, silver air-
craft, with the Air Force symbol visible on the plane's fuselage. Sam had a long,
white scarf with red dots tied around his neck. She could see pure joy in his face.

"Don't they make a great pair?" Nancy said behind Emma.

"Yes," Emma agreed. "When was this photograph taken?"

"When they were in flight school together, down at Marana. That was taken
shortly after they both had been tossed into the pool, after finishing their solo
flights."

Emma turned toward Nancy. "When did you and Jim meet?"

"At Portland University. I was in an experimental program to commission women in the Air Force ROTC. I became an investigator for the Air Force."

"So, you've known Sam a long time, too?" Emma asked, surprised at the small twinge of jealousy in her heart.

"Affirmative."

Nancy looked around her a moment, then said, "Let's go out to the hangar and round up those two, Emma. We could starve waiting for them." She put on a light jacket and opened the door, leading the way to one of the larger buildings outside.

An older man walked past them, talking to a big man who looked like a mechanic. The older man was pointing to a plane with floats used for water landings and was saying, "But, Joey, with some modifications, couldn't my plane look like that?" The big man, who must have been Joey, just shook his head and continued walking away, while the older man followed, saying, "With some modifications..."

As Emma and Nancy entered the hangar, a small, yellow crop-duster plane stood in the center with various parts lying all around it on the floor. When the two women approached the doorway to a smaller room that looked like an office, Emma heard a man's boisterous voice.

"Sure, Sam, a DC-7 could land here. But, you'd need something that big to fly a couple of horses that far. Those crates take a lot of real estate to take off, but our runway could handle it."

When Emma turned the corner into the office after Nancy, the two men looked up and became quiet. The man sitting at the desk hurriedly shoved some papers into a drawer, then brushed his hand through his dark, curly hair and stood up.

"You must be Emma," the man said, as he smiled and reached out his hand. "I'm Jim Barolio. Sam's told me a lot about you."

Emma looked at Sam as she shook Jim's hand.

"It's nice to meet you, Mr. Barolio..." Emma began, but Jim gently patted her back with a smile.

"Just call me Jim."

Nancy had caught the side glance Emma had given Sam and said, "Well, kids, why don't we all go into Mac and get a bite to eat. I'm starving." She began to lead the way and nodded her head at Jim to follow her.

"Great idea," Jim said, walking out after Nancy. He caught up to her and put his arm around her waist, then led the way to a shiny blue Chevy Impala four-door. Jim opened a back seat door for Emma and waited while she slid in, then closed the door after her. Sam got in next to Emma and smiled at her, squeezing her hand gently in the back seat.

"Where're we going, Jim?" Sam asked. Emma saw the same joy in Sam's face that she had seen in the photograph.

"I thought we'd go to the hotel. It doesn't look like much inside right now, but they make a mean burger and fries."

"Their shakes are my favorite," Nancy added.

♦ ♦ ♦ ♦

Emma looked around as they drove into McMinnville's business district and pulled up before a large square building that filled one quarter of the block. The sign above the main entrance said "Hotel Oregon." A beauty shop occupied a portion of the hotel's main floor. Emma saw the Western Union sign and the Greyhound emblem in the window next to the old double doors of the building as they walked into the hotel's lobby and was reminded of home. A large, tall counter, with a long bench nearby, seemed to serve as the local bus depot. An older couple sat on the bench with their suitcases around them, waiting for the next bus to arrive. Jim led the way through an archway to a snack counter, where silver service, white, porcelain coffee cups, and menus with a picture of the hotel on the cover sat waiting. The smell of French fries and burgers cooking filled the air.

"Hello, Steph," Jim said to the tall, red-headed woman behind the counter. "We brought you some extra mouths to feed."

"Good to see you, Jim. Hi, Nancy. You and your friends are always welcome here," she said with a big smile and a pot of coffee in her hand. "Just let me know when you're ready to order. Can I get you some coffee while you decide?"

"No, thank you," Emma said. Sam nodded that he wanted coffee. Stephanie poured the dark liquid and without asking, filled Jim's cup.

Emma thought the menu was simple, like the one at the small ice cream shop back home. After they'd ordered, she asked the waitress where she could wash up.

"I'll show you," Nancy said and took Emma's arm, leading the way back towards where they'd come in.

While the two women were gone, Stephanie came back to the counter and stopped before Sam. "I forgot to ask your wife if she wanted a milk shake, like Nancy."

Sam sat and stared at the waitress for a moment. He liked the sound of the "wife" part, but it also scared the hell out of him. He thought back to the small diner in Chicago, the second time in his life he'd shared a meal with Emma.

"Why don't you bring her a strawberry one," he said with a grin. "I think she likes those."

"Newlyweds, huh?" Stephanie winked at Sam and walked away before he could respond.

"I like Emma," Jim said to Sam after the waitress had disappeared into the kitchen, enjoying the color on Sam's face.

"So do I," Sam said. His stomach was twisted in knots. The only time that had ever happened to him before was the first time he'd met Emma.

"So, how's the investigation coming?" Jim asked, watching his friend.

"I think the vet may be right, but I still haven't seen the colt. I'm working on a way to get Emma to take me to her ranch..." Sam stopped and looked into his coffee cup, his face sullen.

"I just wish this animal wasn't in her stable. It complicates things," Sam continued.

"Why?"

"Remember the girl I told you about at Marana - the one I met in Chicago?"

"Yeah, why?"

"That was Emma."

"Whoa! I see what you mean." Jim knew how hard Sam had fallen. That girl was all Sam could talk about for months, until one day he simply stopped. He'd never explained why, and Jim knew not to ask.

"We flew over an interesting ranch today..." Sam stopped as the waitress came over to refill his cup.

"Did you know Joe Remsky's in Oregon?" Sam continued after she'd gone down the counter to wait on some newcomers.

"Hell, no," Jim said. "If I'd have known that, I'd go kick his ass. How did you find out?"

"I ran into him last night at the same club where I found Emma. He owns the ranch across from hers."

"Well, hot damn." Jim whistled through his teeth.

"As we flew here today, I took a little sidetrack and flew over Joe's ranch. He's got a training track in the woods behind his house. I saw someone riding a black colt while Joe watched on the sidelines."

"Do you know who the rider was?"

"No, but I took some photos and will give you a call when I get them developed."

"Have you talked to Emerson White yet?" Jim asked.

"No. He was out until tomorrow." Sam looked at his friend. "I may need you to bring in the police if this shakes down like I think it will. McMinnville and Aurora are the only two fields without a tower around here that could take something as large as a DC-7. You know I'm only betting on a hunch here."

"Your hunches are usually right on. Just let me know what you need," Jim said.

"Thanks for letting me use your office..." Sam began, but stopped when he saw Emma returning.

Emma noticed that the men grew quiet as she and Nancy sat in their seats. She wondered why that had happened twice today and felt almost as if she'd stepped into a spy movie or something. Shrugging it off, Emma began looking at the high ceilings and dark wood in the room around her. A large case filled with numerous boxes of cigars stood on one side, next to a wide stairway with dark railings and wainscoting, leading to the upper floors. Four Baldwin-style fixtures hung in the high ceiling, giving a soft, warm hue to the room.

"On the way to the restroom," Emma said, "I saw an old photograph of this building from the outside, the road was unpaved. On one side of the road stood a horse and buggy, and on the other, a car that looked like a Model T."

"This is a great old building," Jim said. "Built in 1905. It was called Hotel Elberton then. The third and fourth floors weren't built for another five years, which made it the tallest building in Yamhill County. It's got quite a history."

"Is it still a hotel?" Emma asked.

"Not since the early sixties. There was a freeze one winter and some pipes burst upstairs, so most of the rooms had to be closed. In the 50's and early 60's, a small family lived on the fourth floor and managed the hotel. They had two boys, one was actually born here. Once, I heard a story about the youngest boy. He played the accordion. One day, I guess he'd found a puppy and brought it home – named it Suzie. When he'd asked his dad and mom if he could keep it, his dad said he had to choose between the accordion and the puppy. The boy chose the puppy."

Emma laughed. It was good to be here with Sam and his friends. She felt so at ease with them.

The waitress came back to refill Sam and Jim's coffee cups.

A photograph that hung on the wall next to Jim caught Emma's eye. It was of an old building with a cupola standing at the top. Tall, white columnar entrances opened on two sides behind the crowd of soldiers in uniforms and nurses in white. A statue of a bronze soldier stood next to the crowd.

"What is that building?" Emma asked.

"That's the old courthouse," Nancy said. "It was destroyed in 1965 and was replaced with a more modern building. I think that was taken when they dedicated the statue to the dead soldiers in WW II."

"Oh," Emma said, "that's too bad that it was destroyed. I love old buildings."

"That old courthouse had a great reputation during the war. Dad told me about civil volunteers who would stand up there," Jim said, pointing to the cupola in the photograph, "and spot planes that flew overhead, identifying them from a chart. When they could identify certain ones, they were to call in to the Portland Air Force Squadron and report it. If the Air Force thought there might be a problem, they would send a couple of interceptors in to check it out."

Stephanie came over to the counter with a tray and placed a tall, silver cup that was frosty on the outside before Nancy, then handed her the chocolate milk shake she had ordered, the tall glass topped with whipped cream and a cherry on top. Then, she set a strawberry one in front of Emma.

"I didn't order this," she said.

"He said you liked strawberry," Stephanie said, nodding to Sam. Sam just smiled. Emma was surprised that he remembered that was her favorite.

"Jim and I grew up together," Sam said, looking at Jim with affection. "Then, we were in the same squadron in the Air Force." Emma looked between Jim and Sam, and realized that the history between them bonded them together for life.

"We trained in T-34's and T-28's together at Marana Air Base, near Tucson,

Arizona. We lived in town because the base was privately run. It was contracted to the Air Force. After we finished basic flight training, we went on to Texas for advanced training. Then, we were given our commissions in Texas. That was before Vietnam." Sam was silent for a moment.

Stephanie came out of the kitchen door carrying four plates, three in one arm, one in the other, and placed them on the counter before the foursome. Hungrily, they dove into their food.

"How long were you in Vietnam?" Emma asked, after awhile.

"Too long," Sam said, then was silent. She could see his face change, and she was sorry she had asked.

"Jim, where was your commission?" Emma asked to turn the conversation away from the pain she saw in Sam's face.

"Sam," Jim asked quickly. "How're your folks doing?"

"They're okay," Sam said into his coffee cup. Emma could see the shadow still on Sam's face, but he didn't seem to want to talk about it.

Sam stood up, put money on the counter and said, "Let's walk for a bit."

◆ ◆ ◆ ◆

They walked out into the sunlight. Across from the hotel, Emma saw the Mack Theater, the large marquee announcing *The Love Bug* currently playing. The building reminded Emma of a theater she had gone to in Rockport, Indiana.

As they walked further down Main Street, they stopped outside of a tavern named the Blue Moon. Emma looked up at the large, blue neon sign, with a star and a moon at the top, advertising two New York steak dinners for $6.95.

They passed numerous shops, looking into the windows. Nancy stopped in front of a shop with children's clothing in the window.

"Jim," Nancy said, "Emma and I are going in here a second. I want to pick up a little shirt for Amy."

"I didn't know you had children," Emma said to Nancy as she followed her into the store.

"We have two."

"What ages?" Emma asked. She liked looking at the small baby and toddler's jumpers and dresses.

"Amy is seven and Josh is four."

"How do you find time to take care of them and work at the airport?"

"A neighbor watches them during the day, and I don't work on Wednesdays. Kids grow up pretty fast, though."

"Yes," Emma said, not sure what she meant, but a small part of her was wishing she did know. She was thirty and knew she wanted children of her own someday. Emma felt her stomach tighten when a vision of children with Ted came to her mind. She took a deep breath and relaxed, thankful that had not become a reality.

Nancy chose a small girl's green blouse. When Emma noticed the airplane logo on the pocket, Nancy said, rolling her eyes, "Amy wants to learn to fly, God help her." They laughed as they walked to the checkout counter.

"So, how are you and Sam getting along?" Nancy asked, waiting for a clerk to return to the counter.

Emma was taken by surprise at her words and stared at Nancy.

"I...guess okay," she answered. "We have only known each other for a short while."

"I thought you knew each other a long time ago?" Nancy asked,

"Oh, yes, but that was for only a few days. We met in Chicago. I was going into art school and Sam was going to the Air Force. We haven't seen each other for many years."

"Well, I know he's pretty taken by you," Nancy said, paying the clerk. "I'm surprised he never looked you up before now."

Emma stood silent, unable to think of anything to say. She then followed Nancy back out to the street where the two men stood near Jim's car. She saw that Sam had a brown bag that looked like it contained a bottle of alcohol in his hand. Her stomach knotted. Ted used to drink a lot. She was afraid that Sam did the same, remembering Joe's words. She tried to relax and tell herself that Sam was not Ted.

"I found a great bottle of wine at a small grocery up the street," Sam said to Emma, when he saw the expression on her face. He was confused for a moment, but was glad when he saw her relax and smile.

"Are we ready to head back?" Jim asked.

They all nodded in agreement and climbed back into the car. Jim then drove them back through the city, past a beautiful college, and out amongst the fields to the airport.

"Well, we'd better get back," Sam said.

"It was nice meeting you," Emma said, extending her hand to Nancy.

"Yes, I had a great time." Nancy first shook Emma's hand, then softly leaned over to give her a hug. Emma hugged her back. "You'll have to come back sometime and let Jim cook his famous lasagna for you. You could meet the kids, too."

"I'd like that," Emma said, then turned to Jim and held out her hand to him.

Jim put his arm around her, surprising her, and gave her a big hug. He felt her stiffen, then slowly relax.

"I'm glad we got this chance to meet," Jim said. "Sam's been talking about you, and I needed to see for myself what a beauty you are."

Emma smiled, but sent a side glance at Sam again. She liked Jim and Nancy, but she wondered what Sam had been saying to them.

"Don't mind Jim," Nancy said, giving her husband a playful poke in his side. "He's that way all the time - doesn't know any strangers."

"Goodbye, you two," Sam said, giving both Jim and Nancy big hugs, placing a quick kiss on Nancy's cheek. "See you in a few days. Tell the kids 'Hi' for me."

"Will do," Jim said, waving.

"Goodbye," Emma said, waving back as Sam led her to his plane and helped her inside.

Sam pre-flighted the plane, fired up both engines, taxied to the active runway, and took off. As Sam circled back around the airport, Emma saw Jim and Nancy still waving. Then Jim put his arm around his wife's shoulder and walked into the office with her. Emma smiled, small tears coming to her eyes as her heart swelled. *That's what I want*, Emma thought to herself, "*that kind of love.*"

CHAPTER FIFTEEN

I t was early afternoon, just before their plane was about to land at the Newberg airport. The sun was still high in the western sky. To Emma's dismay, the return ride had been much shorter.

"Thank you, Sam," she said, smiling over at him. "I had a wonderful time."

"My pleasure," he replied, forcing his thoughts back from searching for a way to get inside of Emma's stable.

Seeing the airport ahead, Sam turned his focus onto his final approach for landing. He dropped the landing gear, then adjusted his glide path. He could see he was coming in too high, so he used full flaps to cut his airspeed. Shortly before touchdown, he cut the power to an idle, so that the plane flared over the runway. Once the wheels were on the ground, he applied the brakes and retracted the flaps.

"I don't like that sound," Sam said as he taxied toward one of the hangars. He turned his head to one side and listened to the hum of the left engine, which he knew purred flawlessly.

"What's up?" Emma said nervously.

"I'm not sure," he said. When he saw the look on her face, he placed his hand on hers and added, "I don't think it's anything too serious. Trust me, Em. I've flown these crates for years and know when it's time to get nervous."

Sam brought the plane to a stop and cut the power.

"I'll ask Smitty to check this out before I take her up to Portland," Sam said, as he helped Emma out of the plane. He knew she didn't have far to step, but he liked the feel of her slim hips in his hands and the softness of her hands on his shoulders.

They walked to the hangar where Smitty stood on a ladder with his back to them, hunched over an engine in a Piper.

"Hey, Smitty," Sam said, his back to Emma. "The Shrike started making a strange noise in one of the engines just before I landed. Could you check it out?" Emma didn't see the wink Sam gave to Smitty.

"Sure, Sam," Smitty said. He stepped down from the ladder, grabbed a rag out of his back pocket and wiped his hands.

"Hi, Emma," Smitty said, with a large grin around the cigar butt clenched between his teeth. He blushed and his eyes had that soft, sad look of a puppy in love.

"Hello, Smitty," Emma replied smiling, shaking her head as she watched Smitty and Sam walk to the plane.

While she waited near the hangar, Emma tucked her jacket over her arm and looked around her. She saw two other open hangars standing against a grove of poplar trees next to the runway, with planes waiting to fly. This was a much smaller airstrip than the one they had just left in McMinnville. Emma recalled their flight over her ranch, meeting the Barolios, seeing McMinnville... It felt like she had lived an entire lifetime in just a few hours, a lifetime she knew she didn't want to end.

"There's nothing wrong with my plane, Smitty," Sam said with his voice lowered, so only the small man could hear. "I just need a diversion for a while."

"Sure, Sam," Smitty said, rolling his eyes in Emma's direction. "I'd be looking for one too, if I was you."

"So, will you make something up for me? Nothing serious, just something that looks like the plane will need to stay on the ground for a day or two?"

"No problem."

Sam got into the plane's cockpit and fired up the left engine. Then, he reached under his seat and pulled out his camera. After taking out the film, he placed the roll in his jacket pocket.

◆ ◆ ◆ ◆

Emma watched the two men. Sam was in the cockpit and Smitty stood outside near the left wing with his hands on his hips, shaking his head. Smitty motioned to Sam to shut down the engine. To her, it didn't seem very long to determine what the problem was, but what did she know? Sam came out of the plane, and the two men walked back toward her, deep in discussion.

When they were near the hangar where she stood, she overheard Smitty say to Sam in a loud voice, "Nothing to worry about. But, I really have to get this other job finished today." Smitty pointed his thumb to the blue Piper that he'd been working on. "The owner wants his baby ready to fly out tonight, so I have to keep on it. I'll call in the part I'll need for yours today. I could have her ready for you in a couple of days."

"A couple of days?" Sam moaned, rolling his eyes for effect. He had a pained expression on his face when he stopped next to Emma, his hands deep in his jacket pockets.

Emma looked at Sam and smiled. "I could drive you back to Portland," she said hopefully. She didn't want to let Sam go just yet, and she had seen how she could do just that.

"Would you mind?" Sam asked. "I wouldn't want to impose."

"Not at all. It'd be my pleasure."

"OK, then," Sam said, then he added, "Wait here, I left something in the plane."

Emma watched as Sam ran back to the plane, went in, then walked back to where she was standing, the brown bag containing the bottle of wine he'd purchased in McMinnville under his arm.

Sam turned and winked at the mechanic. "I'll see you in a couple of days, Smitty." Then, he gave Emma a big smile, which made her knees weak. Shakily, she led the way to her car.

Once they were inside, Sam turned to Emma and said, "I would really like to see your ranch sometime, from the ground."

"It's sort of on the way into the city. We can drive over Chehalem Mountain as a side trip."

"That would be great. Are you sure it's no trouble?" Sam asked, taking a chance.

"Yes, no problem."

Sam sat back in the seat, thinking how easy that had been.

As her car wound up the hills back to her ranch, Emma said, "I like your friends, Sam." She placed her hand on his, which lay on the seat between them. Then, feeling awkward by the familiarity, she pulled it away.

"I wanted you to meet them," he said, grinning. He liked her touch and was sorry she had pulled away so quickly. *Something in her life has made her afraid,* he thought. Now, he was determined to find out why. The Emma he had known in Chicago had been more open and trusting. But, then, so had he. He knew he'd have to be very cautious now not to destroy the trust she'd begun to show him. Last night, she had set his heart and body on fire. He wasn't so sure what he'd do if he got that close to her again. But, he was afraid that his job would come between them in the end.

"What did you tell Jim about me?" Emma asked. She'd been watching Sam out of the corner of her eye and knew he was deep in thought.

"What?" he asked, puzzled. He thought for a moment, then said with a shrug, "Oh, that you were a beautiful lady from my past."

Emma blushed and looked out the window to her left.

"So, you dropped art and got into dressage," Sam said to change the subject, seeing how uncomfortable Emma was. Besides, he was supposed to be working.

"I left school because I wanted to continue my father's work," she said, shrugging her shoulders. "When I moved to Oregon and found this place, it was perfect for a riding school. The rest you know."

Oh, there's a lot I don't know, Sam thought to himself.

"Sam," Emma said after a few moments, "are you planning on flying some horses somewhere?"

Sam shot up straight in his seat, shaken from his thoughts. When he turned to look at her, his eyes had turned to the color of light on steel and it frightened her.

"Where'd you get that idea?" he demanded in a harsh tone, then saw the look on her face. He tried to smile, to soften the impact of his words.

"I...I heard Jim say something to you about it as Nancy and I came into the office at the airport before lunch." She couldn't understand what he was so upset about or why he seemed so guarded, but the change had been instantaneous.

"No," he said and looked away. "I'm not shipping horses anywhere today." He couldn't tell her that Jim had heard about a guy who was asking around the airport last week, checking to see if the strip could handle a DC-7. Sam knew that was the size of plane used to fly large cargo out of the country. There was a lot he couldn't tell Emma just now, she might be in the middle of it.

They rode in silence. Sam saw Doc White's animal clinic as they drove back around a hairpin curve, which overlooked the entire valley behind them. Emerson White had been at his dad's ranch the day Ele came into his life. Sam remembered that day, and the pride in his dad's eyes when they were training the young mare together.

I need to get back to work, he thought to himself, wiping his hand over his face. He hoped Sally had made the appointment for him with Doc White for the next day, like he'd asked. Now, he was damning his line of work for getting in the way of what he really wanted to do.

"We're almost there," Emma said to break the silence. The Sam she knew was always calm. It wasn't like him to be so quick to anger. But then, she'd only known him for a short time. She wondered what he was thinking about.

"Tell me again how long you have lived on your ranch?" Sam asked.

"I bought it the year after I moved to Oregon."

"So, it was yours before you and your husband were married?"

"Yes. I had the money from my parents' farm to invest. My friend, Jennifer, found this place for me. I fell in love with it the minute I saw it." She was silent for a moment, then added, "It reminded me of home."

Even though it was still daylight, the forest of fir and deciduous trees created eerie shadows. The trees met overhead, creating a cool and dark tunnel. When Emma's car emerged back into the light, long stretches of white fence appeared along the left side of the road. She pulled into a driveway, and Sam held his breath when he saw the large, dark blue sign with RISING SUN STABLE in gold letters. He slowly exhaled. Sam couldn't believe his eyes. Blue and gold had been his silk colors on the track.

The same white fence, lined by birch, stretched down both sides of the drive. The golden sun danced on the backsides of the waving young leaves that arched over the entire length, ending just short of the house.

The white trim on the house was bright against the dark red of the brick. Emma pulled up in front of it, stopped the car, and turned off the engine. Sam could see why it reminded her of her childhood home. The house was almost a copy of the one he had seen at the farm in Indiana.

"Well, here we are," she said as she stepped from the car. Sam got out and walked to where Emma stood. They stopped in the quiet for a moment, feeling the warm breeze against their faces, the fragrance of the bed of daffodils next to the house surrounding them.

"This is my favorite time of year," Emma said in a soft voice in an attempt not to disturb the peace. "It holds the promise of new beginnings."

After a moment, she turned and said, "Welcome to my home, Sam." She led the way through the wide front door, and slipped her jacket onto a peg of the coat tree near the gun rack. She saw Sam notice the man's black Stetson hat next to her coat and the rifles standing as sentinels by the entrance. Also, her tall, slim riding boots stood under a small, black hunting coat hanging on the rack.

"Yours or your husband's?" Sam asked, nodding his head toward the man's Stetson.

"Ted's."

As she walked toward the kitchen, she smiled and added, "One of the rifles is mine, though."

Sam shook his head and smiled as he followed her through the entry way. *Now, that's the Emma I remember*, he thought as he walked past the large den to his left and continued after her.

Turning into the kitchen, Emma said, "Want some coffee?"

"Sure."

"Make yourself at home," she said, gesturing to the table and chairs. "Black, right?" she asked, filling the bottom of the coffee maker with water from the tap.

Sam looked at her and saw the coffee maker in her hand.

"Right."

Sam settled into a chair so he could watch Emma. He liked the way her hair gleamed in the light coming through the window over the sink. Her long, white hands reached to the top shelf of a cabinet for the coffee filters. When a flash of white skin at her waist was revealed by her reach, he had to look away. His throat was dry and his palms became sweaty.

He looked out of the sunny bay window toward the stark white stable, which stood down the lane from the house. Tall birch, like the ones lining the drive, surrounded it. A large metal roof shaded a fenced, outside arena next to the stable.

"How big is your ranch?" Sam asked, wiping his palms on his jeans.

"Thirty acres. I had fifty acres when I bought it..." Emma stopped what she was doing. Biting her lip, she took a deep breath and turned toward Sam. "Before he died, my husband got into financial trouble, so I had to sell some of the property. I sold it to a farmer who was leasing part of my land. That was when I began boarding horses and closed the training school. I have only one boarder now, but she's making up for the money I'd lose without classes."

"How's that?" Sam asked, trying to keep from showing too much curiosity. He saw the sadness in her eyes and wished he could take it away. But, he had a job to do.

"The owner paid me a tidy sum for one mare's care," she said, turning back to turn on the fire under the coffee. "Much more than the usual fee for boarding. She's an outstanding chestnut. I've never seen a Thoroughbred like her before, except for Frankie."

"Who's Frankie?" Sam asked, his jaw tight as he fought to control his impatience. He wanted this investigation over so he could put his full attention on Emma.

"He's a horse that Ted brought to our stable last year..." Emma stopped, remembering that it had been shortly after Ted had returned from the Derby that Frankie came to her stable. A chill went down her spine.

"Where did she come from -- the mare, I mean?" Sam said, seeing the look on her face. He'd seen her hand shake as she'd reached for coffee mugs in the cabinet. Now, he caught his gaze was on her lips, as she began to speak again.

"I'm not sure. She arrived one day last January by a transport company, with a letter and enough cash to board her for about a year. The letter said we would be contacted sometime this spring by the owner to pick her up." Emma looked away, thinking of the defeat she had felt when she'd closed her riding school.

"Her owner saved me this year," she added.

"Do you know who the owner is?" Sam asked, watching Emma. He'd seen her eyes turn almost black before she'd turned her head and poured the coffee into the cups.

"No. The letter was just signed with the initials 'G. M.' I figured if I had any questions, I could contact the manager of the transport company." Emma walked over and sat down, handing Sam one of the cups.

"What was the name of the company?" Sam asked.

"I think it was Anderson's. Why?"

"Nothing. Just nosey, that's all. You said "we" earlier. I thought you lived alone now," he inquired, watching her face closely.

"I do." She looked at Sam, then looked away again. She'd noticed the strange tone in Sam's voice she had heard earlier. Guarded now, she looked straight ahead, choosing her words carefully.

"Sometimes, I just forget that Ted's gone. I do have a stable hand. Joe sent him to help me after Ted died. I don't know what I would have done without Casey."

Sam was surprised to feel the slight twinge of jealousy. He found himself almost angry that he hadn't been the one here to help her when she needed it.

As the air grew cooler, the smell of rain came in through the open window before he even saw it. Sam loved the rain, and he loved Oregon. It rained here most of the year, and the lush green hillside to the west of the stable was one result of it. The evergreens on the boundary of the property stood tall, a deeper green than the field of young wheat. The faint odor of lavender brought him back into the room.

Emma noticed Sam's gaze and asked, "After the rain stops, would you like to go for a ride?" She knew that in the spring, the rain clouds passed over quickly and the sun would be out again soon.

Sam's face lit up. "Sure. I don't have anything on my schedule this afternoon." In his mind, he'd been working on a way to get inside of Emma's stable. He needed to see the horses. Now, he thought his luck was holding out, and he relaxed.

They sat together and sipped their coffee, watching the breeze dance through the leaves of the birch trees and the wall of gray mist that began to cover everything, changing the colors of the land. Emma loved this, sitting in her home, watching the world outside with someone special sitting quietly and contentedly beside her. She had missed this - for more years than she wanted to remember.

The sky began to lighten and the rain stopped. Once again, the sun burst through the clouds. The shadows from the clouds slid across the land, creating images on the canvas before them. They looked at each other and smiled.

"Are you ready?" Emma asked.

"Lead the way."

The bright sunlight made them flinch at first after being in the house, yet the warmth felt good. The world seemed new after the shower; the grass glistened and vibrant colors splashed everywhere. Even the air smelled clean and sweet.

"I bought some wine back in McMinnville – for dinner tonight. It's still in your car." Sam said. "Would you mind if I put it in your refrigerator, until we leave for Portland? It's best if it's kept cold."

"I guess it's all right," Emma said, a little reluctantly.

Sam quickly went to Emma's Buick and tucked the brown bag under his arm. Smiling, he disappeared into the house, then returned a few seconds later.

"Thanks," he said as he took her elbow in his hand and began to lead her toward the stable.

"How much riding have you done, Sam?" Emma asked as they walked.

"I cut my teeth riding horses. My grandfather had two old Sorrell horses when I was a kid. June and Doodle. One was so gentle - that was June. Doodle was full of fire and mischief. They were mostly used to pull an old buggy that Grandpa kept for fun, but I'd take Doodle out for a ride once in awhile, just to let him exercise. He didn't have much speed, but he had life and strength in him. Every time he and I rode together, he'd test me with some new trick."

"Then, you can ride Flash. He was Ted's horse and has a reputation that is a lot like his name. You never know what he'll try."

Playfully, she watched Sam's face and laughed when he shot a look of disbelief her way. "Just kidding!" She watched as his face turned into an incredible grin. "He does have a bit of a temper," she added, taking a deep breath. "I guess it's because he'll never get used to being broke. He's a mustang from Eastern Oregon,"

"I like a horse with heart," Sam said.

When they walked by the large arena, Sam saw numerous large white cards tacked around the inside walls of the arena. Each card had a single, black letter on it.

"What are the letters on the cards in there for?" Sam asked.

"They are dressage ring letters. During a test, the various movements the horse and rider must follow take place at each letter or between them. I'll show you sometime."

"What do they mean?" Sam asked.

Emma laughed. "No one seems to know. I haven't been able to find out either, but they've been used this way forever. My father once told me he thought they were the initials of kings."

Sam and Emma walked into the stable. The smell of animal flesh, leather, and sweet hay filled the air. These were the smells that Sam loved, smells of his past that filled him with a feeling of peace - of home.

A small room on the right with the door slightly open caught Sam's eye. It looked like someone's living quarters.

"Casey sleeps in that room," Emma explained, after seeing Sam stop before the door.

They continued walking past the tack room. Sam glanced into the large room of saddles and equipment and noticed an old, dusty trunk in a corner.

"Where'd you get that old trunk?" he asked Emma.

She stopped and stared at it, the dark sides and rusted hinges showing its age. "It was my father's. He brought it on the ship with him from Germany in '37, when he and his stallion, Conversano, came to America."

Sam looked down the row of white stalls that stood on both sides of the large aisle. Ropes and bridles hung outside the gates where the horses waited patiently. Shiny brass hardware adorned some of the gates, listing the names of the horses inside.

"I love the smell of a stable," Emma said, walking passed the tack room to the first gate on the right. "It reminds me of the old barn at my parent's farm in Indiana, where I grew up." A large, white stallion came slowly to the gate and nuzzled Emma's hand.

"Hello, Gandolf," Emma said, stroking the horse's high forehead. The stallion nickered softly in response.

Sam stood, watching Emma and the tall, white, stallion. He thought of the joy in her face in the photograph he'd found in that barn in Indiana, the picture that was still in his wallet. Some of that joy was there again as she talked softly to the horse.

"This is Gandolf, son of Conversano," Emma told Sam with pride.

"He's a beautiful animal," Sam said, holding out his hand to the stallion's nose.

"Conversano Sabrina is his registered name, but I like to call him Gandolf."

"So, where is this Flash you plan to test me with?" Sam asked, laughing.

"He's on the other side, down at the end," Emma nodded with her head to the dark stall across the aisle. Then she walked to Ele's stall and stopped.

"Here's my mystery lady, Classy Elegance." Emma stopped before the chestnut beauty standing in the middle of her stall. The mare was weaving her head, gently rocking her body, but she stopped the motion when Sam appeared and brought her head up high, her eyes wide. Her nostrils flared, testing the air around her.

"She's a little shy," Emma said. She noticed that Ele had not eaten all of her food. Usually, the mare ate everything in her rack by now.

Emma looked over at Sam. He was standing still in the middle of the aisle, staring at the mare with a look of shock on his face. Finally, he walked up closer to the gate and stretched out his hand to the red horse. Ele walked up to the gate and put her muzzle in his hand. He leaned closer to the horse's head, then scratched her neck in a way that gave Emma a feeling of familiarity in movement that had taken place many times before. She couldn't explain it, but there was an obvious bonding between man and animal.

"How long did you say you've had her?" Sam asked, glad that his voice was calm. His heart was racing as he leaned over the gate to Ele's stall to get a better look at her. He checked her legs with his eyes, a habit that was as natural to him as breathing.

"About four months now."

She watched in awe as the man and horse seemed to have found each other after a long separation. Knowing this to be impossible and probably a figment of her imagination, Emma turned and walked back to Gandolf. She busied herself with placing the bridle on her horse, trying to sort through the thoughts that raced in her mind. She had an easy feeling with Sam in her house and stable. It was like he belonged here. She looked over and watched as Sam placed his forehead against Ele's while he rubbed her neck and whispered softly to her. It was a gesture Emma used sometimes with Gandolf when she was troubled.

"And," Sam continued, "you said the owner's letter only had the initials 'G.M.' on it?"

"Yes."

Emma turned and walked to the tack room.

G.M. - George Mason! Sam thought with surprise, as he stared at Ele. But, that didn't make sense. *Why would George send Ele to Emma Jacobs for boarding?* None of it made any sense at all. *Unless, George was behind Koenig's Wonder's switch.* Sam wondered if George knew the colt was in this stable. *But, Why?* Sam's head was beginning to pound.

"Are you coming, Sam?" Emma asked from the door.

"Yeah, sure." He followed her toward the tack room.

Emma grabbed her saddle and blanket, then said, "You can use whatever tack you want." Then, she went to Gandolf's stall and led the tall stallion out into the aisle, tethering him to the ring that hung outside his stall.

Seeing that Emma was busy with Gandolf, Sam walked into the open door of Casey's room. He noticed the rifle hanging on the wall rack near the door. It was a military-style rifle, with a dark stock, a metal buttpad, and a large scope mounted over the bolt action. He walked over to it and examined it more closely, noting that "Mod. 98" was stamped on the receiver.

"Wrong door, Sam," Emma called, seeing that Sam had walked into Casey's room.

"Sorry," Sam said. As he began to leave the room, he noted a phone number written on a piece of paper next to the telephone. He made a mental note of the number, then walked across to the tack room. He quickly picked up a Western saddle with one hand and slung it over his shoulder. Grabbing a blanket, he walked out toward Emma.

Emma looked up and saw Sam carrying Ted's saddle and blanket. Sam's plaid shirt and long, blue-jeaned legs gave him the look of a cowboy as he sauntered toward her. She then looked down and saw his tennis shoes and started giggling to herself.

"What's the matter?" he said, stopping a few feet from her.

She put her hand on her hip and, with her best Southern drawl, said, "The only thing missing on you, darlin', is a pair of spurs on those Nike's."

He laughed, bowed, and said with a much deeper southern flair, "Wahl, ma'am, I left my spurs in my other suit. Now, where's this bucking bronco y'all been talkin' 'bout?"

"This way, pardner," she answered in her own drawl.

Leading Gandolf, Emma continued giggling as she walked down the aisle toward the other end of the stable.

"Who's this?" Sam asked, nodding to the smaller grey in the stall across from Gandolf's stall.

"Sonny, sired by Gandolf."

Sam could hear the pride in her voice. Colt and sire nickered softly to each other as Gandolf passed. When Emma and Sam came near the next stall on their left, a high whinny came from inside, then a black head came out over the top of the gate, nostrils flaring, as if he was ready to run. Sam dropped the saddle and blanket he was carrying. He heard Ele return the whinny, as if the two horses were communicating with each other.

"That's Frankie," Emma said. "He's as black as midnight on a moonless night. It's odd that he doesn't have any markings on him."

Sam went over to the horse and began stroking his neck. The horse calmed easily, giving Sam the chance to look him over. He ran his hand upward against the hair on the horse's forehead.

"You're right," Sam said. "There are no markings - that are easily visible."

When Emma went to open the back doors of the stable, Sam quickly looked under Frankie's upper lip at the tattoo. Sam knew that retired racers were used for dressage, and that they would have a tattoo, but this one seemed different somehow. He was rubbing the tall horse's forehead when Emma turned around again.

"Flash is that buckskin in the next stall," Emma said, pointing to the last stall on the same side of the stable where Frankie stood. "He's a mustang Ted adopted from Eastern Oregon. He was almost two when we got him, with a few bad habits."

Sam patted Frankie's neck, then walked over to the gate of Flash's stall. The bright sunlight streaking in from the large, open doors made it difficult to see into the stall. All of a sudden, a great, tan head shot out at them with eyes glaring and loud snorts coming from the great nostrils.

Gandolf stepped back, frightened momentarily, but Emma quieted the white stallion, and looked over at Sam.

"Ted had him gelded," Emma continued, with a smile on her face, "thinking the habits would disappear. They didn't."

Sam grabbed the bridle hanging outside of the mustang's stall and began talking to the horse in his deep, husky voice. Emma couldn't hear what Sam said, he was speaking so softly. Flash snorted, shook his head a few times, then went to the back of his stall. Sam continued his lulling speech, and before Emma knew it, he was in the stall with the horse, slowly placing the bridle on the animal's large head. Leading Flash from the stall, Sam was smiling broadly. He picked up the blanket and saddle and began to place them on the horse's tall back. At first, the horse became agitated and began to prance around, but Sam held him with a firm hand and continued talking softly to him while he cinched up the saddle.

Emma stood dumfounded, Gandolf's reins in her hand. "How did you do that?" she whispered. "He's never been this docile with a stranger. Ted's the only one who usually could control that animal, but he usually used an iron fist..." She stopped, realizing what she had just said, remembering just how strong his fists had felt.

Sam saw her face and realized that something had upset her. Her face was white, her eyes wide and fearful. She lowered her eyes and seemed more interested in the reins she held in her hands than what she'd been talking about. Sam wondered what had caused the change in her.

"Em," he said, softly touching her arm. He could feel the tension in her body. "Are you okay?"

"Sure," she shrugged, looking back up at Sam. She saw the warmth in his eyes and wanted to touch his cheek, but kept her hands locked on Gandolf's reins.

To put her at ease, he flashed his incredible smile and winked. "I just used my magic on the beast!" Then, he added softly, "I don't believe in abuse, of any kind."

He saw Emma's body relax and was glad when she smiled. They walked their horses toward the large open doors. Outside of the stable, Carlos drove up in a Jeep and stopped near them.

"Morning, Mrs.," said the dark-haired, man. He had a day's growth on his face, which was shaded by a cap.

Sam noticed his voice, heavy with an accent Sam couldn't place. He was a small man, with a darkly tanned face and small, brown eyes that pierced like a hawk's.

Carlos looked up at Sam in the bright sun, then seemed to force a smile under the small cap. Sam recognized the type of hat that Carlos was wearing - it was like the ones the jockeys wore during exercise at the tracks.

"Sam, this is Casey Morales, a friend of Joe's. Casey, Sam Parker," Emma said.

Carlos gave a short salute to Sam with his hand to his hat. He was now very glad that he'd changed his name when he'd arrived in Oregon. He remembered Sam Parker and knew he was no friend of Joe's. Sam was someone Carlos needed to watch very closely.

"Nice to meet you, Casey," Sam said, noticing that the small man seemed nervous. Sam had the strange feeling he'd seen this man somewhere. "Have we met before?"

"I doubt it," Carlos said as he put his hands quickly in his pockets.

"Has Doc been around yet?" Emma asked.

"Haven't seen him," Carlos answered shortly.

"Well, if he isn't here in half an hour, would you give him a call? Ele didn't eat all of her food this morning again, and I'm beginning to worry."

"Sure, Mrs."

"Sam and I are going to take Flash and Gandolf out for a ride around the ranch."

Carlos whistled between his teeth and said, "You must be a brave one, Mr. Parker, to tackle that hombre." Looking down, he eyed Sam's tennis shoes. "And without any spurs on!" Shaking his head and chuckling to himself, Carlos walked into the stable. Sam saw him turn to watch them as Emma mounted her horse. Then, the large stable doors were pulled shut.

"He's a curious fellow," Sam said to Emma, nodding back towards the stable.

"I'm not sure I like him, but he's a hard worker." Emma avoided spending much time with Casey. There was something about him that made her skin crawl. She hated needing the help, but was financially unable to hire anyone else. She would never forget that she had almost lost her ranch after Ted's death.

"Do you know where Joe found him?" Sam asked.

"No, I never asked. Are you ready to ride?" Emma said, wanting to change the subject.

"Sure," Sam replied and turned to mount Flash. The horse threw back his head and whinnied loudly, rearing up. Sam had one foot in the stirrup, the reins and both hands on the saddle horn. Leaning forward as best he could, he swung his other leg over the large horse as front hooves pounded back to the ground. Over the horse's cries, Emma could hear the husky tone of Sam's voice as he softly talked to the animal. Flash seemed to begin to settle down, then shook his head, snorting fiercely. Emma saw Sam gently kick the horse's sides and they galloped swiftly up the lane toward the house. Then, Sam pulled the reins to stop the horse. They turned to the left and cantered back to where Emma stood.

"I wish you could see your face." Sam's eyes twinkled with excitement.

"Why?"

"It's lovely."

She melted and smiled. Shaking her head, she gently nudged Gandolf and led the way into the hills behind her property with Sam riding next to her.

"I never know what to expect from you," she said to Sam, looking over at him.

"I guess that makes us even."

"What do you mean?"

"I have a feeling this horse has some surprises stored up for me." He stood up in his saddle and reached over to touch her hair.

"I just noticed that your hair is the same color as Frankie's coat in there," he said.

Feeling flushed and a little shy, Emma said, smiling at his touch. "Come on, you devil, let me show you around."

"Who? Me or the horse?"

"Both of you!" Emma laughed, then gently pressed her knees into Gandolf's sides and began to ride toward the hills, leading Sam away from the stable, the house, to her world.

They rode together at a gentle pace through the meadow and up to the first rise. Soft, white, puffs of cloud held suspended overhead in the blue sky, moving slightly with the gentle, warm breeze that surrounded them. From their viewpoint, they could see a low draping of clouds that clung to the nearby hillside. In the distance, rain fell on the blue hills on the horizon as the gentle spring showers continued eastward, leaving a vivid rainbow in its wake. Sam stopped his horse next to Emma's.

After a few moments, Emma said in a voice that was almost a whisper, "I love this place. It's so peaceful here."

Sam smiled and nodded, then reached over and touched her hand.

"I often ride out this way - to escape," she added.

When he noticed the tear sliding down her cheek, Sam gently wiped it away, saying nothing. Together, they drank in the quietude and beauty.

"What are you escaping from?" Sam asked, after a few moments had passed.

She looked into his eyes, wishing she could lose herself as she had once before when she was young, knowing that it was impossible since she was no longer that same naive girl. She looked away and softly said, "Myself."

He saw that same look she'd had before - a sadness that tore at him. *If it's the last thing I do before I return to Baltimore*, he decided, *I'm going to find out what caused that sadness.*

After awhile, Sam said, "Emma, would you mind showing me what dressage is like?"

"Yes," Emma said, glad he had changed the subject. She looked around her at the large, open field of low grass. She imagined the layout of the arena in her mind and recalled the recent patterns she had used on the last test she had judged at a show. Then, almost imperceptibly, she gently pressed one knee into Gandolf's side to begin his movement. After the horse had taken a few steps, she gave a slight squeeze on the inside rein to begin his turn. To switch sides, she guided the animal in the opposite direction, shifting her left seat bone as the horse seemed to bend around her leg. She turned him completely around and began moving him toward Sam in a leg-yielding pattern, moving him away from her leg in a lateral movement going both forward and sideways at the same time, while the horse's head looked away from the direction he was moving. Gandolf's body remained straight throughout the motion, Emma slightly working him with her right leg and rein. Once she returned to where Sam was, she brought her horse to a halt, stood there for a few seconds, then reached down and patted Gandolf's neck and praised him.

Sam sat in awe. He had watched the pair move together as one. He'd ridden horses since he was five years old, but he had never seen anything so beautiful as this. Training to race was archaic compared to the preciseness of this style of riding. Her horse had looked as if he was enjoying himself, willingly following every slight command she asked of him without any visible sign from Emma.

"That was wonderful," Sam said. "You have truly found your talent."

She blushed and stroked Gandolf's long neck again. "I owe it all to my father. He was the master who taught me the gentle way to work with horses."

"Thank you for sharing that with me. I'd like to see a dressage show sometime," Sam added.

"I could arrange that," she said smiling, "one of these days." She reined her horse to begin the slow climb up the hill, which she knew held the best view on her property. Sam turned his horse and followed her.

Emma led to a place on the crest of the hill. Under a grove of old, oak trees, the skeleton of an old homestead stood next to a small brook. A broken chimney, and steps that led to where a porch must have stood, were all that was left of the house. Sam and Emma stopped beside the brook and tied the horses to a nearby tree.

"Do you know whose place this was?" Sam asked, walking around the steps.

"No. Probably was a couple with a dream, only to end up buried somewhere near here in unmarked graves. These few remains are the only testimony to their existence."

Emma took the small blanket that was always tied to the back of Ted's saddle and laid it out near the water's edge under one of the oak trees. She sat and watched Sam as he walked by the chimney and stood looking around him at a small patch of daffodils. A rusted wagon wheel lay off to the side, almost overgrown by the blackberry vines.

Sam noticed a blue-speckled, metal cup and stooped to pick it up. A large, gaping hole was eroded through one side, where the earth had begun to reclaim it. He sighed and gently laid the cup back where he'd found it. Then, he stood and stared out over the valley below, his hands deep in his pockets. Dotted among the trees were other ranches reaching out to the horizon to the north, where the tips of the tall buildings of the city broke the solid line against the blue sky. The different greens of spring, mingled with the fields of early red clover, wove a tapestry over the land, and the silver thread of a river wound its way through the many colors, the sun reflecting on its surface. In the distance, Sam could see clouds hanging over the snow-covered peak of Mt. St. Helens. To the east was Mt. Adams and Mt. Hood, which he knew were separated by the Columbia River Gorge. He turned south and looked for Mt. Jefferson, and he wasn't disappointed.

"What a great view!" he exclaimed. "My dad always called Oregon 'God's country'."

The trees rustled overhead with a light wind, and he looked up at the cry of a hawk soaring overhead. *Yes*, Sam thought, *peace is carried on the gentle breeze here.*

He walked to where Emma sat and joined her on the blanket. From where he sat, he could see her stable with the thick forest standing dark and tall behind it.

He looked at Emma and smiled. The sound of the gentle brook was soothing, as he drank in her beauty, searching her face.

"Do you have a dream, Emma?" Sam asked, thinking of the abandoned homestead.

She looked up at the sky for a moment, as if searching there for the right words. No one had ever asked her that before. Taking a deep breath, she looked into Sam's eyes.

"I thought I did, once."

"And, now?" Sam asked.

"Now, I'm not so sure."

Her sad, brown eyes cut into his heart. Sam couldn't help himself. He took her in his arms and held her, feeling the jolt to his system with her warmth against him. He reached up and stroked her hair as he held her in silence. *What did she want*? he wondered. *What did he want*? He put his hands on her shoulders and held her so he could look into her eyes.

Emma became frightened of what Sam might see and turned away to distance herself from what she was feeling, her heart racing in her breast. She sat up, shaking herself from his arms, so she could breathe again. She was surprised how easily he released her. Ted would never have done that.

◆ ◆ ◆

Suddenly, they heard rifle shots coming from the direction of Emma's house. Startled, Sam jumped up and looked toward the stable. A flash of light beamed as the sun reflected on the shiny chrome of a black Morris Minor pulling away, the gear's grinding up the lane, quickly leaving Emma's ranch.

"Casey must be target practicing again," Emma said to Sam, walking to where he stood. Sam noticed she seemed relaxed and he tried to, but found it hard.

"Whose car is that?" Sam asked, nodding to the car swiftly passing on the road below them, a cloud of dust billowing in its quake.

"That looks like Doc White's car. He's the only one around here that I know of drives a car like that. He must have had an emergency for him to drive like that."

"Does Casey do that often? Shoot targets, I mean?" Sam asked, still agitated and on guard.

"Yes. He practices whenever he gets a chance and takes pride in being a good shot."

"It doesn't bother you that he shoots so close to the stable?" Sam questioned, still upset.

"He usually doesn't shoot that close. Besides, he says he usually hits what he's aiming at. I'm used to it by now," Emma shrugged, then walked back to the blanket and sat down.

Reluctantly, Sam returned to the blanket with her, but sat facing the direction of the stable.

"You mentioned Doc White. Is that Emerson White?" Sam asked, as he stretched his long legs out in front of him, trying to appear relaxed.

"Yes, why?"

"I've known Doc White for many years. Did you know that he used to be the track vet at Epsom Downs in England?"

"No. I knew he was from England and that his wife died a few years ago. He knows a lot about horses, and he's awfully good with them."

They sat quietly. Emma was actually glad for the diversion, remembering the warmth of Sam's arms.

The gentle breeze sang through the leaves. Emma looked up as a bird cried overhead. She watched a Great Blue Heron fly down toward the meadow, its wings slowly flapping in a graceful ballet until it glided and landed. It came to a standstill and looked like a statue against the prior season's brown, cut hay.

"It's too bad that the peace here can't erase the pain of the past," Emma said with a heavy sigh.

"Emma, you know you can tell me anything. Would you like to talk about it?"

"After my mother died, I felt lost, misplaced for awhile. I was searching for something...or maybe I was running away. I'm not sure. I felt I needed a sense of belonging, a security in a life where there no longer was any. I moved here, thinking that I knew what I wanted."

She stopped for a moment, remembering that at the time, she had thought Sam was what she was searching for. "Then I realized I was wrong," she continued. "When I met Ted, I thought he represented that security. He was so strong and caring, at first. Then, he changed..."

Emma stopped. No, she couldn't go there just yet. Ted was dead and couldn't hurt her again, but she shivered anyway and wrapped her arms around herself. Her eyes went out over the valley, remembering that day. She thought of the heavy mist that she had seen from the window that had hung low in the distant hills, giving the illusion of a large lake that hadn't been there before. The early sun shafts had cut through the temporal wisps to the east, and the colors of harvest exploded in the silence of the dawn just as a distant gunshot had echoed through the air.

"When did he begin to change?" Sam asked.

Emma took a deep breath and began.

"It all seemed to start after Ted brought Frankie here. Something had been bothering Ted a couple of days before he was killed, but he refused to talk to me about it." She stopped and looked away, thinking of the night before he died.

"I heard the shot," she continued. "Ted and Joe were hunting together that morning on Joe's property. Joe told the police later that he and Ted had separated to scout the herd. He said he'd heard a shot and thought Ted had landed a deer. When Joe got to him, Ted was already dead. The hunter who'd fired the shot was never found. The police searched for days, but only found a few footprints. The bullet went through Ted's heart."

"I know that happens out here, trespassers hunting illegally. I'm really sorry." Sam reached out a hand and rubbed it down Emma's back to release some of the tension he'd seen in her body.

"Where did Casey come from?" he asked, after a moment, hoping to get her to open a little more.

"I already told you. I don't know. You sure ask a lot of questions, Sam," she said, turning to look at him. "Someone might think you were a private detective or something."

Sam blushed and looked away from her. He stood up and placed his hands in his pockets, his back turned to her as he looked down at his own reflection in the water. God, he never hated his job more than he did at that moment. He hated that he couldn't be totally honest with Emma, that he couldn't put everything else behind him and hold her close. He knew he'd hurt her by prying, but it was his job. Reaching inside of himself, he tried to find the words that were closest to the truth. Then, he turned and went back to her, kneeling down beside her. He took Emma by the shoulders, so that his eyes once again met hers.

"Emma," he said in the same low, husky voice she'd heard him use the first time with Flash. "Forgive me. I know you've been through a lot. Death is hard to accept, and when it happens so abruptly, it takes longer to let go. I'd like to think I may be able to help."

"You don't know anything about it!" she cried and tried to pull away from him. She couldn't help herself. His sea-blue eyes looked so sad, as if he was afraid he had hurt her. But, she couldn't tell him all of it, not yet.

He let her go, then started picking at the grass in front of him, giving her the time and space she needed.

"You mentioned how Ted had changed," Sam finally said. "All men go through something like that, sometime in their lives. They begin to question everything, their choices, and the results of those choices. Some men, if they aren't strong within themselves, will go to the extreme and run – maybe out of cowardice or fear, or in search of something else.

"This happened to me a few years ago. I was in the racing circuit with my mare, the one I told you about last night. I began to get cocky. She'd won three races in a row, and I just knew she'd win again. I'd had too much to drink, and...well...I put her in a claiming race. I lost everything – my horse, my pride, my dream."

"What did you do?" Emma asked.

"I ran away. I couldn't face my dad, or myself. I started drinking, trying the oldest remedy in the world. I became a pilot for hire. I'd fly anything, anywhere - Europe, Africa, South America. Anywhere - except Oregon - because of my parents. I couldn't face my dad, not after what I'd done. Jim finally found me in New York. He pulled me back and got me started again. That was one of those points in life where someone comes along and changes your path forever."

Sam looked away. "I'll never race again," he added.

Emma smiled and hugged him, placing her face into his broad chest. She listened to the rhythm of his heart. His arms felt so safe around her – a feeling she realized now that she had missed tremendously.

A flock of Northern Geese flew in formation overhead, returning home. For the first time in a long while, Emma truly felt as if she was home.

"Life is never what we expect it to be, is it?" she asked softly.

Sam waited for a moment, seeing the pain in her eyes. "One of the things I learned is that sometimes what we thought was a dream can be replaced with another. It's sort of life's way of directing us in the way we're destined to go. Don't give up on your dreams, Emma. You never know -- they may someday come true."

"I had a dream once, but it shattered into a million pieces. Now, I don't dare dream. It's too painful."

"What do you mean?"

She sat up and looked at him, a fire behind her eyes. "You walked away from me for a blonde once, Sam Parker. Remember?" Her voice cut into Sam's heart.

"Yes, but..." he began to explain, then looked down at the grass around them. He remembered her father's face as he'd left the hotel in Chicago. "I wrote to you later, trying to explain—"

"You wrote to me?" Emma looked at Sam in disbelief. Her heart shifted in her breast. She'd spent all those years thinking that he didn't care. "When?"

"Shortly after I arrived in Arizona. I wrote a couple of times. But, I never heard from you. Then, Oliver Stenson told me you never wanted to hear from me again."

"Oliver? You never received my letters?" she asked softly.

"You wrote to me?" Sam's heart began to jump for joy.

"Yes. I wonder why Oliver would have said that to you." Emma thought for a moment. She remembered her father's fury at the Drake Hotel the morning after she had slipped out to go to the movies with Sam. It was the first time in her life he had ever yelled at her. *Could he possibly...?* she began to wonder, but dismissed it quickly.

"It doesn't really matter now," Sam said, taking her in his arms. "What did you say in your letters?"

I love you, was on the tip of her tongue, but she held back. She wasn't sure why. "Oh, things about my new school, and my friend, Jennifer, that I'd met at the riding stables. I told you about her last night. Silly school-girl stuff." She paused for a moment, then added, "I also thanked you for taking me to the movies and for my locket. It was a wonderful time for me. I never forgot it." She was fingering the chain of the necklace that she always wore now.

She searched his face with her eyes, noticing for the first time the small scar on the left side of his chin.

"Where'd you get that?" Emma asked, lightly touching the scar.

"In a crash over the gulf. I was testing an F-4 and the fuel control meter failed."

She watched his mouth as he talked, soft and inviting.

Sam saw her eyes drop to his mouth and lowered his head slowly to hers until their lips almost touched. Her heart moved within her breast, but then she quickly stiffened. It was too soon to trust so fully again.

"You don't need to be afraid of me, Emma," Sam said as he pressed his lips against her temple. The look in her eyes was like a frightened animal. He gently took her in his arms. "I will never hurt you. Just let me hold you."

She slowly allowed herself to become enveloped within his arms. They sat holding each other under the shade tree, the horses grazing nearby. The gentle trickle of the water and Sam's warmth eventually calmed her heart and soul.

CHAPTER SIXTEEN

*T*he sleek, black colt, led by the small man, strode into the circle of horses in the Paddock area. The man wore a brown leather jacket, zipped tightly against the cool, early morning air, his small wool hat sat cocked low over one eye as he held the reins of the great steed in his hands. A slight fog swirled about the legs of the players, giving an eerie effect in the faint light of the rising sun. The other horses were tense in anticipation of the game to come, their breaths clouding the area where they stood. It was the day of the great race. In just a few short minutes, these animals would test their abilities, their bodies straining to fulfill the only purpose for their being...to run.

Sam stood at the side gate and watched. Everything he owned rode on this race, including his mare. He was a gambler of sport, of life. He couldn't remember when he began the game, but knew he would one day be dealt a hand he would not be prepared to accept. He could see George Mason in the distance, talking to his trainer.

"I must have been out of my mind to bet with that man," Sam thought to himself. The pounding in his head reminded him that he'd drunk too many whiskeys at the tavern the night before, where he'd bet his horse against Mason's young black.

The horses were led out onto the track by the runners. When Ele returned in front of the grandstand, pride swelled in Sam's chest as he watched his chestnut mare walk to the gate.

Then, Mason's colt walked by, owned by no one. That horse needed no training, he knew exactly what to do. The wind was on his heels and fire was in his eyes. This animal seemed to be the devil himself, possessed by no one, master of his world - holding all the cards of the game, head high above the others, sure of the win.

But, then Sam knew that this wasn't Koenig's Pride, the horse entered in the race. He saw it was Koenig's Wonder! Sam had witnessed this colt's birth, the foal with the white star.

Sam jumped up. He had to stop this race. Mason had slipped another horse into the race. Everything Sam had been working for, his one chance at his dream, would be lost if Ele ran that race. He was afraid that he was going to lose Ele...

Sam. Sam. Emma was calling his name from the other side of the fence.

How can that be? Sam thought to himself. *She can't be at the race.*

Then, he realized he had been asleep and saw that he was sitting up. Emma was looking at him with wide eyes and a look of concern on her face. He looked behind her and saw her house in the valley and remembered where he was. Running his fingers through his hair, he tried to shake the nightmare from him and smile at Emma.

"I'm sorry," he said. "I must have fallen asleep. Did I say anything incriminating?"

"No."

She had watched Sam sleep, the way his long, dark eyelashes just brushed against his cheek, the soft rhythm of his breathing as his strong hands lay folded on his chest. She'd felt her heart stir, as if it had finally come alive again from a deep sleep and was surprised that she wasn't afraid. It was as if she'd been waiting for that moment all her life. Then, she'd seen the confusion and fear in Sam's face and wondered what had walked through his dream to cause it, remembering the many nightmares she'd walked through over the past few years.

Sam stood up and stretched.

"We'd better be going," he said, as Emma stood next to him.

Without even thinking, Sam gently placed his arm around her shoulders and pulled her to him, in a gesture that felt so natural. They looked out over the meadow toward her ranch.

The sun was setting low in the sky, just above the grove of fir trees in the distance. A cool breeze was beginning to stir the leaves of the old oak tree overhead. With the warm glow of the day still in her heart, Emma reached her hand out to Sam. He took it in his, turned it over and gently touched the palm with his lips.

Reluctantly, they slowly rolled up the blanket and replaced it on Sam's saddle. They mounted the horses and began the ride back.

"The wind's coming from the south," Sam said. "There'll be rain soon."

"I've never heard that one," Emma said with a laugh. "Back in Indiana, the old farmers always believed that you never go fishing when the cows are lying down."

Sam laughed heartily. Emma's face beamed and Sam could only stare at her. Her beauty paled everything around her.

"A lot has happened since Chicago, huh?" Sam said as the horses walked side by side.

"Yes," Emma replied, a little sad that so much time had past – time without Sam in her life. She liked him being here on her ranch. She liked it very much. Then, she thought of the first time she had seen Sam.

"Do you remember when we met at Arlington Park?" Emma asked.

"You bet. That was the best day I've ever had in my life. I'll never forget when you asked me if I was a touter."

Sam liked the sound of Emma's laughter. The excitement in her voice and the joy on her face reminded him of her spontaneity that had drawn him to her from the beginning.

"Yes," she said. "We had a lot of fun then."

She felt sad as the reminder brought memories of her parents and how much she missed them, but she shook it off as she always did when an emotion slipped into her heart that she was unable to do anything about. She loved the reminder, but not the ache it left behind.

"You were so beautiful when I first met you at the track," Sam said, reaching his hand to her face. "But, it doesn't compare to the beauty I now see."

Emma didn't know what to say. She felt embarrassed and naive. Here Sam was once again in her life. *But*, she thought to herself, *how long would it last this time*? She knew she would have to ask, but couldn't find the words.

They rode on in silence. A pale, golden light slipped sideways onto everything around them, softening the edges and bringing small details into focus that were normally missed in the full daylight. Warm colors, soft like watercolors, washed over the land. It was a light that artists waited patiently for, so they could capture the true essence of nature. The sun set behind the fir trees, and the air grew cooler. The clouds overhead and the snow on Mount Hood began to turn coral in the descending sunlight.

"Sam?" Emma asked, after considering it for some time in her mind while they rode. "Would you like to stay for dinner? I have some fresh salmon."

"I'd love to, as long as you let me cook." Sam sighed, relieved that the day with Emma wasn't over yet.

"You cook?" she asked in surprise. Ted had never set foot in the kitchen when they were married, except to eat what was on the table.

"Yes, I like to."

"Great! I can drive you back into the city after dinner."

◆ ◆ ◆ ◆

Carlos came out of the stable as they approached in the waning light.

"Have a good ride?" he said as he reached out a hand for Gandolf's reins.

"Yes, thanks," Emma said as she and Sam dismounted. "Would you mind brushing and feeding these two? I'm going to take Sam back to the city later."

"Yes, Mrs."

"Oh, by the way," she said. "What did Doc have to say?"

Carlos seemed a little startled that she even knew Doc had been there.

"Yes. He had a call while he was here and had to go." Carlos paused, removed his hat, and ran his fingers through his dark hair. "He didn't say much."

"What time was Doc here?" Sam asked.

Carlos gave him a long side look, then shrugged his shoulders. "I got back from Joe's 'round three or so. Why do you want to know?"

Sam looked him straight in the eye and said, "We heard gun shots coming from this direction, then we saw Doc White's car leaving quickly."

Carlos' eyes flared. His face darkened with anger as he turned to Emma.

"What's this all about, Mrs.?"

"We just wondered if you knew anything about the shots," Emma said. "I don't like you target practicing so near the horses."

"Well, I was just cleaning my gun out by the Jeep when it went off by accident. You know I wouldn't shoot near the horses on purpose."

Carlos looked away, and took Flash's reins from Sam. Flash became agitated and began snorting and thrashing his head. As the reins broke free from the small man's hands, Sam reached out and caught them.

"I'll lead him in if you want," Sam said.

"No, I'll do it," Carlos snapped at Sam. "It's my job." He grabbed the horse's reins from Sam. Flash strained against Carlos' hold on the reins, but the man persisted.

"Will there be anything else, Mrs.?" Carlos asked.

"No."

Sam and Emma walked to the house.

"He's a curious fellow," Sam said. "I wonder what he was doing over at Joe's today."

Emma stopped in the drive and looked at Sam. His jaw was set hard. She had never seen him so tense before, except for when they'd heard the gun shots. All of his questions had a similar tension growing inside of her now.

"Why don't you go ask Joe," she snapped, not sure why.

For the first time, a strange silence came between them. A terrible distance hung suspended that neither one of them knew how to bridge. The only sound was the frogs down at the pond singing to the full moon that had now risen over the horizon in the east. A cool wind was beginning to stir. As Sam looked back at the stable, he saw a faint, yellow light beaming from a window. He knew that was the groom's window and wondered what this man's part was in his investigation.

"I'm sorry I snapped at you, Sam," Emma finally said.

"It's okay. I'm still going to cook, if you still want me to." Sam took her hand and smiled at her in the evening light.

Emma smiled back, then looked up toward the house and noticed smoke circling from the chimney. Her hand tightened in Sam's. She'd have to talk to Joe again about going into her house when she wasn't there.

◆ ◆ ◆ ◆

Once inside the house, Emma turned before the long stairway and slid open the double doors to the den. The welcoming glow of the fire danced across the oiled, wooden floor and furniture. Emma had to admit that the warmth of the fire felt good after the cool night air. The rose-colored light from the lampshade of a tall floor lamp, sitting by an old rocking chair on one side of the fireplace, softened the light in the room. She motioned to Sam to have a seat in the great, wing-backed red upholstered chair on the other side of the fire, but noticed that Shadow lay curled on the soft cushion of the chair. The cat opened her yellow eyes, stretched out one paw, yawned, then pretended to go back to sleep, keeping one eye on Sam as he walked toward the fire.

"This is Shadow," Emma said, rubbing the soft, ebony fur gently with her hand. The cat mewed softly in response to her touch. "She takes time getting used to strangers, but once she knows you, you won't be able to resist her."

"Sort of like her owner," Sam said with a twinkle in his eye. "Who started the fire?"

"Joe. He sometimes does things like that for me."

Sam stood with his back to the fireplace and his hands behind his back, facing the opposite wall of numerous shelves of books. Emma thought to herself how her father used to stand just like that at their home in Indiana when he'd first come in from working with the horses.

"Would you mind if I made a phone call?" Sam asked. The mention of Joe's name reminded him that it was time to get back to work. It riled Sam to think that Joe came into Emma's house whenever he felt like it.

"No problem," Emma said. "The phone's over there on the desk. I need to go upstairs for a minute, then I'll make some coffee." She left the room, leaving one of the doors of the den open.

She heard him dial, then could hear his deep voice sifting through the hallway from the den, but couldn't hear what he was saying. Her thoughts danced around in her head. She really liked Sam, but was afraid of the feelings she was beginning to allow to open once again. That door on her heart had been closed for a long while.

You silly schoolgirl, she thought to herself as she climbed the stairs. She went into her bedroom and took off her boots. Slipping her feet into soft slippers, she looked at herself in the mirror. Her hair was wild from the wind and she had a glow in her cheeks from the ride. *Was this from the elements or from being with Sam today*? Emma wondered, as she smiled to herself.

◆ ◆ ◆ ◆

After he had dialed, Sam cradled the phone on his shoulder so he could rifle through the papers on Emma's desk.

"Hello," a female voice said in the receiver.

"Sally, you're supposed to answer with the Commission's name, remember?" Sam shook his head. Sally had worked for Jim for a few months now, but she never could get the greeting on the office phone correct.

"I'm sorry. I keep forgetting. Where have you been, Sam?"

"I've been at the Jacobs' ranch. What do you have for me?"

"Not much to report yet," the sultry voice on the other end said. "Baltimore called, checking up on you, making sure you were still on track. I told them I was sure you were, just like you told me to."

"Good, I'm still working on it. I've seen him and he's magnificent. Call in this lip tattoo number for me, J4879. Also, did you call Doc White and make an appointment for me?"

"Yes, but he isn't available until around four, tomorrow afternoon."

"OK. Also, would you find out when Joe Remsky bought the property across from Emma Jacobs and who handled the deal?"

"Sure, Sam."

"Thanks, Sally."

"Sam, honey," Sally's voice pouted. "When are you coming back?"

"I'm not sure," Sam said. "It may not be until tomorrow – if I play my cards right here tonight."

Sam heard Emma coming down the stairs.

"I can't talk now," Sam said into the phone. "I'll see you tomorrow." Then, he hung up. He listened until he heard Emma turn into the kitchen, the soft click of the light switch being turned on echoed down the hall.

On the desk, Sam found feed bills and invoices. He came across a letter from the Anderson Transport Company out of Louisville, Kentucky. Quickly, he noted the name and address into a small notebook he had in his pants pocket. He skimmed quietly through the small desk drawers, but found nothing else interesting. He jotted down the number he'd seen in Casey's room, then re-placed the notebook back into his pocket and walked over to the shelves. Scanning the stockpile of old, leather-bound poetry books and novels, he saw titles by Camus, Thoreau, and Du Maurier. Numerous volumes of books on horses, equine medicines, stable management, and dressage training stood in the center, while the two lower shelves held numerous art books.

Interesting, he thought to himself. He'd found that a person's true character was shown mostly in the books on their shelves.

He noticed a box of books sitting in a corner near the shelves. He pulled out a book from the box that looked unread, entitled "*Famous Horses of the World.*" An envelope fell from the back of the book. Sam heard Emma's footsteps. Quickly, he picked up the envelope, folded it, and placed it in his back pants pocket. He figured he'd get a chance to look at it later, when he knew Emma wouldn't be around.

When she didn't come into the room, he relaxed and walked to the large chair, carrying the book. He gently pushed the black cat to one side of the cushion and sat down. The cat jumped out of the chair and sat by the fire, slowly cleaning her fur, then left the room with her tail in the air in the curious form of a question mark.

Sam settled back into the big chair and opened the book, slowly turning the pages. Suddenly, he stopped and stared at the photograph on the last page. The black colt stood in the Winner's Circle, draped with a blanket of red roses, his head held high. His tail and mane blew in a strong wind, the bright, white star on his forehead the only visible mark on him. Standing next to this champion was a man that Sam knew - George Mason. Astride the tall colt, the mud-spattered jockey sat smiling in the gold and red silks, his goggles on top of his cap, leaving only the skin around his eyes visible. Sam read the caption. There was something about the jockey's eyes that made the hair on the back of Sam's neck stand up. Sam had seen those eyes somewhere before.

◆ ◆ ◆ ◆

The brightness of the kitchen light against the white walls and cabinets startled Emma. She'd chosen white when she moved in, then added ivy-covered wallpaper on one wall to bring life into the room. Plants hung by the bay windows where the oval, Formica-top table sat that faced the stable.

She began the coffee and pulled the salmon from the refrigerator to warm a little, seeing the bottle of wine Sam had brought. Then, she found herself thinking about Ted. There were similarities between Sam and Ted. Ted had been tall, like Sam, but much thinner, his features harsh, like a lean wolf in the wild. Ted was gentle, like Sam – at first.

Since the accident, she often thought she'd heard Ted come in late at night, just as he did after he was out late with Joe. She would become afraid and sit in her room and wait, barely able to breathe, waiting for him to come to her room and begin hurting her again. But then, she'd remind herself that he was dead. She had felt so alone.

One day, she'd come across her father's gun and remembered the last time she'd held it. That was when she'd decided it was time to put it all away - Ted, the fear, the heartbreak. She'd placed the gun in the glove compartment of her father's truck, where he'd always kept it.

Shadow softly walked into the kitchen and rubbed up against Emma's leg, purring.

"Hi, Shadow," Emma said to the cat. The cat meowed in answer. Then, she went to her food dish near the side door, sat down, and began to eat, her tail curled around her feet.

Emma wondered what it was about Sam that made her feel like a young girl again. A lot of years had passed and there was still a lot about him she didn't know. *He could be another man who can hurt me*, she thought. *Oh, why did I ever ask him to stay in the first place? What is wrong with me tonight?*

She put her hands in her hair and shook it as if to shake her scrambled thoughts out to make them disappear. Setting up the tray, Emma resolved to herself, *I'll just feed this man, and take him back to the city. You can't go back in time. Chicago is in the past.*

Shadow rubbed against her leg again, bringing Emma back to reality. She went to the door at the side of the kitchen and let the cat outside. Emma stood on the small landing and looked up at the night sky, smiling as she saw Venus chasing the full moon, just as her father had described in his favorite Friedrich painting. Then, she turned and went back inside.

She walked into the den with the tray of coffee mugs in her hand, the wonderful aroma of fresh coffee preceding her. She set the tray on the table before the couch.

Sam, leaving the book open, stood and placed it on the same table. He picked up a mug and sipped the strong liquid, feeling the warmth as it traveled down his throat.

"Good coffee," he said, looking at Emma over the top of his mug.

"Thanks. Sam, —" Emma stopped. She saw the photograph on the opened page of the book. She picked it up and stared at the man standing next to the horse and took in a quick breath. The face could have been her father's staring back at her, his smile and the lines around his eyes.

"What's up?" Sam asked, noticing her reaction to the picture.

"I feel I know this man. He reminds me of my father."

She read the caption aloud.

"George Mason's Koenig's Wonder, Carlos Madera up, won the 94th Kentucky Derby. Koenig's Wonder was the first horse to ever win six consecutive races before a Derby win. He disappeared right after winning the Kentucky Derby and hasn't been seen since."

"I don't remember seeing this book before," Emma said as she looked at Sam. She turned to the copyright page. "It was just printed last September." Then, she saw the cover. It was the book that she had tossed into the public library donation box on the morning Ted was shot. She handed the book back to Sam.

"I saw that horse at the Derby," Sam said, looking back at the photograph, filing away in his mind Emma's reaction to it. "He was magnificent. The owner didn't discover the imposter until after the Belmont race, the following June. Damnedest thing. The lip tattoo was the same as the champion, but the horse was not the same."

Emma picked up her coffee cup, her hand shaking slightly. "Ted and Joe were at that race, too," she said, after taking a sip with the cup in both hands.

Sam's head shot up. Just then, he remembered seeing a guy who he'd thought was Joe at that Derby. He'd seen him with a horse that looked almost identical to Koenig's Wonder, but was scratched a few minutes before the race. Sam had later found the reason "Frank's Revenge" had been scratched was due to a sprain. *Could that possibly have been the horse used in the swap?* Sam thought to himself. Now, he wondered how the horse would have ended up in Emma's stable, if that was the case.

"It was after that race when Ted brought Frankie here. That was a couple of months before he died," Emma continued, hating the reminder.

Sam looked at Emma, and saw her face was white.

"What were you going to ask me, when you came into the room?" Sam asked to change the subject. He was itching to press on, to find out what Emma knew, but the one thing he'd learned in his job was to be patient with a witness. *Later, I'll ask her*, he thought.

"Hm?" she asked, then remembered. "Oh, I was going to see if you were ready to cook."

He smiled. "You bet."

"Then, follow me," she said as she picked up the coffee tray.

◆ ◆ ◆ ◆

"What do you need?" Emma asked, once they were in the kitchen.

"I make a pretty mean broiled salmon. Do you have a broiler pan?"

"Here's the broiler pan," she said, pulling the pan from the bottom drawer of the stove. "The salmon's over there on the counter. What else do you need?"

"Some butter, lemon, garlic, salt, pepper, and a small saucepan."

Emma began gathering the items and watched Sam as he peeled the garlic cloves, slicing them. He slid the slivers of garlic into the flesh of the salmon.

Then he cut the lemon in half and squeezed it over the fish just before he placed it under the broiler. He started to melt the butter over a low heat on the top of the stove, adding the salt and pepper.

"How much time do you need?" Emma asked as she watched in wonder.

"About five minutes each side, once it really starts to cook."

"I'll make a salad."

"Good, I'll open the bottle of wine I bought after lunch. It'll go great with the salmon. Do you like white wine?"

"Yes," Emma said, frowning, even though she only had it when she went out to dinner in the city. She stared at the bottle, feeling uneasy around the alcohol.

Sam saw Emma's face and wondered what Ted Jacobs had been like. "I only like a small amount of wine with dinner. I drink very little, usually." He noticed Emma's shoulders relax and smiled. He'd been right on target. The son-of-a-bitch had been a drinker, and probably a mean drunk.

Emma returned Sam's smile and began pulling out the lettuce, tomato, mushroom, red onion, and Calamata olives for the salad. Sharing her kitchen was new for her, and she decided she liked it.

Sam began opening the wine, while Emma pulled down two tall-stemmed wine glasses from the cabinet in front of him.

"Nice glasses," Sam said, noticing the intricately cut glass.

"Thanks. They were presents that my parents received at their wedding."

He poured the slightly golden-colored liquid into the tall glasses, and handed one to Emma. As he gently touched the rim of his glass to hers, a delicate ring echoed through the room. Emma noticed that the light from overhead shone through the cut glass like soft rays of sunlight.

"What type of wine is this?" Emma asked.

"Chardonnay."

She watched as Sam swirled the wine slightly in the glass, then held his nose over the lip to catch the odors. Emma followed his lead.

"What do you smell?" he asked.

"The soft aroma of summer," was all Emma could think of. The fruit was different from anything she had smelled before.

"I like that. Now, take just a sip and close your eyes, swirling it in your mouth for a second before swallowing." Sam watched Emma's face as she took her first sip. When she closed her eyes, he had an urge to kiss her soft lips, but waited.

The first taste was fresh, almost buttery, with a lingering fruity flavor that rested lightly at the back of her throat. When she swallowed, she licked her lips in a sensuous fashion, savoring the last bit of the wine. She smiled as she opened her eyes. Before she knew it, Sam was kissing her. She could taste the wine from his mouth and felt a wave of desire rush over her.

"Why did you do that?" she asked when he released her, her body shaking.

"Because you looked so inviting and I wanted to taste the wine on your lips." Sam smiled, then went to the stove and brushed the butter mixture onto the salmon fillets before turning them over. He closed the oven door and turned to Emma.

"Did you like it?" Sam asked, raising his glass to her.

"Like what?"

"The wine?"

She took a deep breath and answered, "Oh, yes, very much. I don't think I have ever had anything like it."

"Have you ever been wine tasting?"

"No."

"I'll take you someday."

Emma liked the thought of 'some day' with Sam.

"Where're your plates?" he asked, setting his glass down on the counter.

"Over here." Emma took two plates from the cabinet, deciding to use her mother's china. She used it every so often over the years, on special occasions. She loved the soft, white color with the small ivy design around the edges, the gold plating on the rim shone in the light.

Sam turned on the tap and ran water in the sink until it was hot, then he closed the stopper and placed the dishes in the sink, letting the hot water wash over them.

"They will be warm by the time the salmon is done."

"Do you like blue-cheese dressing, Sam?"

"You bet - that's my favorite."

She finished the salads, placing the long, cut slices of plum tomatoes on the plate, around the lettuce and mushrooms, then dropped the red onion rings on top of the olives in the center. She was pleased with the way they looked, as she drizzled the dressing over it all.

"Where did you learn to cook, Sam?" Emma asked.

"My friend, in New York. He taught me a few tricks at his restaurant." Sam saw the salads and said, "It looks like you have a few tricks of your own. That's a great looking salad."

"Thanks, I guess it's the artist in me. How's the salmon coming?"

"Almost done." Sam poured more wine into their glasses.

"Here's to old friends," he said, raising his glass in a toast and tapping it lightly against hers, the sound of the crystal ringing again softly in the air.

"To friends," Emma said, then took a sip, as she watched Sam over the rim of her glass. He tipped his glass up and closed his eyes, savoring the flavors that were exploding in his mouth, the same flavors she was now tasting herself.

The smell of the salmon filled the air.

"It's time," Sam said. "The nose is always the best timer." He pulled the salmon from the oven and placed the broiler pan on top of the stove. Emma dried the plates as he buttered the tops of the fish.

"Where would you like to eat?" Sam asked.

"Let's take these into the den by the fire." Emma pulled out a large tray from below the counter.

"I'd hoped that's what you'd say."

Together, they put everything onto the tray.

"Why don't you carry the wine glasses," Sam said. "I'll bring the tray."

Emma saw him put the bottle of wine on the tray, then he followed her to the den.

Sam set the tray on the low, coffee table. After setting down the wine glasses, Emma went to the radio and turned to a Portland jazz station she loved. Carmen McRae was singing about it being *Too Late Now*." Sam took a salad plate and sat in the large red chair near the fireplace. Seeing him in that chair gave Emma a familiar feeling in her stomach. She decided it was a good feeling. The chair had been her father's. All of her earlier resolutions to herself in the kitchen were forgotten and she decided to wait and see what happened.

"You make a fantastic salad," Sam said. "I like the dressing."

"Thanks," Emma said, as she sat on the couch and watched Sam. Like all his movements, he ate with gusto, stopping once in awhile to sip his wine.

He noticed her watching him and stopped.

"You're not eating," he said. "Anything wrong?"

"No. I just enjoy watching you. I keep thinking how little I really know about you." She took a bite. "You're different from my husband."

"Different? In what way?"

"Ted had an annoying way of slipping into his own little world when he wanted to avoid something." She stopped to take a small bite of tomato, then added, "You totally focus on whatever you are doing. There doesn't seem to be any regrets of the past and no anticipation of the future. You live now, this moment. I felt it when you kissed me the very first time, and I can see it now in the way you are attacking that salad. You enjoy whatever you're doing to the fullest."

"Well, I usually try," he said a little shyly.

It was the first time she had seen his strong confidence waiver.

"Just wait until you see me attack that salmon," Sam said as he got up and walked to the tray of food. Back in the chair with the plate of salmon in his hand, he dug in and smiled at her.

Emma did the same and settled back onto the couch, taking her first bite.

"Mmm, this is great," she said. "It's perfect. So light and buttery, it melts in my mouth."

"Glad you like it."

They ate in silence for a while, savoring the tastes in their mouths, sipping wine, listening to the crackle of the fire and the soft jazz.

"You've changed quite a bit from that shy girl I met in Chicago," Sam said.

Emma put her fork down and looked at Sam. Images of the young girl she had been flashed through her mind and she smiled. Her hand went to the locket Sam had given her as she remembered sitting in the dark theater, and Sam's first kiss.

"I decided long ago that life is too short to waste even a moment in time.

Some, I find, are very precious." *And, this is one of those moments,* she thought to herself. She had to look away. He had once again captivated her with his eyes, and she was afraid that he would see the tiny drops at the corners of her eyes. No one, except Sam, had ever gotten this close to her heart. She'd tried to let Ted into her world. At first, he'd seemed to want in. But, then, he closed himself from her and became someone she no longer knew.

Sam saw the shadow cross over Emma's face and vowed again to himself to find out why.

"I have something for you," Sam said.

Emma watched as he reached into his pocket and pulled out his wallet. Inside, she saw a black and white photo of herself and recognized it as the one Jennifer had taken in her barn in Indiana. Next to the photo was a shiny dime. Sam reached in and retrieved the dime.

"I drove to Indiana a few years ago, before I was out of the Air Force. I was hoping to find you. However, you had already sold your family's farm and moved out west, according to some nice old fellows I met at the diner in Grandview."

"You went to Grandview?"

"Yep. Well, when I found you were gone, I was devastated. I stopped beside the river that runs just outside of town and wondered what to do next. I was about to leave, when I looked down and found this dime. I've always believed that when you find a coin, you should always pick it up, and it'll bring you luck."

Sam ran his thumb over the coin, making it shine even more in the firelight.

"I vowed then, when I found it, that I would someday find you again. And, look where we are now."

Emma smiled as Sam took her hand, placed the coin in her palm, and slowly curled her fingers around it.

"Thank you, Sam," Emma said, opening her hand and looking down again at the coin.

"I noticed you also have my photo in your wallet," she added, looking up at him.

"Yeah," he said smiling, looking at the photo again before he put his wallet back into his pocket. "I found that in your old barn. It's been everywhere with me."

"I don't know what to say..." she began.

"You don't have to say anything, Em." Sam picked up his plate and began eating again, smiling to himself as he watched her.

Emma laid the dime on the table in front of her. She opened her locket and placed the dime inside, then slowly snapped it shut. It fit perfectly. She was overwhelmed to know that Sam had carried her photo all these years and felt a little awkward and shy all of a sudden – almost as if she was a young girl again.

In silence, they finished their dinner. Emma then stretched out on the rug in front of the fire and watched the flames, her head resting on her forearms. Sam sat in the chair, stretched his long legs in front of him and watched her face.

Emma thought it was rare when two people can be together in silence and know peace. In the beginning, she had that with Ted until they were married. Here, now, it filled the room she loved most in the house. Peace can be so fleeting, yet here it remained.

Gerry Mulligan was playing *"Night Lights"* on the radio. Sam remembered that they had listened to this before on the waterfront in Chicago. He had wanted to dance with Emma then, but her parents had been there. He got up now and reached out a hand to her.

"We never got to dance to this before," he said. "Would you like to now?"

She nodded and rose, slipping slowly into his arms. The gentle music flowed around them, carrying them back to a time when they were young, learning about each other, their fingers interlocking and caressing. Emma laid her head on Sam's shoulder and followed his lead in a small circle in the center of the room. She liked the smell of his skin and the feel of his arm wrapped around her, holding her close to him. She allowed her heart to slowly open the dream again, the one that she had closed a long time ago, of her and Sam forever.

After the music stopped, they stood, looking into each other's eyes, searching. Sam placed his hand under her chin and softly kissed her, their lips barely touching. She let him in, tasting his breath, his lips, his soul. She was beginning to feel lost, to feel abandonment, to feel love. Then, she felt a chill and turned away. She walked over and sat down before the fireplace again, wrapping her arms around herself.

A little confused, Sam went to pour more wine into their glasses. His hand touched hers as he handed Emma her glass, and his touch sparked a fire deep in her stomach, a familiar warmth. He then lay on the floor next to her, raised up on one elbow so that he could see the firelight on her face. He kicked off his shoes and reached up a hand to caress her cheek. His piercing, blue eyes penetrated her soul, speaking silently of gentle embraces and summer kisses stolen in the night.

"What do you want, Emma?" Sam asked softly in his husky voice, as if for her ears alone.

She looked into the flames. After a moment, she set down her wine glass and said, "The love like my parents had." She wanted the fantasy to come true, like the strong love her parents had between them. That was true love. They had spent their young lives raising Emma, and she knew throughout their lives together, they spent every day caring for each other.

Sam's eyes met hers in the warm light as tears welled up in hers.

"What's wrong?" Sam asked her, gently brushing the tears away.

She was quiet for a moment.

"Ted was a good man, before he began drinking. When I first met him, he was warm and gentle, so attentive and caring, a lot like you," she said, then looked away.

Sam sat still, waiting for her to continue.

"Maybe I was just searching for someone like you. Shortly after I bought this ranch, I drove down to Eugene – to look for you." She smiled at Sam. Emma didn't know why she felt she had to tell him, but found she couldn't stop the words. "I found the phone number for your parents' home and I called from a diner near the highway. That's when your mother told me over the phone that you were getting married. I felt lost and alone, like a dream had died inside of me.

"A few months later, I met Ted. We dated for a while. Then one day, out of the blue, he asked me to marry him. I gave Ted what was left of my heart and he broke it into pieces."

She stopped and turned away from Sam, her throat knotting up.

He waited.

"That was when I realized Ted didn't really love me. He had only married me because I would be able to give him what he needed – money to support his habits that he had carefully hidden from me. But, by then, it was too late."

Emma wiped the tears that had begun to fall down her cheeks. It was time, she felt. Time to share what had happened to her. She had been afraid to before, but she didn't feel afraid any longer. She heaved a sigh, releasing a pressure from her breast that she had harbored too long.

"There's a fine line between passion and pain," she continued. "At first, I was excited by his passion and strength, but the alcohol turned him into an animal and he'd lose control. The dream was shattered as I tried to fight him, but he was too strong. All I could do was lie there and cry...until he was finished. I wanted him dead...the next day, he was." Tears streamed now down her cheeks and she began to sob, her whole body shaking as she released the pain.

Sam held her gently in his arms and wiped her tears away. *No wonder you've been so afraid*, he thought. Anger grabbed him at the thought of anyone hurting her.

"I'm sorry, Sam. I've never told anyone about this. Please don't repeat it."

"Never, I promise."

He kissed her forehead softly and gently pulled her closer to him in comfort. She wanted nothing more than to be in his arms, feeling his strength cradle her as he caressed her hair with his hand.

Time, once again, stood still for them – they were alone in the world at that moment with their pasts bared and unable to hurt them any longer. They lay quietly in each other's arms.

Emma relaxed, feeling safe for the first time in a long time. She was suddenly very tired, and soon fell asleep.

Sam reached for a blanket on the couch and laid it over Emma, holding her gently against him with her head on his shoulder. He listened to the gentle sound of her breath and let out a long, silent sigh.

He thought about Emma's words, her dreams, her desires for love. He, too, had been searching for it, but was always comparing everyone to Emma.

"Em," he whispered softly, but there was no response. He realized she was asleep. "I love you," he said softly.

Eventually, with Dinah Washington's voice on the radio softly singing *"What a Difference a Day Makes,"* Sam fell sound asleep.

CHAPTER SEVENTEEN

T he sound of distant thunder aroused Emma. She awoke next to Sam and remembered that he'd held her in his arms all night. She watched him sleep now, the sound of his relaxed breath reminding her of the gentle waves of the ocean.

When he awoke, he smiled and began caressing her face with his eyes and his hands. He seemed to want to capture every possible detail of her, using his eyes like the lens of a camera. His lips softly touched her forehead, kindling the fire that had been burning ever so slowly within her since they had first kissed in the city.

Was that only yesterday? Emma thought.

Sam was burning to touch her, but he knew he needed to go very slowly with Emma. The first move had to come from her. He waited and watched as her eyes changed, growing darker in the soft light.

She reached up and gently took his face in her hands, kissing his cheeks, and running her fingers through his hair. She knew there was no stopping the yearning that was growing inside of her and she was no longer afraid.

"I'll never hurt you, Em," he whispered in her ear, and she surrendered to him.

Their passions met the fury of the thunder and lightning nearby, their bodies intertwining in a dance of hearts and flesh, flooding their bodies as sheets of rain poured onto the land. The full force of the storm and their passions washed over them, taking them to a place they had only dreamed of until now. Then, just as suddenly as it had arrived, the storm passed on, the soft thunder echoing their heartbeats as they clung to each other.

If only moments like this never ended, Emma thought to herself. She sighed contentedly, her head lying on his chest with his arms wrapped around her, their legs entangled, feet touching. Neither of them spoke, afraid it would break the spell. The sun burst through the clouds, warming them with its rays through the window as they lay in their private world. Sam began to caress her softly. Emma could feel the affection in his heart flowing through his fingertips into her skin. She laid her hand on his and pressed it gently against her heart, feeling his warmth. They momentarily slipped into a world of clouds and sunbeams, dozing lazily in each other's arms.

"Are you awake, Emma?"

It was Sam's voice. Emma heard it from a distance, then realized she was still walking in her dream world, where they had been lying on the hilltop near the stream with the sun glowing on them.

"Mmhmm," she sighed, then stretched lazily like a cat. She felt new and alive. Sharing her past and herself with Sam seemed to have lifted a huge weight from her, and she wondered if it would last. She just knew she had never been truly happy, until now.

"Good morning, sunshine." He touched her face with his hand.

"Morning. What time is it?"

Sam looked at the clock on the mantle above the fireplace. "Almost eleven. What're your plans for today?" he asked as he raised himself up on one elbow, wishing he didn't have a job to do.

"To keep you here all day," she said with a big grin. The dark hair on his chest glistened in the sun filling the room. She reached over and felt his heart beating.

"I have no objections to that," he said, feeling the tug on his heart, wishing it were true. "As long as you feed me once in awhile," he added as he winked and flashed his marvelous smile at her.

She yawned and stretched, waking more fully. Her mind began to give way to reality. She hated the way it raced ahead with visions of a thousand different things that needed to be done that day. Consciously, she began to slow her mind, focusing on the one vision that had appealed to her. Sam was now stroking her hair.

"Unfortunately, I have to judge a show in Portland today." She was wishing she could share it with Sam. "When do you need to get back to the city?"

"I probably should get back by noon," Sam said. "I have some business I need to take care of." He leaned back and pulled on his jeans, then stood up to slip into his shirt.

"Sure," she said, gathering the blanket around her that Sam had lain over them the night before. "I'll just go take a quick shower and be right down." She gathered her clothes and went upstairs, knowing the dream was now over.

While Emma showered, Sam took the dinner tray from the den to the kitchen. Out of habit, he looked in the freezer for the coffee and smiled to himself when he found it there. After starting to brew the coffee, he washed the dishes, then placed them in the dish drainer.

Sam turned when Emma entered the kitchen. She was wearing jeans and a light blue shirt, which set off the color of her dark hair. He walked over to her and took her into his arms. He kissed her gently and smelled the sweet, familiar lavender scent in her hair.

She felt the hard muscles in his back with her hands and let his strength flow through her. She placed her head against his chest; the smell of his skin where his shirt was unbuttoned was like sweet hay to her, his heartbeat pulsated in her ear.

Sam stepped back, holding her at arms' length, but the distance didn't help his need. "Do you mind if I clean up a bit?" he asked.

"Not at all. I'll show you where the bathroom is upstairs."

Emma took his hand and led him out into the hallway and up the stairs lined with dark, oiled wood. There were four rooms; the door on one of them was closed. To the left was an open room with large windows, the sunlight exploding throughout it. An unfinished painting stood on an easel facing the light.

"I'm glad you still paint" Sam said, hesitating at the door. The smell of paint thinner and Linseed oil was in the air; a palette of colors and a ceramic jar with brushes stood next to the easel. He could see the white horse on the dark background of the canvas, the seats of the unfinished stadium behind the horse and man. The horse and the man's face were more complete than the rest of the painting. He walked over to it and saw the small photograph of the same pair taped to the top of the easel.

"When I first saw this room," Emma said as she walked into the bright room after Sam, "I knew it had to be my studio. I started this when I found the photograph, shortly after moving here." The large white stallion in the painting leaped into the air, his mane flying behind him, as the man stood on the ground in his uniform, holding the lead to the horse in his hand as if the animal was a large kite flying in the air. "It's been difficult for me to finish it."

Sam remembered her words from the previous night and gently placed his arm around her. They stood in the light, watching the colors on the canvas change as the sun rose higher in the sky. He knew that, in the past, the Spanish Riding School had displayed their best-trained horses in these performances for the emperors of Austria. Sam stood in awe when he recognized the man in the photograph was Emma's father.

"This is marvelous," he said. "You have captured those two beautifully."

"That's my father in Verden," she said. Sam noticed Emma's voice had softened, and when he looked at her, a small tear slowly fell down one side of her face. He reached over and gently wiped away the tear.

Emma smiled and turned, walking out of the room and continued down the hall. Sam watched as she silently passed the closed door, then went to the end of the hall.

"The bathroom's in here. Each room upstairs shares it." Emma stepped into a room painted white with green ivy wallpaper above the wainscoting. The fixtures were white porcelain with brass hardware, a striking contrast to the green-tiled floor. A six-foot, white, claw-foot tub with a brass shower attachment stood on the outside wall. The same sweet smell of lavender filled the room and a corner of the mirror still held the moisture from Emma's shower.

Sam saw the open, white door to the right and walked into a large bedroom.

"That's my room," she said, a little embarrassed as she followed him. "Sorry it's such a mess."

He looked quickly around the room as she talked, noticing a couple boxes of men's clothes sitting next to a dresser and a tall armoire with bevel-mirrored doors standing against the far wall. When he saw the gray-tone photo of a woman's profile sitting next to a telephone on the bed stand, he recognized Emma's mother in the photo.

"Help yourself to anything you need," Emma said as she walked back into the bathroom. She laid clean, white towels over the edge of the tub. "There's a new toothbrush in the cabinet."

"Thanks," Sam said, coming up behind her. He turned her around and looked into her eyes, the steamy air circling around them. He took her chin in his hand and gently kissed her. "I'll only be a moment."

After Emma left, Sam turned on the water in the sink. Once he knew she was downstairs, he went into her bedroom. He sat on the bed, picked up the receiver of the telephone, and dialed, pulling the notebook from his pocket.

"Hello," a female voice said in the receiver.

"Sally, it's Sam. I need you to check on the Anderson Transport Company. Here's the address and phone number. Don't tell them where you work, just act like you're going to ship a horse to Washington and get what you can out of them." Sam gave her the information.

"Okay, Sam."

"Also, please call George Mason for me and tell him to get out here now. I think I've found his horse for him. I'll explain later." He hung up.

Sam sat and looked at the photograph next to the phone. He'd met Emma's mother in Chicago, but this was a younger photograph of her. The face had the same angelic smile and dreamy look in her eyes he had seen in Emma's when they had first met years ago. He wished he could bring that back for her. He then noticed the riding clothes lying on the Bentwood rocker and tall boots sitting nearby. He smiled, then went back into the bathroom, washed his hands and face, and brushed his teeth.

◆ ◆ ◆ ◆

Emma took down two cups and poured herself some coffee. She could hear the water running upstairs. When she saw that Sam had put the dinner dishes in the drainer, she smiled. She enjoyed washing them in the deep kitchen sink full of sudsy, warm water. This came from something her mother had taught her when she had become impatient to be done with the dishes so she could go ride her horse. 'It's part of the process of life,' her mother had said in her broken German accent. 'Don't be in such a rush that you miss the simplest of life's pleasures.'

Emma knew her mother lived on in her heart. Looking into the far corner of the kitchen, she saw the rocker that her mother had re-finished for her after that day when they had found it in a man's garage for five dollars, proud of themselves for finding such a bargain. The beautiful rosewood, that had been hidden beneath the rippled, old, black varnish, now gleamed through the shellac.

Sam walked in.

"That was fast," Emma said, pouring him a cup of coffee and handing it to him.

"Didn't want to miss anything," he said with a big smile, brushing his lips softly against hers.

"Thanks for making the coffee and doing the dishes," she said, looking at him over her cup. She noticed her hand was shaking from the jolt she'd received from his kiss.

"No problem."

"Are you hungry?" Emma asked.

"Not really. We ate so late last night. How about you?"

"No." They carried their coffee to the oval table and sat down, looking out toward the stable.

◆ ◆ ◆ ◆

"Anybody home?" Emma heard Joe call out as he walked in her front door.

"In here, Joe," Emma answered, wishing she didn't have to share this precious time with Sam. She frowned at Sam and rolled her eyes.

Joe walked in and stopped, seeing Sam sitting at the table.

"Sam!" Joe exclaimed as he turned, his eyes glancing sideways at Sam. "What're you doing here?" Carlos had called him last night to tell him that Sam had been there looking around the stable, but he hadn't mentioned that Sam was still here. Joe looked over at Emma with a disapproving look, walked to the coffee pot and poured himself a cup of coffee without being asked.

"I was having trouble with my plane," Sam said, watching Joe walk to the table, turn a chair around and sit next to Emma. Joe straddled the seat and pulled it towards Emma, so his knee touched her thigh. Sam saw Emma move her chair closer to the wall, away from Joe's knee.

"Emma offered to take me to Portland," Sam added, omitting the day and night they had just spent together.

"Next time, Joe, knock first," Emma said. "What're you doing here?" she asked after a moment.

Joe looked at Emma. She'd never spoken to him like that before. He glanced at Sam and knew he was the reason she was being so snippy.

"I came over to talk to...uh...Casey."

"Emma told me you sent him to help her after her husband died."

"Yeah, I just wanted to do anything I could to help." Joe patted Emma's hand, which she pulled away. "Why do you want to know?" Joe added.

"You know me," Sam said, winking at Emma. "Curious as a cat."

Joe had caught the wink and fumed quietly inside. He wanted to smash Sam's face.

Sam saw the anger flare in the smaller man's eyes. He took the advantage, looked at his watch, stood up, then said to Emma, "I'd better get back to the city. Good to see you again, Joe." Sam waved to Joe and walked out of the kitchen. He stopped in the hall where he could still hear Emma and Joe.

Emma was glad for the excuse to get away from Joe. She walked to the counter and picked up her purse.

"I won't be back until later this afternoon," she said.

"No problem," Joe said as he came up next to Emma. "I'll be waiting for you." He ran a hand up her arm.

A chill ran over her skin and she hugged herself. She heard his breath coming in short gasps, like Ted used to do when he was angry.

"I don't like you being with Sam," Joe added. "Stay away from him."

She looked him in the eye and said, "Joe, I can do whatever I want. You can't tell me what to do. Besides, I like Sam. I always have."

"He'll only break your heart."

"It's my heart."

Sam walked back into the kitchen.

"Are you coming, Em?" Sam asked, watching Joe.

"Yes." She grabbed her things and turned. "I'll let you out, Joe," she said with confidence, now that Sam stood near her.

The warmth of the bright sunlight felt good. To Emma, the world seemed new after the storm, the grass glistened; vibrant colors splashed everywhere, the air smelled clean and sweet.

Sam watched as Joe walked down toward the stable. He saw a black truck and trailer parked near the large double doors of the building and remembered seeing that rig yesterday as they'd flown over Joe's ranch. The hair on the back of his neck stood up.

"Sam, are you coming?" Emma called from her car.

He turned and climbed in next to Emma. She drove off down the lane away from the house.

"Thank you," Emma said, placing her hand on his knee. He took her hand in his and brought it to his lips.

"What'd I do?" he asked, pretending innocence while he kept her hand in his.

"Joe makes me uncomfortable sometimes. I don't like the way he just walks into my house - like he owned the place."

"I noticed. Has he always done that?"

"Yes, since he and Ted became friends. I've asked him before to stop, but he just ignores me." She thought of the scene in her house the other day that had shaken her.

"Well," Sam said, looking at Emma while she drove. "I'll talk to him, if you'd like me to. I know Joe." He knew how Joe treated women, which made Sam's blood boil. He rolled his window down. *Yes, I'll talk to Joe, indeed*, he thought to himself. He still had a little unfinished business himself with the man.

"No, I can handle it. But, it was nice that you were here today."

Emma smiled at Sam, then pulled her hand back and placed it on the steering wheel to steer around a sharp curve. She drove past the store in Scholls, then turned her car north and headed over the Sylvan hills into the city.

"Where is the show today?" Sam asked after awhile.

"Columbia Stables."

"How long do these take?"

"It depends on the number of entries we have. These events can sometimes go on for eight to nine hours, but I will probably only be judging for two or three hours today. Then, one of the other judges will take over."

Emma thought of not having Sam with her and took a deep breath. "Would you like to come with me?" she asked.

"I'd love to, but I've got some things I have to do. Turn here," he said, as they approached the west side of Portland. The traffic was heavy as people drove to their jobs. Emma thought of their flight over her property, seeing it from the air.

"When will you have the photos from yesterday?" Emma asked.

"I'll send them in today and try to push a rush on it. Maybe I'll have them by tomorrow."

"How can you get them that fast?"

"I have a friend who has a darkroom, and I used black and white film. This is it," Sam said as he nodded towards a brown-tone building with white Grecian sculptures on the front.

Emma pulled up in front of the building and stopped the car. Sam took her hand. His incredible blue eyes pulled her in again and he gave her a deep kiss. The world disappeared and she heard the buzzing around her she'd heard earlier that morning.

"Thanks for everything," Sam said, smiling. He got out of the car and shut the door, leaning down on his elbows to look at Emma through the window. "It was wonderful," he added.

"It was my pleasure," Emma said when she found her voice again.

"I'm going to be busy for a couple of days. I was wondering if I could give you a call when I get finished?"

Behind Sam, Emma noticed a pretty blonde appear from the front door of his building, wearing a short, tight, red dress. Even though her hair was pulled up, Emma recognized the woman from the jazz club the other night. The woman turned to look into her mailbox, then looked their way. She smiled and came over to Emma's car, swinging her hips.

"Why, Sam, honey," the woman said with the same sweet southern accent Emma had heard in the club. "Where've you been? You didn't come back last night."

Sam became nervous and awkward, hating the familiar way Sally took with him. He cleared his throat. "Emma, this is Sally, my...uh..., secretary."

Sally leaned over next to Sam and looked at Emma with her brown eyes. Emma noticed Sam's eyes drop to Sally's deep cleavage.

"Hello, sugar," Sally said to Emma. "It's real nice to meet you." Then, she put her arm around Sam in a possessive manner.

Before Emma could reply, she saw Sally wink at Sam and walk back to the entrance of the building, back to the row of mailboxes.

Sam looked back at Emma, clasping his hands together. "So, can I give you a call later?" he asked again nervously.

"Sure," Emma said, knowing in her heart that he wouldn't. She reached over and brushed back a dark curl that had fallen onto his forehead, then she looked into his eyes. She wondered if her eyes revealed the thoughts circling through her mind and the ache in her heart.

His face lit up with his intoxicating smile, then he stood and waved as Emma slowly pulled away. Glancing in the rear-view mirror, she saw Sam go up to Sally and place his hand on her back as they disappeared together into the building.

◆ ◆ ◆ ◆

The dream was shattered as Emma drove with tears streaming down her cheeks. She felt like such a fool as she turned onto the highway, heading toward the fairgrounds.

Later, when she had parked her car, she wiped her face with a tissue and looked herself in the eye in the mirror. Sam had broken her heart once before, and here she was - repeating history.

"You idiot!" she said to herself. Angry with herself now, she grabbed her bag and went into the women's restroom to clean up her face. It was time to go to work.

◆ ◆ ◆ ◆

Joe banged into the door to Emma's stable, opened it, then slammed it shut again.

"So, why the hell didn't you tell me he was still here?" Joe yelled at Carlos angrily.

"He, who?" Carlos said as he touched up the dye on the hair of the colt's forehead. From his window, he'd seen Emma and Sam Parker leave together. He was going to enjoy this, knowing how Joe salivated over that woman.

"Sam, you idiot." Joe's fury was bursting inside of him. If he couldn't smash Sam's face, he was going to smash something else.

Carlos dropped the dye equipment and quickly turned to Joe, grabbing him by the collar. He walked Joe backwards until Joe's back was against a wall. Carlos was Joe's height, but he was much stronger.

"Don't call me 'idiot,' you worm," Carlos spat into Joe's face. "We wouldn't be in this mess now if you hadn't been so stupid as to bring this horse here. Parker wouldn't be coming to your place, since he's obviously sniffing after the Mrs." He pushed Joe harder against the wall, banging his head back to make it hit against the wood.

Joe put his hands in the air in surrender. He had been furious after seeing Emma with Sam. He wanted Emma for himself. But, Carlos had his attention now.

"Gee, pal, I'm sorry," Joe said, his eyes wide. He knew Carlos had a short fuse, but had never seen him this angry before. "I didn't mean anything by it. Besides, I thought it was a great move, until Parker showed up asking questions. No one would think to look for Koenig's Wonder here. I'm just getting a little nervous about Sam. I don't like him snooping around here too much."

Joe knew Sam would recognize the mare and maybe put the pieces of the puzzle together before they could get out tonight, but he decided to keep that to himself. Joe had tolerated Carlos only because Reichmann seemed to like him, which irritated Joe.

"You're in this thing as deep as I am," Carlos said, walking away from Joe. "If anything goes wrong, I'll personally see that you're taken care of. Mr. Reichmann won't like it if this Sam guy gets in the way, so maybe you need to make sure that doesn't happen."

"So, when's the boss flying in?" Joe asked, walking around Carlos to put more distance between them.

"This afternoon. As soon as I finish this job, I'm driving in to pick him up."

"Who is this guy, anyway?" Joe asked. He shivered as he thought of his first encounter with Reichmann.

"You know as much as I need to," Carlos said. He knew a lot more than he was going to tell Joe, but he'd been instructed to keep it very quiet. Joe would know soon enough. "Just be ready when it's time. Now, bring your truck and trailer down here so we can load this animal."

Joe walked out of the stable, pushing both doors open. He was beginning to get a little nervous around this trigger-happy pot shot. He'd seen Carlos shoot before. He'd stood next to Carlos when he'd pulled the trigger on the gun that had killed Ted.

Joe got into his pickup and backed the trailer to the large, open doors. Then he stopped and turned off the engine as Carlos had instructed so the diesel engine wouldn't spook the colt as he was loaded into the trailer.

Carlos walked back to the stall where the colt stood. He took the horse's reins, opened the gate to the stall, and led the colt down the aisle to the waiting trailer, talking gently to the animal as he went. This was the only time Joe saw Carlos gentle with anything since they'd started working together.

"What time are we going to the airport?" Joe asked, after the colt was loaded.

"You're not going," Carlos answered. He turned and pointed his finger into Joe's chest. "The pilot will call you when they've landed. Remember, the horses are to not receive any hay before they arrive at the plane, and make sure you're ready."

"I'll be ready," Joe said. *Yeah*, Joe thought to himself. *I'll be ready to get rid of all of you.*

◆ ◆ ◆

Sam opened the door marked OREGON RACING COMMISSION in gold letters on the window. Sally followed him into the outer office and sat on the top of her desk, crossing her long, slender legs. She picked up a pile of messages and held them out to Sam.

"Sally, why'd you have to go and do that?" Sam was upset.

"Do what, honey?" She smiled.

Sam realized she either didn't have a clue or knew exactly what she was doing and decided to drop it.

"Okay, Sally. What do you have for me?" he asked abruptly, walking into the next office. He placed his jacket on the back of the chair and sat down at Jim's large desk.

"I called Baltimore and gave them that lip tattoo number, like you asked," Sally said, as she followed Sam. "Simon said it was the wrong number. The number was registered to Frank's Revenge."

"Good girl, Sal," Sam said. He knew in his gut that Koenig's Wonder was in Emma's stable, but something still bothered him - something he'd seen yesterday when he'd looked at the colt. He wanted so badly to believe that Emma had nothing to do with this case, but the pieces to the puzzle still just didn't quite fit.

"So, what have you been up to?" Sally asked with a pout on her thick, red lips.

"I've been working on the case," Sam said, as he quickly rifled through the messages.

"Sure, honey," Sally said, shrugging a shoulder. "I recognized her from the club the other night."

"Knock it off, Sally," Sam said shortly, looking up at Sally with fire in his eyes. "That was Emma Jacobs. Our missing colt is at her ranch, I can feel it." Sam saw the look on Sally's face and cooled down. "I just have to prove it. What about the other stuff I phoned you about?"

"I checked on Anderson's. They're very congenial and told me they ship horses anywhere, for the right fee. I tried to sound like I was concerned about shipping a horse as far as Kentucky, but the guy assured me that they've done it in the past with no problems. He told me about a horse they brought to Oregon from there just this year."

"Good going. At least we know we've got the right group. I'll have Simon send someone out on it. Did you get hold of Doc White?"

"Oh, yeah," she swooned. "He was real sweet. I think he's a widower. He loves to talk, and I love his accent."

"Sally," Sam said abruptly, stopping her rambling. "What did you find out?"

"I made the appointment for you to meet him at his office today at four."

Sam looked at his watch. It was almost two.

"What did George Mason say when you told him I wanted him out here?"

"I never talked to him. His trainer told me he'd left on a vacation this morning."

"Vacation?" Sam asked, staring at Sally. "I'm knee deep in the middle of an investigation, and when I need him here to identify a horse that I think is his, he takes a vacation?"

"Sorry, that's all I know."

"Did his trainer say where he went?"

"No, he wouldn't say. He just said Mr. Mason told him he wanted some time to himself, said something about going to meet his niece."

"Niece? I didn't think the old guy had any family. Well, call his trainer and get him out here, then."

Sally nodded and started to leave the room. "Oh, by the way, Joe Remsky moved into the ranch across from the Jacobs woman in the summer of '67."

"I wonder where he got the money?" Sam said, thinking out loud.

"It was purchased by some guy named Reichmann."

"Would you call Jim and give him that info on Remsky? Have him check on it for me."

"Sure. Do you want some coffee?" she asked.

"Yes, thanks. Also, would you mind getting me a ham and cheese on rye at the deli downstairs?" he asked as he handed Sally a ten dollar bill.

"No problem. Too busy to eat?" Sally asked with a twinkle in her eye.

Sam just scowled at her until she left. Then, he picked up the phone and dialed his Baltimore office.

"Thoroughbred Racing Protective Bureau," a female voice answered on the other end of the line.

"Georgia, this is Sam Parker. Would you ring Simon for me, please?"

"Anything for you, Sam," the voice purred. Then, there was silence for a moment.

"Simon," Sam said, when a man answered. "I need you to get some records for me that I can't get out here."

"Sure thing, Sam. What do you need?" Simon Day and Sam had worked together as a team shortly after Sam had started for the Bureau.

"Sally told me that the lip tattoo I called in was for Frank's Revenge, number J4879. Can you check further on the background of this horse, his lineage, markings, owners, races, his present owner - anything you can get on him? I need it pronto."

"No problem. I'll get back to you later today."

"Great. Oh, and would you send someone in Louisville to visit the Anderson Transport Company? They're the ones who shipped a horse out here earlier this year."

"Sure will."

"Thanks, Simon. I owe you one."

"No, you don't, Sam," the man at the other end said, before he hung up.

Sam thought for a moment of the accident when Simon had been injured on another investigation. He had stepped in just before Sam's head was about to get kicked in by a New York trainer that had gone nuts over the charges Sam had brought against him. 'All in the line of duty,' Simon had said later in the hospital, his arm in a sling. But, Sam knew that he would never forget what Simon had done for him.

Shaking his head, Sam got back to work. He called the archives section of the Newberg Gazette.

"This is Sam Parker with the Thoroughbred Racing Protective Bureau. I'm looking for any information you have on the shooting of Ted Jacobs sometime last fall."

"I remember that shooting," the woman said. "It will take me a little while to look this up, but I will call you back shortly. What is your phone number?"

"I'm at the Oregon Racing Commission in Portland," Sam said and gave her the number. Then, he thanked her and hung up.

Sam leaned back in Jim's chair and placed his feet up on the desk. He sat, staring into space, his mind jumping between images of the past two days. He methodically went over what he had seen in Emma's stable, his shock at seeing Ele again. He never thought he would see her again in his life and the ache in his gut knotted again. He sighed and realized that was part of his past and he could never expect it to change. He thought of the colt and pondered over the fact that there were no markings on him. Something wasn't right, but he couldn't put his finger on it.

Then, he remembered seeing the child-like excitement in Emma's eyes, as they had raced over her property on their ride. A smile came to his lips when he thought of holding Emma in his arms in her den.

Just then, the photograph he'd seen in the book at Emma's flashed in his mind - the mud splattered face of a jockey, the eyes that Sam couldn't forget. All of a sudden, Sam sat straight up, and he called Simon's number again.

"Simon," Sam said after his friend answered. "I'm glad I caught you. I need another favor."

"What's up?" Simon liked it when he heard this excitement in Sam's voice, but it always meant work for him.

"Would you check the name of the jockey that rode Koenig's Wonder in the Derby for me? I think I've just seen him out here, going by the name of Casey Morales."

"Sure. Let me get Mason's file for you right now." Sam could hear Simon lay the receiver down and open a file cabinet drawer nearby. Then, Simon picked up the receiver and said, "Carlos Madera."

"How long had he been riding for Mason just before the Kentucky Derby?" Sam asked. He remembered now that Madera had been George's jockey at Del Mar.

"I think it was just days before the race. Mason's other jockey disappeared...," Simon stopped, the gears in his mind now churning. "Sam, you don't think that something happened to Mason's first jockey, do you?"

"Simon, at this point, anything is possible. Find out where this Madera came from and if there's any news on the disappearing jockey. Also, see when and where Madera rode his last race."

"I'll get right on it." Simon hung up the phone.

Sam got up and began pacing the floor, asking himself questions in his mind. If Casey was the same as Mason's jockey, he was beginning to worry. *How was Emma involved in this theft? And, how did this colt end up in her stable? Had Ted been involved? Was that why he was shot?*

The phone rang. Sally was still out, so Sam answered.

"Mr. Parker, please," said the voice on the other end.

"This is Sam Parker."

"Mr. Parker, this is Amy Reynolds at the Gazette. I found the information you were asking about on the Ted Jacobs shooting." The woman's voice was low and dusty.

"I'm listening," Sam said, pulling a large notepad to him, poising his pen over the paper.

"Ted Jacobs was shot on October 21, 1968, on Joe Remsky's property shortly after dawn. Remsky's statement was that they had been hunting and separated to locate the herd. Remsky said he heard the shot, but was too far away to see anything."

Sam was making notes as the woman talked. There wasn't much here Sam didn't already know.

"The Portland police investigated," Amy continued, "but were unable to find any other hunter out there with a gun that matched the caliber of the shell the forensics dug out of Jacobs. It was a rare type of gun." This was news to Sam.

"Thanks, Ms. Reynolds, that helps me a lot," Sam said, then thanked the woman.

After he hung up, he placed another call to the police department's records division.

"Hello Harry, this is Sam Parker." Sam had known Harry Davidson since they were kids. He thought of the day Harry had been shot during a drug bust. "I need you to pull a report for me. October twenty-first of last year - Ted Jacobs' shooting."

"Sure, Sam, give me your number and I'll call you back." Sam gave him the number and hung up. Then, he got up and went to change his shirt.

A small sink stood in a large closet in Jim's office. Sam went over and quickly shaved, then pulled out a clean shirt from his bag.

After he sat back down at the desk, Sam brought out his notebook and looked up the number he'd seen in Casey's room. He picked up the phone and dialed it. When Sam heard Joe's voice, he hung up. *It's about time to pay Mr. Remsky a little visit*, Sam thought.

Sally returned with a sandwich and some coffee. Sam thanked her and dug in.

Then, the phone rang again. Sally answered it and called out to Sam that it was Harry.

"Okay, Sam," Harry said on the other line, "I've got it. I was on this one before my last case, when I was wounded." There was silence for a moment, then Harry continued. "I wrote this report. What do you want to know, Sam?"

"I understand from the newspaper that the gun used was rare. What does your report say about the gun?"

"From the projectile found in Jacobs' body, it was fired from an 8mm Mauser."

"How can you tell that from a bullet?" Sam asked.

"My dad used to own a Mauser FR-8, which was a German design built by the Spanish in the fifties. The rifle used in this case had a strange bore; the standard is .311 inches in diameter. This was a gun that probably came from South America. They were used in the German army after WWI, but were discontinued around 1938."

Sam sat in silence for a moment. The skin at the back of his neck began to crawl, but he couldn't figure out why. "What does this type of gun look like?"

"Like any military-style rifle, but they were built with un-checkered European walnut stock to reinforce the strength of the long barrel, had a bolt action, with a five-shot box magazine. The butt pad on the M98 Mauser usually was a stamped metal. Those babies were built to last."

"Thanks, Harry."

"Sam, to tell you the truth, I never really was satisfied that it had been a hunting accident, but there wasn't any proof to show otherwise. Jacobs had some debts, but his wife had taken care of those by selling some of their property. There were a couple of prior reports in California of domestic violence, but the cases were dismissed - his ex-wife was a reluctant plaintiff. Otherwise, the man was clean, with little history. Do you have something on this case, Sam? "

"I might, but I have a couple of things to do before I know for sure. I'll let you know as soon as I do. Thanks again, Harry."

Sam hung up, the muscles in his jaw working hard. *Reluctant plaintiff,* he thought to himself. He now knew why. Anger stirred inside of him and he almost wished that Jacobs was still alive, so he could beat the shit out of him.

He looked at his watch and saw it was almost three-thirty. Grabbing his coat, he took the rest of his sandwich and started to run out.

"Gotta go," he said as he rushed past Sally, tugging on his jacket. "Would you please call Doc White and let him know I will be a little late? I have to make a stop on the way to his place. Also, if Simon calls, take down the information and call me at Doc's."

"Will do," Sally said, hoping she'd get to speak to Doc White herself.

Sam put his free hand into his jacket pocket and pulled out the roll of film. He tossed it to Sally.

"Would you take this to Bennie Morris for me right away and ask him to put a rush on it? I'd like them back by tomorrow. It's very important!"

"Okay, Sam." Sally smiled to herself. She really liked Bennie.

◆ ◆ ◆ ◆

At the Portland airport, Carlos stopped the Jeep at the arrival area. As he got out, two men approached him with small carry-on bags. They wore corduroy slacks and wool jackets, attire that was much too heavy for the Oregon springtime.

"Hello, Carlos," the older man said in a heavy German accent, extending his gloved hand to the smaller man.

Carlos shook his hand and said, "Hello, Mr. Reichmann. I hope you had a pleasant flight." Carlos noticed the man's hand felt cold, even through the leather.

"It was as well as could be expected, for a commercial flight. I prefer my own jet, but this had to do under the circumstances. I think you may call me by my real name, Carlos, since there no longer is any need for pretense."

"Yes, Mr. Maseman." Carlos was one of the few who knew this man's true identity. He had been in his employ for the past three years. He'd first met these two men at the track in Venezuela, where Carlos was a jockey, a damned good one. But, he'd gotten into trouble over drugging a horse with a syringe that had been handed to him by the owner's trainer. Carlos took the fall when the drug was discovered. Mr. Maseman had found Carlos after he'd been fired and gave him this job.

Maseman looked at the other man next to him. "The flight home will be much more pleasant, wouldn't you say, Dr. Strauss?"

Karl Strauss, wearing dark glasses, was shorter and stouter than the other man. When he smiled, his square jaw line became more severe. "Yes, I would agree. I hope our plane arrives safely later this evening for us, and all is prepared for the horses."

"Remsky's working on that right now," Carlos said. "Are these all the baggage you have with you?" he asked, taking the two small cases from the men.

"Yes," Maseman said. "Did you make the other arrangements we discussed?"

"Yes," Carlos answered. "John Anderson made the phone call, as I instructed."

"Good. Then, let us go to the ranch. I am anxious to see my magnificent animal."

The men got into the Jeep. Then, Carlos drove off, heading west out of the city.

◆ ◆ ◆ ◆

Sam drove Jim's '65 red Mustang into the southwestern hills. Sam had been in this car numerous times when he was young. It had been stored in Jim's father's garage, while Jim was in the service. Sam had always told Jim he was nuts to buy a convertible in Oregon, but on days like today, it was worth its weight in gold. The earth was alive. Daffodils were beginning to bloom along the roadsides, and the purple plum trees dressed up the countryside like a woman's bonnet.

He finished his sandwich as he approached the boundaries of Emma's ranch. He liked the feeling in his gut right now when he thought of her, the same feeling that had grabbed him in Chicago when he'd first met her. It had never really disappeared. Seeing her again had awakened a part of him that he'd tried to bury a long time ago. He remembered now the vow he'd made at the side of the river in Indiana. He'd found Emma again, but he hated the reason he was here.

Noticing that Casey's Jeep was gone, Sam remembered the gun he'd seen in the small man's room. He'd need to find a way to go back there and take a better look at it.

As Sam pulled into Joe's lane, he saw Joe standing next to a black colt in the corral. He was surprised to see that the horse looked like Frankie. Sam parked his car and walked over to where Joe was standing. He saw the charred remains of Joe's stable on the other side of the corral.

"Hello, Joe," Sam said, with a smile on his face.

"Sam," Joe said with a nod, then turned back to adjust the blanket he'd placed on the colt for protection on the long ride that night. Joe wanted to get rid of Sam as quickly as possible, before the Germans arrived.

Sam saw the blood red 'M' on the black blanket and thought it was odd that Joe would have it on the animal this time of day, but dismissed it. "He looks like Frankie, Emma's horse."

"Yeah." Joe smiled to himself.

"What're you doing with him?" Sam asked, nodding toward the colt. He kept his eyes on Joe, to see his reaction.

"Emma wanted me to take care of him for a few days, while she was gone." Joe snickered to himself. *She'll be with me and not you, pal*, he thought.

"Where's Emma going?" Sam was surprised that Emma hadn't told him she was leaving.

"This morning, she told me she was going to take a little vacation. She said she needed to get away from everything." Joe's mouth curved up as he lied to Sam, watching the other man's face drop.

Sam was confused. He looked over at her ranch, but didn't see her car. Maybe Emma had called Joe after she'd dropped him off at his office, but he didn't understand why she would do that. Sam walked over to the corral and hiked one foot up onto the lower board on the fence. He looked at the sun shining on the black hair of the colt's neck.

"Joe, Emma mentioned that you and her husband had taken this guy to the Kentucky Derby last spring to sell," Sam said, nodding toward the horse. He could see Joe's face turn white and his fingers shake as he adjusted the bindings on the blanket.

"Yep, that's right," Joe said, taking deep breaths and keeping his eyes on the horse, trying to steady his hands. He wished he had a drink.

"So, what happened? Why did you two bring him back to Oregon?"

"The guy that was going to buy him never showed," Joe said with a jerk of his shoulder. "So, Ted and I brought him back here."

"Where did this horse come from to begin with?"

Joe looked at Sam for a second, then turned and said, "The owner was from out of state, boarding him for a few months before Ted and I took him to the Derby."

"I thought I'd seen you at the Kentucky Derby last year."

"Yeah, what about it?" Joe nervously looked over at the road as a truck approached, then let out a sigh as the truck passed on by.

"Well, I was thinking," Sam said, "that it was a little odd that we were there at the same time when Koenig's Wonder disappeared. You remember him - the black colt that was swapped for a good look-alike? Frankie here looks a lot like him, wouldn't you say?" Sam saw Joe's jaw working, even though the expression on his face hadn't changed. Oh, he liked to see Joe squirm.

"Did you happen to see anything that might have seemed odd to you that night, like any kind of commotion down at the shedrow?" Sam continued.

"I didn't see nothing. What are you, Sam, some kind of investigator now?" he snapped at Sam, looking him up and down. Then, he laughed. "Naw," Joe continued, "I doubt you'd go that direction. You like to gamble and drink too much, and they don't hire the likes of you."

Joe's words brought back the pain Sam had inflicted upon himself after he'd lost Ele. *But, that's over*, he thought to himself and tried to stuff the pain back where it had been hiding. *That was old business*, he thought. *This is new*. Sam replaced the pain with anger.

"I understand that no gun or hunter was ever found in connection to Emma's husband's death," Sam asked, quickly changing the subject. He was on duty now. His fight with Joe over Ele would have to wait.

Joe stopped fidgeting with Frankie's blanket and stood next to the horse, his hands still on the bindings. He sighed heavily, as if disgusted by the question, but Sam had seen his eyes widen with fear. Joe walked the horse to the gate of the corral, then tied him up.

"I've been all through this again and again with the police. Now, do I have to do it again with you, Sam? What's this all about?"

"I just care about Emma and want to find out all I can about her husband's death."

Joe then turned and walked to where Sam stood, anger flashing from his eyes. "You leave Emma alone, Sam. She deserves better than a drunk and a gambler."

"Who does she deserve, Joe?" Sam said with a slight grin. "You?"

Sam saw Joe's eyes and watched as the man's hands turned into fists.

"Get off my property!" Joe yelled.

"Okay, but I'll be back. We still have some unfinished business between us."

Sam turned and got back into the Mustang and drove away. He now knew what he needed to know about Joe Remsky.

◆ ◆ ◆ ◆

The forest floor, green from the winter rains and dotted with bursts of early color from the blooming rhododendrons and azaleas, passed by Sam as he wound around the hairpin turns. The thick canopy overhead cooled the air, causing fingers of mist to linger through the trees, giving a feeling of mystery and enchantment. An occasional dogwood splashed pink and white color against the many shades of greens, and the sunlight shimmered on the wet moss clinging to the trees. Once he was near the top, the trees opened on a switchback in the road. The valley lay out below him, reminding him of his ride with Emma.

Doc White lived on the south side of Chehalem Mountain. As Sam descended, he saw the southern valley open, the large, billowing clouds of steam from the wood mill flowing over the small city below. When he saw Doc's sign, he turned into the drive and pulled his car up in front of the office and kennel. Numerous barks and whinnies came at Sam as he stepped out, announcing his arrival.

The rustic office building, covered with weathered shakes, was adjacent to a building that looked like Doc's house. A red barn stood back behind what was left of a filbert orchard, a few old trees still dotting the area. Sam walked into the office. A young woman in a white clinical jacket was struggling in an attempt to leash a large, excited shepherd. Her wavy, red hair had fallen over her face. When she looked up and smiled as Sam came in, her hazel eyes crinkled at the corners.

"May I help you?" she asked with a hint of an English accent, giving the leash that now held the dog, a firm jerk. The dog responded to her signal and sat next to her.

"Hello, Wanda," Sam said, noticing the name tag on her jacket. "I'm Sam Parker. I have an appointment with Doc White."

Wanda Eaton flinched. Ever since she had come to America and began working for Dr. White, she could not get used to people addressing him as 'Doc.' It seemed so unprofessional and disrespectful to her, but even the doctor had insisted that she address him with the nickname. She still refused to call him 'Doc.'

"Yes, Mr. Parker," she said in her sweet voice. "Dr. White told me you were coming. He's in the barn, behind the kennel. Do you want me to take you to him?"

"No, thanks. I think I can find it."

Sam walked out and followed the path around the kennel toward the barn, which had the same weathered look as the other buildings. The dogs in the kennel cages came to their gates and began yelping at him. Above the noise, Sam looked up at the sound of the low drum of a plane's engine. A small yellow biplane with a large red target on the tail flew overhead, similar to one he used to fly when he was young. Anyone with flying in their blood always looked up when they heard a plane's engine. It was an instinct that never went away, jarring memories of the world's view from the eyes of a bird soaring on the winds of time. He wished at that moment he was up there in that plane.

Walking into the barn, Sam saw Doc White washing a large, gray mustang. The horse had a wild look in its eyes, pulling at the restraints of the halter, yet he stood still while the old man talked to him. Doc's gray, curly hair was covered with a dark woolen cap. His old, tan sweater was buttoned over his shirt and the sleeves of his tweed jacket were pushed up to his elbows. Tall boots covered his brown corduroy trousers. In a low voice, he gently talked to the animal as he rinsed its body, running his hands down the muscles of the strong legs to extract the last of the soap. Sam watched the small man as he wiped down the horse with care. Then, the horse whinnied.

Doc looked up and saw Sam watching him. "Well, Sam Parker. It has been a long time," he said, as he wiped his hand on his trousers, then reached it out to Sam.

"Hello, Doc," Sam replied, shaking his hand.

Sam knew that Doc White had lived in the states for many years, but he was glad that his British accent had never wavered. Doc's face was weathered with lines of life traced across his skin. His large, brown eyes twinkled with hidden mischief that stemmed from within the soul of the man. His hands were strong, yet covered with deep veins traversing up his firm forearms. Sam found it strange to see the changes of age in this powerful man, yet the essence of the man was the same.

A large, dark red Irish setter, that had been sleeping when Sam came in, sauntered over to Sam and sniffed around his ankles. Sam reached down and scratched behind one of the setter's ears.

"It's been a few years since we saw each other," Doc said.

"Yes, it has." Sam remembered the last time he'd seen Emerson White. It was the day he'd returned home from the service, in his father's stable - the day his dad had given him Ele. That seemed so long ago now.

"And, how are your parents, Sam?" Doc asked.

"They're doing well, thanks. How've you been?" The setter ambled back to curl up and resume its sleep on a burlap sack that lay near the tack room door.

"I have never been better. Since my Maggie died, each new day gets me closer to her." He winked at Sam. Sam knew Doc had lost his wife a couple of years before to cancer. It had been a long, hard illness for Maggie, but Sam's dad had told him that Doc never lost his love of life and optimistic attitude. He seemed to know something that escaped Sam. But, whenever he was near Doc, he could feel the strength and wisdom inside. There were times Sam wished he had that strength.

Sam looked around the barn as Doc walked the gray to his stall.

"I acquired this old boy through the "Adopt-A-Mustang" program in Eastern Oregon, after I learned the ranges don't have enough food for the number of horses born every year. The ranchers round up these beautiful animals late each spring and place them for adoption. It's a most uncommon practice, but a good one."

After a moment's silence, Doc continued. "A strange country, this America, but I like it."

Sam noticed the bay mare with a white blaze down her forehead in the stall to his right. She gently rolled her head from side to side, her eyes closed as her body rocked to a silent rhythm.

"Why is this mare weaving like that, Doc?" Sam asked. He recognized the same habit in Ele, which now had him concerned.

"She is a retired race horse. Generally, they are nervous when they are retired from racing, and the rocking releases an endorphin in the animal. She does it much less now than when she first arrived. The weaving calms her down. It's similar to our rocking in a chair."

"I know someone else who has a mare that weaves like that," Sam said.

"Oh, and who would that be?" Doc White asked.

"Emma Jacobs."

"Emma. Oh, yes. What a lovely girl. I don't like seeing her alone like she is. Her husband was not the right man for her, you know." Doc watched Sam out of the corner of his eye.

Sam was silent, but he knew that nothing escaped Doc.

"She has that wonderful mare she's boarding," Doc continued. "And, that black colt, what a fine specimen. I have seen numerous outstanding race horses in my days on the track at Epsom, but that one is truly a champion."

"Yes," Sam said. "I have to agree with you." Sam wasn't sure what part he was agreeing to, the part about the colt or about Emma.

"That was the reason I sent the local Commission office the information on the markings and lip tattoo. There was something different about that tattoo. I knew something was not right the first day I saw him in Emma's stable. She has no idea of the winner that she has there. I never understood how Joe Remsky obtained Frankie in the first place. He's a neighbor of Emma's, you know."

"Yes, I know Joe. We were in the service together years ago," Sam answered, then stopped and stared at Doc.

"What do you mean about Joe obtaining Frankie?" Sam finally asked.

"Why, Frankie is Joe's horse. Didn't you know that?"

"No. Then, how did the colt get in the Jacobs stable?"

"I understand that Joe brought him over to Ted and Emma's while he was doing some repairs to his stable."

Doc sat down on a chest outside of the mare's stall, then leaned back against the wall placing his hands on his knees.

"I remember the day of the fire at Joe's ranch," Doc said, his eyes looking toward the rafters in the barn. "It was the same day that Emma's husband, Ted, was shot in the hunting accident. Ted's death was most unfortunate. The police believed it was someone hunting illegally on Joe's property, but no traces were ever found. Her husband was a hard man to get to know, very private and guarded. I understand he began drinking and gambling after Joe moved in across from Emma's ranch.

"The fire started after sunrise, I think it was. I heard that luck was with Joe that day- he didn't have horses in his stable. Seth Halverson, a vet over by Hillsboro, had told me earlier that Joe had talked about having two or three horses to train for the pre-Derby races last spring. I don't know where he planned to get the horses. Since Joe used Seth as his veterinarian, I never had a reason to go to his ranch. However, I was curious, being from a background with the track myself. So, one day I went to Joe's ranch. He is a most disagreeable fellow, but very shrewd."

"I know," Sam said, an old anger stirring inside.

"I never liked it when Emma's husband began spending so much time with him." Doc shook his head and took out a pipe, filling the bowl while he continued. "The trouble all started when Joe and Ted went to the Kentucky Derby together, taking the colt with them. Seth had told me that Joe had a buyer in Louisville. Later, I heard that the buyer never arrived and they had to bring the colt back to Oregon." He lit his pipe, and the sweet smell of tobacco filtered through the air in the barn, with a hint of cherries in it.

"Doc," Sam began, "Emma and I were riding on her property yesterday and we heard gunshots. We saw your car driving away from her ranch."

"Oh yes, that was Casey. He's a strange man, guarded and, I think, very dangerous. I was on my usual rounds and had stopped in to check on Ele. She hasn't been eating well."

"What is wrong with Ele?" Sam asked with concern in his voice. He remembered Emma talking about it the prior day.

"Oh, nothing, that a few bouts around a track wouldn't cure. She's just simply bored, standing in her stall all day. If one isn't careful, the difficulty of black water can begin, if a horse does not get enough exercise. I was planning to recommend a ride each day to Emma, the first chance I get."

"Where did Casey come from?" Sam asked, realizing that Ele was in good hands.

"I understand he is from Venezuela. I think he is a friend of Joe's. Joe had sent him to work with Emma, to help her out after Ted was killed."

"Was Casey shooting at you?"

"No, he was firing into the air as I drove away. I took it to be a sort of warning."

"Why a warning?"

"I had said something to him about Frankie's validity. That was my mistake. He became enraged, grabbed his rifle, and told me to leave, yelling that I should keep my nose out of other people's business. I didn't ask questions. As I raced out of there, I heard the gunshots." Doc laughed. "That's not the first time I've been run off at gun point. Maggie's father tried to run me off, too."

Sam laughed with him, remembering the look on Emma's father's face that he'd seen through the lobby window in front of the Drake Hotel. If her father'd had a gun, he'd probably shot at Sam that night.

"Are you married, Sam?" Doc asked, looking at him sideways with a twinkle in his eyes, while smoke circled above their heads.

"No," Sam answered shyly, looking down. "Life kept getting in the way."

Doc smiled, nodding his head. "I don't like to see young people alone."

"Doc, can you tell me if someone could dye the hair on a horse to change his markings?" Sam asked, quickly changing the subject.

"Oh, yes. I've seen it done before. The problem is, you can color the hair, but not the skin beneath it. If the hair is white, the skin underneath will also be white."

Sam remembered seeing this on Frankie, as he was looking him over when Emma was busy with Gandolf's tack before their ride.

"Well, I've taken up enough of your time, Doc," Sam said as he reached out a hand. "Thanks for all of your help."

Doc stood up and shook Sam's hand, then began to walk with him to the office, the Irish setter closely following.

"It has been my pleasure, son," Doc said, placing his hand on Sam's back as they walked together. "Just let me know if I can help any further. And, tell your dear mother and father hello for me the next time you see them."

"Will do."

Wanda came out of the office door and said, "Mr. Parker, your secretary called and asked you to ring her back as soon as possible."

Sam looked at Doc White and asked, "Would you mind if I made a quick phone call?"

"Not at all," Doc said, "Wanda, I'd like Mr. Parker to use my office to make his call. I need your assistance with this new shipment of hay, so would you please call my son, Ian, down from the house on the intercom?"

"Yes, Doctor," Wanda said.

Doc winced at the formal name, then left the building.

Wanda led Sam into the interior office, closing the door after him as he entered. Books lined the wall behind the large, oak, roll-top desk. Sam sat down in the red leather chair and dialed Jim's office number. Through the window, Sam watched Doc White walking with the red setter trotting happily beside him.

"Hello," Sally answered.

"What's up?" Sam asked, forgetting to remind Sally where she worked.

"Simon Day wanted me to give you this information right away. He sounded worried when he called."

"What did he say?"

"He said that you're on the right track. Mason's first jockey, Juan Martinez, was found a month after the Derby in Venezuela, dead of a drug overdose."

"Venezuela?" Sam asked, a chill running down his back. "What the hell was he doing down there?"

"Simon didn't know."

"How did they find him?"

"Simon was pretty excited," Sally said, stopping to take a second glance over her notes. "He said he asked a friend, who's a journalist, to check on any information about Martinez. The guy found an article about his death down in Caracas. They also found a woman in the room, dead from the same drug. Her name was Maria Sanchez. She was pregnant. Oh, Simon also said the Anderson Transport Company had been hired earlier this year by George Mason at Essen Farms to deliver a mare to Rising Sun Stable in Oregon."

Sam was silent for a moment.

"Sam, honey," Sally said. "Are you still there?"

"Yes," Sam said, his mind turning over this new bit of news.

"Before I forget," Sally continued, "Jim Barolio called from McMinnville and said to tell you that your DC-7 just landed."

CHAPTER EIGHTEEN

T he driving rain, smashing into the windshield, and the hypnotic thump of the wiper blades that swung back and forth in front of Emma, mirrored the ache in her heart. She had just begun to believe that dreams could come true - until she'd seen Sam with Sally.

As she made a sharp turn in the road, Emma saw the mist in the trees above. In her mind, memories surfaced, as if she was watching a movie; visions of meeting Sam in Chicago, her parents' farm in Indiana, Ted when they were married, Ted's abuse and death, sharing her ranch with Sam. She noticed that when her mind circled back to Sam, her heart moved in her breast. He was the only man who had that effect on her. Now she saw she was in the middle of the same confusion she had when he left her in Chicago. Her heart and body tried to convince her that he was good for her, yet her mind told her otherwise. She knew she couldn't trust her heart now, not after seeing him with the other woman.

In Chicago, she never told Sam that she loved him. At one point, she was very close to revealing it, just before he left in the taxi with another woman. She wasn't sure if she could ever trust Sam.

Emma drove into her driveway and parked her car in front of the house. She saw a strange white car near the stable and walked down the lane. The white car had Oregon plates and a rental sticker on the back bumper.

As she stepped inside the stable door, she stopped. A tall man stood at Ele's gate, talking to the horse in a soft tone. For a moment, Emma thought it was her father standing there, his silver hair glistening in the sunlight, but this man was broader in the shoulders.

The man turned and saw Emma, smiled, and walked over to her. She could see his smile was like her father's, but his eyes were not her father's steel blue color. This man's eyes were dark brown, like hers.

He reached out his large hand. "Hello, Emma," he said in a deep voice. Emma could hear the underlying accent that she had grown up with.

"Yes, I'm Emma Jacobs," she said, as she shook his hand, unable to take her eyes off him. "And you are?" Emma asked, feeling a little awkward.

"George Mason. I'm the owner of Classy Elegance." He looked at her square jaw, her high forehead. "It is time we met," he said with a smile. When they had touched, George knew that she was Hermann's daughter. He could feel Hermann's strength in her.

"Oh," Emma said. She felt the warmth in his big hand, and thought she had stepped back in time and could only stare. The resemblance was uncanny. Something in the back of her mind recognized him, but she couldn't remember where.

Then, she remembered the man she'd seen in the club a couple of nights ago. Suddenly, it dawned on her - the photograph in the book.

"You look like you have seen a ghost," George said, still smiling and holding her hand. George looked into his niece's face, seeing the beauty of her mother. The last time he had seen her was twelve years ago at Arlington Park in Chicago. Emma had been eighteen then. Now, she was a beautiful woman.

She shook her head and pulled her hand free. "I'm sorry," she said. "It's just that you remind me so much of my father."

"Ah," George said, "I understand."

"Have you been waiting long?" she asked, looking around her, searching for something familiar of her own real world.

"No, not very long," he said, "I wanted to see how Ele was doing." He had received a phone call from John Anderson, the transport company he'd used to send Ele to Emma's ranch. The message had said that Ele had been injured and that he needed to go to Oregon, because a decision needed to be made about the mare's future.

"She looks very fit," he continued. George would take the matter up with Mr. Anderson, when he returned to Kentucky. "You have taken special care of her for me, as I knew you would."

"She's a great horse." Emma noticed that the gate to Frankie's stall stood open. She figured that Joe had taken him. She thought of Joe's words about Sam and hated that she had to admit to herself that they had come true.

George saw the shadow in Emma's eyes and wondered what had caused it. "Are you okay?" he asked, placing his hand on Emma's shoulder.

"Yes," she lied and tried to smile. His hand felt warm. She remembered her father standing next to her in the stable on their farm in Indiana. He had placed his hand in the same gentle way after she had lost at a competition.

Ele whinnied and bobbed her head for attention. George reached his hand to the chestnut horse and she nickered gently as she placed her muzzle in his hand.

"Doc White," Emma said, "the vet who's been watching Ele, said she is in good health. I did notice, though, that she did not eat all of her feed. I need to call and see if he can come out later today to check her."

"I would like to meet him."

"How did you learn about my ranch, Mr. Mason?" Emma asked, watching George stroke Ele's neck, the same gesture she had seen Sam do just yesterday. So much time had seemed to pass since then, and so much had happened.

"Please, call me George," he said, flashing his wide smile back to her. "I have known about you most of your life."

Emma stopped and stared at the large man. "How do you know me?"

"I knew your father."

Emma was intrigued now to learn more about this man. "Would you like to come up to the house for a cup of coffee?" she asked.

"Yes," he said. "I would like that."

George followed her toward the stable door, then stopped when he came to the door to the tack room. He walked in and stood in front of Hermann's trunk.

"That's my father's trunk," Emma said, behind him.

"I know. I haven't seen this since we separated in New York." He looked at Emma. "May I look inside?"

"Sure." Her mind was going back to something her mother had said years ago. She watched as George gently touched the trunk, slowly running his fingers over the top.

He opened the lid and got down on one knee, looking at the contents inside. Hermann's hat lay on top of his red jacket. George fingered through the items, lifting up the clothes to look further into the trunk's depths. George was fighting the emotions inside that surfaced as he looked through his brother's things again after all this time. When he reached the bottom, he smiled slightly to himself. Now he knew where Hermann had hidden the painting, unless it was in the house. He closed the lid and stood up.

"Come on, George," Emma said, after seeing his face. "Let's go have that coffee." She led the way out of the stable toward the red-brick house.

◆ ◆ ◆ ◆

"Please come in," Emma said as she walked through the front door, opening it further for him to pass through. George stopped before the open doors of the den and glanced around the walls of the room, then followed Emma into the kitchen. She began making the coffee while George sat in a chair at the table, watching her.

"How did you know my father, George?" Emma asked, her back against the counter as she waited for the coffee to brew.

"I am his brother."

Emma stared at George. *George Mason was her uncle?* Thoughts rolled inside her head. *Why hadn't he come forward all these years? Why now?* He was her last living relative. She didn't know what to say.

"I understand your silence," George said, smiling. He stood and walked over to her. "Your father and I separated once we arrived in New York. Come, sit, and I will tell you."

He turned off the fire under the coffee and took her hand, leading her to the kitchen table. Then, he sat down opposite her.

"Your father and I came together to America in nineteen thirty-seven from Germany. Our father had sent us to find a new home. Then, we were to send for our family. When your father and I arrived in New York...," he paused, his voice wavering. "Life had separated us on different paths and we never had the opportunity to meet again."

"Why did you separate?"

George looked away for a moment. "Your father had become very angry at me and said he never wanted to see me again."

"But, what made him so angry?"

"I had lied to him to get him to come with me to America, as our parents wanted. I later learned, when I returned to Germany to find our parents..." He stopped for a moment, a sadness coming over his face. "I learned that our parents and Franz, our small brother, had been killed during the war."

Emma's heart went out to George. She thought of the shock of her father's accident and could imagine George's feelings of terrible loss. She put her hand on his. Loss is difficult to share with someone, unless they had experienced it themselves. Emma understood this. What she didn't know was the terrible guilt George kept locked inside.

"I'm so sorry," she said. "I knew my father had something about his past that he never shared with Mother and me. He told me once about your parents and brother, but he never told me about you. My mother finally told me, after he died. She had said that he'd searched for you, but there had been no record of you coming into the country."

Her words circled in his mind and warmed his heart. "Hermann had searched for me?" he asked.

"That's what Mom said. You were listed on the ship's manifest, but your name never appeared on the Immigration list. Dad hardly ever talked about his past."

"A lot of people that came here from other countries at that time kept their dark secrets to themselves," George said, without revealing all of his.

They sat in silence for a moment. Outside, the rain had started again, washing over the land in large drops, beating against the metal roof of the arena as it passed over.

George placed his hand upon Emma's and patted it softly. Emma felt that he was a gentle creature, more sensitive than her father.

"I saw you at Hermann's funeral," George said softly, amongst the torrents of rain.

Emma remembered the man she had seen standing off by himself that day. "That was you?" she asked.

"Yes."

"Why didn't you come forward then?"

He simply shrugged his shoulders and tried to smile.

"What happened to you after New York, George? How did you get the name Mason?" Emma asked. She wasn't sure if she should call him 'uncle' or not.

"When I went through Immigration, my name was inadvertently changed to Mason. I understand it happened to a lot of people when they entered this country. I thought about correcting it, but then decided that...maybe it was best to leave it, that it was a slip of fate that now separated me from my family, just as Hermann had separated from me. Yet, through all those years, I watched Hermann. I knew where he was at all times..." He stopped and looked away. He stared out of the window for a moment.

"We had been around horses all of our lives in Germany, as you probably know," George added.

"Yes, Dad told me about the horses your family raised for the military."

"Many years ago, when I was just a lad, I worked on our farm, while Hermann went to study at the Austrian school. Then, afterwards, he taught riding in Verden. He was their most advanced trainer," George said with pride in his voice and a smile that seemed to remove the years from his face.

"He used to tell me stories about Verden," Emma said, then paused. "There always was a sadness in his voice when he spoke of it," she added. She watched George's face. A shadow had come over it and the youth she had seen when he was talking had vanished and the tired, older man sat again before her.

George looked at Emma. He knew the reason for his brother's sadness, but he wasn't ready to reveal it to Hermann's daughter. There was still something he had to do.

"After arriving in America, I became interested in Thoroughbred racing. Later, I moved to Kentucky and started working on a breeding farm. After a few years, I bought the farm and renamed it Essen Farms."

That name was familiar to Emma, but she couldn't remember why. Her thoughts were circling on his words about knowing where her father was over the years, but never contacting him.

"I never married," George continued, "but became very successful at the races. Then I started racing my own horses. Koenig was my favorite colt. He won the Kentucky Derby..." George stopped. A pain shot through his heart. He added, "His blood line is carried now through many other winners."

"Koenig," Emma said. "I know that name. That was the name of a horse that my mother and I bet on when we were at Arlington Park in Chicago on my eighteenth birthday."

"That was my horse," George said with pride again in his voice. "He's a fine stallion."

Emma smiled at George.

"You have a lovely home, Emma," George said to change the conversation. "May I see the rest?" He was becoming anxious to see if the Friedrich painting was hanging somewhere inside of her home. That was one of his reasons for coming.

"Certainly." She led the way to the den. George admired the books that were on the tall shelves, noting the authors' names.

"Camus is also one of my favorite authors," he said as he looked more thoroughly around the room. The Friedrich was not visibly displayed on any of the walls.

Emma proceeded down the hallway, past the kitchen, to a large room that George could tell was used very little. The furniture were pieces of a more contemporary style, which simply filled the space more than being useful. "This is the living room," she explained. "But, I don't use it very much. I prefer the den."

As Emma ushered George from room to room, she watched as his eyes gazed around the walls, as if he was looking for something. She led him upstairs and opened the door to her studio. He walked up to the painting on the easel.

"Ah, I remember this performance. Hermann was so proud of Conversano." He looked at Emma.

"Yes, I know."

"Did Hermann ever show you the Friedrich?"

"What Friedrich?" Emma knew the name, and remembered her father telling her about his favorite painter and the one painting that he loved, but she had never seen it.

"The painting by Friedrich, that belonged to our parents." He didn't tell her he had been the one to steal it first from their parents' home before coming to America, but that his brother had taken it from him before leaving the ship in New York.

"I've never seen it," Emma answered.

"He must have given it to you, where else could it be?"

"I have no idea."

Emma saw that George was becoming agitated, so she turned and began walking back down the hallway.

"May I use your facilities?" George asked, taking a deep breath to control his anger.

"Yes, it is down the hall. I'll go finish the coffee."

In the kitchen, the coffee perked. Emma stood with her arms wrapped around herself as she thought about George's reaction. When the coffee was finished, she poured some for both her and George, then set the cups on the table. She thought of the change in George when he began talking about the painting. She remembered the same change in her father, as if something about the painting had an effect on the people whose lives it touched.

George returned to the kitchen, after having looked in each of the other rooms. He sat and looked at her from across the table once more. He could see that she was deep in thought.

"When I found that you had closed your riding school, I wanted to do what I could to help you." He patted her hand and smiled. "You will let me know if there is any more I can do for you. You are all I have left of my family."

"Thank you." Emma's mind was reeling.

George looked at his watch and stood. He hadn't touched his coffee.

"I'm sorry," he said, "but I must leave. I have an appointment to make. I would like to come back soon, if I may."

"Of course you may," Emma said, as she began to walk out of her house with him.

"You need not walk me to my car."

"Okay. I will call Doc White and find out what time he is coming today, if you'd like. Where can I reach you?"

"I will be staying at the Benson Hotel. You may leave a message there for me."

George placed his hand on Emma's. "I was sorry to hear about your husband's death."

"Thank you," Emma said, averting her eyes. She wanted to let that part of her life stay buried. "I will call you."

♦ ♦ ♦ ♦

Emma watched as George got into his car. Then, she walked back into her house and up to her bedroom. She hadn't yet changed from the show. She placed a call to Doc White from her bedroom phone and asked if he could stop by later that day to check on Ele. Then, she called the Benson and left the message for her uncle.

Deciding to take a shower, she began to run the water and take off her clothes. When she stepped under the water, she thought of the things George had said to her. Suddenly, she stopped cold. Even though the water was hot, chills went up her spine, as questions circled around her.

How had George helped her? How did he know where to find her? And, if he was from Kentucky, how did he know she was married and about Ted's death?

"*I have known about you most of your life*," he had said. "*I watched Hermann. I knew where he was at all times*," he had said about her father.

All at once, she knew. Essen Farms. Chris Schmidt. Chris had been a spy for George all those years, his eyes and ears at her father's farm. She remembered the phone call she had made to Chris on the night Ted had raped her. They had answered 'Essen Farms,' when she'd dialed the number that Chris had given her. She had always felt that Chris was her friend. Now, she wasn't so sure.

"*Why?*" Emma asked herself.

Suddenly, it came to her. "The Friedrich," she yelled. In her mind, she saw her house in Indiana ransacked, the paintings pulled out of their frames, her father's trunk in the stable emptied. Chris had been on vacation, but appeared shortly after she had returned to the house. It now made sense. Someone had been looking for the Friedrich. Had Chris done it?

With the water running, she didn't hear the gunshot from Joe's ranch.

♦ ♦ ♦ ♦

George sat in his car for a few moments, smiling to himself at his wonderful fortune today. Then, he slowly drove away from Emma's stable and stopped at the end of her lane. The sunset behind him cast a golden sideways light, bringing every detail of grass and leaf to life, like the soft, warm colors of a Monet painting. The tip of Mount Hood in the distant east and the surrounding clouds were beginning to turn a soft coral with the backwash of the lowering sun's reflection. He saw a small rain cloud to the north, gently washing the earth. A full double rainbow followed in its wake, as the light passed through the vivid colors reflected on the surface of the lake in the valley below.

At that moment, George heard a high whinny. He looked at the ranch across from Emma's and saw a large, black colt standing at the corral's edge, looking in his direction with his muzzle raised, testing the air. George drove his car out of Emma's drive and pulled over to the roadside, parking near the end of the lane to the other ranch. He watched the large colt in the corral, the proud, high head.

George stepped out of his car. He let out a soft, slow whistle, a signal he'd used since Koenig's Wonder was born. The horse's ears came forward, and he began to nod his head up and down, his black mane blowing in the gentle, evening breeze. The horse whinnied into the air in answer to the man's whistle. George knew this was his colt. He didn't see the men standing near the truck; he was only watching the magnificent animal that he knew was his.

At that moment, a shot rang out, and George fell to the ground.

♦ ♦ ♦ ♦

"I have wanted to do that ever since I was young." Franz Maseman grinned, as he handed the rifle back to Carlos. "Your contact at Anderson's brought my brother here, as planned. You have done well."

Franz stood for a moment, looking at where his brother lay on the ground. He remembered the day when he'd begged George to take him to America and George's refusal. Later, his father had discovered the Friedrich missing, and vowed he would kill the thief. But, when Franz had survived the bomb that fell near their home, destroying everything and everyone he ever loved, Franz had vowed then for revenge upon his brothers, blaming them. A surge of energy went through him, just as it had at the concentration camp, after he had fulfilled an assignment.

Franz turned to the others standing around him. He could see the shock in their faces - all except one. Karl Strauss smiled and nodded his head to Franz. Karl had known the purpose of this mission all along. He also knew that it wasn't over, yet.

"Come," Franz said. "Let us continue."

Joe and Carlos shook their heads, as if they were coming out of a dream. They walked stiffly to the corral. Carlos went through the gate, while Joe prepared the trailer. The gunshot had startled the colt. He struggled against the hold on his reins, rearing in the air and lashing out with his forelegs, making it impossible for Carlos to get him into the trailer. Carlos kept side-stepping away from the dangerously sharp hooves. Joe ran up to grab a rein that had slipped out of Carlos's hand, and the two men struggled to subdue the angry horse.

"Give him something, Doc!" Joe yelled, holding on with all his strength. "This fella's going to kill us all before the night's over."

Karl had already gone to the Jeep and opened his bag. He went to the rearing colt and waited with a hypodermic needle in his hand. Just as the colt came back down to the ground with his front hooves, the vet plunged the needle quickly into the animal. Koenig's Wonder reared again, screaming, his eyes wide in fury, then spun around again, attempting to shake the hold on his reins. Joe and Carlos held on, scurrying out of the way of the colt's slashing teeth. In a few moments, the horse began to slow. Then, he finally stood still with his head hanging down.

"That will keep him quiet during the ride to the airport," Karl said.

"I hope you did not give him too much," Franz said with concern in his voice. This animal was very valuable to him. He had been planning for this moment for a long time.

"No, it will wear off in about an hour, and he will be his wonderful self again. Then, I will give him more as needed, during the flight, so he does not hurt himself."

Carlos walked up to the animal and patted his neck. He talked softly to

Koenig's Wonder as he had done before, and walked the animal toward the trailer. Carlos was glad that they no longer needed to pretend that this horse was Frankie. Frank's Revenge, the imposter that took Koenig's Wonder's place after the Kentucky Derby, was now in the hands of Essen Farms and had served his purpose.

Once Koenig's Wonder was in the trailer, Carlos closed the gate behind him, then walked up to the driver's door of the truck and got in.

"You know what to do," Franz said to Karl.

"Yes. We'll be right behind you."

Franz got into the passenger side of the black truck and Carlos drove off.

As the truck neared where George lay, Franz told Carlos to stop. He stepped from the vehicle and stood, looking down at his brother lying motionless, face down in the tall grass, his shirt bloody. Franz began to laugh, a sick sort of laugh. He was surprised that he did not feel the release he had expected when his last brother was dead. Franz had begun planning his revenge ever since he had witnessed his parents' death. He knew that if his brothers had arranged to get their family out of Germany before the fighting had begun, they would not be dead.

Then, in his strong accent, Franz said, "It is a pity, my brother, that you did not know it was me who shot you, unlike the night I killed Hermann." Franz looked toward the darkening sky and said, "Finally, both of my brothers are dead and my work here is almost finished. Soon, I will have destroyed her, and the painting will be mine. Only then will I have my revenge."

He got back into the truck and motioned for Carlos to continue. The vehicle turned to the west.

◆ ◆ ◆ ◆

Joe and Karl got into Carlos' Jeep and drove to Emma's. As they came up to her house, Karl said, "Stop here. I'm getting out. Go down to the stable and load the mare. I have some business to tend to."

Joe didn't like this creep going into Emma's house, but he did as he was told – for now.

◆ ◆ ◆ ◆

Emma quickly finished her shower and dressed in a pair of jeans and a crisp, white, shirt. She was frightened now and didn't know where to turn. She realized that she needed to have the painting - to have an ace in the hole. *Where could this painting be*? Emma wondered. She remembered George lovingly caressing the tack trunk, smiling to himself. *Could it be in the trunk*? She doubted it, simply because it had been ransacked once before. Maybe there was some secret hiding place in it that she didn't know of, maybe a false bottom...

As she sat down and put on her tennis shoes, she heard the front door open and close. Thinking it was Joe, she quickly tied her shoes and pulled her hair back into a ponytail, then went downstairs.

No one was in the entry.

"Joe?" Emma called. "Is anyone here?" A strange feeling came over her in the silence.

"Hello, my dear," said a man with a heavy accent as he walked out of the den, a face she'd never seen before. He stood with his hands on his hips and a strange look on his face - a sort of loathing in his eyes that made her skin crawl.

"Who are you?" she asked, looking past him to where her rifle stood near the door.

"I'm a friend of your uncle. I have come to claim his property."

Uncle? Emma thought. *George*?

"What's your name?" she asked. Her heart raced and her palms were sweaty.

"I am Dr. Karl Strauss," he said with a bow. *She was a beautiful thing*, he thought, *soft and well developed. It will be a shame to destroy her.*

"What do you want?" She really didn't want to hear the answer, but she hoped she could keep him talking while she slowly began to walk around him, one slow step at a time, trying to get to where she could run for her rifle.

"I want you...and the Friedrich."

"I don't have the Friedrich. My father destroyed it," she lied. She kept slowly walking around him in a wide circle.

"I don't believe you. Hermann would never do that." The man shook his head, a sick smile coming to his lips.

Emma's stomach began to turn as she slowly circled near the door of the den. *Almost*, she thought, *I'm almost there.*

Karl noticed where Emma was looking and saw the rifle standing to his right. He realized what she was doing. He grabbed her roughly and pushed her into the den, a fury in his eyes.

She could feel his fingers bruising her arms. When she saw the madness in his face, she froze.

"You stupid woman," he spat at her. "Do you think I do not know what you are planning? You underestimate me. I have killed numerous, useless people in my life without any regret. Don't tempt me into adding another, until it is time. Now, tell me, where is the painting?"

She shook with fear and her knees threatened to buckle. *What did he mean by 'until it is time'*? Emma wondered. Then, an image of George and the trunk in the tack room flashed through her mind. She took a deep breath and decided quickly to try anything to get away from him so she could escape.

"It's...it's in my father's trunk - in the tack room down in the stable."

"I am not a fool. We have looked there before - after Hermann was out of the way." He turned her back against him, one arm across her throat and twisting her arm behind her back.

Pain ripped through her arm and she could hardly breathe, but her mind raced. She had been right. Her father had been murdered! Panic grabbed at her throat as she felt the man's hot breath against her cheek. He tightened his grip as she struggled against him.

"Did you kill my father?" she managed, gasping for air.

"I was not the one who ended his useless life." Karl pulled up again on her arm and enjoyed her scream of pain. "Now, tell me where the Friedrich is," he yelled.

"No...stop," she begged, barely able to speak. Tears ran down her cheeks. "George told me...just today. He said there was a...a false bottom in the trunk. That's where it's hidden."

Just then, Joe came into the room.

"Joe," she screamed, thankful for the first time to see him. "Please, help me—"

Karl threw Emma at Joe.

"Watch her," Karl said, then turned and walked out the door.

◆ ◆ ◆ ◆

"Joe, let's get out of here. That man is mad!" Emma started to pull away, her arm throbbing with pain, but Joe held her tighter against him, his arms wrapped around her. He liked the way she smelled, her hair still wet from the shower, her warm, soft breasts wriggling against him. His body began to harden and ache. *God*, he thought, *I've waited a long time for this moment*. He held her closer against him and felt her body tense.

"What's going on?" she protested, trying to wriggle free. "Let go of me."

"Calm down, honey," Joe said, licking his lips, thinking of her in the shower. "We're all going to go for a little ride in a bit."

"What? Where?" Emma twisted her body, trying to loosen his hold, as her fear turned into panic.

"To Venezuela," he whispered in her ear, smelling the lavender in her hair. Her movements excited him even more, feeling her body rubbing against his. His blood raced in his veins.

"Venezuela? I'm not going anywhere - especially with you...and that killer."

"You'll come, baby, just like I said you would. I'll take care of the others later. Then, it'll just be you and me – and the horses."

"Horses?"

"I've waited too long for this..." he said, lowering his head.

You're crazy!"

Emma had seen the lust in his eyes and her fear was now replaced by anger. She tried to bring her knee up into his groin, but Joe blocked it. He grabbed a handful of her hair and pulled her head back, bringing his mouth down hard on hers, bruising her lips. He pushed her back until she was off balance and she fell back onto the couch, with him on top of her. He pinned her arms down, and held her body with his, while she struggled under him.

"Ted was never good enough for you," his voice raspy and his breath coming in quick gasps as he ripped at her blouse, revealing her full breasts. "I know how to put out your fire, baby. I know how hot you are." Joe kissed her to stifle her screams, as he pulled at her clothes. He couldn't stop himself, he'd dreamt of this moment every night since he'd met her. He was about to explode.

"Get off of me, Joe," Emma screamed when she freed her mouth from his. "Leave me alone." She twisted her head to avoid his mouth, hating the taste and the smell of him.

Joe arched back and slapped her, and stars flashed behind her eyes.

◆ ◆ ◆ ◆

Sam, driving back from Doc White's, saw Joe's truck and trailer approaching around an oncoming curve. He knew the red stripe down the side of the black vehicle, but he couldn't see the driver in the flash of the passing headlights.

He thought of Casey and the rifle he'd seen hanging on the wall in his room. Then, it clicked! Sam remembered seeing the 'Mod.98' on the gun's receiver. The M98 Mauser used in Ted's death. Sam floored the gas peddle and the Mustang raced toward Emma's.

As Sam neared Joe's ranch, he noticed a white car parked on the edge of Joe's lane. Just as he was about to go by, he slammed on his brakes. He'd seen the white shirt of a man lying on the ground. Sam turned into Joe's lane and got out, the car still running. The man began to stir as Sam turned him over. Sam saw the pool of blood soaking into the ground and the blood-stained shoulder. Then, he stared at the man's face. It was George Mason.

"George!" Sam yelled, stunned. "How the hell did you get here? What happened to you?"

George didn't respond. In the car's headlights, Sam tore at George's shirt and saw that the wound was from a bullet.

"Who shot you?" Sam asked.

"I.....," George stammered, slowly returning to consciousness. Then, he remembered. How could he tell Sam that his own brother had shot him? He'd thought he'd died when he was shot, but later realized he'd only fainted. He'd regained consciousness long enough to hear Franz's words, then had passed out again. Slowly, now, he sat up and placed his hand on his throbbing shoulder. Then, as he saw the blood on his hand, he looked at Sam and said, "I think I need some help."

Sam helped George up and into the passenger seat of the Mustang, then ran around and got in. "I'm taking you to Emma's and calling an ambulance."

"Emma..." George began. "Hurry..." George felt himself fading again and slumped back against the seat of Sam's car.

Sam gunned the Mustang, threw it in reverse and spun the back tires, shooting gravel under them as he backed out of Joe's. Then, he raced forward to Emma's lane. He turned in and stopped his car in front of her house. When he looked over at George, he saw that he was out.

Sam noticed that Carlos' Jeep was parked down by the stable. Emma's truck and trailer were backed up to the open doors, as the light from inside streamed out into the night. Sam heard Ele's whinny and was about to run to the stable, when he heard Emma scream.

Sam ran into the house. He heard Emma's cries coming from the den and raced to the door. He saw Joe on top of Emma on the couch, her blouse torn and open. Joe's hand was raised, about to slap her. Sam ran over to them and reached out, catching Joe's arm in mid air.

Surprised, Joe turned around as he was being pulled off of Emma and saw Sam.

"You son of a bitch!" Joe yelled as he swung at Sam's face, anger flashing in his eyes. "Trying to horn in on me, huh? She's mine."

"You're crazy," Sam said, warding off the swing from Joe.

"Watch out, Sam," Emma screamed, but it was too late. Karl Strauss had knocked Sam out with the butt of a rifle.

"Sam." Emma jumped up from the couch and started to run to Sam.

"Not so fast, honey," Joe said, grabbing her by the hair and locking his arms around hers. "Like it or not, you're coming with me."

Emma looked from Joe to the other man, her eyes wide like a trapped animal. Then a rage grew deep inside of her and she began to fight harder than ever.

"No way," she yelled, kicking her feet, the force turning both her and Joe around. "I'm not going anywhere with you.....", then she slumped to the floor out of Joe's arms.

Joe looked at the needle in Karl's hand.

"What the hell did you do that for?" Joe yelled at the man.

"To shut her up. I have what we came for; now help me pick her up. We need to leave for the airport."

Karl adjusted Emma's clothes. They didn't need a nearly naked woman attracting attention when they arrived at the airport. He would deal with Joe Remsky later. Karl nodded for Joe to lift Emma's shoulders while Karl grabbed her legs. They took her out to the waiting truck and put her in the middle of the bench seat. Karl, sitting next to her, looked at the treasure in his hands. Franz Maseman had killed two men to get this painting, his blood brothers, who had abandoned him. Soon, the painting would be Franz's again.

Joe got in next to Emma in the driver's seat and looked in the rear-view mirror. He saw the head of the mare through the window in the trailer behind them. He was hard as a rock and frustrated as hell. *Parker is going to pay for this*, he thought. *I almost had her.*

Without a word, Joe yanked the gear shift into position and drove the truck down Emma's lane. Then, he turned toward McMinnville.

◆ ◆ ◆ ◆

Emerson White's small black, Morris Minor turned into Emma's property and parked in front of the house, next to the red Mustang that he recognized as the vehicle Sam Parker had been driving earlier that day.

Doc had seen Emma's truck and trailer pass him before he'd reached her lane and wondered where Casey was.

As he got out, Doc reached into the back seat of his car to get his bag.

"Wanda," he said to his young assistant as he stepped from the car. "Run in and tell Emma that we have arrived, would you dear?"

"Sure, Doctor," Wanda said and walked up to the house. Shadow, the black cat, followed her.

Doc started to walk down to the stable, then stopped as he looked over at the red Mustang and saw the large man slumped over in the passenger seat. Quickly, he went to the man. When he opened the door, Doc saw the blood on the man's shirt. He opened the shirt and took out his handkerchief to wipe away the blood, to see the extent of the wound. In the overhead light of the car, he could tell it was a flesh wound in the man's left shoulder, caused by a bullet.

"Hold it there now, fellow," Doc said, trying to keep the man still as he moaned and stirred.

Wanda yelled from the house, "Doc, Emma's not here, but I think you need to come in here. Quickly!"

"Wanda, first come here and help me get this man out of the car. We need to take him in and lay him down somewhere. He's been shot."

As Doc swung the man's legs out onto the ground, Wanda ran over to where Doc stood.

"Watch his head now for me as I try to pull him out." Doc put his arms under the injured man's armpits and pulled him out of the car, while Wanda placed her hand over his head to keep it from bumping into the car's frame. George came to again.

"Can you walk, old boy?" Doc asked, once George was standing.

"Yes," George answered in a weak voice. "Who are you?" he asked, looking over at the small man holding him.

"Now is not the time for introductions. Let's get you inside."

Wanda placed her arm around George on the opposite side, and she and Doc slowly walked George into the house. As they entered the den, Doc saw Sam lying on the floor, the rifle lying next to him.

"Good lord, what has been going on here?" Doc asked, not really expecting a reply.

"That's what I was trying to tell you," Wanda said. They took George to the couch and gently laid him down. George passed out again. Doc pulled a blanket off the back of the couch and covered him.

"Wanda, go into the kitchen and get some towels, and water in a glass. Then, come back and place one of the towels on this man's arm, applying pressure to stop the bleeding. When he wakes up again, make him drink the water."

He then went to Sam. He could see the blood on the floor at the back of Sam's head. When he opened Sam's eyes and saw that they were slightly dilated, he exhaled a sigh of relief. He gently rolled Sam over onto his side and saw that the gash on his head was not very deep. Opening his bag, he took out some gauze and disinfectant and began cleaning the wound. Sam began to stir at the sting of the disinfectant and came up fighting. Doc and Wanda together calmed him and sat him back down on the floor.

"Now sit still, young man," Doc ordered.

"Ow! What the hell are you doing?" Sam yelled groggily, reaching up with his hand to stop the pain.

"Saving your life, Mr. Parker," Doc said, pulling Sam's arm down to keep him from touching his head until he was finished cleaning the wound. He then began wrapping Sam's head. He put the last strip of tape against the gauze to hold it in place.

"Now, how many fingers do you see?" Doc asked, holding up two fingers in front of Sam.

"Two," Sam replied, holding his head.

"Do you think you can stand?" Doc asked, then he helped Sam to his feet.

Sam's mind was beginning to clear. Frantically, he looked around the room. Frightened now, he shouted, "Where's Emma?"

"Maybe she's down at the stable," Doc said. He looked at George and saw that Wanda was helping him take small sips of water.

"Wanda, dear, would you mind running down and see for us?"

"Okay," Wanda said. She ran out of the front door, the cat following her again.

Sam ran through the house, calling for Emma. He checked upstairs, looking in every room. His stomach was beginning to tighten, and his head throbbed.

"You're a lucky fellow, this is only a flesh wound," Doc told George, glad that the bleeding had stopped. "It looks as if the bullet has gone through the muscle, but probably missed the bone. I'll need an x-ray to be sure. You've lost quite a bit of blood."

George slowly sat up, looking around him in a daze. "What happened?" he asked.

"That's what I'd like to know," Doc said. He began to bandage George, placing his left arm in a make-shift sling with an extra large dish towel Wanda had brought from the kitchen.

Then, George remembered and his body shook. *My own brother...* he thought.

"Sam, what has been going on here?" Doc demanded, when Sam ran back into the den.

"I'm not sure, but I think I know where they're headed," Sam said.

"Who, Sam?" Doc was still confused.

"The men that abducted Emma..." Sam began.

"Emma?" George cried, a pained expression on his face. His shock was now replaced with anger and he tried to stand, but Doc held him back.

Wanda ran in at that moment out of breath. "Doc, she's not at the stable," she said in gasps. "The black colt and the mare are gone, too."

"Oh God," Sam yelled, "I need to call Jim." Sam ran to the desk and began dialing.

"Who's Jim?" Doc asked.

"He's the Oregon Racing Commissioner. He also manages the airport in McMinnville."

"You're talking in riddles, Sam," Doc said.

"Jim," Sam said into the receiver. "It's begun. They have Emma with them and should be there in a few minutes. Call the police, and I'll meet you there in..." Sam looked at his watch, "twenty minutes." Sam was about to hang up, but stopped and added, "Oh, and Jim...call Smitty in Newberg and have him get my plane ready." Then, Sam hung up the phone.

"Come on, Doc," Sam yelled, as he started running to the front door. "I'll need you. I'll explain all of this on the way."

"Wait!" George yelled, trying to stand again. "I must go, too."

Doc ran over and put his arm around George to steady him.

Sam looked at Doc.

"Is he okay?" Sam asked.

"Yes, but he needs medical attention. We need to get him to a hospital soon."

"I'm fine," George said, trying to stand more on his own now. "We Germans are made of strong stuff," he sniffed into the air.

Sam nodded, looking into George's eyes. He knew George Mason's strength and saw that George could hold his own, for now.

Doc and Sam hurried out into the night air, helping George between them. Wanda followed closely on their heels, carrying Doc's bag.

Once they had placed George in the passenger seat, Doc and Wanda got into the back seat. Doc looked at Sam's face. He saw the set jaw and his tight, white knuckles on the steering wheel as the car raced out of Emma's lane onto the roadway.

"Sam," Doc said, as they were speeding over Chehalem Mountain. "Will you kindly explain to me what is going on?"

"Joe and Carlos have taken Emma, Classy Elegance, and the black colt to the McMinnville airport to fly them out of the country tonight."

"Who is Carlos?" Doc asked.

"Casey is Carlos Madera," Sam said, seeing George's head snap around to him as he spoke. "Carlos is a jockey that George used in the last Kentucky Derby."

"Who is George?"

"George Mason," Sam said, nodding at the man sitting next to him. "The owner of Koenig's Wonder."

"You are George Mason, of Essen Farms?" Doc asked George.

"I am," George answered, trying to sit a little straighter in his seat. Then, he winced as pain shot down his arm.

"But, I don't understand why Emma and the horses have been taken?" Doc asked, grabbing the back of George's seat as Sam swerved around a sharp corner. Doc could see the anger now in George's face.

"That's what we're going to find out," Sam said.

Doc was silent for a while, closing his eyes as Sam screeched around the hairpin turns on the winding road down into the valley. Then he asked, "Sam, you like Emma, don't you?"

Sam tried to concentrate on the road. He didn't want to make a false move – to lose precious time. 'Like' was too small a word for what Sam felt. He knew now that he had loved her ever since he'd first met her.

"Yes," was all he said.

Sam pulled into the Newberg airport and drove his car up to his plane near the runway. The engines were running and Smitty stood nearby.

"Thanks Smitty," Sam yelled above the noise of the engines. "Would you call Jim and have him get a medical team to the Mac airport. We will need their help when we get there."

"Will do, Sam," Smitty saluted, seeing the makeshift sling on the larger man's shoulder. "Take care of yourself," Smitty said to Sam.

Sam jumped into the cockpit and quickly checked the instruments while Doc and Wanda helped George into the plane. Doc came up and sat beside Sam in the co-pilot's seat.

"I just hope we're not too late," Sam said, as he taxied for takeoff.

CHAPTER NINETEEN

he DC-7 sat near the large hangar at the McMinnville airport, the propellers of the four turbo-compound engines stopped. Jim Barolio saw it was a 1954 Douglas Mainliner with cargo door modifications, much like the one he'd flown one summer when he'd ferried fish from Alaska to California. It looked like an old battered air freighter, probably stripped down inside and the pressurizing equipment removed, with a history of numerous missions since its maiden flight, but Jim knew these birds were built to last.

Earlier that evening, just before six o'clock – before the last of the airport crew left for the day, the DC-7 had landed at Mac Air. Jim had received numerous calls from residents living near the airstrip, complaining about the noise this plane had caused. He'd driven out to the airport to see the enormous machine sitting on the tarmac, the fuel truck still attached to it. The parking lot was full of curious townspeople who had come out to see the attraction. This didn't happen every day in McMinnville, and it was like a Christmas parade to this quiet community.

Nancy was working in the office and was about to leave.

"What time did that bucket arrive?" Jim asked Nancy.

"Before eighteen hundred. I received a call on the 122.8 frequency requesting to land for refueling. The pilot requested twelve thousand gallons of fuel, which the airport crew were very happy about, since they were getting cash."

Jim knew they were from Australia, by the plane's call numbers. He left the office and walked out to the plane, just before a strange pilot slipped into the office behind him.

◆ ◆ ◆ ◆

Charlie Fletcher was a salty old dog, and a renegade by trade. Over the years, he'd become a crude man, an ex-veteran who'd lost any morals left in him during the Vietnam War. He'd fly his DC-7 anywhere, as long as the money was right. He didn't ask any questions of his clients, and he'd go wherever the job was.

He noticed a man walking towards him. By the way he walked, Charlie recognized that this guy must run the place. Charlie had seen a thousand men like him – ex-Air Force pilots who, when their duty was over, found some way to stay near the world they loved – flying, but in a safe way, always staying within regulations, afraid to try anything illegal.

This guy probably wore a tie and had boards on his shoulders at one time. Not me, Charlie thought to himself. *I just like to fly – for profit.*

"Hi, I'm Jim Barolio," Jim said to the pilot, extending a hand. "Where're you headed?" Jim looked at the older man with the sky blue eyes that creased the suntanned skin at the sides when he smiled. Those eyes, Jim knew, had seen things most men only dream of. This was a man unafraid to try anything. *And probably for any price*, Jim thought to himself.

"Call me Charlie," the pilot said, shaking Jim's hand roughly. "Just flew in from Australia. We're headed for Africa."

Charlie looked behind Jim and saw Bill Isaac, his flight engineer and partner, walking back from the airport office. Charlie knew that he must have charmed a pretty lady by the big grin on his face. Bill was a tall, slender man with dark hair and big brown eyes like a puppy. The women liked him. His long arms swung loosely at his sides as he walked toward Charlie and Jim.

"We're going over there to do some relief work," Charlie told Jim with a private wink toward Bill as he passed. Bill and Charlie had been working in South America for a cheap outfit. But, when the German offered them the large bundle of cash for this job, they'd jumped at it.

"You sure caused some excitement coming in here today," Jim said.

Charlie laughed heartily. "I usually do!"

"When are you planning on taking off?"

"Bill and me probably won't be taking off until about eight o'clock tomorrow morning," Charlie lied, knowing they'd hopefully be leaving within the hour. "We are both in need of a good hot meal and some shuteye. Where's a good place to eat in town?"

"You could try the Overnighter out on 99W," Jim offered, watching the other pilot walk toward the tanker. "It's kind of a truck stop, but the café next door's not bad and the motel there's clean." Jim saw the tanker crew release the fuel hose from the airplane.

"Thanks, Jim," Charlie said. "Is there any live entertainment?"

"Well, there's black jack and craps at the Western Tavern, if you're inclined. Tonight, a country band will come in, so you may find something there to interest you. The tavern's not far from the motel. Do you want a ride into town?" Jim asked. Pilots took care of pilots. It was the code they all worked by.

"Thanks for the offer," Charlie said. "But, Bill and I've got a few things to do here before we're done tonight. Is there a cab service in town we can call later?"

"Sure is. Their number's written on the outside of the book in the phone booth over there," Jim said, pointing to a booth standing under a street lamp.

Charlie nodded, then asked, "Which runway would you suggest we use to take this bird out of here in the morning?"

"You'll probably want to use Number thirty four over there," Jim said, waving his hand to the small lights near the ground in the distance. "It's our longest one. You can get to it by using the old taxiway over there. It was built in '42 by the military, but is still in good condition today. We use it mainly to get between the two main runways."

"Thanks for your help."

"Okay," Jim said. Then, before he began to walk away, he added, "I'll probably see you later."

"Sure," Charlie said, with a slight chuckle under his breath. Charlie watched as Jim walked into the airport office, then shortly emerged with a woman. The pair walked to a Chevrolet and drove off together.

Bill paid the fuel man and watched the tanker leave. The parking lot began to empty, as the curious people went back to their homes. That was the reason they'd chosen McMinnville. Joe Remsky had checked it out before they'd made their final plans. The small airport didn't have a tower, and Joe had told Charlie the entire crew left after six o'clock.

"Bill," Charlie said, as his partner walked up to him. "Did you get all the tanks filled?"

"Sure thing. All eight of them." Bill gave Charlie a big grin. "I had the extra tanks jury rigged with some sophisticated household plumbing, so we'll be able to pump it forward into the wings as we need it on this non-stop flight. Maseman said he didn't want us landing anywhere for any reason, once we have our cargo on aboard."

◆ ◆ ◆ ◆

When they were alone, when the sky fell to a darker blue and before the hangar floodlights came on, Bill quickly pulled off the call letters on the plane, revealing the new letters underneath. Then, he and Charlie stood outside of the plane, watching the first arrival of their cargo and passengers.

The truck pulled into the airport and stopped. Franz smiled at the sight of the DC-7, lit by the floodlight near the largest hangar. It was an impressive piece of equipment. Then, he got out and walked over to the pilot.

"Hello, Mr. Fletcher," Franz said with a nod, but not offering his hand. He detested being touched. "I hope you had a pleasant flight and all went well upon your arrival here."

"Yeah, no problems. We caused quite a show for a while, when we landed here. But, that didn't last long. We're ready for you."

Charlie didn't like this man. He reminded him of a weasel and sometimes smelled like one. There was something about Maseman's eyes that made his skin crawl and imagine the terrible things he was capable of. Charlie noticed the leather gloves on Maseman's hands, and wondered what he was covering up, since it wasn't that cold here. *But*, Charlie thought to himself, *I'm not getting paid to like him.*

Franz and Charlie watched as Carlos loaded Koenig's Wonder onto the plane. The horse was led up a steep, make-shift ramp, which stood twelve feet off the ground, leading into the large cargo door of the plane.

"What a fine animal," Franz sighed, not so much to Charlie, but to himself. He was finally allowing himself to believe that this colt was now his.

"Yes, I think you have a winner there, Frank," Charlie said.

"You may call me Mr. Maseman," Franz shot back at the pilot, his eyes angry and threatening.

"Sure," the pilot said, raising his hands in a surrendering gesture. "Anything you say, Mr. Maseman."

"You will pay me our second installment before takeoff, right?" Charlie asked.

"Here it is," Franz said, placing a bundle of bills into Charlie's hand. "I will pay you the remainder when we land in Caracas," he added, lighting a dark, thin cigarette. "Now, make sure the plane is ready for flight. The others will be here soon."

Charlie nodded and climbed into the plane through the open cargo door. He stopped to see that the animal was secure in his make-shift stall, then walked toward the cockpit. Bill was inside, leaning over charts, checking his flight plan again.

"That's a testy fellow we work for," Charlie said. "Watch your backside with him. I don't trust him any farther than I can throw him."

"Did he give you the money?" Bill asked, as hungry for the cash as Charlie. It'd been a long dry spell since a job like this one had come along, and he'd already spent most of his share of the first installment.

"Only the second installment. Maseman says we get the rest when we arrive in Venezuela. Let's make damn sure he does, okay?"

Charlie slapped Bill on the back, then slid into his seat and began the routine of checking the gauges in front of him.

"You're sure we're going to be okay with the fuel?" Charlie called back to Bill.

"I'm sure. I can manage the refueling and oiling from up here with the flip of a switch or two, the way I rigged it up. Pretty proud of myself," Bill said, puffing himself up in his seat. He'd learned many tricks in the service, before working with Charlie. They were a good team.

◆ ◆ ◆ ◆

Franz saw that Joe and Karl were driving in at that moment. Joe parked the truck near the plane, while Karl walked over to talk with Franz, leaving Joe to unload the mare.

Emma was still unconscious in the cab of the truck.

"Did you get it?" Franz's eyes glowed in the faint light, the greed widening them into a hungry stare at the bundle in Karl's hands. Franz had removed his gloves, opening and closing his hands, as if he was about to receive a long-awaited present.

"Yes." Karl handed the muslin-covered painting to Franz. He looked at Franz's hands and sighed.

"Where did you find it?" Franz asked, his breath coming in short gasps now.

"It was in a false bottom of Hermann's tack trunk. That's why we didn't find it before."

Franz's hands shook as he slowly removed the outer cloth. When the dark paint on the canvas came to life in the dim light, he sighed. It was as he'd remembered it – the solitary man standing at the foot of a stone grave site in the eerie moonlight. His heart beat fast and his breath came quickly as he gazed into it. When his father had brought this home, Franz had immediately known that it must one day be his. It was as if the painting had called his name the first moment he saw it. When it had been stolen from his father's house, Franz had vowed he would get it back – no matter what the cost.

"Mine. At last, this is mine."

Karl watched his friend's face while he looked at the painting. He knew how much this meant to him. Franz had told Karl how he'd seen his brother, George, steal the Friedrich painting from their parents' home, just before the two older boys left for America. Karl had carefully searched George's house in Kentucky, but had found nothing. When Karl had returned to Venezuela, after drugging George's colt at Churchill, he had found Franz in Caracas.

Karl looked again at the scars on the backs of Franz's hands. Guilt grabbed at his heart when he remembered the accident that had caused the scars. He hadn't known that Franz was standing behind him, shielding him when the land mine had gone off on the way to one of the camps.

After a moment, Karl said, "We had a little trouble at the woman's house."

"What kind of trouble?" Franz asked, not looking up from the painting.

"Remsky must have been fooling around with the woman while I was in the stable getting the painting. When I came into the house, the American cowboy, Sam Parker, was there. He and Joe were fighting. I had to knock Parker out so we could leave. I sedated the girl to keep her quiet during the drive here."

"I don't like Joe Remsky," Franz hissed into the night air. "I think we will need to take care of him before we land, along with my new niece." He was covering the painting again and gently rolling it. "I don't like the way he uses his own ideas."

"Yes," Karl said, thinking to himself of the similarities between Joe and Franz. "I'll tell the pilot."

"No, Karl," Franz said, placing a hand on his friend's arm with a smile on his face. There was affection in the gesture and his voice, but Karl knew what the smile meant. He had seen it numerous times before – just before Franz would pull the lever next to the door of the room that was jammed full with naked bodies.

"Let me tell him when it is time," Franz added. "Now, go tell Carlos to help Remsky with the mare. I don't want anything to happen to her. She and the colt will bring me millions in the future."

Karl walked into the plane as Carlos finished adjusting the restraints in Koenig's Wonder's stall.

"Mr. Maseman wants you to help Joe with the mare," Karl said to Carlos, nodding his head back toward Emma's truck.

Carlos nodded.

After Carlos left the plane, the colt next to Karl snorted, shaking his head. Karl checked the horse's eyes to make sure he was still sedated and that the pupils responded correctly.

◆ ◆ ◆ ◆

Emma slowly awoke from a dream where everything was dark and quiet. A cool, gentle wind crossed her face through the open window, clearing her mind. The familiar smell of fuel came into the truck's cab on the breeze. A bad taste in her mouth told her she had been drugged. She realized her hands were tied in front of her and that a bandana was tied across her mouth. Then, she saw the plane through the windshield, its metal sides gleaming in the low lights around it. Joe stood by a strange man outside of the gaping cargo door of the plane.

She looked around her and saw the office building Nancy had worked in and realized that they were at the McMinnville airport. It seemed abandoned. Her stomach knotted as she remembered what had happened. She thought of Sam lying on the floor of her home and her heart began to ache. *Was Sam dead?*

At that moment, Carlos emerged from the plane and walked over to the two men. Emma took that moment to push the button of the glove compartment. The small door opened and she reached inside with her tied hands. She groped through the small compartment until her hands wrapped around the handle of her father's small revolver. She pushed it down inside her jeans, under her panties, gasping as the cold steel touched her warm skin. Then, she softly closed the small door until it clicked into place.

◆ ◆ ◆ ◆

"I think we need to stop off in Mexico for fuel, Mr. Maseman," Carlos heard Joe say. "I don't think this bucket is going to take us that many miles without it."

"The pilot assures me that we will not need to stop. I trust his judgment with his own equipment, Mr. Remsky."

Carlos could see that Maseman was beginning to get irritated with Joe, and so was he. He walked up to Joe and pulled on his arm to get him to follow him. "We need to get the mare loaded, Joe," he said, keeping his hand on Joe's arm.

When Emma saw the two men walking back to her truck, she slumped back against the seat and closed her eyes, pretending she was still under the drug. She could hear Joe and Carlos talking as they approached the horse trailer behind her.

"I don't like that German," Joe said to Carlos, jerking his head back toward Maseman.

Carlos remained quiet, not responding to Joe. He just listened.

"I tell you one thing," Joe continued. "This plane ain't going to make it all the way to Venezuela without a refuel. We've got hot cargo here and every airport in the country will be watching for us to come down. I know of a small airstrip we could use. Besides, I hadn't figured on getting into murder with this. When you shot Ted – that was one thing. Ted was getting too suspicious. But, when Maseman shot that guy at my ranch and just left him lying there, they're going to think I did it. I wanted out then and there."

Emma gasped. *Carlos shot Ted! Who had been shot at Joe's?* she wondered, frightened and confused.

Joe stopped and looked around to make sure no one was listening as they stood at the back of the horse trailer. "I've got some plans with my share of the money," he continued to Carlos. "As soon as we get to Venezuela, I'm going to catch the next plane to Australia. I've got a brother there."

Carlos didn't answer.

Emma heard the trailer ramp drop to the ground and someone was walking inside. Then, she heard Carlos' voice, talking to the mare behind her.

Carlos could tell that Karl had given the mare a small injection to keep her calm during the ride to the airport. Her eyes and motions were slow and she breathed deeply. Slowly, Carlos backed her out of the trailer, then led her to the plane.

"Hello, darling," Joe's voice startled Emma as he opened the passengers' door of her truck. "I see you are among us again. Too bad that Sam had to come in when he did. We could have had a lot more fun before we had to leave."

Joe licked his lips again and touched Emma's arm. Her skin crawled at his touch and she pulled away from him. Then, his hands caught her arms and began pulling her out of the truck. "Maybe you'll change your mind about coming with me," he said, his lips against her cheek, "when you see what I have planned for us. It's time to go."

She pulled away from him, and began to kick at his face, his arms, anything she could reach. She could see the same fire come into his eyes that she'd seen at her ranch, and she tried to scream through the cloth across her mouth. Joe reached down and pulled on her heels, making her slide back onto the bench seat, bumping her head against the steering wheel. The pain stopped her long enough for Joe to finish pulling her out and wrapping his arms around her. He grabbed a handful of her hair and pulled hard.

"Now listen, you wildcat," Joe hissed. "Settle down. We'll finish this later." He kissed her neck, sucking and biting her skin.

Emma tried to pull away from him, twisting and kicking even though Joe had her pinned against him. Coarse groans came out of her, her lips hurting from the tight bandana. She caught a movement out of the corner of her eye before she felt the fist on her jaw, which caused her neck to jerk back and white, shooting stars, flooded her eyes. Her blood roared in her ears before she blacked out.

"You idiot!" Karl yelled at Joe. "This is the kind of thing that could bring someone here!"

"She's a wild animal, Strauss," Joe said, wiping the back of his hand against his mouth. He could still taste her. "You didn't have to go and hit her like that. I had her under control."

"Right," Karl said as he leaned down and grabbed Emma's waist, throwing her over his back. He carried her into the plane and sat her down on an aisle seat near the cockpit, while Joe followed close behind. There were only four passenger seats. The rest of the plane inside had been stripped to accommodate the horses' stalls.

"Here, Remsky, strap her in, if you think you can handle that without letting your hormones get in the way." Karl was beginning to get nervous about the whole thing – too many people and too many complications. He liked it better when he was in control. He walked back to check the horses.

Joe took his time with Emma's restraints, enjoying the warmth of her body through her jeans, while she lay bound and helpless. Images flashed through his mind of what he planned to do with her when he got her alone again. Then, his hand stopped, and he looked at her and smiled. Emma began to slowly shake her head, feeling the numb pain in her jaw as she started to come to and realized where she was. She could taste the blood from a cut on her lip. Joe looked into her eyes as he reached under her shirt and pulled out the gun from her underwear. In a quick movement, he placed it into his own trousers, grinning to himself. She looked down and saw that her hands were still tied and that her seat belt was tight across her lap.

"Thanks, sweetheart," Joe whispered into Emma's ear. "We may need this later when you and I split this game. I'm taking you with me, you know. You're mine, now."

She tried to kick at him, but Joe stepped aside and grinned as he walked across the aisle and sat down, putting on his seatbelt.

The engines started up and Emma looked around her, staring at the pilot's back in front of her. Another man sat next to him, looking over charts. She noticed a door on the floor between the cockpit and where she sat. Then, she turned to look at the back of the plane and almost cried. The horses stood side by side, while Carlos checked their bindings.

The lunatic from her house and another man got onto the plane and stood at the back.

"Bill," Emma heard the pilot say. "Close the door. It's time we blow this burg."

The man sitting next to the pilot went to the back and pushed a button. The narrow ramp came up to the plane, closing the cargo door. He walked back up to the front of the plane to his seat, as the other men got into their seats, all except for one. Emma stared at the stranger, still standing at the back. He was a copy of her father when he was young, blond and blue-eyed. But, this man's eyes threw a chill up her spine. She could see from his evil stare that he despised her.

The man slowly walked up to Emma. She saw something rolled up in one of his hands, which he carried as if it were made of fine porcelain.

"It is a pleasure to finally meet you, my dear," the man said in heavy German, much like Emma's father had used when she was very young. He had the same high forehead and deep eyebrows like her father, high cheekbones and square jaw, but there was something about his mouth that scared her. There was a smile on his face, but not in his eyes. He placed his hand under her chin. She tried to pull away, but his grip tightened and held her face so that she had to look at him. He grinned and said, "I am your Uncle Franz. You and I are all we have, now that George and your father are both dead. What an unfortunate accident your father had on that dark night – with that nasty rock. And your Uncle George, well, he got in the way of a bullet today."

Tears rolled down Emma's cheeks as she stared at his face, the face of the man who had killed her father.

"You'd better get into your seat and strap in back there," the pilot's voice shouted. "We're ready to get in the air."

The engines grew louder as the crew performed the run-up and pre-take-off checks. Then, the large plane began to taxi toward the long runway.

"But, why?" Emma asked, looking at Franz.

Franz gently took the muslin from the rolled cloth in his hands, watching Emma's eyes as he slowly opened it for Emma to see. Her eyes widened when she recognized the Friedrich painting that her father had described to her. She'd guessed right, it had been in her father's trunk! The small light in the cabin brought life to the image of the man, standing in a long, red, velvet cloak by a large stone. The dark trees in the foreground stood against the lighter colors of the sky at dusk, the moon and star that her father had described as a sign of hope.

◆ ◆ ◆

"What the hell?" the pilot yelled, as bright lights shone into the cockpit when the DC-7 turned onto the runway. Franz, still standing in the aisle, looked up, just as the plane jerked to the left sharply, throwing him off balance. The engines raced, forcing him to stumble to the back of the plane. Emma screamed through the bandana. Then, she heard the horses cry and turned, just as the restraints on the colt broke loose and the man fell under the sharp hooves of the rearing black colt. She tried to close her ears to the screams of animal and man, shutting her eyes tight to the bloody scene she had just witnessed.

The plane finally stopped. Emma could see red lights flashing in the cockpit and heard someone outside the plane. Joe, Carlos, and Karl jumped out of their seats and ran back to pull the trampled man from under the horse. Emma pulled down the bandana, then tried to undo her seatbelt with her bound hands.

◆ ◆ ◆

Sam jumped from his plane that was standing on the runway in the path of the large plane and ran under the belly of the DC-7, followed by the police. He opened a small access door and crawled into the unused baggage compartment. Then, he found the small hatch that allowed him to look up into the small area between the cockpit and passenger seating. Sam saw the fear in Emma's face. Their eyes met for a moment.

Then, Sam saw the men at the back of the plane, and hoisted himself up.

Joe saw Sam pull himself into the plane and he rushed at him. Emma saw Joe reach into his jeans and pull out her gun.

"He has my gun," Emma screamed at Sam.

"Get down," Sam yelled at Emma as he dove down the aisle at Joe's feet.

She crouched down in front of the seat. When she heard the gunshot, she looked up and saw the pilot slump forward in his seat, then she looked back to see that Sam had knocked Joe down. Emma screamed as the two men rolled closer to where the horses were standing. The colt's eyes were wild and he reared nervously on his hind legs as the men fought in front of him. She saw the gun in Joe's hand, Sam holding on to Joe's arm. Before Carlos or Karl could do anything, the gun went off during the struggle.

Then, there was silence.

After a few seconds, Joe went limp and lay quietly on the floor. Sam stood up and looked down at Joe in disbelief.

Two policemen went into the cockpit, while others ran past Emma, taking Carlos into custody and removing the gun from Joe's lifeless fingers. Doc White followed and went immediately to the horses.

An officer stood next to Karl Strauss, who was kneeling over Franz, lying on the floor, while two other men opened the cargo door and lowered the ramp.

Sam ran back to Emma and helped her out of her bindings. She jumped into his arms, crying. "Oh God, Sam, I thought you were dead. I was so frightened."

"Sh," he said to her, slowly caressing her long hair while his other arm held her tightly. "It's okay, now. It's over." Sam saw the bruise beginning on Emma's face and the cut on her lip. Anger welled inside of him.

"Oh, Em, who did this to you?"

"I didn't see who did it. He came up from behind when I was kicking Joe, trying to get away." She saw the hurt in Sam's eyes, and then she saw the anger. "It's okay," she said, putting her hand to her face. It didn't hurt as much now. "But," she said as she gulped in air between sobs, "that man back there. He said he was my Uncle Franz. I've never seen him before in my life. He killed my father, and he said that George was dead."

"It's okay," Sam said softly.

"I'm not dead," a voice said behind Emma. She turned and saw George standing there, blood on his white shirt, his left arm in a sling. Emma ran up to him and hugged him. He winced, but held her with his free arm.

"What happened to you?" Emma asked.

"I was shot."

"You two know each other?" Sam asked, looking between Emma and George.

From the back of the plane, Emma and George heard Karl Strauss say in German, "Oh, Franz, my brother. Can you hear me?" He was sobbing, holding onto Franz's hand.

George ran to where the man kneeled. He grabbed the man by his collar, forgetting the pain in his shoulder, and pulled him to his feet, shaking him.

"Strauss, I've waited a long time for this moment. I should have known you'd be behind this." George's rage burst and he slugged Strauss, enjoying how the man's head snapped back from the blow. Strauss fell to the floor of the plane, just as Sam came up and grabbed George from behind.

"Let me go," George yelled. "This is the man who drugged Koenig before the Derby..."

"Let the officials handle it, George," Sam said in a calm voice.

George turned toward Sam, then stopped. He stared down at the face of the other man lying on the floor. George's face went white. It was a face he had not seen for many years, a face he never expected to ever see again. It was the face of his younger brother, Franz. George went down on one knee next to him. Franz's face and body were covered with blood, his chest sunken and his breathing shallow and raspy.

"Franz?" George said in German, tears streaming down his face. "You are alive! But how can this be?"

Franz's eyes flickered and slowly opened. He turned his head slightly toward George and stared at him. George could see the hatred in them and was stunned.

"I thought you were dead," Franz said slowly in German so softly that George had to lean down to hear him.

"No, little brother..." George began. Then, he swallowed and wiped his tears. "I am alive."

"You don't deserve to live," Franz spat at George, blood running down the side of his mouth.

George stared at him and remembered that moment, after he'd been shot, what his younger brother had said. "Franz, what is the meaning of all of this? How is it that you are alive? What did you mean about Hermann?"

"You abandoned me. You, and Hermann. You left me and our parents to die. Only, I survived. You are to blame for their deaths. I vowed then to find the two of you and kill you, as you had killed our parents. The painting was rightfully mine. Father told me it was mine, and you took it from me."

Franz's blue eyes flashed with anger, then he closed them and breathed heavily for a moment, his mind seeing the image of his parents' house exploding after the bomb dropped nearby, his own small body being thrown like a rag doll tossed aside. He was now very tired. He didn't want to continue any longer.

He opened his eyes and looked at George. Then he took a deep breath and said, "I killed Hermann that night, beside his car on that road. When I shot you, I thought I finally had my revenge on you, as well. But, the Friedrich is mine again." He was silent for a moment. Then, in a whisper, he said, "Now, I have everything."

George saw Franz look over at Karl Strauss with love in his eyes. Then, with what little strength he had left, Franz told Karl, "Farewell, my brother." His eyes closed again for the last time.

George looked at Karl and saw the pain in his face. He didn't understand why Franz had called Karl his brother, but George had felt the hatred in Franz for his own blood brother. Now, he understood why Karl had drugged Koenig.

Emma and Sam watched in silence.

Large tears fell over the rims of George's dark eyes and down his cheeks, dripping onto his shirt, as he silently grieved for the loss of his last brother, for the ache in his heart that he knew would never leave him as long as he lived, for the mistakes made in his own lifetime that could have turned the fate of his family, if he had only been strong enough to do what he believed was right.

He leaned over the dead man. In a whisper, as his lips brushed Franz's sunken cheek, George said, "Forgive me, little brother."

◆ ◆ ◆ ◆

Doc White jerked Strauss to his feet with a surprising strength. Sam was surprised at the anger in Doc's face as he shook the man.

"These horses have been drugged, you devil!" Doc yelled. "What have they been given? Tell me," Doc demanded.

"A mild sedative," Karl said, his voice quivering from both his grief and the shaking he was receiving from Doc.

"How much?" Doc demanded.

"Just enough to keep them quiet until we were in the air. I was to administer to them as needed until we arrived in Venezuela."

Doc threw the man at the police standing nearby and went back to the horses. Wanda walked up the ramp toward him, followed by the ambulance attendants.

A doctor quickly checked Franz.

"Good lord, what happened to this man?" he asked, looking at each person standing around him.

"He was trampled by the colt back there," Emma said, her voice quivering.

The doctor examined Franz's temple and ear, which was cut and bleeding. Then he pulled the soaked shirt open. It was obvious that the man's ribs were broken, which probably also had punctured a lung. It was the severed vein that had been the cause of his quick death.

"I'm sorry," the doctor said, standing. "He is dead." He nodded to the ambulance attendants, then went to where Joe was lying.

The attendants placed Franz onto a stretcher; his bloody body was limp and lifeless. As George began to follow them out of the plane, he stopped as a flash of white caught his eye. He walked to the back row of seats and picked up something that was lying on the floor. It was the Friedrich painting. He saw that there was a small tear at the top left corner. He closed his eyes and wept, knowing that all of his brothers had died and his family had been ruined over this piece of canvas.

Emma walked to where George stood. She could see his shoulders shaking, and reached up to touch his arm. Then, she looked down and saw the painting in his hands. Her heart ached as she turned to hug him, knowing that he was all she had left of her family, realizing now how important he was to her. She also knew that the canvas had been one of the reasons her father had died. No words came. All she could do was hold the large man and let him sob on her shoulder.

Sam watched as the doctor shook his head, indicating that Joe was also dead. As a new set of attendants took Joe's body from the plane, Sam's stomach tightened at the thought of his responsibility in Joe's death, even though his head tried to tell him otherwise. He stood for a moment, trying to make some sense of it all. He had to do something.

"Come on, you two," Sam finally said softly to Emma and George. "Let's get you out of here." He ushered both of them out of the plane to where an attendant stood near another ambulance. He could see Emma beginning to shake from shock. He handed her over to the attendant. Another medic was already helping George, checking his wound.

Sam saw Nancy Barolio running toward them from the parking lot and was glad to see a familiar face. "Hi, Nanc, will you watch Emma for me?" Sam asked.

"Sure, Sam," Nancy replied, placing her arm on Emma's shoulders.

"Where're you going?" Emma asked Sam.

"I'll be right back," he said, touching her cheek softly with his hand. "I need to see if Doc needs help with the horses."

◆ ◆ ◆ ◆

As Sam walked back up the ramp, he heard Doc White's gentle voice.

"Hello, big fellow," Doc said to the colt as he stroked his long neck. The horse whinnied softly in answer. "You're going to be just fine, as soon as I get you back to your own stall."

Sam walked up to Ele. His stomach tightened to see the frightened and confused look in her eyes. He placed his forehead against hers and stood in silence.

"It looks like you two know each other," Wanda said to Sam, as she stood next to Doc.

"You could say that. Doc, what can I do?" Sam asked, feeling helpless.

"You could bring Emma's truck and trailer up to the ramp, so that we can load these two and take them back to Emma's."

"No problem," Sam said and walked down the ramp.

As he reached Emma's truck, Jim Barolio came up to Sam and put his arm across his shoulders and hugged him.

"Sam," Jim said, glad to see his friend alive. "Is everyone okay?" His eyes were dark with concern as he saw Sam's jaw working, knowing that was how Sam worked through his tension.

"I think we're going to be fine now," Sam said. "Thanks, pal, for getting the troops here on time. I knew you'd come through. I'm just thankful I got here when I did."

"That was a great stunt, cowboy," Jim laughed, shaking his head. "I got here just as your Commander came down straight at that big tank. I thought you were going to be dog meat, but I guess you've played chicken more times than that pilot had."

Sam laughed, too, feeling the knot in his jaw finally release.

"I did too, for a while, till he turned off the runway. His hand must have slipped on the throttle. That's probably what threw that fellow to the back of the plane, where the horses were. I'm glad it's all over."

Sam knew now that there was nothing he could have done to prevent what had happened. He flinched as he thought of the gun going off while he and Joe had struggled on the plane. Sam had never killed a man point blank before. Flying over an area in Vietnam and dropping bombs was one thing, but this was totally unreal. He stuffed the guilt back, deep inside.

"You okay, Sam?" Jim had seen Sam's eyes darken. He'd heard about the scuffle between Sam and Joe Remsky – and the result of that scuffle.

Sam looked away into the darkness. Then, he turned and tried to smile. "Yeah, just haven't absorbed it all yet."

"I understand. You did what you had to do. The police are already talking to George. They have Carlos and Strauss in my office here at the airport, waiting to be interrogated. Do you want me to take care of it?"

"Thanks. I've got to take this truck to Doc, for the horses. I'll come over there in a couple of minutes. I want to be in on it." Sam had some questions he wanted to ask those two men.

"Okay," Jim said. "See you in a few."

Sam climbed into the truck and backed the trailer up to the cargo ramp. He was surprised to see Emma standing at the top of the cargo door with a blanket over her shoulders.

"What are you doing here?" Sam asked gruffly, as he climbed up the ramp. "You should have stayed with the medics."

His concern for her was showing on his face, and she loved it.

"I needed to see that the horses were all right," she said, still shaking a little, but much less than when Sam had last seen her. "They gave me something to help me settle down, so I'm going to be fine."

"I'm just worried about you," Sam said, gently taking her shoulders into his hands and looked deeply into her eyes. He could see the hurt behind them, the dark circles beginning to form under them.

Emma shivered at his touch, but this time it was not from shock. "I'm stronger than you think, Mr. Parker," she said.

"Mrs. Jacobs," an officer said from the bottom of the ramp. "May I have a few words with you?"

"Yes, Officer," Emma said.

Sam kissed her forehead and gave her a smile as she walked down the ramp and followed the officer to the airport office.

"Do you need help loading them, Doc?" Sam asked.

"No, Sam. Wanda will help me."

◆ ◆ ◆ ◆

When Sam walked in, Jim sat behind his desk, while Carlos sat across from him. Sam watched the small man's eyes nervously flit between them as he sat handcuffed. An officer stood just inside the door.

Jim asked, "How're you involved in this scheme, Madera?"

"I don't know anything."

"Then, tell me how you happen to be here with Joe Remsky's truck and trailer tonight? Sight-seeing, I suppose?"

Carlos was quiet for a moment, his eyes dropping to the ground. Jim could see his hands opening and closing, as his mind churned to come up with some lame excuse. He remembered this from the notes on Carlos' interrogation after the drug was discovered in Sam's mare at Del Mar.

"I wonder whose prints we'll find in that truck..." Jim began, then stopped and waited.

"Those guys came to Joe's ranch and stole Mr. Jacobs' colt," Carlos blurted out. "They made me drive."

"When was this?" Sam asked as he leaned his hands on Jim's desk, giving the impression he was interested.

"Just today." Carlos looked between Jim and Sam, thinking they may be buying this after all. He relaxed a little, as he created more of the illusion in his mind.

"Had you ever met them before?" Sam asked, turning Carlos so he could see his eyes.

Carlos looked away. "No. They just showed up and forced me and Joe to come with them at gunpoint."

"What were you doing at Joe's?" Jim asked.

"He'd asked me to bring Frankie there, after Mrs. Jacobs went into the city." Carlos looked at Sam. "Why's he here?"

"He's in charge of this investigation."

Carlos' face went pale. He knew Sam Parker was the owner of the horse he'd conned Joe into drugging at Del Mar, but he didn't know he was an investigator.

"Where'd Ted Jacobs get the colt, Carlos?" Sam asked, stepping closer to Carlos' chair. The blood in his veins was thundering, as he remembered the notes on the investigation of Ele's race. He wanted to take this little creep and toss him across the room, but he knew his job.

"Joe told me Mr. Jacobs had bought him from the owner," he lied.

"Are you sure Frankie isn't Joe's horse?" Sam asked.

"Doc White told me he was..."

"Why were you using the name Casey Morales at the Jacobs' ranch?" Sam questioned, leaning more closely into Carlos' face. "You were George Mason's jockey at the last Derby, weren't you?"

Carlos' hands were working quickly. He knew he was dead if he said anymore. These two knew too much about him. "I want to see my attorney."

Sam exploded. He grabbed Carlos by his shirt and jerked him out of the chair. "You little shit," he yelled in Carlos' face. "You'd better tell me everything you know about this or I'll break you into pieces."

"Whoa, Sam," Jim was saying behind him, trying to get hold of Carlos. "Let him go. Maybe he's telling us the truth." Jim and Sam had worked together enough to know how to get information. Jim pulled Carlos free of Sam's large hands and pushed him back into the chair. Sam paced in the back of the room like a wild animal in a cage.

"Now, Carlos," Jim said, leaning over him. "If you want your attorney, we'll get him for you. What's his number?" Jim began pulling the phone over closer to Carlos.

"I.....don't know. I need time to look it up." Carlos needed time to talk to Strauss. Sweat was beginning to role down his face and his hands were shaking.

"Okay, we'll give you time," Jim said, as he calmly walked around his desk. "But, we know Joe and Ted Jacobs were at the Derby last spring with Frank's Revenge. You were there, too. It'd be easy to run a blood test on this horse to find out just which one we have here."

Sam smiled as he watched Carlos' eyes bulge and goose bumps popping up on his forearms. *We've got him*, Sam thought to himself. *Now, I'll come in for the kill.*

Sam spun Carlos' chair around, leaning down into his face with such fire in his eyes that Satan would be frightened.

"You helped Joe swap Koenig's Wonder for Frank's Revenge, didn't you?" Sam said softly.

"No," Carlos lied, his voice quivering slightly.

"Don't lie to me. I saw you and Joe there that night," Sam yelled now. It wasn't a lie, he had seen them both at Churchill Downs.

Carlos remained silent.

"Did you kill Ted Jacobs?" Sam shot at him.

Carlos looked up at Sam, then quickly looked away. "No."

"We can have that gun of yours checked that I saw at Emma Jacob's stable."

Sam could see Carlos beginning to shut down, his eyes glazing over. He decided to make one more stab at getting to the truth.

"Did you know that Juan Martinez, Mason's first jockey, and Maria Sanchez were found in a motel room together down in Caracas, about a month after the Kentucky Derby? They were both dead from a drug overdose."

Sam saw Carlos' eyes when he'd mentioned Maria's name. He waited a few beats, then added, "Did you know Maria was pregnant?"

Carlos' face turned white, and he stared into Sam's face. Then he looked frantically around the room. "Maria?" was all he kept saying.

♦ ♦ ♦ ♦

In the plane, Doc White could tell that the colt was in pain, his ears were bent back and he was favoring his right hoof. Instinctively, Wanda placed Doc's bag on the floor next to him, then went to take Ele to the trailer.

Emma returned to the door of the plane and watched as Doc looked at the colt's front legs. There was blood on his right hoof and it had started to swell. Doc wiped some of the blood off and noticed a small cut on the horse's right pastern. Doc could see that the cut did not need any sutures. He softly talked to the large animal as he cleaned the wound with Bedadine soap, and painted it with an iodine-based ointment. Gently, he placed a Telfa pad bandage with brown gauze over the area. Then, he wrapped it, while the colt waited patiently, as if he was used to this type of treatment.

"There you are, big fellow," Doc said, closing his bag. Then he stood up and stretched his back. "He's ready to load now, Wanda. The sooner we get these two back home, the better."

"The sooner we get these three," Sam said, as he came up the ramp and placed an arm protectively around Emma's shoulders.

"How're you doing?" Sam asked Emma. She saw the concern in his eyes and smiled.

"I'm going to be okay."

Sam then walked over to the tall colt. He needed to stay busy, to choke down the anger still surging through him. He took the horse's reins in one hand and stroked the large, black neck with the other.

"Hey, big boy," Sam said in a soothing voice. "You're the victor here, the hero of the day."

"No, Sam," Emma said softly. "You are."

Sam blushed. Then, he and the colt walked down to the trailer where Ele was waiting.

Emma watched as George walked up to Sam, his left arm in a clean sling. The two men began to talk between them. Then George went down on one knee and touched the bandage on the horse's leg. He stood and nodded to Sam. Sam took the colt into the trailer.

"Doc, are they really going to be all right?" Emma asked, her eyes filled with worry. She wasn't sure if she was asking about the horses or the two men standing at the trailer.

Doc was wiping his hands on a towel. He dropped the towel on the plane's floor, picked up his bag and walked to her. He put his arm around her shoulder and led her from the plane and the reminders of that terrible scene.

"Yes, my dear," he said gently, leading her to where George stood. "Everyone will be all right. Don't worry your pretty little head."

"Hey, Doc," Sam said, as he came out of the trailer. "Would you and Wanda mind driving these two on your own? I'd like to take Emma and George back to her ranch."

"Not at all, we'd be delighted."

"Hi, Uncle George," Emma said, as she hugged the big man gently.

Sam stood stunned. "George Mason is your uncle?" Sam asked, looking from one to the other.

"No," Emma said. "George Maseman is my uncle. His name was changed to Mason when he arrived in America."

Sam felt a little awkward, now that he knew George and Emma were related. He had quite a bit of history with both of them, but he wasn't sure either knew about it.

"Will the horses be all right?" George asked Doc.

"Yes," Doc assured him.

"Then, are we able to leave now?" George's voice suddenly sounded very tired.

"I'll fly you and Emma to Newberg," Sam said. "Then, we'll drive back to Emma's."

"I hope, young man," Doc said, with a twinkle in his eye for Sam, "that you will be more careful than when I was a passenger."

"No problem," Sam said, grinning at Doc and winking at Emma. "I won't be playing chicken with any planes this time."

The black colt whinnied from the small enclosure.

"Well, I guess we'd better be off," Doc said to Sam. "I'm proud of you, Sam. Take care of these two." There was true affection in his voice.

"Okay, Doc," Sam said.

Doc climbed into the truck, where Wanda was waiting. He waved as he drove the truck out of the airport gates. "I like seeing those two young people together," he sighed to Wanda.

◆ ◆ ◆ ◆

Emma watched as Sam and Jim turned Sam's plane around on the runway. She was amazed that it only took the two men.

"Sorry we didn't get much out of Strauss, before we had to turn them over to the police. You were great in there," Jim said to Sam, grunting as he put his back into the tail section.

Sam didn't answer. His gut was in knots again, as he thought of the evidence they had on this case. He wanted this night to be over, but he had no idea what tomorrow was going to bring. Carlos wouldn't say what Emma's involvement was.

"Thanks," Sam said, shaking Jim's hand when they were finished. Then, Sam walked to where Emma and George stood. He saw that the rolled painting the policeman had released to George was now inside of George's sling.

"Sam," Emma said, as they walked to his plane, which now stood on the runway facing away from the DC-7. "What did you mean about playing chicken with planes?"

"It was Sam's plane that made that big one stop," George said, nodding toward the DC-7. "He said it was the only way to keep it on the ground."

Emma looked at Sam. "You mean you flew your plane straight at us?" She saw the larger, four-prop plane standing near Sam's small, twin-engine Commander. Then, she imagined the two planes facing each other down, like a couple of gun fighters in an old ghost town.

"Yep," Sam answered in a Southern drawl. "Did it with my eyes closed," he began to laugh, then he looked at Emma.

He placed his arm around Emma and opened the plane's door. He smiled and said, "Damned glad I did."

CHAPTER TWENTY

S am drove his car into Emma's lane and parked next to the Morris Minor. He looked in the rear-view mirror and saw her sitting in the seat behind him. A loose strand of hair fell from the band she had used to pull her hair back when they'd left the Newberg airport. From the dash lights, he could see her eyes were dry now, as she stared ahead. His heart had ached when he'd seen her silent tears falling down her cheeks and how exhausted she now looked.

In the seat next to him, George rested his head against the door's window. Dark, dried, blood stains were visible on his white shirt. These two people had come back into his life in a matter of two days, and he knew at this very moment, as he parked his car in front of Emma's house, that his life would never be the same again.

This had been the longest day in Sam's life. His fear that he could lose Emma again, had spurred him into action. When he had stared up at the nose of that DC-7, Sam knew that nothing would stop him from getting her back or he would die trying. He hadn't even been sure that she was still alive, until he'd seen her when he'd entered the DC-7. The wave of relief had stunned him.

Just then, a shiver ran through Sam. In the need to protect Emma, and in the line of duty, he'd done one thing he wasn't proud of. He'd killed Joe. Once again, in his mind he heard the gun fire and felt Joe's body go limp under him. He knew it had been an accident during his struggle with Joe, but it surprised Sam how sorry he was that it had been Joe. For years, Sam'd thought of how he would get even with Joe, after he'd learned that Joe had been the one who'd drugged Ele. But, he'd never expected it would end this way.

Emma gently touched Sam's shoulder. She smiled as he turned to her, then she saw his face in the light of the overhead yard light. Ever since he'd arrived at the airport, he'd seemed so strong and in control. But, now, there was a vulnerable, frightened look on his face, and it scared her. She needed his strength now more than ever. Just in touching him, part of the nightmare she'd just experienced began to fade.

Sam reached up and held her hand. He felt her warmth run up through his arm and soften his heart.

"Thanks," he whispered and smiled at her.

"For what?"

"For being you."

She smiled and gently touched her uncle's bandaged arm through the bucket seats.

"We're home, Uncle George," she said softly, surprised at how naturally his name now rolled from her tongue.

Sam opened his car door and pulled the seat forward for Emma.

When the car's dome light came on, George jumped as he awoke with a start. He looked around, trying to get his bearings. When he saw Emma's face as she opened his door, he smiled. He pulled his large frame from the seat of the small American car. The cool, fresh night air, with the distant smell of rain, felt good on his face as he stood for a moment.

"How do you feel?" Emma asked George.

"Very well. Thank you, my dear." George didn't tell her that his arm was beginning to ache again in the sling. He placed the painting inside of the cloth of the sling, resting it on his forearm.

"George," Sam said. "Where are the keys to your car?"

George felt his pants pockets, then shook his head. "They must still be in the automobile."

Sam nodded. "I'll walk over and bring it back here for you." It was a good excuse to walk off the tightness still in his gut. Then, Sam saw the lights in the stable. Emma's truck and trailer stood just outside of it.

"Doc must be down with the horses," Sam said.

Emma and George looked in the direction of the stable.

"I need to see him," George said, as he started toward the stable. Emma followed closely at his heels.

Sam left to retrieve George's car.

◆ ◆ ◆ ◆

Doc looked up over the gate of the colt's stall as George and Emma entered. Wanda stood just outside the gate.

"Hello, there," Doc said in a jovial voice, then he saw the weariness in their faces.

"How is he?" George asked as he walked up to the gate. He saw that the colt was pacing back and forth.

"Oh, he is doing quite well, at the moment," Doc said cheerfully, in hopes of lifting the heaviness in the air. "The excitement has made him nervous, but that doesn't surprise me."

"Is his leg all right?" George asked, glancing down at the horse's front legs. "Sam told me you had bandaged it at the airport."

"Yes," Doc said, watching George's eyes. "He had a small cut and some swelling on one leg, but not to worry. He will be just fine in a few days."

"Will there be any complications?" George asked, his brow furrowed and his eyes intense on Doc. This horse was very valuable to him.

"No, I don't think so," Doc said, peering at George over his low-cut glasses. "I re-bandaged it after we arrived here, just to have another look at the wound." Doc plunged his hands into a bucket of water and washed up, then after drying them, he walked over to where George stood, reaching out his hand.

"We haven't formally met," he said to George. "I'm Emerson White, Emma's veterinarian."

"I'm pleased to meet you, Dr. White. I am Emma's uncle, George Maseman."

"Call me 'Doc,' please."

"Doc," George said, shaking the man's hand with his right, wincing slightly as the motion shot a pain in his left shoulder, reminding him of his wound.

Doc noticed George's face. "Are you in much pain?" he asked.

"No, thank you, I will be all right," George said, remembering Doc's care after he'd been shot. "I am in your debt."

"Maseman?" Doc looked puzzled. "But, I thought your name is Mason, of Essen Farms?"

"Maseman is my family name. It was changed by an Immigration clerk when I entered this country."

"What did you mean that you are Emma's uncle?"

"Maseman was my maiden name, Doc," Emma explained.

Doc smiled, as he saw the look that had exchanged between George and Emma. Then, he looked at the colt again. "George, you have a long line of magnificent Thoroughbreds that have come out of Essen Farms. I'm very pleased to know you."

◆ ◆ ◆ ◆

Just then, Sam walked into the stable. "Your car's just outside, George," Sam said, handing him the keys.

"Thank you, Sam."

Sam walked into Carlos' room and did a quick survey. Just as he thought, the gun was no longer hanging on the wall. Then, he left the small room and walked over to Ele's stall. Once inside, he talked softly to the mare. George watched as Sam lovingly caressed her long, chestnut neck, looking her over for signs of injury. He could hear Sam's soft voice, as he stood with his forehead on the mare's, the same way that George usually stood with each of his horses before a race. George knew then what he must do.

"Uncle George is the owner of Ele," Emma said to Doc. She was pleased that George had used their family name, when he introduced himself.

"I know," Doc said, as he slowly left the colt's stall. He and George had discussed the horses while flying to McMinnville. Doc also had told George of his experience at Epsom in England. "These are fine animals you have here, George."

"Thanks to your help, Doc," George said, with a large smile on his weary face. Sam walked up next to them, and George patted him on the back. "And, to this young man," George added. Sam looked down at the ground shyly.

"Sam," Doc said. "You've done your job well."

Emma stood in shock as she watched George walk into Frankie's stall. Placing his hand on the horse's forehead, he raised the hair and looked at the skin below. Then, he looked under the horse's upper lip. George reached down, touching the colt's right front leg, talking gently to the large, dark animal as he rubbed the tendons. The horse watched the man and nickered in a low tone. Then, the horse jerked his leg, and the man released it.

"When do you think he'll be ready to race again?" George asked Doc, respectfully.

"I'd say in about a month or two," Doc said. "He's a strong animal and the wound is quite superficial. Yet, I wouldn't start training again until after the swelling goes down." George nodded in agreement.

"What are you two talking about?" Emma asked, looking from Doc to George. Doc's words to Sam were still circling through her mind.

"Emma, dear, this is Koenig's Wonder," George said proudly, patting the black colt's long neck. The horse nodded his dark head and whinnied.

Emma stood in amazement, pondering the pieces of the puzzle, trying to fit them together in her mind. Then, a light came into her eyes. "Koenig's Wonder?" she asked. "The Kentucky Derby winner?"

"Yes," George replied, smiling. "I lost him just after the race last year."

"You lost him..." she started, then stopped. Remembering the book on famous Thoroughbreds, she now made the connection. "You are the George Mason who owns Koenig's Wonder?"

"Yes."

"But," Emma continued, "Ted told me he was Frankie."

George broke in. "At the McMinnville airport, Sam learned, during an interrogation, that Frank's Revenge was switched with Koenig's Wonder. I think that's the horse that you know as Frankie."

"Sam?" Emma looked at Sam. Her heart was pounding. She didn't want to hear this, but she had to ask. "What are you, some kind of investigator?"

Sam looked deeply into Emma's eyes. It was going to hurt him to say this, but he knew he had to. "Yes."

"What?"

"I work for the Thoroughbred Racing Protective Bureau, Emma. I was assigned to this case about a year ago, but Doc was the one who gave us the tip we needed to locate this horse."

"How do you know he's Koenig's Wonder?" Emma asked, pieces were still missing to the puzzle in her mind.

Doc placed his hand on the horse's muzzle and pulled back his upper lip, revealing a tattoo. "Sam told me that he'd found it the first day he'd seen him here at your ranch. See these numbers?" he asked.

Emma nodded. She was numb with disbelief.

"The champion's numbers are J4619. This horse's number is J4879, but see how the ink on the tops of the 8 and 7 are a slightly different color?" Emma looked more closely.

"Yes," she said. "But, what does that mean?"

"The horse that I had," George added, "the one that had been switched with Koenig's Wonder, had J4619 tattooed on his lip. His forehead had a white star, just like Koenig's Wonder and was almost identical to him. We found later that he was an imposter when my vet ran a blood test on him. The other horse was Frank's Revenge, born of Koenig, the same sire as Koenig's Wonder, but from a different mare."

"But," Emma said, still confused. "This horse doesn't have any white star."

"Come, look more closely," Doc said, with a sparkle in his eyes and a grin on his tired face. He put his hand on the horse's forehead and separated some of the hair, revealing whiter roots on the hair and pale skin underneath.

"I had noticed this when I was here one day, during a checkup on the mare. The skin underneath the black hair is what convinced me we had some sort of criminal act going on here. That was when I reported it to the Oregon Racing Commission. They must have contacted the Bureau. That was why Sam came here."

Emma stood, looking from man to man to horse. Her head was spinning, she was too tired to comprehend all of this. The only thing she remembered was the reason Sam was here – he was investigating the theft of this horse. He was investigating her! Anger started low in her belly, while at the same time, her heart ached. She quickly turned to Sam. Her eyes, wild with rage and fists clenched, she began yelling at him, marching toward him, backing him toward the door of the stable.

"You have been investigating me all this time?"

"Well, yes. The horse was in your stable, but—"

"So, everything you said and did was so that you could get the information you needed for your investigation?"

"No, that's not exactly true—"

"Sam Parker, I hate you. I never want to see you again as long as I live." She quickly opened the door and pushed him out into the night, then slammed the door shut and locked it, as Sam yelled and pounded against the door. Turning around, she threw herself back against it, with tears streaming down her cheeks.

"Emma," Sam's voice pleaded through the closed door. "Let me explain—"

"Go away, and leave me alone," she yelled. She saw the expressions on everyone's face inside of the stable as Sam continued to pound on the door, talking to her. She closed her eyes to shut it all out, her body blocking the door so that no one could unlock it.

George stood frozen. He was back on the ship in New York, when his brother had said those exact words to him. The pain in his heart now was not for himself, but for his young niece. It saddened him to see Emma so upset, and knew she was making a big mistake, just as he and his brother had, many years ago. He slowly walked up to Emma and placed his hand on her shoulder.

"Emma," he said in a soft voice. "Sam was only doing his job. I'm sure—"

"That's just it," she said, her voice low and steady. "He was doing his job, and he did a damned good one, at that." Her anger continued to fire inside of her, burning through her veins as she remembered the things he'd said, what she had given him. She'd allowed him back into her heart.

Then, she heard Sam's car start up and race away. She wrapped her arms around herself, protecting herself.

Doc saw the fatigue in George's face, which was beginning to pale. Emma had dark circles under her heavy eyes, and her anger was wearing her down even more.

"Emma," Doc said gently, after a moment of silence. "I think it is best that you and your uncle get some rest. It has been a long day. We can talk more about this tomorrow."

He picked up his bag, then motioned to Wanda to follow him as he walked toward the stable door. He gently moved Emma to one side, unlocked it, and walked out. Then, he turned to make sure that Emma and George were following his direction.

Outside, under the light in the drive, Doc turned and held out his hand to George.

"It has been a pleasure meeting you, Mr. Maseman," he said.

"Please, call me George," George said softly, taking the man's hand again in his right. "I can never repay you," he added, "for all of your assistance today. I will have my bookkeeper send you a check for your expenses."

"Thank you, George," Doc said. "But, that won't be necessary. I'll be back tomorrow afternoon, Emma," Doc added, placing his hand on her shoulder, "to look in on the horses. I suggest that your uncle does not drive tonight, because of his shoulder."

He and Wanda walked to his Morris Minor, and Wanda got in. Standing outside of the black car, Doc looked at Emma. "Emma, I've known Sam Parker for a number of years. He's a good man."

Then, Doc got into the driver's seat, and started the engine. As he drove away, he waved to Emma and her uncle, who were still standing together under the light.

◆ ◆ ◆ ◆

George turned to look at Emma. "Is it all right with you if I stay tonight? I think Doc is correct. I should not be driving now."

Emma saw her uncle sigh heavily. She tried to forget Sam Parker for the moment, and smiled softly. "Of course it is," she said, as she placed her arm in his and gently guided him to her door. "I have a spare room that you may use. Do you have any bags in your car that I can get for you?"

"Unfortunately, no. They are at my hotel in the city."

"I'm sure I can find something for you to wear in the morning," Emma said, looking at his blood-stained clothes. Then, she continued to the house.

She led the way through the entrance hall and stopped just before the double doors of the den. The hall light was shining on the rifle lying on the floor that Strauss had used on Sam, a small, dark stain, visible on the rug where Sam had lain. Emma's stomach tightened as she relived that moment, when she thought that Sam might be dead. The thought of losing him had broken her heart. Now, her heart was bleeding. She went into the den and turned on the light. Then, she reached down and slowly picked up the gun. Tears came to her eyes. It was Carlos' rifle that he'd kept in his room in her stable, and she saw Sam's blood still on the butt.

George went to her and took the rifle from her. He walked out and placed it in the gun rack next to the door, then returned to his niece.

"Emma. It's been a long day, hasn't it?" George said in a soft voice.

She looked at her uncle and saw the pain and weariness in his eyes. "Yes," she sighed, wiping the tears away.

"Come on, Uncle George. I'll show you to your room." She led the way up the stairs.

On the second floor, George paused at the doorway to the room where moonlight streamed over the painting of Hermann. He walked in and stood before the man and horse, tears filling his eyes. He suddenly felt tired and very old.

"Are you OK?" Emma asked next to him, placing her hand on his arm.

"In one's life, as we grow older, we realize how very important family is to us. I walked away from mine years ago, but I have always regretted it. I'm sorry I did not take that first step to meet with Hermann before he died."

"You had said that you always knew where we were. Why didn't you come forward until now?"

George looked away and walked to the window. "I was ashamed," he said softly into the darkness. He could see in the moonlight the outline of Joe's corral where he'd first seen Koenig's Wonder standing. He realized he'd been closer to his horses than to his own family.

"Come on," Emma said, placing her arm around him and steering him out of the room. "We both need to get some rest."

When she stopped at what was now the spare bedroom door, her heart skipped a beat. She hadn't been in that room since the last night she'd seen Ted alive. That had been their room then. She had arranged for it to be totally remodeled, in an attempt to erase that night, but it would always be a part of her past.

"Don't be angry with Sam," George said gently, watching her. He had seen her tension, but had misread it. She didn't say anything, but simply opened the door and walked into the room, switching on the light. George followed her.

The room was warm with different shades of blue. She had read somewhere that blue was a calming color, so she had used it when making her choices on the fabrics. The larger, darker furniture stood out against the lighter colors. She had asked the decorator to make sure it no longer looked like a bedroom, but more like a sitting room with large, stuffed chairs, tables, and floor lamps. Against one wall sat a daybed with a dark blue cover.

"This is a very nice room," George said.

"The daybed pulls out to make a queen-size bed. I hope that it will be okay."

"Of course, my dear." George sank down into the large, overstuffed chair. "Ah, I like this chair."

"Can I get you anything, Uncle George? Is your arm hurting you?"

He had been too proud to admit it before, but now the ache in his shoulder was beginning to throb and his head hurt. "Yes, a little. May I have some water? The doctor at the airport gave me some tablets to take before retiring."

"Yes, I'll get you some." She walked out to the hallway and into the bathroom at the end of the hall.

While she was gone, George took the painting carefully out of his sling and placed it in a drawer in a small table beside the bed. Then, he went back to sit in the chair.

After Emma returned and gave George the water, she pulled out the daybed, smoothing the covers. Then, she turned on the floor lamp next to George, which cast a soft light around him. She sat in the chair across from him and looked around her. Yes, she preferred this room this way now. Sharing it with her uncle seemed to chase any ghosts away that may have still lurked there. They both kicked off their shoes and placed their feet on the large ottoman in front of the two chairs, laying their heads against the high backs of their chairs.

After a few moments' silence, Emma finally said, "I'm not angry at Sam, Uncle George. Just disappointed – and hurt."

"But why, because of his work?"

"Yes, but it is much more than that." She closed her eyes and sighed heavily. "I met Sam in Chicago, at Arlington Park, when I was eighteen."

"I know," George said with a smile. "I was there, too."

Emma opened her eyes and looked at him in disbelief, then she remembered that he had told her that his horse, Koenig, had won at Arlington. "You were there that day."

"Yes. I watched you and your family claiming your betting money after Koenig had won the race. It was your birthday, wasn't it?"

"Yes." Emma thought for a moment, then said, "Why didn't you let us know you were there?"

"The same reason I did not approach you at your father's funeral. I was ashamed of what I had done to my brother – to my family." He looked at her face and his heart swelled. He knew he could not tell her now what he needed to say.

"Tell me more about you and Sam," he said quickly to return the conversation to Emma, instead of himself and his past.

A shadow fell over her face. She looked away toward the dark windows and into the night, fingering the locket around her neck. "I defied my parents and went out with Sam to the movies one night. I, uh, fell in love with Sam then, at least what I thought was love at the time. I was still so young."

"Then what happened?"

"Sam took me back to my hotel. He was leaving for the Air Force that night. Just before I could tell him I loved him, a taxi pulled up with a woman in it. She called to Sam and he left with her, leaving me standing there like some idiot.

"Now, over ten years later, here he is in my life. I was beginning to trust him again," then she stopped. Anger was beginning to rise in her again as she thought of him using her. "Until tonight." She rolled her eyes to the ceiling. "Oh, the things I said to him, I could just die. He was only doing his job the entire time."

George sat quietly watching his niece. He smiled softly and nodded. "Yes, I can now understand why you might have been so angry at him, but that is no reason to shut him out of your life. I saw how hurt he was when you pushed him away."

"Oh, Uncle George, you just don't understand."

They sat in silence, looking at the dark window. Then, Emma asked, "Why did you never marry?"

George thought for a moment. He had only met one woman that he wanted to share his life with, but she was dead.

"I haven't met the right woman here," he said, trying to smile, the ache in his heart cutting deeper.

Emma smiled and stood, then went over and kissed him on the cheek. She noticed again the dried blood on his shirt and pants.

"Let's see what clothes I can find for you." She walked to her room and opened one of the boxes next to her dresser. These were the only clothes she had left of Ted's. She chose a bath robe, some sweats, a pair of khaki trousers, and a wool Pendleton shirt. She wasn't sure why she'd kept them, but now she was glad she had.

"I think these may fit you," she said, walking back to where George sat. "They may be a little short in the sleeves, but they will at least be clean."

"Are these your husband's?" George asked, holding the shirt up to him.

"Yes."

"Was he a good man, Emma?" George asked. He'd heard the hesitation in her voice and remembered her telephone call one night the previous year, when she had called Chris at his farm.

"At first," was all she said, after a long silence. He could tell by her face that she did not want to talk about him. Now, he thought he knew why she had called Chris that night at Essen Farms.

"The bathroom is next door," she said, to change the subject. "But there is no door to it from in here. You'll have to use the hall to get to it. Funny, how some people plan their homes."

George stood and placed his free arm around Emma, gently pulling her to him. She allowed him to hold her. It felt very natural and very right, like coming home. Her nerves were raw, and she was sure George felt the same.

"I wish I could erase all the hurt that has happened in your life, my dear. But, I know that is not possible," he said softly. "I would like you to know that I will do anything I can to help you be happy."

"Thank you, Uncle George," she smiled and kissed him lightly on the cheek. "I am so glad we finally met."

After Emma left the room, George laid the clothes down and sat heavily in the big chair again. Sam had told him what little he'd learned from Karl Strauss - how Karl had found Franz in Caracas, Venezuela after leaving Essen Farms in Kentucky, surprised that Franz had survived the war. Sam had also said that Franz had been one of Hitler's men.

If only..., George thought, shaking his head.

With a deep sigh, he saw Hermann's face in his mind. George wanted to tell Emma about Hannah, but didn't know how to tell his niece that he had been the cause of their family's destruction.

◆ ◆ ◆ ◆

The office was dark, except for the small lamp on the desk. Sam sat with his head in his hands, going through everything in his mind. It didn't make sense. Jim had left a message with the answering service that Strauss wouldn't say any more during their interrogation without talking to an attorney first. Carlos would only tell them that he'd seen someone walking another horse around Koenig's Wonder's stall late that night at the Derby. He said he couldn't tell who it was, it was too dark. Sam knew he was lying, but Carlos had broken down in tears when he'd heard what had happened to Maria Sanchez. He kept blaming Joe for her pregnancy and wouldn't say anymore.

Sam didn't think Emma could be involved in this mess, but he didn't know how he was going to be able to separate himself from his feelings and finish the case. He'd watched her in the stable, when George and Doc were telling her about Koenig's Wonder, but Sam still wasn't sure she was truly in the dark about the horse.

He stood up and turned, facing the window. The colored lights of the city did nothing to ease the ache in his heart as he remembered Emma's face when she'd slammed the stable door. She was right. His job had come first, at least in the beginning. He'd schemed all along to get to see her ranch and get near the colt. Yet, he knew that hadn't been his only motive.

Sighing, he shoved his hands in his back pockets. Then he stopped, his hand wrapping around the paper there. When he pulled it out, he saw the envelope that had fallen from the book at Emma's. Emma's name was scrawled across the face, the handwriting was unfamiliar, and it was still sealed at the point of the flap. He walked to the desk and sat down. He wondered if he should read it or not, since it was addressed to Emma. *It could be pertinent evidence to the case*, he thought to himself, justifying his actions. He took the chance, and carefully opened it. He noted the letter was dated October 20, 1968 and began to read:

> *Emma, I didn't mean to hurt you. It's the drink. It's always had a power over me that I can't control, ever since my dad gave me my first whiskey, right after he'd beaten my mom. It's in my blood, and I know now it's bad blood. I watched it happen too many times, with Susan, my first wife. I thought it'd be different with you. I know now that I can't change who I am, but I don't want to ever hurt you again.*
>
> *I've got something I need to tell you - to tell someone. You know that Joe Remsky and I took Frankie to the Kentucky Derby last spring. I didn't know then that we didn't bring Frankie back. After seeing the article in this horse book, I figured that somehow he was swapped for the winner, Koenig's Wonder.*
>
> *I don't think Joe's in charge of this. He's too weak. I overheard Joe talking to that Venezuelan, Casey Morales, last week at his ranch. Joe said something about a German guy named Franz Reichmann being behind it all, to get his revenge and what was rightfully his. Casey had admitted that he and Joe*

would both be convicted if anyone found out they were the ones that had made the swap. When I bought this book on race horses, I realized that Casey was really Carlos Madera, George Mason's jockey. He must have been the inside man who'd helped with the switch at the Derby. I didn't know anything about the swap. When I looked the colt over and saw the white skin on his forehead, I knew I was right. I'm going to talk to Joe about it today, while we're hunting, to see what he's going to do with this horse.

If I don't return after today, take this letter to the police. Watch out for Joe and Carlos. I don't trust Carlos, he makes me nervous. I've got a feeling that something's about to happen.

Ted

Sam re-read the letter. It was all here, written the night before Ted was killed, the night he must have raped her. Sam's gut tightened as he thought of Emma, how some men think they have a right to take advantage of a woman. It was a good thing that Ted Jacobs was dead or Sam would find himself in jail for murder. He was certain now that Emma had nothing to do with the theft of Koenig's Wonder. She couldn't have known anything about it. With a sigh of relief, he carefully placed the letter and the envelope in an evidence bag.

Sam noticed a large, manila envelope lying on the desk that he hadn't seen when he first came in. He picked it up and opened it. It contained the photos he'd taken on the flight to McMinnville the prior day. Sam's hands began to shake as he looked at Emma's smiling face staring back at him, her long, black hair glistening in the sunlight, her large, brown eyes, filled with tears as she smiled at the camera. It was the moment she'd turned back to look at him after seeing her ranch for the first time from the air. She was so beautiful.

He stopped, staring at the photo. All of the walls that he'd built around his heart began to slowly crumble, revealing to him something he'd locked away. There in front of him was the face of the woman he loved, the only woman he'd ever loved. Tears stung in his eyes and her image blurred. Then, he remembered her last words to him.

Sam sighed and slowly thumbed through the rest of the photos, stopping when he saw the oval track on Joe's property. The zoom lens had captured both Joe and Carlos standing next to Koenig's Wonder. Carlos had a rifle in his hand that had a large scope.

The rifle! All of a sudden, Sam remembered the rifle he'd seen in Carlos' room in the stable, with the 'M98' stamped on it. Sam knew he needed to go back to Emma's, to retrieve the rifle and have it tested with the bullet found in Ted Jacobs. He also knew this was only an excuse. The rifle wasn't the real reason he needed to go back. Then, he remembered her words and slumped back into the chair.

He'd seen the look in Emma's eyes, the fury and hatred he'd never expected to see there. It had scared him to the bone. He was no longer sure of what she felt – if there was any way, any chance he could make it up to her.

Sam put a call into Jim.

"I've got a full confession here," Sam said, "from Ted Jacobs in a letter he left for Emma. I'll leave it with Sally on my way out."

"Wait a minute, Sam. What's happened?" Jim read the tone of defeat in Sam's voice. He'd only heard that tone once before – when he'd found Sam in New York after the Del Mar race.

"There's also a rifle at Em's..." Sam's voice wavered. He took a deep breath and continued. "It's a Spanish M98 Mauser that Carlos used to kill Ted. You may want to go pick it up. My job's finished here."

"Wait a minute, buddy," Jim yelled into the phone. "What the hell's going on here?"

"I gotta go," Sam said.

"Sam, just wait till tomorrow," Jim said, "I could come by the office. I think you and I need to talk—"

"I'll call you from Baltimore."

Sam hung up the phone and began to pack.

CHAPTER TWENTY-ONE

Emma awoke with a start, breathless and sweating, her heart pounding in her chest. Someone had been chasing her, but she couldn't run - her legs had felt weighted down, as if she were running through a bog. She sat up and looked around her, relieved to see that she was in her own bedroom and that it had only been a dream. Sighing heavily, she fell back against her pillow, waiting for her heart to settle down.

The sunshine outside of her window came in across her chenille bedspread, as it inched its way toward her. Shadow lay curled up in the warm light next to her. Emma ran her fingers through the soft, sable fur. A purr emitted from the seemingly sleeping cat.

Emma smiled when she heard footsteps in the bathroom, remembering that George had stayed with her the previous night. She felt as if she was back in her home in Indiana with her parents, and that she was not alone.

When she realized George had returned to his room, she arose and walked into the bathroom. Locking the hallway door, she took a shower. While the water ran over her body, visions of the previous night, the fear, the horror came back to her. She vigorously washed her long hair, in an attempt to wash it all away from her mind. After awhile, the warm water helped her to begin to relax as she remembered that it was all over. She then felt a peace that she hadn't known since her father died.

Sam's face flashed before her, and she felt the disappointment and hurt all over again. She had believed him. She'd thought he was being truthful with her, until she had learned his real motive. She turned off the water and towel-dried her hair. Unlocking the door so George could use the room, she walked back into her own bedroom.

Emma braided her wet hair, and pulled it to one side over her shoulder. She liked the ripples the braid left when she released her hair after it had fully dried. Slipping into jeans, and a cotton blouse of a bright coral color, she looked in the long mirror. The color gave her cheeks a nice blush, but there was sadness in her eyes this morning. She sighed and went downstairs.

She thought of Sam again, as she walked to the open door of the den. Thoughts of the previous few days circled in her head, Sam's ploys to get to see her ranch - flying over her ranch and taking photos, the wine he'd bought in McMinnville, the engine problem with his plane. It had all been part of his plan - for his work.

Shaking her head, she went into the kitchen and began brewing strong coffee. She wasn't ready to deal with Sam yet, but her heart began to ache and she rubbed her hand over it. She had left Sam's locket in her dresser drawer, where she'd placed it the night before. She was still sure, now in the morning light, that she had done the right thing with Sam. He had used her for his investigation. That was all she could think of. She didn't understand why her heart hurt so.

"*Guten morgen, mein leibchen*," George said as he entered the kitchen, just as Emma was pouring a cup of coffee.

"Good morning, Uncle George," Emma said with a smile. She hadn't heard the old German in a long time. George was wearing Ted's shirt and trousers, which were a little tight on him. He looked rested, but Emma could see the dark circles under his eyes.

"Did you sleep well?" she asked, as she reached for a second cup and poured coffee for him.

"Yes, thank you," he replied, sipping the dark liquid. The strong flavor helped to dissolve the ugly taste in his mouth. He looked out of the window over the sink. The medication had helped him to fall asleep quickly. Yet, sometime during the night, he'd awoken and relived seeing Franz again. He'd tried to understand the hatred he'd seen in his younger brother's eyes and the realization that Franz had killed Hermann. But, George only realized that he had failed his family.

"Would you like something to eat?" Emma asked. She had seen the shadows cross over George's face.

"No, thank you. I'll get something later."

They walked to the table and sat where they had the first day they'd met. Emma realized that had only been yesterday and that she had come very close to losing her last relative. She noticed that he rubbed his left arm, which was still in the sling the doctor had given him.

"How is your shoulder?" she asked.

"It is fine," he said, even though it ached. The pain was a reminder that he was still alive.

George reached out his hand and placed it on Emma's arm on the table. He looked into her eyes with a sad look. "I will have to leave soon," he said with sorrow in his voice. "I telephoned the airport and my farm last night before falling asleep..." he then stopped and looked at her. "I hope that is not a problem?"

"Of course not," she said. She didn't want to hear what he was going to say next.

"My plane leaves in two hours. I must return to Kentucky – to my business."

"Yes." She placed both hands around her coffee cup and looked down into the dark liquid. "I'm sure you must," she said with regret.

"I must also see to my brother's body."

She looked up at him, then said, "If there is anything I can do to help, please let me know."

"Thank you, but I must do this myself."

He was silent for a moment, then added, "I do not really wish to go, but many people rely on me." He paused and looked at her. "Emma, will you come with me? Will you come to Kentucky to live with me?"

Emma was stunned for a moment, weighing what he'd said in her mind. Her first thought was *leave Oregon*? Her second was *lose Uncle George*?

"I....I don't know," she stuttered, unsure of her own voice. "I love it here so much, but I also want to be near my family – what's left of it."

"I feel the same way," George said. "That is why I asked you to come with me." He placed his hand on her cheek, relieved to hear her words. He'd been afraid she would think he was like his brother, Franz. "I thought about many things last night."

George was quiet for a moment, his face grave while he searched for the right words. He settled back into his chair and looked Emma in the eye.

"Remember what I told you about my family, my lie to your father?"

"Yes," she said, holding her breath – a tension hung suspended in the still air.

"I never was able to tell my brother that I was doing what our father ordered me to do..." George hesitated. He'd never told anyone this before. "My father told me to do whatever was necessary to get Hermann to agree to come to America with me. From that moment, I hated my father. Hermann was engaged to marry Hannah Siemens, a young woman from Hannover. My father was against the engagement. I lied to my brother..." He stopped, remembering the anger in his brother's eyes on the deck of the ship.

"What was the lie?" It was a question that had been in the back of her mind since the first day she'd met George.

George was quiet for some time, searching for the right words. He'd rehearsed them for years, for the moment when he met Hermann again. This was different. Tears came to his eyes as he thought of never being able to explain the truth to his brother. This young woman sitting before him was his brother's daughter, and she had a right to know.

"I told Hermann that Hannah had tempted me to join her at an inn near Wiesbaden, but that I refused her. In truth, she had never approached me in that manner. I ruined the lives of two people very dear to me..." He stopped, wiping his face with his handkerchief. "Your father said some very terrible things to Hannah when he confronted her, not believing her when she denied it. She was heartbroken and took the next train back to Hannover. I'll never forget my brother's face on the ship when he said he never wanted to see me again."

George paused, looking out the window. Emma could see the pain in his face.

"When I returned to Germany to find our parents..." George stopped. "I did not learn until many years later that Hannah had been killed in a train accident shortly after she had left Hermann and I that fateful day." He looked down at the tiled floor. A tear fell as he said, "When I told Hermann the lie about Hannah, I knew that it would not only break my brother's heart, but hers as well. You see, I was in love with her."

Emma sat in silence. She was beginning to understand.

"I also learned that my parents and younger brother, Franz, had been killed. Now, I know that Franz survived, only to have a terrible bitterness that grew in his heart that almost destroyed us all."

"But, you can't blame yourself for this any longer—" Emma began.

"I am responsible," George said with anger in his voice. "It was because of my lie, because I did not send for my family in Germany..." He stopped for a moment and looked out of the window.

Eventually, his gaze returned to Emma. "There is another thing...I had been the one to take the Friedrich from our parents' home. I was young and frightened by the idea of going to a new land that I'd only heard of in rumors. I felt the painting would be security for my brother and me. It also was something I knew would hurt my father – he had loved that painting more than his family. I am so very sorry."

She now understood that her father's silence had been due to his own hatred. That was why he had never brought the Friedrich out of its hiding place. She now also saw the guilt and pain that George had carried with him all those years.

George felt relief and peace, to finally admit it to Emma - his last living relative. He had been afraid to tell her; afraid he would lose her and die alone. Finally, he felt a strong connection with his niece, as if she was the daughter he'd never had. Joy and love surged through him as he looked at her, and he felt peace at last.

When he saw her face, the innocence and love, he knew now what he must do.

"Wait here a moment," George said, patting her hand. He went upstairs and returned with the painting, gently rolling it out on the table before Emma.

She looked at the soft colors, the exquisite, masterful hand that had captured this moment in time in oil. The red, velvet robe on the man bowing his head shone in the soft light of the crescent moon. Then, she saw the star and knew why her father had loved the painting. She sighed and looked at George.

"I have never seen this, until yesterday," she said. "Dad had always kept it hidden from mom and me."

"Yes," George said with a sigh. "That is what I was afraid of." He stopped and looked at the painting for a moment. "My father sold numerous acres of our farm in Germany to possess this. As I said, he soon became very possessive of it. I took it from my father. I only had it for a short time in my possession, before Hermann took it from me. My brother, Franz, killed for it. This painting was what destroyed my family – the greed and obsession that comes with it."

They sat quietly together, looking at the Friedrich. George silently quarreled with himself, seeing the power that this painting had over his family. He realized he was very lucky that he had not had it very long in his possession.

"I've decided to destroy it – before it can destroy anyone else," George said, shaking his head. "I just wanted you to see it before I do."

"No!" Emma exclaimed, placing her hand on George's arm. "You can't destroy it. This belongs to the world, not just us."

"What do you mean?" George asked, bewildered for a moment.

"This painting belongs in a museum, for the world to see and appreciate."

George finally realized that his niece was stronger than anyone else in his family. *She has the strength to break the obsession*! George thought. He slid the painting closer to Emma.

"Would you please see to it?" he asked, his voice breaking. He knew that if he did not leave it with Emma, he would never let it go again.

"Yes, I will contact the museum tomorrow." Emma sighed as she looked at it again, then carefully rolled it back in the outer cloth.

"Thank you," George said. Emma could see the relief in his eyes. "You will contact me when it is to be placed in the museum? I would like to be there." He also wanted to make sure that Emma would not be stricken by the power it had seemed to have over the rest of his family.

"Of course."

George looked at his watch and stood up. "I must leave now."

Emma got up and walked with George. Stepping outside, she felt as if she was coming out into the afternoon light after watching a matinee in a dark theater, the scenes of the movie still running through her mind of the past few days on the big screen.

"Would you like me to drive you to the airport?" Emma asked as they neared George's car. Suddenly, she did not want to be alone.

"No, that is not necessary." He stopped and turned. "Unless, of course, you wish to come to Kentucky with me?" George asked, with a smile and hope in his eyes.

"Thank you, but I will have to think about it. I have so much work here..." She let it drop. She still wasn't entirely sure what she wanted.

"I will send Fred Jamison, my trainer, here next week to help with Koenig's Wonder's return later. Also, another man will accompany Fred, to help you with the other horses. Would that be all right?" George wanted to surprise Emma when Chris Schmidt arrived. He had made the arrangements over the phone the prior evening.

"Yes, I would like that." Emma hadn't yet realized that she no longer had anyone to help her with the horses.

George turned to her. "Emma, there is one more thing I want you to do for me. Let me tell you a small story," George said as he settled himself back against his car.

"A few years ago, at the Del Mar track in California, I met a remarkable young man, cocky, sure of himself and his mare. He did not think she could lose. He had placed his mare in a claiming race. However, before the race, I had claimed the man's mare." He paused for a moment, then added, "That man was Sam Parker."

Emma's eyes widened.

"Classy Elegance was Sam's mare," he said, smiling.

Emma's mouth dropped open. She remembered the mare's reaction the first time Sam had been in her stable.

George reached out and put his hand under her chin, gently closing her mouth.

"I have thought about that race many times and wished that it had never happened. After the race, I learned that Joe Remsky, Sam's jockey, had injected Ele with a drug, which caused her to lose the race. She's now worth a considerable amount of money, well over what I had paid for her then."

"Joe was Sam's jockey?" Emma asked, not believing her ears.

"Yes. I have decided to sell Ele back to Sam for the same price I had bought her for. He would not receive her as a gift. He is too proud. She really belongs to him. I could see that last night in the stable. However, I would like to have the opportunity to breed Koenig's Wonder to her, before I have him returned to Kentucky. A foal between those two will be outstanding." He waited for a moment, silently watching Emma. He had decided to give Emma Ele's first foal, but he would tell her that later.

"Will you please tell Sam of my wishes?" George asked. He saw her face change immediately, just as he knew it would.

"I can't," she cried, turning to pace. "I never want to see Sam again," she said, then she looked away.

"I saw the love that is between you two young people," George added.

Emma looked at George, trying to remember what he may have seen that she had not the night before.

"What do you mean?" she asked.

"I saw the way you held Sam when we first arrived at the airport. I also saw the fear in his eyes when you were throwing him out."

"Yes, and for a damned good reason," Emma quickly snapped. Her voice had a sharp edge on it, one that she'd never heard before – until last night.

"You are still angry, then?" George asked with one eyebrow raised, a sadness in his eyes. "Anger is an ugly demon. It causes people to do things they do not really mean, but then it is too late."

"No," Emma shot back, then turned and walked back to where George stood. "I told you last night about meeting Sam in Chicago and the woman he left with."

"Yes."

"Well, earlier this week, Sam introduced a pretty blonde to me – as his secretary. Yesterday, I saw them together again. They looked like there was more than a working relationship between them." She tried to ignore the ache in her heart.

"And you did not believe him?" George asked.

"I don't know," she replied. "I'm not sure I can ever trust him again. He could have been lying to me, just as he lied about the investigation."

"There is one thing I have learned in my life," George said, again taking Emma's chin in his hand. "Do not always trust what your eyes see, or what you hear. Look inside of your heart for the truth. That is where the answers lie."

He looked away, embarrassed by the tears that threatened to fall. "If I had only done that, our family would not have suffered as we have. If I had possessed the courage to do what I knew was right, my younger brother would not have lived with the hatred in his heart."

George sighed, then smiled at his niece. "Sam is a good man, Emma," he said. "Do not be afraid to let go of your anger and learn to trust again."

Finally, she felt she had to say what had been in the back of her mind ever since she'd met her uncle.

"Mom had told me about you, after Dad's funeral. That was the first I'd heard you even existed. When Conversano was dying, she said that Dad had begun to talk about his family to her. He said that if he'd ever gotten the chance to see you again, he would have told you he understood – that he'd forgiven you."

George could only stare at Emma. For many years, he'd hoped one day to hear those words, to hear his brother say them to him. He reached over and hugged Emma with his free arm, letting the silent tears fall as he finally bridged the gap in their family, flooding them each with the sense of belonging that they both had yearned for.

"You have given me the most precious of gifts, *liebchen*," he said after a few moments. "I do not know how to thank you."

"You just did," she smiled at him through her own tears.

They wiped their eyes and hugged again.

"You will let me know if there is anything you need?" George asked after a few moments.

"Yes, I have your number," she smiled, remembering the number that Chris had given her years ago.

"I will call you when I arrive in Louisville." He gave her a quick kiss on her cheek and patted her arm, then slid into the car. He rolled down the window with his right hand.

"Be safe," she said, placing her hand over his as he pulled the door shut and started the car.

"Don't forget to call Sam and tell him about Ele," he called from the open window, then drove away before she could respond.

◆ ◆ ◆ ◆

Emma slowly walked into the house and closed the door, leaning back against it. *It's too quiet now*, she thought. As she walked past the gun rack toward the den, she saw the rifle that Karl Strauss had used on Sam standing next to hers and found her heart ached.

She walked into the den, turned on the radio, and sat down in the large chair by the fireplace. As the newscaster talked, George's words circled through her mind. "*Learn to trust again*," he'd said. "*Listen to your heart*," he'd said. She had done all of that again, and now look where she was - alone and empty. The recent events had taken their toll on her and suddenly she felt numb.

Before she knew it, she found her thoughts beginning to move away to another place, a place where she had family. The idea of moving to Kentucky, where her uncle lived, did tempt her. Yet, something kept pulling her back. She had learned to love Oregon, and she really didn't want to leave her ranch. It had become her home. She looked around the room and knew that this house carried many memories for her, both good and bad; but, she needed the feeling of history, of belonging somewhere – to someone.

Restless and torn, she got up and began to pace. Shadow came into the room and mewed, her tail in the air. The cat walked up and rubbed against Emma's leg, purring loudly. Emma smiled and sat again in the large chair. The cat jumped onto her lap and curled up. Emma sat staring across the room, not really looking at anything, slowly petting the soft fur of the animal. All she could see was Sam's face.

Slowly, she thought of first seeing Sam again. Once in awhile, she'd smile, remembering something he'd said or did that had made her laugh. It was as if they had spent a lifetime together, the sweet memories that were crammed into three days. Like Chicago, each moment was caught in a time capsule, which could be played back again in slow motion, whenever it was needed. Then, she remembered the bitter one, the one that had caused her to become so angry that she had thrown him out of her stable.

Oh, he must hate me, she thought to herself, trying to put herself in his place. After all, she did have a stolen Derby winner in her stable. Yet, had she changed so much that he could have suspected her of having some involvement in the theft of the horse? She nodded her head. Yes, she had changed from the innocent girl Sam had met in Chicago. Life had changed her.

A bossa nova song began playing over the radio, a woman's soft, sultry voice singing "*Only Trust Your Heart.*" Emma smiled slightly, remembering her uncle's words. When the song was finished, she stuffed her pride deep inside of her and decided to call Sam. She could use the excuse of giving him Uncle George's message about Ele.

She gently nudged Shadow from her lap and walked to the desk. After finding the note with Sam's number on it, she took a deep breath, picked up the receiver, and dialed.

Just as the other end was picked up, Emma was about to say what she had quickly rehearsed in her mind, but stopped.

"Hello," a woman's voice said on the other end.

Emma recognized the voice – it was the woman outside of Sam's building. Emma stood, shaking and nervous, sorry now that she had even dialed. This all felt very familiar.

"Is Sam Parker there?" Emma asked, straightening her shoulders.

"No, he just left."

"Do you know where he went?"

"Baltimore. He'll be calling me tonight when he arrives, honey. Would you like me to—"

Emma hung up before the woman could continue. She swallowed, trying to choke back the tears and the pain in her heart. Once again, she felt very foolish.

"Uncle George can just tell him about Ele himself," she said out loud. She had work to do. She stormed out of the house toward the stable to begin the daily routine to keep busy – to try to forget.

♦ ♦ ♦ ♦

Emma absent-mindedly went through the routine of cleaning the stalls and feeding the horses. Ele had met her at the stall gate, expecting her usual treat.

"Sorry, girl," Emma said to the chestnut mare, scratching behind her ear. "I forgot."

The black colt whinnied for attention. As Emma walked up to him, she stopped. This animal had been the catalyst that had brought all of this into her life – Ted's death, her uncle, Sam.

"Hello, Frankie...or Koenig's Wonder, that is," Emma said as she walked to his stall. "How's your leg today?"

She looked down at his foreleg and saw a small stain on the wrap around the wound. She remembered that Doc had said he was coming back today to check on the horses and was thankful. At least it was somebody.

She went into Gandolf's stall, threw her arms around the tall stallion's neck, and sobbed into his white mane, finally allowing herself to let down her guard and release the pent-up emotions that were racing inside of her. The horse stood quietly, patiently allowing her to hold onto him, as he had done many times before. When she was empty, she wiped her eyes and nose, picked up his brush, and began to slowly brush him, the continuous, long strokes, which always helped her to relax.

"Thanks, old friend," she said to the horse. "I needed that." Gandolf nickered softly in response. Emma walked out of Gandolf's stall to the back of the stable. She opened the large, double doors to let in fresh air, thankful for the warm sunshine that flooded the aisle. She watched as dust particles danced in the light. Then, she turned, picked up a bridle that was lying on the floor and went into the tack room.

At the door, she stopped and dropped the bridle. The contents of her father's old trunk were strewn on the ground around it. She shivered, when she thought of Joe and Karl Strauss. Then, she saw a slim board standing up at one end of the trunk that she had never seen before. She remembered that she had guessed right – there was a false bottom in the trunk.

She knelt down and looked inside.

The face of a beautiful woman smiled up at her from a photograph of someone she had never seen before in a tarnished gold frame. Emma kneeled and picked up the brown-toned picture. She saw an inscription in the lower right corner of the photograph written in German, which Emma had learned to read as a child. Looking more closely, she read, *"To Hermann, with all my love. Hannah."*

Emma sat back on her heels and stared at the face. *So, this was Hannah*, she thought. She could see why her father and uncle had both loved her. The woman was stunning, her eyes penetrating, even from this faded photograph.

Emma carefully laid the photograph on the floor next to her and looked back inside the trunk. A cloth of soft, white muslin lay over something. She picked up the cloth and found a small bundle of letters carefully wrapped with a pink ribbon. Since her mother never wore ribbons, Emma assumed the ribbon was probably from Hannah's hair. She gently untied the silk and noted that the letter on top was from her father's mother in Germany, written to an address in New York shortly after he had arrived in America. The letter explained that they were glad that Hermann and George had arrived in the new country safely. His mother explained that they were anxiously awaiting the message from Hermann that everything was ready for them so they could leave Germany. She told him that she hoped it would be soon, because the turmoil in their country was growing graver every day. Hermann's mother mentioned her appreciation of his explanation of the disappearance of the Friedrich. She said she forgave George, and hoped that Hermann could also forgive him.

♦ ♦ ♦ ♦

Tears came to Emma's eyes when she realized that it had probably been written shortly before they were killed – all except for Franz. She thought for a moment of how the confusion of George's name, changed on Ellis Island, had prevented her father from being able to contact him. Emma decided to send this letter to George later.

The next letter was to her father from Hannah, dated in 1937. It was in response to his accusations about George. Hannah must have written and posted the letter before she had stepped onto the train that would lead to her death. Emma now understood the pain she had seen in her father's eyes when he talked of his homeland.

When she set these letters aside, she could not believe her eyes. Another small bundle of letters stared back at her in her own handwriting. They were her letters to Sam. A short note from the dean of her college was attached, explaining that he had done as her father had requested. Then, the realization hit her. Her father had arranged to intercept them, preventing them from ever reaching Sam. Staring at the unread letters in her hand, tears came to her eyes as anger rose in her. Any future that she might have had with Sam years ago was barred because of her father's interference.

She was about to replace the stack of letters into the trunk, when she noticed the return address of the last letter. It was a letter from Sam, written to her at her Chicago address of her school twelve years ago. It had been opened. Her hands shook as she pulled out the letter.

> *Emma, I'm not sure I understand why you haven't written to me, but I figured I'd give it one more try. Before we parted in Chicago, there was something I was about to tell you, but I didn't have the guts. Then, it was too late. The taxi arrived before I could say it. Now, I may never get the chance. I'm getting shipped out tomorrow.*
>
> *What I wanted to say was, I love you, Em. I loved you from the first moment I saw you. That's why I had to see you again, alone. Somehow, you got inside of me before I even knew what happened.*
>
> *I hope that you feel something for me, too. Otherwise, I'm going to feel pretty foolish here at my end. Please write me at*

*the address below and let me know if there's a chance we can
ever be together again. If I don't hear from you, I'll try to understand. It'll hurt like hell, because I don't want anyone except
you in my life.*

Love always, Sam

Emma sat stunned, holding Sam's letter in her hands. Her eyes stung and her
heart ached. She looked around her, unsure of what to do. Quickly, she shoved
Sam's letter into her pocket, grabbed Gandolf's bridle, and ran to his stall. After
leading him out into the aisle, she placed his bridle on him. Then, she wrapped
her fingers into his thick mane, jumped onto his bare back, and raced out through
the open doors into the bright sunlight. The wind blew through her hair that had
fallen loose down her back, and she rode up into the hills of her property with
such a fury that Gandolf's muscles tightened beneath her.

Dismounting, she tied Gandolf to a tree and sat down at the edge of the hilltop, watching the clouds create shadows over the valley floor below. She felt
confused, lost, empty, exhilarated. Words circled in her head – her father's request to the dean of her school; Ted's parting words at her door, the morning he
was shot; Uncle George, begging her to leave Oregon and move to Kentucky; the
woman's voice on the telephone today; Sam's letter, telling her he loved her.

Emma took Sam's letter out of her pocket and re-read it, examining each
word. She cried, she laughed; then she stopped and listened to the wind in the
trees. Finally, she knew in her heart what she wanted; but, then, she grew sad
when she realized that it was no longer possible. She had thrown it all away - she
had pushed Sam away.

She looked down for the locket that Sam had given her on her eighteenth
birthday and remembered she'd taken it off yesterday. Tears flowed softly and
silently down her cheeks as she looked out over her property and wondered what
it all was for, what was the reason of having all of these things in life, if there
was no one to share it with? Quietly, she sat, staring out over the valley at Mount
Hood in the distance.

Finding George in her life was the one thing she'd dreamt of - a family. But,
somehow, it wasn't enough. Now, she wanted more - a family of her own, here,
where she had made a home for herself.

She had tried once before, but failed. She knew now in her heart that she had
always loved Sam. Yet, she'd let her second chance slip through her fingers.
She'd pushed him away with her own blind jealousy and anger. Her heart ached
to think that it would never come again.

◆ ◆ ◆

Sam parked the Mustang in front of Emma's house. As he'd driven toward
the airport that morning, he knew he couldn't leave without first seeing Emma
one more time. He'd made one stop in the city and now stood on Emma's door-
step with the photos in his hand.

I'm taking a big chance this time, he thought with a sigh.

Sam knocked, but there was no answer. Slowly, he opened the door.

"Emma?" Sam called and walked into the house, leaving the door open. He waited, but heard nothing.

"Em, are you here?" he called again, louder. Still, there was no answer.

Sam walked through the house, checking both upstairs and down. As he was about to walk out, he saw Carlos' rifle in the gun rack. He took out his handkerchief and grabbed it, trying not to disturb what fingerprints remained. He then went out and placed it in the trunk of Jim's car, deciding he'd take care of it later.

When he entered the stable, Sam saw the trunk contents spread everywhere in the tack room. Noticing that Gandolf was gone, he knew where Emma was. Quickly, he saddled Flash and rode up to the hill where they had ridden the other day, the envelope of photos caught between his teeth. As he approached the top, he saw Emma sitting on the grass with her back to him, staring out before her. He was glad she hadn't seen him ride up.

Gandolf stood off to one side, eating the grass around him. Sam noticed there was no saddle on him. He stopped Flash a little distance from Gandolf and dismounted. When Flash whinnied to Gandolf, Emma turned.

She quickly wiped her eyes and raised her hand to smooth her hair as she tucked Sam's letter into her pocket.

Sam tied Flash next to Gandolf, then walked over and sat down on the grass next to her. He laid the large envelope containing the pictures between them.

"Hi," he said softly, placing his arms on his knees. He looked straight ahead, his body shook and his heart swelled. He knew what he had to do.

"Hi." Emma looked over at Sam and saw the sadness in his face, the dark circles under his eyes. She stood up.

"I thought I said I never wanted to see you again," she said, her pulse racing. It wasn't what she wanted to say, but it just came out before she could catch herself.

Sam stood next to her. "Yeah, but I found these on my desk and figured you might want them." He handed her the photos.

She slowly looked through them one by one, pride swelled in her heart as she saw her ranch in the black and white photos, her house, her stable, her riding arena. Everything that she had worked for was here in her hands. Now, she knew she couldn't leave it and tears rolled softly down her cheeks.

She looked up at Sam and said, "Thank you."

"About my job—" Sam began. He wanted to touch her, but didn't dare.

"No," Emma said. "Uncle George explained everything to me. I understand that you had your job to do and the fact that I had a stolen racehorse in my stable was a big part of it." She stopped for a moment, then continued. "Uncle George has asked me to move to Kentucky – to live with him."

A fist clenched around Sam's heart. He looked at her, seeing the dried tears on her cheeks. Then, he looked back over the buildings on her ranch, seeing her home.

"Are you going?" he asked, turning to her again, his hands in his pockets.

"I don't know. He's all the family I've got left," she said. Then, she looked into Sam's eyes and said, "It all depends on you."

"I'm transferring to Oregon," Sam blurted out. "Jim came by to see me last night and said that he's decided to quit the Commission and work on planes full time. There's too much here for me to leave."

He stopped, swallowed hard, and added, "Besides, there's one more thing of yours I have."

"What?" she asked.

Sam's right hand had wrapped around the box containing the ring in his pocket that he'd bought that morning, but stopped when he saw the look on her face. Sam saw the Emma he'd first met, her eyes wide and hopeful. He walked closer to her and touched his hand to her cheek.

"My heart," he said softly, smiling.

"Do you suppose we could start over?" he asked. "I mean, can we forget all the years that have happened since we first met? Forget the things that got in the way, like my stupidity and fears?"

"And my stubbornness...," she added.

"I'd like to pick up where we left off in Chicago..."

"Or, yesterday, before I threw you out..."

"And, be able to finally tell you how much I love you, Em. I've loved you since I first saw you."

"I know," she said, pulling his letter out of her pocket. "You said that in your letter years ago. My father had intercepted our letters. I never saw this, until now."

"He was probably just trying to protect you. You should have seen his face when he saw me leave in that taxi in Chicago with Nancy—"

"Nancy?"

"Yeah. Nancy Barolio, only she wasn't married to Jim yet. The three of us were leaving for Arizona."

Emma looked at Sam, stunned. "I...I thought she was the woman you were engaged to – the one you almost married."

"No, I couldn't marry Susan." He stopped and gently touched her cheek again. Then, he held her hand. "Not when I was in love with you."

"Oh, Sam," Emma cried.

"I love you, Em. I always have."

"I wanted to tell you in Chicago that I love you, but I never got the chance..." Emma began, then stopped as Sam pulled a ring box out of his pocket and flipped the lid open, the sun glinting on the emerald stone surrounded by diamonds.

"Do you suppose..." he started, his voice breaking, "if it's not too late...you might consider marrying me?"

Emma looked down at the ring, at their hands joined together, and tears ran down her cheeks. Those were the words she'd dreamt of hearing. This was the moment she'd wanted all her life.

"Yes," she said, laughing through her tears as Sam placed the ring on her finger. "We still have a lifetime ahead of us – together."

THE END

About the Author

This is Linda Kuhlmann's first novel. The story is based on her family history, which began when her great-grandfather and his brother arrived in New York from Germany. The two brothers were separated and never saw each other again. This is her fabricated version of their lives. Ms. Kuhlmann lives in Oregon with her husband.

Printed in the United States
35412LVS00002B/7-33

9 781595 262592